W I D

 **CANADA WATER LIBRARY**
Council 21 Surrey Quays Road
London SE16 7AR

www.southwark.gov.uk/libraries @SouthwarkLibs

Please return/renew this item by
the last date shown.
Books may also be renewed by
phone and Internet.

DARWIN'S

GHOSTS

a novel

ARIEL DORFMAN

 new york · oakland · london

First trade paperback edition March 2020.

Seven Stories Press
140 Watts Street
New York, NY 10013
www.sevenstories.com

Library of Congress Cataloging-in-Publication Data

Names: Dorfman, Ariel, author.
Title: Darwin's ghosts : a novel / Ariel Dorfman.
Description: Seven Stories Press first edition. | New York : Seven Stories
    Press, 2018.
Identifiers: LCCN 2018002021 | ISBN 9781609808242 (hardcover) | ISBN
9781609809874 (paperback)
Subjects: LCSH: Voyages and travels--Fiction. | Family secrets--Fiction. |
    Human zoos--Fiction.
Classification: LCC PR9309.9.D67 D37 2018 | DDC 813/.54--dc23
LC record available at https://lccn.loc.gov/2018002021

Printed in the USA.

9 8 7 6 5 4 3 2 1

For Angélica, always.

Darwin's Ghosts was inspired by a series of true events that effectively happened in the nineteenth century. However improbable they may seem at first glance, these have all been rigorously documented. Readers will have to decide for themselves whether the same can be ventured about the narrator of this story and his fate.

"Any attempt to know the past is a voyage
to the world of the dead."

—Carlo Ginzberg

"The only hope is to be the daylight."

—W. S. Merwin

ONE

It came a bit after dawn, the dark condition that was to plague me, so sudden that I was unable at first to give it a name. How to know right away that it had been incubating inside some ancient zone of myself and my ancestors for one hundred years, begin to guess that it had infected the vast, blind world for far longer? All the more unfathomable because its advent, as with many another subsequent terror in my life, was so entirely unforeseen.

I searched, almost from the start, for signs that might have announced its emergence, might have prepared me for the catastrophe. I can remember my adolescent hands leafing through our Foster family album, page after page, a ritual consolation that allowed me to stop and diagnose each previous, untainted appearance of mine, pinpointing with my index finger what used to be my sunshine face, lingering on it.

Until my fourteenth birthday, when it disappears. The image disappears, my face disappears, not the family album. That continues to fill up with father and younger brothers and for a while my mother, they continue to find habitation in that endless chronology of endless ordinary life, graduations and celebrations, engagements and games and vacations, most of my family growing, blossoming, blooming in the album without me. To think that as a child I thought that was boring, for one day to be like the next one, that I prayed, as I voraciously read stories of the sea and odysseys in exotic lands, that something adventurous might befall me. It did, it did—but not until that dawn of contagion when everything changed.

So innocent, I had been so innocent in the first photo my father snapped of me suckling at my mother's breast, the derisive welcome the camera offered, though not instantly, not yet a Polaroid, then and there in 1967. Like all babies just arrived in this world I am barely recognizable in that photo and yet recognizable enough that I can identify that infant with myself, not that different from what my father had distinguished through the viewfinder and the camera bagged and froze in time while I was drawing pleasure and milk from my mother, Mom so radiant and jubilant at her first-born child, look at me, just look, luminous in all my suckling glory, ecstatic to be alive. The image of me that my father's camera and every other camera would continue to display during the initial phase of my life, normal, so exceedingly, delightfully, yawningly normal. My involvement in that album concluded with the last snapshot taken the day before my fourteenth birthday, the photo that I pinned up, enlarged, above my desk, to perpetually remind me of what I had been, could no longer be. Next to the photo Cam Wood, the one love of my one life, had given me—another reminder of what I thought I had lost forever.

How effortless it all was while it lasted, the photographic trail left behind by that early buoyant life: performing each stage of existence for others, for myself, for posterity, for the lens of a cold machine. My first toy duck in my mouth, the first tooth peering forth like an interloper, my first step holding a hand, my first step without a helping hand, my second step, all the etceteras that my parents kept lapping up, *oh isn't he the cutest little monkey?*, *oh you little savage you.* Yes, that's how they used to describe me, not knowing that the joke would be on them, unaware as they dispatched photo upon photo to grandparents and uncles, showed to willing and unwilling neighbors, unaware as the tired attendant at the AAA office who nipped my first official picture for a passport (can it be that they really took me to Paris—Paris of all places—when I was six, so small next to the Arc de Triomphe with hands in pants, so curious and grimacing at the chimps in the zoo of the Jardin d'Acclimatation in the Bois de Boulogne, indeed, indeed, they took me there), unaware and oblivious and heedless as the folks at the kindergarten when they demanded a large print of me to put on the board with all the drawings of flowers. So easy, compliant. Snap, click, ready, here you go, here he is.

Just as I was unaware. No intimation, let me insist, of the fate ahead, the horror my life would become when I reached puberty. When something happened, somebody happened. He happened, my visitor.

I remember the day as if it were yesterday. For all purposes it was yesterday, never ceased being one day ago, became in my mind the day I was expelled from modern life.

It started as such days did for millions of boys my age or thereabouts.

For that first light of September 11, 1981—my fourteenth birthday—I gave myself an early present, just as the sun was rising. I masturbated for the first time. I thought of Camilla Wood, how just the previous night—her dad was out to see some movie, *American Werewolf in London,* I think it was—we had gone as far as she wanted to go, the pang of kisses and the touch and tip of her breasts, and something more, but not enough, not enough, I thought of Cam's unexplored depths the next morning when I did it by my solitary self as I listened to Peter Gabriel's "Games Without Frontiers" and the spasm of that verse, that foreboding verse, *If looks could kill they probably will.*

I have told myself that it was the sex that brought on that punishment, the fact that I could from that shuddering moment onward certifiably produce offspring, as my parents were able to conceive me, repeating the coupling of generations before us, so many men and women making and unmaking me in the distant and less distant past. It's difficult to doubt that conjunction of sex and sickness, and yet, how many boys have inaugurally fondled their genitals for their first and abiding time—and girls, and girls like Cam—how many have joined in a panting bout of sex, how many kids had watched with hot amazement their sperm jetting thick and white into whatever sweet receptacle was available, while they melted all over, from the slope of their toes to the expanding universe of their brain, and thanked the stars and Peter Gabriel that they would soon repeat the experience? How many ended up afflicted like me? How many descended, as I did—wanly and proudly descended the staircase to breakfast, where my dad awaited with the latest model of his SX-70 camera to catch the exact second when I would gawk at what lay next to my plate: the keys to a small motorbike, my dream vehicle. And two tickets to the upcoming Rolling Stones private pre-tour concert at Sir Morgan's Cove in Worcester. My father wanted to fix in eternity that Polaroid moment of familial bliss, of the kind that he himself had devised and presented to millions of TV viewers with the stellar presence of James Garner. Click!

That was it. The click that divides my existence. Before the click and after the click. I remember the exact aftermath so well. One second after my father eagerly received into his hands the spool of instant celluloid and, shooing the rest of us away, watched something arise as always from the gray like a ghost, that's all it took, while my mother kissed and hugged me with her overwhelming warmth and my siblings sang their stupid happy birthday anthem, good wishes meant for everybody else on this earth, but never again for me.

My father's face. Gaping into the abscess of that Polaroid likeness of me as if it were the devil incarnate. It was, it was, I was certain that it was for many a year. But he did not believe his own eyes, he muttered *No, no, no,* and stashed the incriminating evidence in his pocket, squished it there as if it were a venomous worm rather than a photo—so alarmed and disgusted that I wondered if my recent erotic initiation had not been revealed in my reddened cheeks, if the author of my days had not somehow guessed by some efflorescence of features, some telltale pimple, some leering dribble from my lips, what had transpired in my room upstairs some brief minutes ago while Peter Gabriel crooned about kissing baboons in the jungle, but it was not that, I have often prayed that it would have been something so inconsequential. *No, no, no.* What he said, and then: *I need another shot, this one came out sort of blurry. I'll have to tell the guys at the lab that they haven't fixed the glitches on this latest model. Wouldn't want to have to recall the whole batch.* As if the only trouble was technical and the only entity requiring protection, his precious Polaroid company.

So he herded us, the whole family, into one frame and again, click. The second momentous click of my existence. The second click, perhaps worse than the first one, because it governed all else that was to follow. Because this time he showed the photo, he was compelled to do so, showed it to my mother, and the revulsion on her exquisite face as she tried to keep it from me, but I was too quick, I snatched it from her hands and . . .

There I was.

Not me. In the middle of all those other commonplace, conventional faces, only mine—well, not mine—stood out.

My body. My place at the table. My mother on my left, my brother Hugh on my right, both of them beaming at the camera, while my other brother, Vic, crowded eagerly in.

Instead of what had been for fourteen years my face was another face, the face of a young stranger.

The eyes of that man, his wild overgrown mop of black hair, his snub nose and high cheekbones, his thick aboriginal lips with barely a white hint of teeth flickering between them, his sultry enigmatic defiant look—oh if looks could kill, if looks . . .

The eyes, the dark eyes.

My visitor.

Though I did not yet call him that, did not know that he would mutely reappear over and over again, each time any photo of me was snapped, any film, any portrait, solo or in a group, any replica, that he would not go away, would crop up incessantly, unrelentingly, twinned to me as if we had been born together of the same soundless matrix.

Peering out from my neck and shoulders, parked on me like a quiet, mad totem. The only thing familiar about him: that short dense mane of his that seemed a bad imitation of a Beatles hairdo—a slight contemporary touch and echo that made his face even weirder and more threatening, perhaps because his hair almost reached the eyebrows, shadowing them, making their orbits gleam all the more starkly.

"If this is another one of your pranks," my father said. Not because he believed it but because he needed to say something, anything, and I was a mischief maker, the carefree sort, the good fun favorite of everyone and especially my impish mother and practical jokester Cam. My dad was playing for time, trying to squeeze this aberrant incident into some semblance of order, ready to blame anything but his saintly and sacred SX-70 Sun 600 Series model.

I was also playing for time. Taking my cue from my father, I asked my brothers if they were pulling a stunt, had conspired to flash a mask in front of me without anyone realizing it, I was also doing my best to rationalize what had just happened when I showed them the photo and accused them directly of . . .

"We didn't do anything, Roy," they cried out, "swear to God and hope to die, we'd never . . ."

"A mistake, a mistake, Fitzroy," my mother added, but her eyes were as wild as the stranger's in the Polaroid, not as full of night but as wild and with far more fear. "This latest model your dad brought home just yesterday, who knows what quirks it may have, try another one, Jerry."

Click. Number three. A close-up. Only of my face, nothing more.

His face, nothing more.

I grabbed it, the photo, grabbed it before anyone could stop me, rushed to the door, came back for the keys to the motorcycle, eluded my father's hands vainly attempting to block me and then the clutching claws of my siblings who by now were beginning to enjoy the spectacle, *Me too, me too*, each of them screeched, *I also wanna see the monkey man, I also wanna see the Roy ape*, and Mom shushing them horrified and I allotted them just one look and they were silent, if looks could kill, they knew that I was older and stronger and would eventually exact revenge. But not now, not yet, now I careened out to the driveway and was on my way, heading for Cam's house. Who else could I show this to, who else could give me comfort, lift whatever evil spell had been cast, decree that this was only an accident, something that would slink away, that somebody else's camera, yesterday's or tomorrow's model, would not repeat.

She'd be there. I knew she would be waiting for me so we

could go to school together, that she'd awoken that morning thinking of me and my birthday, thinking of me as she made breakfast for her father, saw him off in his Mustang, left the front door open so that I wouldn't even need to ring the bell, I always, always would be welcome.

Though not the photo I showed her.

"Who is it?" she asked.

I told her that I did not know, did not care.

She insisted: "Who is he? What does he want?"

To fuck me over, that's what he wants. Words I didn't bother to spit out.

Already feeling a chasm yawning between us, that primate's face separating me from her, setting me apart. Because I could not even reveal that I suspected that this had leeched onto me due to that morning's transgression, that I had betrayed her, had engaged in sex with myself instead of showing patience, bestowing on an empty room what I should have been depositing inside her, listening to Peter Gabriel instead of hearing her murmur and gasp into my ear, I could not tell her that truth or any other truth. Maybe this happened to every boy who—maybe this was the most arcane rite of initiation, the secret of sex and puberty that no one wanted to talk about, maybe she would hate me for having spent myself, maybe if I pretended nothing much had happened it would go away by itself, tomorrow I would wake up and a different photo would announce my return to normality. Maybe I had been wrong to flee to her, trust that she would have a solution. When all she had was the question: Who is it?

It was the right question but I was not ready for it, I could only think of myself, why me?, why me?, that was my blundering and dumb response to her query, dumb because I did not articulate those words to her, just let them shape and slap my mind, breaching an even darker chasm between us, she was interested in who that man was and I didn't give a damn, all I wanted was for him to be gone and for her to take me in her arms and offer my stained body refuge, but he was already digging a pit around me, a wall forged from his eyes and hair and brown skin, he had made me and therefore her into strangers.

I looked at Cam as if I had never seen her before, as if I could already predict what lay ahead of us, the Rolling Stones tickets thrown into the garbage, the days and then weeks and months and years when we wouldn't speak to each other, avoid each other's company—as if I could come by and lavish a kiss from her lips, as if only the two of us were in the room or under the stars or on her bed, when there would always be three, yes, his poison was beginning to seep into every cranny, starting with her.

"You," I stuttered, "you," and I could barely manage to breathe out what ensued, but she could picture it in my eyes, she wasn't afraid and yet took a step back, such was the violence of my frustration, "You can't tell anyone about this, no one, no one, not your dad, not one soul, or . . ." Or what? Would I despise her, abduct her, maim her, kill her, cage her like a wild animal?

Cam's response was gentle, and for the click and snap and instant of a tick of time I managed to hold onto the illusion I was not turning into somebody else, into him, into the man whose face had ravaged mine, that it would all work out, that she still loved me as she had the night before and that I could still be whole, because she said:

"You can count on me," that is what she promised, that is what years later I would discover was the truth, but that interlude of peace dissolved and I knew it was too late, I had let some monster out or in and she had asked who it was, who is it, what does he want? And so I backed off. Instead of falling into her arms and sobbing there and planning by her side what to do, I snatched the Polaroid print and turned and left her without any promise on my part, she could not count on me because there was no me anymore, just us, just the young barbarian and this contaminated fourteen-year-old condemned for reasons he did not understand, clinging to memories of the girl he had just broken with, as if remembering could bring salvation.

We liked to joke that it had been love at first splash. Or first stroke, which had a more erotic loop to it.

At the tryout for the swim team at our school, that's when we recognized each other. We both loved swimming, we were both good at it, we were paired together by Coach Griselda, a former Olympic bronze medalist who wanted to mix boys and girls up, considered it stimulating for competition.

I barely spared a glance at the petite damsel by my side, this partner who had been foisted upon me—hey, I was ten years old and often vented about how stupid girls were, overcompensating for my fear of the other sex, their pert looks, their gossipy mouths, their giggling conspiracies, the mysterious attraction of slim legs as they ran or, in the case of the swimmer perched next to me at the pool's edge, fleshing provocatively from the contours of a bathing suit. So I just nodded in a perfunctory manner, indicative of my obvious superiority, when the coach introduced us, this is Cam Wood, this is Roy Foster, hello, hello, hello and goodbye, I hoped, I'd leave her behind me in the water soon enough.

And then we dove in and were swimming vigorously, furiously, doing our best to beat the rival, clock the best time, make the team. But it turned out that we were synchronized perfectly, matched as if by some magical hand of God, her left arm and mine swinging like the bending necks of two swans, cupped hands hitting the water at the same lilting instant and our mouths breathing in and out simultaneously, and the next stroke again, and then again, as if there were not two of us but one, one body sharing four arms and four legs, skimming on top of the liquid challenge of the pool, one just as vibrant and tired as the other, unable to gain an inch in our race, unwilling really because it was too wondrous how these parallel lines and lives and torsos converged in one sweet savage rhythm. Unwilling because when she started, for the squish of a second to advance and edge forward, break away, reach the goal sooner, she immediately relinquished her lead, something in the tips of her fingers sighed to her not to outclass me and stay in that mutual, common cadence our lungs had discovered before either of us had ever exchanged a true word, letting our bodies speak for us, already yearning for a different song.

Not my imagination that she was relenting when she should have pressed her advantage. I did the same thing. When she eased up a bit so our arms could once again dip into the water and surface in harmony, when I managed, thanks to her delicate hesitation, to forge forward, I also surrendered my speed right away so my frame would coincide millimetrically with hers, we both made sure we would arrive at the end of the pool absolutely, completely, amazingly together.

And amazing was the very word that Coach Griselda used to describe our performance. "Like two peas in a pod," she enthused. "Two dolphins! Two orcas! Two seals! What a team, what a team, made for each other."

Then I looked for the first time at the glory that was Cam Wood and she blinked back at me. We both knew what the coach meant, that we could pace each other, contest each other, bring out the best in our teammate. But dripping with water, glistening my eyes over her face, her smile slipping into mine, we did not need to express with words the deep-sea meaning beneath the surface of that word *team*, those words *made for each other*. And we dared to divine that the rest of our lives would be nothing more than the exploration of what our bodies by now knew.

And this paradise was what that horrible leering image had robbed from me.

I must have spent the next nine hours wandering around, given that I exhausted almost all the gas in the motorbike. I probably rode along the Charles River back and forth, back and forth, as if caged and trapped between water and land, rather than enjoying the clear blue of the late summer sky, the glorious breeze, a perfect day to play hooky. I had always wanted to visit my favorite nature spots when there was nobody spoiling them, I am sure that I stopped and lulled myself to sleep under those enormous oaks by water that Thoreau had venerated, but what came before is speculation as I have no memory of where I went, what I did, even who I was, losing myself, lost, until I awoke to the murmurs of a nearby stream and looked at my watch and it informed me that it was five o'clock in the afternoon.

I extracted the photo from my pocket. I rubbed his mug with my fingernail. Nothing. I scratched harder. For one instant, it seemed to fade, then slowly surfaced again, recomposed itself entirely. I used a pen to scrawl a beard on him, a florid moustache, horns, stupid eyebrows. And observed how the puerile cartoonish defacement vanished, his face reemerging as if from a fog.

I grabbed a stick and punched a hole where his features gloated out at me.

That did it. He could not fill a void. But of what use was that to me, exterminating my image along with his? Like killing yourself to get rid of cancer or banging your head to stop a headache. Nor would such defilement deter him. The next time somebody snapped a photo of me, he would be back. Unless I cut my own face out, shredded and cut my face into shards. Killed myself.

Five fifteen.

Time to head home for whatever reckoning awaited me, my violated face.

My face?

Was it still there, could I still see it?

I looked at myself in the motorbike's rearview mirror and the very features that the camera had refused to capture stared back at me, unaltered. I turned to the river, crept to the water's edge until I found a pond among the reeds and searched for my reflection, and again recognized the young man who had awoken to his birthday that very morning, an eternity ago. Something at least to celebrate, that the monster had not infected everything, though I could not know, of course, the pain that glancing at my own face would cause me in the years to come, could not guess that I would spend hours on end staring at my image with mocking, masochistic self-scrutiny in the morning mirror, as if to assure my mind that I had not disappeared, that the curse had not spread, leper-like, to my skin, until finally, one day, I stopped hurting myself, I repudiated looking glasses and replicating ponds, I would no longer squint out of a window when it grew dark outside for fear of being reminded yet once more of what I had lost, one day I drastically decided to avoid the horror of watching my face grow older, the changes that no camera or video or film registered once the plague took up residence in my skin.

Did I have any hope as I sped home that evening? Did I expect that maybe something miraculous would happen once I was under the protective wings of my family?

Skulking outside the door, I could hear a full-blown war of words, angry arguments cascading to and fro. Of course, as soon as I entered the living room, silence possessed the antagonists— my father cool and cutting, my mother flushed and spilling over with anxiety, while my two brothers watched from the sofa, transfixed as if they were onlookers at a wrestling match. That major scuffle had probably been fermenting since my departure, probably my father had called in sick, not caring that he had to put the finishing touches on the new Danny Kaye commercial, my mother must have phoned her book club pals that she could not meet them, neither of them even realizing that Hugh and Vic had missed school.

There were forced smiles all around and an extra-special bear hug from Mom, everything as it should have been on the eldest son's birthday, except for the question my father directed to me: *Did you show it to anybody?*, and my lie just as quick: *Of course not.* And his retort: *Good. Let's start then. Soonest is better.*

That's when I saw, piled up in a corner, twelve cameras, the seven that belonged to my dad, plus the four different versions of the Polaroid SX-70 delivered on separate and solemn occasions to my mother, my brothers, and me, as well as one old piece of German equipment that Mom had inherited from who knows what ancestor and that nobody had ever figured out how to use, that's how old it was.

There followed the first of what was to be an endless array of photographic sessions in the years to come. Starting, that night, with all the Polaroid devices, which spewed out the same primitive countenance pasted onto mine. No matter the distance between me and the lens, no matter who else was in or out of range, no matter how much light or shadow was cast upon me, the result was invariably the same. And the more those visual testimonials of the travesty piled up, the paler my father grew, the more red and embarrassed my mother, the more withdrawn my brothers.

When that phase was done, the ceremony was repeated with each of my father's machines that had not been manufactured by Polaroid. He loved cameras of all sorts, even the ones the Kodak rivals had released, and other brands as well, and he had fully loaded each one and now proceeded to shoot me all over again, family group, then by myself, then in a chair, then lying down, finally a close-up, and then all over again with the lights down, and with sunglasses that, he liked to remind us, came straight from the genius of Dr. Edwin Land and Polaroid Research and Development, and even dressed me up with the goggles Grandpa Bert had brought back from the war, hundreds of frames, the full pictorial pursuit carried out with not a sound in the room except the faint clack of shutter and button and my dad clearing his throat after each take.

Once it was over, he nodded, and finally spoke: "I'll be back soonest." He loved that word, *soonest*, expected the world to quicken at his command or persuasiveness, always in a hurry, my dad, always so sure of himself, always scripting everything.

We knew where he was going, with that bag brimming over with cameras and film, and could calculate how long it would take him to drive from our Waltham home to the Polaroid building on Memorial Drive in Cambridge, stealthily creep into it without being disturbed, descend into the bowels of the lab and develop the many rolls of film, I could imagine him scrutinizing each photo and then stuffing each one in the bag along with the cameras and returning to the darkened living room where we all awaited him on tenterhooks, my hand in my mom's, our hearts beating as if one.

He tried putting a good face, so to speak, on the disaster that was befalling the tribe, as he liked to call it.

"It's every photo from every camera," he said when he returned. "All brands are equally liable! Look, look, look!" If I repressed my resentment at such glee it was because I was aware how much it mattered that the blame for my savage's malevolent raid be shared by other companies, saving both Edwin Land's photographic empire and Dad's income. Though as we looked, per his

instructions, at the hundreds of photos where that young, primitive alien subjugated me, as our dismay grew, so did Dad's, his
realization that Polaroid would not easily escape a barrage of bad
publicity, far from it.

And here is where the quarrel I had interrupted came back
full blast. Now that it was clear that a plague—my mother was
the first to use that word, my father avoided it, preferring the less
medical term *catastrophe*—had indeed mortified our family, the
question was what to do with me.

Mom wanted to raise the alarm. She didn't quite manage
to recommend calling out the Army, the Navy, the Air Force,
the Coast Guard, but that was the caliber of intervention she
was demanding. Our doctor, for starters, to see if he could discover the causes of this sickness. He'd know if anyone else was
infested. Though better perhaps the ER, the police, lawyers, the
Boy Scouts—and also uncles and aunts, her mother, my father's
parents, ever more hysterical as she added names and professions
and contacts, my teachers, they would know if any students had
reported in sick, the school principal, everybody, anybody who
might shed some light on Fitzroy's ailment, and then there were
the neighbors and the PTA so parents could quarantine their
children. And the media, she said resolutely, the public had the
right to be on the lookout and collaborate in a campaign to—

And that's when my dad cut the torrent off. Precisely now was
when prudence and caution were needed. To panic could bring irreparable harm to Roy. Did she realize what it meant if this shameful
episode was revealed to the ravenous media, whose hunger for
scandal he knew all too well—he was paid, after all, to feed it selec-
tively, make sure Polaroid's image remained intact and unblemished.

We knew, he said, the delicate position that the company was
in. He didn't need to elaborate. We had all lived through the traumatic Polavision fiasco of the last years: many millions invested

to develop a soundless instant film had almost bankrupted the company, leading to Dr. Edwin Land's resignation as CEO, unsettling the company's stock and status. And this "creature from hell"—my father's exact words—could not have picked a more perverse moment to infest me, precisely when next month's upcoming patent trial against Eastman Kodak guaranteed a media frenzy. Reporters, searching for rumors to juice up the story, wouldn't care if other cameras, non-instant photographic systems displayed the same horrible effects. The first manifestation of this fiendish child molester had coiled out of an SX-70, choosing the son of Polaroid's marketing vice president, sullying the cheerful image of families basking in American bliss that he had strived to create. The company could not survive such a blow.

Mom was about to reply, when I piped up.

"What about me?"

I wasn't surprised that my dad's priority was Polaroid. His loyalty to Dr. Land's legacy could be traced back to his own father: "I wouldn't exist, you boys wouldn't exist, if it hadn't been for Edwin Land and his invention of wartime darkness goggles." Grandpa Bert had started working in the Land laboratory in 1940 and claimed that his life had been saved by the use, five years later, in the war zone of France, of the same eye equipment he had helped design. To give the story a twist of drama and romance, my dad's dad would add that it was through that very device that he had first espied his future wife, Berénice Briant, gazing in wonder at the night sky aglow with rockets and blazing bombs, and that he had rushed to her, thrown her down on the rich soil of France. And, of course, both he and she had taken their time in raising themselves up, the noise and the havoc a perfect pretext for the process of mutual exploration that would lead, nine months later, to the birth of my father, in the States, as by then Bert had been sent back with shrapnel in his knee—and

a young Parisian bride. His only regret: that he had not liber-
ated the concentration camps, having promised Dr. Land that he
would kick kraut ass and free whatever Jew he found imprisoned
by the Nazis. Instead he was limited to looking at those photos
of emaciated humans. Not that Land ever reproached him
with dereliction of duty. He accepted Bert Foster back into the
Polaroid family—showed him the old draughtsman's desk that
awaited his skills along with his old salary. And then, decades
later, welcomed Bert's son into the fold as well. Though Jerry
Foster was too proud to use his father's credentials to secure a job
at the company. This he did on his own, sidling up to Dr. Land
as he was leaving a shareholder meeting (our family had shares
in the company, of course) and whispering into his ear: "We had
fun inventing it. Now it's your turn." Land only grasped what this
meant—he was never any good at marketing—when my father
elaborated: "It's your new slogan, sir, for the next model." Land
hired him on the spot—just out of Harvard Business School
though he might be—and had nurtured him carefully over the
years. More so when he discovered that he was the product of
Bert's loins and Polaroid goggles.

And also took a liking to me at the age of eleven when my
father, without the slightest hint of the irony in the words he
was choosing, introduced me to the great genius as *the boy who's
being groomed to follow in his forefathers' footsteps*. Dr. Land had
responded by musing to himself, *steps, yes, steps*—and then, *so tell
me, lad, are you ready to create the impossible, are you ready, Fitzroy
Foster, to take five thousand steps before you reach it?* He must have
appreciated my response, *as many steps as required, sir*, because the
next day he sent me, written in his own hand, some lines about
those five thousand steps—neither of us guessing that there
would be a day when his advice would come in handy.

So my "What about me?" was not judgmental, merely inquisitive. However much I had been trained to privilege the company over my own desires, I still had the right to know what was in store for me.

Like any superb marketing executive, my father had answers to everything.

"You, Roy? This is all about protecting you. Even a whisper about this illness and you'll be sequestered by the government, picked apart by bureaucrats and researchers and medical personnel, displayed like a freak till the end of your days. My Lord, they might even confine the whole family for who knows how long. Your mother and I only have your best interests at heart. Tell him, Margaretta!"

"So, according to you," she said, "what happens next?" The calmness in her voice indicated that she seemed ready to defer to him—for now, at least.

"First, we need to investigate this—this phenomenon. Unobtrusively. Test every piece of photographic equipment out there—and film, of course, Super-8, the works. Polaroid has models of each and every camera. We can sneak in after hours."

"Isn't it careless not to warn anyone else?" Mom insisted.

"If any other child or adult is afflicted, we'll know soon enough—"

"Not if everyone decides to keep quiet like us."

"And we'll need to ferret out from both sides of the family," Dad continued, ignoring Mom's objection, "if anyone's heard of any anomaly that involves taking pictures."

"The pictures. What do we do with the pictures?"

"Destroy them, burn the fuckers, every last one. No incriminating evidence. We can't risk letting Kodak get ahold of even one sample. Nobody's ever going to say that our family was responsible for the downfall of the Polaroid empire."

I wondered if his craving for an auto-da-fé might derive from something more than a tactic to shelter the company. Could this supernatural, inexplicable portent have delivered my habitually, excruciatingly rational, ultra-scientific progenitor into the grip of superstition? Did my father really believe that reducing the miscreant to ashes would rid us of his crimes and sins?

Anyway, Mom wasn't about to reenact the Inquisition in our own home. Now it was her turn to be adamant: she intended to collect every item, every photo, make an archive, day by day and hour by hour, document the whole infestation, just as she had kept the school reports in a box, vaccination certificates, medical history of her three boys, just as she had measured height and weight, all, all of it there, a sort of family anti-album, so that when Fitzroy was cured she would be able to point to the origin of the sickness, the stages of its progress and ultimate rout and defeat. And that day—

And Dad began shaking his head violently, that day what?, pass this on to the press, be accused of having hidden something so explosive and dangerous?—and I could see where this was heading and decided to leave them to it, and climbed the stairs to my room.

There, awaiting me, imperturbable, was all that I had abandoned a mere few hours ago, each pillow and poster and book and piece of clothing and drawings and mathematical equations on my desk. And Cam's glorious photo snapped by her father, as crazy about taking pictures as my own dad—"my parents decided that when they called me Cameron," he would joke, "so what else could we name our daughter but Camilla, huh?, be sure to take good care of her, Fitz, or I'll snap something else, eh, come and shoot you with something heftier than a camera, right?," oh if he had known what we had been up to in her bedroom just the night before. And also there, on top of my sheets, the cover to the Peter Gabriel album, containing the song that had started it all this morning. I had fallen in love with that cover by Hipgnosis as soon as I had glimpsed it in a store and loved it all the more because my father hated the artwork. The designers had used a Polaroid shot of the singer to deform his face, melt half of it ferociously—Cool, I thought, terrifyingly perfect, was Camilla's reaction—but now that I was the monster, now that "Games Without Frontiers" was associated and always would be with this disease, I felt disgust, the intuition that I had brought this upon myself, not just the solitary sex, but the fact that before the act itself I had dabbled in this fascination with the monstrous without fully understanding what was behind it, that I had let myself be caught in something that was not a game, that I had passed a frontier, was discovering that if looks could kill they probably will.

I vomited on the cover. There was not much in my stomach but enough bile to smear the side of Peter Gabriel's face that was whole and intact, and I immediately realized that this was wrong, that the singer had nothing to do with my cataclysm. I had to hold onto something from my former life, could not destroy everything I cared for as that indigenous invader wanted—but what, what, what did he want?

I took the cover to the bathroom where eighteen hours before I had burst my innocence and entered the world of adulthood with a joy I no longer felt, I cleaned the artwork, scrubbed Peter Gabriel's face spotless, returned the album to its venerable place in my room.

And descended the stairs for the second time on that fateful birthday.

Dad and Mom had attained a truce.

Mom agreed that we should not go public. And Dad had consented to my seeing our family doctor—we'd tell him that I was assailed by sudden blinding headaches, so that a barrage of tests could be ordered. Strange how they were deciding my fate, the next decades of my life, without consulting me, treating me more like a captive than a minor. And Mom had won another battle: she would keep all the offending images, save them from incineration under lock and key up in the attic, and furthermore she was given permission to surreptitiously investigate the possible identity of this devil who had come to disturb the peace and quiet of a happy and law-abiding American family.

The next days brought me a taste of what my life would be like from now on.

Being probed by machines, that's what.

Medical devices of all sorts, including, of course, X-rays. Though the savage seemed to specialize in exteriors and skin, we feared that his real, cavernous habitat was deep inside me, that he'd somehow infiltrated my brain, leering out from the skull or the stomach, we feared he was hidden in some cancerous growth. The X-rays came back absolutely normal, incongruous that this should be about the only normal thing in my existence, the inside of my vulnerable body.

I was also one of the first humans to be scanned by an MRI machine, not yet available to the public. But Cameron Wood had been the liaison between Polaroid and General Electric on several military projects, and when my dad told him that I was ill, he responded that he'd be glad to get me tested up at the medical facility in Schenectady, New York, and added, *So that's why Cam's been so depressed lately.* Again, the sonar waves revealed no problems. Other medical tests were equally noncommittal—they measured every last limb and protuberance, length of fingers, arms, thighs, cranium, nose, mouth, and checked my blood for sugar, cholesterol, mineral content, liver function, triglyceride levels, possible drug use. My cells were analyzed in petri dishes, electrocardiograms monitored my heart, the screenings seemed endless, all returning negative, each of them telling the truth about my health, that there was no visible cause for my condition. Not a surprise, as we had lied about what was really ailing me, insisting to staff and doctors and our health insurance company that the headaches would not go away, elaborating ever grander untruths to secure further assessments, inventing hallucinations that made me see monkeys and gorillas in the place of people. Until they finally gave up, certified me in perfect physical health and recommended psychiatry. Could they be right? Was I crazy? No. The monster I was forbidden from divulging to the world, he was the crazy one, crazy with rage, envy, vindictiveness.

As the cameras proved in the many secret photographic sessions that ran parallel to those medical exams. The morning after my birthday, I was greeted by my parents, at last united in their strategy. While I had slept well, visited by nothing other than the usual bizarre dreams entertained by our species for the last two million years, they had been up all night compiling a list of questions that my increasingly unwilling body had to answer. Would a similar invasion be inscribed on film or on the video recorders that were being tested by Sony and JVC, according to Polaroid's spies? Did anything change if the photos were in black and white? With one flash, with two flashes, with green lights and red lights and filters and black drapes? At different locations and landscapes? At night, when I was asleep and the prowler might be less vigilant? Beneath a canopy of trees or at the zoo or at an ethnographical museum? Wouldn't a more natural habitat, the sort the Neanderthal was accustomed to, placate whatever bloodthirsty reasons he had for this foray? What if I closed my eyes? Covered my face with one hand, with two hands, only with a few fingers? Disfigured myself with clown makeup, made my countenance cartoonish with the sort of moustache and scars and heavy eyebrows I had carved into his image by the Charles River? What if I wore a mask like Zorro or Flash Gordon, placed my heroes Spider-Man or Batman between us? Foiled him with Porky Pig or Mickey Mouse? Entirely disappeared inside a burlap bag?

Of all the alternatives, only the latter stopped this unknown native's intrusions. He ignored every obstacle we put in place, every modified circumstance, every shift from Konica to Minolta to Kodak and back to Polaroid and its multiple models. Only when I was entirely ensconced away, not one inch of skin visible, did he refuse to impose his features on mine. Much help that was—I couldn't go stumbling through the rest of life inside a bag. Though one ephemeral pleasure was afforded to me: as he seemed to tolerate the two slits for my eyes, six weeks after my catastrophic fourteenth birthday, I was able to freely roam the streets for Halloween. This was eight months before Spielberg's *E.T.* was released in the States, the movie where the cute little alien, walks a California suburb without calling attention to himself. My mom snuck me into the Cineplex to see it with my brothers, and there it was, the same trick I had anticipated in my own life.

But I never wandered freely like that again. It had been so exhilarating while I was trick-or-treating—telling one and all that I was dressed up as a simple burlap bag, a shopping bag hungry for candy—when what I was hungry for was company and normalcy, the anonymous liberty to play with other boys, fantasize that I was like them, that tomorrow I would go to school like them and kiss girls like them and play baseball like them and attend dances and picnics and beach parties, like them, like them. Except I wasn't. I returned home and saw it as my prison, its walls and windows the true limits of my world. So that taste of freedom was bitter. The momentary experience— not even affording a glimpse of Camilla, unless she was hiding her sorrow under a mask of her own—was not thrilling enough to compensate for the next 364 days of misery and simulation.

Better to accept that real captives were not given a day's sur-cease. All those kids out there could play at being monsters for one night because they were nothing like me, this paranoid shadow whose every Kodak moment was a Walpurgis night, the hallowed evening when the dead rise from the grave—every day and every one of my nights haunted by that dead man, ruining my existence.

Because that is what he had come to do, that is what I thought for many years.

I had dropped out of school, of course. Something decided by my parents that first weekend, not even letting me go there to say goodbye to friends and teachers, coaches and swim-ming pool and baseball field. Homeschooling from now on, my mom explained, until I got better. Not just school forbidden but everywhere and anywhere that ubiquitous cameras roamed, each last inhabitant of this planet a potential predator. The planet! As if I could get anywhere on my own, without a driv-er's license or a passport. Confined and cocooned, much like someone indeed suffering from the plague. My parents system-atically turned away friends who came to check out what might have gone wrong, why was the most popular and boldest boy in the class suddenly a pariah?

Camilla herself did not stop by—she knew I would turn her away—but her father did, to inquire how the tests had gone in upstate New York. Not friends, our two dads, though they respected each other, complemented each other. Cameron Wood specialized in the long-term architecture of the eye and how it could be projected onto paper and Jerry Foster tried to make sure the eyes of millions of consumers instantly fell in love with the images on those pieces of paper. On that visit, Dr. Wood informed them that his daughter, though heartbroken, wanted the Fosters to know she was ready to help if they needed her.

I didn't come down to speak to him, didn't send a message back. I had made the mistake of trusting her with my secret. I wasn't going down that road again. And even if I had wanted to reconnect, each day that I was caged and she was free pushed her farther away. She had asked for me, of course she had—how else to salve her conscience as she tasted life and liberty and the pursuit of happiness, but soon, like someone sent into the ice of exile, I would fade from her memory, not even a silhouette on her horizon. She would find another swimming partner, other lips under other trees and the same stars, other hands to soften her muscles and explore her sex.

Depression started to set in. Staved off during the initial month and a half by collaborating voraciously in the medical and photographic sessions, as eager as my parents for some reprieve, animated by the ever fainter hope that some dawn the savage would decamp as abruptly as he had arrived. Perhaps it was fatigue that punctured that transitory elation—or just the dejected aftermath of my Halloween outing, which forced me to accept that my habitual, receding self was not going to return to anything resembling that photo pinned to my desk.

It was to shield myself from the sting of incessant regrets that I rebelled.

Not by demanding to go out. My parents had convinced me that such audacity could lead to far worse forms of incarceration than the bittersweet safety of our own home. No, what I insisted on was some order in those photo opps, a reasonable schedule.

"I feel like an animal in a zoo," I protested—yes, I really did use that term of comparison, "always on call, you guys looking at me through the viewfinder whenever you feel like it, snapping pictures, turned into a souvenir. I hate that moment when we hold our breath to see if we'll win this time—and we never do!"

Once a week, once a week and no more.

My parents pleaded with me—why make it easy for the ghoul, why give him a timetable he could count on? What if we were missing an opportunity to surprise him, evade his vigilance, seize the odd moment in the day when he dozed off or his attention wandered?

I was deaf to their entreaties. By then I was certain that the visitor did not sleep. He was burrowed inside, irremediably there, under my skin or wafting over me like a malevolent mist. I did not share that disquieting intuition with my progenitors, telling them, instead, that I needed to govern something in my own life, limit his influence to one hour a week, pretend that he had no access to me the rest of the time. It might be an illusion, but at least it would offer him the gift of existence solely in the brief interlude when he inserted his image between me and the camera.

It was almost like a pact.

He would know when he was expected to show up—and I would know that he would keep his appointment, no longer scheming to trick him. We'd each settle into our assigned role: he as a ghost that could not be mollified, poor Fitzroy Foster as the victim who could not escape.

Not entirely true, that I could not escape.

Like a werewolf, I came to love the night, though I preferred my nights moonless and dark. My dad and mom didn't know it, but I would often sneak out, slink down abandoned alleyways, learning the arts of infinite stealth, careful not to tread near streets patrolled by the police. It would have been disastrous to be caught and photographed at the precinct station, though I savored the astonishment I'd cause, how I would caution the officer not to snap my picture, that he didn't know what he was getting into. But no matter how much I relished the imaginary dialogue where I played the tough guy and the police the pansies about to be horrified by my devilish cohort, it made sense to stay away from trouble.

I didn't want to imperil the entrancement and independence that nightfall provided—joining all the monsters of history who creep out into the crevices of society when they believe nobody is watching. Those hours under the starlit or overcast skies with nobody to bother me, no importune camera to nail me to its lens.

Not the only rules I broke.

On those autumn junkets, I would find myself irresistibly drawn to a range of self-service photo booths that Polaroid had strewn in the grittier parts of town. I'd enter that neon cubicle, stupidly read the instructions as if I had never before registered them, feed the coins into the slot, let the camera do its job, and wait for my image to be coughed up.

Why did I subject myself to this ceremony, destined to incessant disappointment, allowing the figment of my invisibility to be demolished again and yet again? Did I truly think that, alone with the machine, he would find himself stymied? That he required human eyes to usher his face into existence? But it was only my solitary eyes he required, the frightened invitation of my face and the cold shuttering whir and clicks of the camera to snake himself onto me, with his sad black eyes and those thick inscrutable lips.

Don't let him beat you, my mother said, as I sank into the listlessness and docility of easy victimhood, rarely rising from my bed, paying only perfunctory consideration to her lessons in history, chemistry, English, or even my favorite of favorites, math. Of what use were they to someone like me, banned from everything a lad of my age should have been enjoying? Don't let him beat me? What did she know? What did my father know when he urged me to fight back? Against an apparition? Dominating my every act?

He rose with me at dawn and breakfasted by my side and snickered at the long conversations with my parents as we sought fruitlessly to outwit him, the timid and ridiculous suggestions of my brothers. He was there when I pissed and when I defecated and when I shut myself in my room for hours doodling with algorithms. And, of course, when I engaged in endless chess matches with myself. He dictated the moves of the other side, he whispered that I should sacrifice my bishop, save my knight for better times, he cheered my pawns as they were crowned queens, I checkmated him over and over, checkmated myself, lost even when I won. He was me. How could I beat him? There was no place to hide from his eyes of night—like a mouse or a chimpanzee in a laboratory, I was always under surveillance. No longer by doctors, but by his gaze, I could feel him measuring me, analyzing my cartilage and gait and elbows. My master. How to beat him?

Only by ridding the world of the body he had infected.

You want my life, you fucker? Well, here it is. I'm surrendering it to you, may it be as useless to you as it will soon be to me. My revenge: never again to be the vessel for your malice. Drown myself and drown him—and send a message to Cam. For some absurd reason I assumed she'd be the one to identify my corpse—oh would she feel sorry when she understood that the water that had blessed us together had now claimed me forever.

And I knew just the place. That lost landscape of paradise next to the Charles River where I had attempted to erase the visitor's image and had realized that only by destroying his face, and mine, and mine, could he be placated.

What I should have done then.

I waited for the family to fall asleep and revved up the motorbike for what I swore would be my last ride. It was cold that winter night—Christmas was only two weeks away—and I bundled a couple of blankets in my backpack. A decision that should have made me wary of how sincerely I was arranging my suicide. Why worry about catching a cold if you're about to die by your own hand? And my suspicions should have redoubled when, upon arriving at that spot, I placed the blankets carefully on the ground and lay down—only for a few seconds I told myself, only to review my life, focus on one memory I wanted to take to the other world, one instant of pleasure that I could remember as I sank into the deep, rushing waters.

And there it was, inside some zone of myself, the very last time I had been free of his atavistic face, and my hand knew what to do to bring that moment back. It crept furtively downward and strayed toward my genitals and nestled there, rummaged gently for a touch, ready to repeat the rhythm that had culminated with that initiation into manhood. Yes, that was it, one ultimate act of self-love to indulge in before terminating my life and his enigma, bring to a fitting close the infernal circle that had opened on the morning of my fourteenth birthday. What better way to say goodbye? After that final expiring orgasm I'd find the courage to slip, still panting and hot with my own fruitless sperm, into the icy river.

And then, before my fingers could continue with their preliminary stroking, Camilla Wood came to me. Not true that she was gone forever. She had remained behind in some labyrinth of my brain, lingered like an aftertaste of perfume that refuses to dissipate. There, under that glacial wind, fighting against the desire to die, I held onto her image like a life raft. There was, in that memory of the woman I had lost, a breathtaking purity that returned me to who I had once been, someday might be, a glimmer of hope in the last corner of the last recess of my mind that things could change. Reminded that an alternative future still might await me somewhere at the confines of the earth. Like a prisoner remembers the mountain he once climbed and the glint of the sun falling into the sea. Like an animal in a zoo must recall the free scent of trees and light. Like a man struck blind evokes colors he will never see again. Where did those images come from? Had she been sending them to me so I could choose life and not death?

I stood up from the ground, shivering, wrapped myself in both blankets like a newborn child, recoiling from the sin I had been about to commit—against myself, against life, against my love.

Warmed by her voice from afar.

And yet, it was not merely her memory that made me cease that sexual ceremony before it had culminated. I also did it to spite my visitor. He had foraged into my secret core, become my twin, my equal, my obdurate companion, the only one who knew my real thoughts. The place of trust that I had always conjectured Cam would occupy: to be my confidante, my mind reader, my pillow, the swimming maiden I'd conceal nothing from. Well, there was one thing, this one private thing that belonged only to me, that I would keep from him.

I headed home.

He could hover above me like rotten breath all he wanted, he could wait till the ebbing of time for me to masturbate for his voyeuristic eyes. I would not perform in his peep show. I would not give him that satisfaction, not now, not ever, not repeat in his presence that instant when I filled the cup of my fancy with Camilla Wood and our dream of swimming through life together, side by side, stroke by stroke, forever, the true forever. I would not let him share what was reserved for her, that intimacy.

I would not betray her.

It was madness, a delusion. What chance did I have of spending a night, much less a lifetime, with that splendid woman, when she was free to pursue her cravings and I was restricted to festering inside that stranger's stare?

Madness, a delusion, but it saved me, allowed me to live for something other than to be a depository of pictures retched on my countenance. By that river of death, I had been struck by the revelation that she could be a visitor as well, at least in my mind, in my forlorn heart. You can stop me from being with her, but not from dreaming about her, you cannot stop her from visiting me.

All the more reason for me to not immediately, that night or in the months and years that followed, try to resolve the questions Cam had posed when shown the photo, who is it, who is he, what does he want? No, I would not honor that fiend by searching for his identity.

That was a task my mother had taken on with such verve and determination that she had eventually found what she believed to be an answer. How was she to know, how was I, that it would lead to even worse injury, a deepening of our tragedy?

Her search had begun tentatively, reaching out to family members. She needed to explain anyway my sudden absence from the flock of pictures periodically sent their way. "These headaches," she wrote, favoring letters over the perilous give and take of a phone conversation, "have made Fitzroy extraordinarily shy of cameras. Each time a photo is snapped, he feels his head is about to explode. So we'd appreciate, if you come for Thanksgiving or Christmas, that you abstain from mentioning this traumatic condition to him, let alone take photos. He requires peace and quiet and affection." And in a nonchalant postscript, a scrawled afterthought: "Just wondering if you know of any such adverse reactions in our family. Any gossip would be most welcome."

The responses were unanimously sympathetic, swearing dis-

cretion, but unable to shed light on any family member who had
ever shunned cameras. Mom's mother added, a touch acerbically,
that she could not imagine anyone in her past or her husband's
who behaved like "one of those savages from Africa, afraid that
a camera will steal his soul." My father's mother was less sharp
in her reply, but equally unhelpful: "I feel so sorry for poor Roy.
This impenetrable desire to escape being photographed goes
against everything I've heard in family lore, photography being,
according to legend, central to our prosperity many generations
back. I wish I had paid more attention to my grandparents, those
snatches of conversation I barely registered when I visited them
in France before they died."

With our tribal past closed, the only piece of evidence left to
my mom was the likeness of the invader himself.

The man was some sort of barbarian, an uncivilized brute who
must have been immortalized in a photograph long ago, and was
therefore presumably dead. Natural then that she should begin her
investigation at the Harvard library, going through stacks of books
on native peoples from everywhere on the planet—and months
later, had to admit that she had come up short. There was nobody
who looked exactly like this specter—though his features vaguely
brought to mind those of some Indians of the Americas.

She decided that it made sense to confer with some anthropologist who specialized in the field, preferably someone far from the
Boston area, so as to keep him at bay if he grew overly inquisitive.
For that she would have to send out the face, making sure to cut
out my neck and shoulders, so no one could link the image to
me. This instantly led to another round of altercations between my
parents. My father reminded his dear wife that their agreement
did not include showing the photocopy to foxy academics who
might well extricate its secret. Dad only relented after wresting
from my obstinate mother a promise to be extra tactful.

Mom enlisted the services of her brother Carl Bailey, a physicist at UC Berkeley. Lately she had been thinking, she wrote, about studying anthropology, maybe obtaining a Master's degree. He probably recalled her childhood dream of being a vet—a calling made impossible by her husband's allergy to fur and the hot breath of carnivorous creatures. *You were the one who counseled me, Carl, remember?—that if I couldn't heal animals, then why not study primitive people one step up the evolutionary scale.* And having spent oodles of time with my father and his Polaroid colleagues she wondered if photography and aboriginal tribes might not make for an intriguing area of research. Did he know of anyone who might offer some orientation?

Uncle Carl—the only member of the family to sport an academic career—replied with the address of Dr. Sheridan Beck, who had helped create an Indigenous Study Center at Berkeley in the seventies but had now retired to Denver, where he taught an emeritus course on Amerindians at the University of Colorado.

In the letter Mom fired off to Colorado, along with asking for guidance regarding future studies, she included the photocopy of the cutout face, inquiring if he might have some notion of its origin or tribal identity, as she found it mysterious and compelling.

Months passed. Just when Mom had lost all expectation of a reply, a letter arrived. Dr. Beck would be glad to help a relative of Professor Bailey's, and listed several institutions of higher learning where she might pursue her studies. Regarding the bizarre photocopy he had, despite lapses in recollection due to his age, some preliminary answers to her query. At first glance, there was a remote resemblance to a tribesman from the Ket ethnic group whose features he had snapped during a trip to Siberia twenty years ago. More likely candidates, however, were members of the Kuikoro and Kalapalo in Brazil, tribes recently relocated inside the Xingu reservation in order to save them from extinction. Here was the conundrum. No camera had been present at the first fleeting encounter with the Kuikoro in 1884, and only in 1945 did his good friends, the Villas-Bôas brothers, establish the first Western contact with the Kalapalo. Given the graininess of the image, however, it had to be earlier than that—shot in the 1870s, in some European country or the States, certainly not in the Amazon. Where, then, had Mrs. Foster come across such a specimen, indeed mysterious and compelling, more so because the body of the subject was missing? In what year had it been taken? If there was an expedition into the Amazon in the middle of the nineteenth century, carrying sophisticated photographic equipment, he would appreciate learning about what might turn out to be a ground-breaking discovery. Would she mind keeping in touch?

"Ha!" Dad cried out when he read Dr. Beck's letter. "You see, you see. I told you not to send it out. He'll show up at our doorstep any day now, announcing that he's figured out how that face is connected to the family."

Mom calmed him down, brandished her thank-you note to Dr. Beck, stipulating that she couldn't remember—she was also having her senior moments, she joked—who had sent along that photo. Once she'd tracked that person down, she'd respond more fully to his query. When the anthropologist excitedly answered, begging her to make an effort, and Mom simply ignored his pleas, several frantic letters from him followed.

And then, abruptly, no more communications from Colorado. Uncle Carl mentioned the reason, passingly, in a phone call: Dr. Beck had died of a heart attack. "Maybe that guy in the photo, your Mr. Monkeyman, killed him," my brother Hugh suggested, echoed by truculent Vic. If that savage could infiltrate my photos, why couldn't he engage in more dire actions? They began dancing around as if possessed by simians.

Mom, secretly relieved that our worries regarding Dr. Beck were over, contained her fury at such unbecoming behavior. Poor man. She had been rude to him whereas he had been so generous, providing real clues to the identity of our intruder. Clues she would diligently pursue for the next years.

Margaretta Foster had interrupted her studies at Boston College in order to support her husband while he finished Harvard Business School. I was now the pretext for a return to her frustrated vocation. Strange twists and turns of life: the monster had ruined my life but was offering a new lease on hers. She plunged into the history and geography, the religious and cultural customs, of the Amazonian Indians, quickly dispatching the vulnerable Ket people of Siberia—a red herring, she decreed, a waste of time.

During the first year of what she called, without realizing the irony, her voyage of discovery, she supplied once a week—precisely after the photographic session that I had to endure and that invariably ended with the same face plastered on top of my body—a report about her findings. What started, however, as a detached comment, neutral in voice and tone, gradually began to be colored by passion, spilling over into dinner conversations, flavored ever more frequently with allusions in Portuguese, a language she had started to learn with furious devotion.

It was not merely, I realized, that she had resolved that this was the path to save me. She was also saving herself, erasing an inexplicable guilt that lurked inside. When each passing day brought me no remedy, she increasingly felt—oh, Mom always took everything too much to heart—that she must be responsible for my disorder, had done something wrong and was being punished. To engage in that research was a relief, the certainty that she could get to the root of what had transpired.

"There must be an image somewhere," she would tell us, upon

returning from her library expeditions. The Amazon had been explored by many travelers in the nineteenth century and she seemed bent on exploring them, each and every one, with equal determination. She would not give up, no matter how impenetrable the thicket of bibliographic references became. When the obvious choices, the drawings of Henry Bates and the photos of Louis Agassiz ("He must be the one who took the photo, he came from the Boston Area, he took his wife Elizabeth Cary with him, you see how women also opened up those rivers?"), yielded no match with my visitor's visage, she spent weeks looking for a hint that perhaps the collection of Alfred Russel Wallace—the naturalist who had surmised before Darwin the evolutionary origin of species—had not really been lost when his ship back to England caught fire. When that trail and so many others led nowhere, she leapt to the twentieth century, to Percy Fawcett and his search for El Dorado, and then on to the expeditions of Euclides da Cunha and the Villas-Bôas brothers and so many others, the search seemed endless and, invariably, she came up empty.

"Maybe I should not be concentrating on the explorers," she said, "but on the dead."

This mystifying phrase was slowly clarified over the next two years, as she plummeted into the predatory exploitation of those unfortunate Amazonian creatures, how they had been robbed of their land and habitat by successive generations of conquistadors and then cultivators of *drogas do sertão*, did we know that the Indians were obliged to dig up cloves, cinnamon, vanilla, cacao, sarsaparilla, all sorts of seeds, for export, all for export, Brazil nuts and copaiba oil, forced to cut down trees on land where their ancestors had hunted, laboring because their women and children were held hostage in filthy encampments, enslaved by rubber barons and iron ore companies and diamond magnates and petty thieves and missionaries. Missionaries! Mom almost frothed at the mouth when she spat out the word. They were the worst—destroying the aboriginal culture under the guise of saving souls. Victimized by epidemics, smallpox, measles, tuberculosis, influenza, sexually transmitted diseases. The horrors went on and on and on. *Descimentos* and *resgates* and *guerras justas* became words as habitual to us as corn flakes and french fries. Turtle butter, she would exclaim at dinner, passing the ordinary cow's butter to smear on our corn on the cob or mix into her al dente linguini. Her eyes blazed: they were obliged to make butter out of the turtles, their amphibian friends.

But I really became conscious of how extreme was her transformation when she ceased to refer to my visitor as a fiend, a ghoul, a savage, a barbarian, a demon. He became that poor boy.

Her stories of oppression, rather than assuage my attitude toward him, made me more resentful: he had stolen my face and now was stealing my mother. I was sorry that his tribe had been exterminated, but why was that my business? Had I invaded his Amazon territory as he had invaded mine? Why hadn't he chosen some descendant of conquistadors or better still a contemporary logger who seemed to be the villain, why not someone ravaging the rain forest? Why me? It always came back to that question.

To which I had added another one, more specific to my own family.

Why not one of my brothers? Both of them?

I waited anxiously for Hugh and Vic to reach puberty. *Wait* is not the right word. I urged them to masturbate, fed them *Playboy* magazines and pornographic pictures and dirty jokes and innuendoes and positions, anything that might entice a visitor to come for them as he had come for me, the same visitor or one of his brothers if he had them, anyone would do. Mitigate my loneliness, join the club, in fact make it into a club, an entity with more than one member. But they hit thirteen and then fourteen and indulged in pleasures that I had given up on and yet showed no signs of infiltration, nothing more irregular than pimples, nothing more drastic than high-pitched vocal chords, a knowing smirk.

So that was that: this curse only descended upon the firstborn of this family. I was to carry the burden by myself.

Not only by myself. Mom also, she was also condemned.

Unlike my visitor's sudden initial incursion, this time we should have been prepared for the impending calamity. The signs were all there, made themselves manifest one night just after she had served each of us a habitually generous portion of dessert.

"Vanilla and cinnamon," she spewed the words as if they were insults. "The four of you like them, eh, vanilla and cinnamon, eh, like I did, like I did?"

We looked down at the bread pudding, delicious as ever.

"Made from Wonder Bread," she said. "Wonder, wonder, no wonder," she said. "No wonder," she said, "no wonder those people fled to the forests and the headwaters of the hinterland. No wonder," she breathed each word out as she pointed to the bread pudding, "that they wanted revenge. No wonder they sent an emissary to our comfortable world, living off their rubber and oxygen, munching their nuts, gobbling up their meat, sprinkling their dessert with vanilla and cinnamon. No wonder, no wonder."

Several minutes of silence followed this tirade, until my father spoke for the four men of his tribe: "You're taking his side. After all that he's done to us."

As if he hadn't made the accusation, as if I wasn't beholding her with amazement, she let us know what really puzzled her. These marauders had been Dutch and Spanish, Brazilian and Portuguese, but not of remote French or German ancestry as she and her husband were, so why should that young man have chosen their eldest son to exact vengeance, why Roy, why our family? And only then: "Yes, I'm taking his side. Not against you. Against the world that made him do this. I'm taking his side because it's the only way to convince him to stop haunting our boy. Or do you happen to have a better idea?"

"In fact, I do," Dad answered. "We both do."

It was a plan that we'd been hatching covertly for the last year. Dad had left Polaroid after Dr. Land's retirement, ending up at Negroponte's MIT lab, helping to explore how personal computers might revolutionize the media. One night, he'd brought home a Commodore 64 and hooked it up to a startup screen.

"This device or some future model will someday cure you," he said, stroking the computer as if it were the Venus de Milo. "It won't be long, the lab folks say, before we're able to manipulate images digitally, not requiring negatives or even light to process and reproduce a face. Just a series of binary codes inside a machine. Once that happens, the bastard's fucked. Whatever he is, whoever he is, he belongs to the past. Born into a world of photography, like we were. But humanity is about to leave him behind. Computer imaging will stop him from smuggling his ugly mug into your pictures. His primitive tactics and knowledge, wiped out for good, made obsolete."

"So what, Dad? This invention and that invention and this camera and that one and the latest newfangled device and a damn paradigm shift. I'll believe it when I see it. When your solution is as real as he is. So let's talk again when somebody truly manages to capture images through this digital shift, this digital shit."

"They've already started," Dad said, ignoring my profanity. "The military and NASA have been scanning scenery into their computers. It's only a matter of time until everybody is able to do something similar from their homes and personal computers, anybody who can afford it, just one more ordinary task. With microchips and miniaturization advancing the way they have lately, we—but that's not the point. The point is that you don't have to wait passively for salvation to arrive from the sky. It's up to you to accelerate that development. See what you can learn from this, Fitz—the latest books and papers, these confidential instruction manuals I borrowed from our lab."

I looked at the pile he hauled from his briefcase. It seemed an awful lot of reading.

"Up to me?" I said dully.

"You're smart, your teachers always said you were a genius at mathematics, how you knew how to talk to machines as if they were people. Read this literature, let me know what else you need, what equipment. Show him what you're made of, kiddo. Hell, you're American, not a loser."

I wasn't sure if he was just trying to shake me out of my depression, but it made sense, it tingled a fiber, long dormant, inside me. Perhaps that is why I was dumbfounded when Mom confessed that she had indeed changed sides. She had sort of fallen off my radar during the year or so dedicated to my new digital labors, most of my waking hours spent trying to defeat with science my Amazonian visitor's witch-doctor magic. I had, in fact, discovered just a month before the cinnamon-and-vanilla bread pudding incident a way to code images on a Mac and then engineer and display them on the startup screen. Dad was thrilled, wanted to show the program to the folks at the MIT computer science lab—though not before patenting my designs in DC under the name *Imageplus*—"We're going to be rich, Fitz! That savage may have done us a favor, set you up for life!"

I did not share Dad's enthusiasm, knew this was merely a modest first step, but it did help convince me that soon—perhaps some years down the road—I would be able to scan the photo from just before I was fourteen onto a computer and manipulate the image to simulate what the years had wrought on my real face. Though I still would be fettered by my need to hide from millions of practitioners of traditional photography, I could begin to envisage a future when I might be able to obtain a passport, create an ID for myself, perhaps even travel if I took every precaution.

We had not revealed any of this to Mom. If her delusionary quest for an outcome in the faraway Amazon jungle spared her from further dejection and guilt, why bring her down to earth? But after her outburst that night over dessert, she needed to know there was another solution to my problem.

"The way," Dad said, "to rid oneself of a curse is more science, not less science. Do your thing, Margaretta Foster. You'll never hear a word of reproach from me. But this monster won't be defeated by good intentions. You can't cure a plague by embracing it." And he proceeded to give her details of our plans.

She was not swayed. "We'll see who's right," she said. "You two, who want to scratch the surface of this crisis, or someone like me, who understands that you have to go to the roots, the origins, address the underlying cause."

And that's how Mom and I, over the next two years, went our separate ways. I plunged into computing and digital imaging with the ferocity of an explorer hacking his way through a thicket of trees and she navigated atrocities as if she had been born to document them. I studied spectrographs and pixels and binary formulas and she studied indigenous customs and religious ceremonies and shamanic rituals, she ever deeper into the past while I voyaged to what I thought was the future. Her new language: Portuguese. My old language: mathematics. A contrast in lifestyles as well: I ensconced myself in my room, and she expanded into the wide vast world, joined Survival International, organized a local Boston chapter to help the indigenous peoples of the world, particularly centered on the Amazon, an unremitting devotion that gained her the confidence of activists and leaders of the cause.

So this time, when she dropped her next bombshell, I was not entirely caught by surprise.

Mom announced, again at dinner, again as dessert was being served, that she was leaving for Brazil in a week. Part of a mission, she said, to confront the loggers, put white, Western bodies between their machines and weapons and the forests they were bent on destroying with the complicity of the government and the multinationals.

Again, absolute silence.

Fractured, finally, by my father's tremulous voice.

"And this is supposed to stop this man and his destruction of our tribe, our tribe, Margaretta, and not his, to save him you're ready to destroy our family?"

"I'm doing this for all of you, for us. I've made arrangements through Claudio and Orlando Villas-Bôas to meet the chiefs of the Kalapalo and Kuikoro and their shamans. I will plead for their intervention, to shut the portal that was opened by Western meddling in their culture, the looting of their souls."

"I forbid it, I forbid this insane trip."

"You know how the loggers decide what parts of the forest to cut down? Do you, Jerry? By aerial photography, Jerry, that's how they mapped out the Amazon and the Matto Grosso. You know who invented that form of surveillance, Jerry? Your precious Edwin Land, your divine Polaroid lab. You're in no position to forbid anything or anyone. You and your accomplices in genocide. Just be happy I'll be coming back to this house. And by the time I am back our Roy will be free. Or has your science found the solution you promised two years ago?"

"This is crazy."

"Crazy? I'll show you something crazy."

She went to the living room and came back with a large portfolio. Pulled out a sepia photo of an indigenous family under a thatched roof in what we presumed was a clearing in the Amazon: an older man, a woman showing her breasts, two younger boys verging on adolescence. "Look at him," Mom said, pointing at one of the youngsters. He shimmered with the faintest resemblance to my visitor, the shadows playing across his face making it difficult to establish a definite correspondence.

"Maybe yes, maybe not," my dad said. "So what?"

"So this photo and fifty-three others were taken by Albert Frisch, a German explorer, in 1867. The first ever snapped of the Amazon Indians. Captured for all time inside a camera and transported for everyone to see, at the mercy of anybody's eyes. 1867. Albert Frisch."

"And this justifies your trip because . . . ?"

"Because the photo was snapped exactly one hundred years before Roy was born. Because you once mentioned that a certain Frosch was one of your forebears, and your grandfather's name was Albert and your dad is Bert—"

"Frosch isn't Frisch and millions of people are called Albert or Bert and Frosch wasn't German but French Alsatian and the photo doesn't really correspond to the man who keeps cropping up and—and—oh what's the use?" Dad stopped, then pounced with another argument: "Didn't your Dr. Beck say that the photo couldn't have been taken of the tribe you're going to visit, that they weren't even discovered until the middle of our century?"

"Dr. Beck was old and his memory was fading."

"The hell to Dr. Beck! What I really resent is you blaming my family history for this malevolence. Why not your ancestors?"

"Yours, mine, that doesn't matter. The only thing that matters is that it's him in the photo. Poor young man. You understand what he must have gone through, right, Roy? That we can't free you until we free that boy from whatever curse is weighing down on him. Don't you? Don't you?"

Her words reminded me of another traumatic moment. Like Camilla, she was more interested in my visitor than in me. She'd chosen to champion some savage stranger over her own son.

I wheeled around, left the room, did not speak a word to her for the rest of the week.

The night before Mom was to depart, I left the door of my room unlocked on purpose, knowing she would come. I hardly heard her enter, so silently did she sidle up to my bed. As she used to when I was a child, as she still did from time to time to give me a good night hug.

But I was not a child anymore. I was almost nineteen and had endured years of agony and she, my own mother, had betrayed me.

I pretended to be asleep.

Maybe she knew I was faking it. Maybe she didn't care. She needed to speak to me, whether I was listening or not. Needed to hear her own voice. To feel that she had tried to make me understand, forgive her: it's about love, love for you, Roy, love for those who suffer just as you're suffering. I'd realize, she said, that the meeting with the shaman had been successful, she'd been able to persuade at least one of them to lift the spell, the haunting from 1867, I'd realize this because any photo of my face snapped at home after that remote exorcism would be clean of interference and I'd then see myself in that image as if in a mirror or a lake, as she was seeing me now with her eyes so full of compassion. Next time I greeted her, we'd all be free, she and Dad and the boys and me, her darling Fitzroy.

She kissed me, stood up, I could hear her tip-toeing to the door. Then she must have paused there to take one last look, because she glided back and I felt her hand caress me, the fingers parting the hair that I had inherited from her, the color and the strands and the lock that kept pushing itself out of place.

I still didn't move.

And then she was gone.

A glimmer in me wanted to believe that she would succeed, that love would win the day.

A week later we received a phone call from the US consul in Manaus.

TWO

"All I know is a door into the dark."
—Seamus Heaney

I answered the phone that night, it would have to be me, of course, so insistent, ten rings and it would stop and then start over again—and I thought that maybe it was Dad or one of my brothers, they would have to be away from home, off to the Schubert Theatre in Boston to see the first touring production of *Les Miz*—there was an extra ticket, Mom's seat, and Dad had suggested that maybe I'd like to use it, we could find a way of sneaking me in once the lights had dimmed, photography was prohibited during the show anyway, make it an all boys' night out, his voice exasperated because Mom was not with him to share the occasion. He'd been wanting to see the show for so long, his favorite author, Victor Hugo, and *Les Miserables*, his favorite novel. He'd read it to me when I was ten, one page him, one page me, decrying Javert and cheering Jean Valjean on and crying for Cosette. Dad had even brought down from the attic a picture of the great French author that we had inherited from

Dad's grandmother. So he wasn't home, nobody was home but me that night, they were listening to *Do you hear the people sing? Singing a song of angry men?* Not me, I wasn't listening to anybody singing, I had my own anger to deal with, and I picked up the receiver with irritation, expecting Dad to tell me how much they had enjoyed the show and what a fool I was not to have joined them, Dad belting out, *It is the music of a people who will not be slaves again.*

But it was not Dad. It was the consul in Manaus.

An accident, he said, the boat had capsized. My mother had not survived the river. Foul play, the consul insisted, had been ruled out.

I bit so hard into my hand that blood sprouted from the wound.

"Mr. Foster?"

"It was murder," I said.

"No, sir. An accident. We've investigated thoroughly and there is no doubt that there was no outside intervention that—"

"Murder," I said.

"Can I speak to someone else in the house, sir?"

I told him my father would be home soon with my brothers, got his number, watched the blood drip from my hand onto the floorboards, carefully placed the receiver back in its cradle.

Are you happy now, you bastard? Now that you killed my mother, used me to kill her, you bastard, you sonofabitching motherfucking savage! It wasn't enough to destroy me, you had to go and seduce her, drown her. Drown her because I wouldn't drown myself. I'll get you, I'll track you down, I'll burn down every tree you ever loved, make the goddamn Amazon jungle go up in flames!

But I did not track him down, I could not.

And he did not, could not, abandon me.

The photos were there, he was still there.

He and me, motherless, each of us now without the woman who had given us birth, stranded, both of us, in different centuries, with nobody near to take care of us, detesting each other across time, miserable, miserable, both of us.

I was not, however, as bereft as I imagined myself to be.

Months after my mother's death—more months than I could even begin to count—the phone rang again in our house. It was for me, my brother Vic said, a puzzled look in his eyes. Nobody ever called me.

I almost didn't answer. I had spent the time since the news about Mom in my room, blaming myself for her death, venturing out only for evening meals with what was left of our mourning and resentful family and, once a week, for the sterile photo sessions that Dad and I continued to hold, not because we had any hope that something would change, but out of respect for Mom, because that was what she would have wanted. I had advanced not a bit in Dad's project of digital imaging as a response to my dilemma. That's how disheartened and guilt ridden I felt. Lifting my little finger seemed to be harder than raising the *Titanic*. And besides, success at ridding ourselves of the intruder through computing would have proven even more how stupid and pointless had been my mother's sacrifice. I did not want to say to her tomb or her face that smiled at me from the living room, from the family album that I masochistically kept examining: Why didn't you wait? Why didn't you trust that we could solve this with rational means instead of traipsing off to a jungle where you did not belong to meet strangers who couldn't care less about me or our troubles?

So I was not in the mood to speak to anyone that Saturday.

"Who is it?" I asked apathetically.

"A girl," my brother answered. "She wouldn't say her name. An old friend, that's all she said. And that she really needed to speak to you."

It was Cam.

"I don't expect you to remember me, Fitzroy Foster, but—"

She waited for me to say *yes, I do*, or *no, who the hell are you*, but I couldn't possibly articulate what was racing through my blood, not just my astonishment at this voice from the past, but everything she had meant to me, her incessant phantasmagoric company all these seven years. Yes. Seven years. Tomorrow was my birthday, I would be twenty-one years old.

She must have tired of the silence, because she said: "I have something for you, something I need to show you. Can I come by? I mean, I know you don't go out anymore, nobody has seen you for ages, so you'd probably rather we met at your home."

"What for?" I asked.

"It's important," and though her voice was calm, there was a gentle urgency in each word, and I conjured up her image as I had done so often in my solitude, as I had by the Charles River when she had come to rescue me from those waters, and said, "Yes, of course, come by whenever. Tomorrow is best."

"Tomorrow," she said. "Sunday. Better still. It'll be a birthday present."

She remembered! How could she remember? Why would she?

I understood the answer when she stood in front of me and gave me a hug and saw in her eyes how I had changed as she saw in mine how she had grown. And yet, we were still the same, as if only one second had passed since she had asked who that man was and what he wanted and I had retreated, as if keeping my swimmer girl alive inside had produced the miracle that she had not forgotten me, not for one instant, she said. And had something to prove it.

We were up in my room, in my refuge, among the computers

and lab equipment, away from prying eyes. It was peaceful, having her there, perched on the chair by my desk while I sat on the bed, a good distance away. As if, in effect, the demon was in abeyance, excluded from this relationship, perhaps averting his gaze, perhaps I had earned that interlude by abstaining from any sexual activity for these seven monastic years. Had she banished him? Was that why I did not sense his dark eyes boring into my skull, watching me as he did all day long, all night long, cannibalizing me, eating my light, chewing my life up, then spitting me out exhausted and drained? Would it have been enough to have invited her into my room, nothing more, just once for the monster to be vanquished?

It was not that at all.

He was there, but did not need to make his presence felt in his ordinary, invasive way.

Because Cam took out an envelope from her handbag and passed it to me.

"Your birthday present," she said.

I trembled at the touch of the envelope, almost handed it back to her, anticipating that if I opened it everything would be altered from that moment onward, altered, inevitably, for the worse. These seven fallow years had made me fearful of the future, any future, scared of being hurt.

"Go ahead," Camilla said, with a smile. "He won't bite. He never could, you know."

It was him.

An old postcard.

His portrait. There. The first time I had ever seen part of his body, something more than the face he had shown me. The short neck below the chin and its shadow, the naked torso, the sloping shoulders and bare arms. The bottom of the picture had been cropped off or perhaps merely framed in such a way that it stopped just above his belly button. One arm, the left one, was hanging down next to his body and the other one jutted slightly outward, with the elbow crooked, so that the unseen hand seemed to be covering his genitals, shielding them from photographer and viewers. Just a surmise, but that merest inclination of the elbow and the forearm toward the juncture between unseen legs revealed a sense of vulnerability that startled me, so accustomed was I to the defiant look, the omnipotence of his glare, the wildness of his hair. Floating by itself, the face that had infiltrated my photos was ghostly and daunting. Now that it was attached to a body, it appeared more like that of a helpless child, without defense against a world that was invading him, plundering his life, stripping him naked in order to take the shot. That nakedness made him look so much younger, as if he was calling for someone to rescue him and knew, the eyes knew, the eyes I knew too well, that there would be no rescue, no salvation, nobody was coming for him except death.

"Where? How?"

These had been strange years for her. Though I was the victim of that assault, she had also been haunted by the image. He came to her, that young man, at night, just before she fell asleep, those hovering eyes in the morning. And she had asked him over and over what she had asked me, but this time directly, who are you? And: Why have you taken Fitz from me? And also: How do you manage it? From where do you come? What do you want?

Just as his presence had shattered my life and twisted the fate of my mother, it had also fundamentally transformed Cam's destiny. As a girl who had lost her mother to cancer at age five, she could remember being terrified and at the same time curious that someone she loved so much could live or die according to what tiny, invisible cells mandated in a body that had given her birth and milk and caresses. And how could it be that her father, a doctor, an expert, a researcher, had not been able to save his own wife? Since that early misfortune, in order to tame that terror, Cam had developed a magnetic attraction to everything relating to the anatomy of the body and its function. Biology and its attendant intricacies were already a vocation when my ailment had impressed itself on her, confronting her mind with a challenge that she had been preparing to meet since childhood. Something secret in Fitzroy Foster had removed him from her life, a secret that had to be tied to biochemistry and molecular biology in some way, of this she was increasingly certain as she delved farther into her high school studies, began to map out the mechanisms of cell signaling and protein molecules, ligands and peptides and many another name that meant nothing whatsoever to me.

"Your malady couldn't be due to anything you'd perpetrated in your life, Fitzroy Foster," she said to me, leaving her chair to sit next to me on the bed and taking my hand in hers—familiar with me as though we had been kissing the night before instead of seven years ago. "You were—perfect, well, maybe a bit perfectible, maybe you could improve your swimming technique, ha!, but about as impeccable a human as anyone could wish for. Cheerful and smart, a math whiz, nice to a fault, perhaps too nice, Fitz, not pressing me for sex, you know, when, hey, I'd have gone along, just needed one more nudge of encouragement. At least we'd have had that memory to keep us warm all this time. But maybe it's better this way. Maybe that kept me going, kept me clean and focused. Knowing that this—this young man had not come because of anything you'd done wrong, a sin you'd committed, some crime, who knows what. And I don't believe that he threw some dice in the other world and you ended up being selected by chance, no, there had to be a subterranean link. Something in your DNA, you understand, something in your family history, that was inviting such an incursion. Something transmitted to you by your forebears, embedded by them, sent on to you. And the more I thought about it, the more I realized that this was to be my life's work. If I could not have you, then I would do the next best thing: find the cause and perhaps, along with the cause, the cure. Rummage deep into how memory affects proteins and neurotransmitters."

I watched her, dazed, amazed, utterly in love. I treasured every word dropping from her mouth into my ear and my memory—the very memory that held, according to her, the key to my condition. Entrenched in our genes, she said, are visual memories from the past that surface from time to time, visions that those who came before us witnessed and have communicated down the generations, just as the color of our skin and the slant of our nose and the delicacy of the fingers and a freckle on a precise spot of the cheek have been transferred, just as we know how to swim without having learned it because of the amphibian brain still pulsating inside.

"Each human," she added, "contains within himself, within herself, all their ancestors, a trove of what was seen and heard and smelled and touched, residues of certain experiences that drastically impressed them, pressed into them, expressed who they were. We encompass in some tangle of our DNA the silent documentation of an incessant, hidden past. We can travel back in time, Fitz—all we need is to go inside ourselves. We can't change that dead, distant past, my dear, dear Fitzroy Foster—but we can retrieve it. That's what I believe. That's why I've forged a career dedicated to the proposition that some ancestral memories never die."

"And my visitor?"

"Is that what you call him? That's interesting, there must be a reason why you chose that term, we'll figure that out as well now that we have his image. Your visitor? Just the projection of a lost, underlying memory, affecting the way light reflects and refracts on your skin."

"But how, how does he do it?"

"If I knew that . . . Maybe he changes the cells on your face for an instant—precisely when an image is captured, like his was, years ago. During an instant that is so infinitesimal, so indiscernible to the human eye, outside the spectrum of our senses, that we don't realize it's happening, can't measure it yet. But this we know: somebody took that photo. An image burnt into that watcher's nervous system so intensely that it lodged in his cells and was transmitted like liquid fire to descendants, eventually flaring into you. One of your forebears is responsible, I always thought. And your mother agreed with me."

I had been reeling ever since I had laid eyes on Cam in her present incarnation, lurching like a drunken sailor from one revelation to the next, but this? Mom? Camilla had been in touch with my mother?

They had run into each other a few years ago at the Harvard Library. My mom had tried to avoid her, this lovely girl who had always been a favorite, suddenly cut off due to the family tragedy. I could see Mom hesitate, envision her assessing the danger of engaging with Camilla Wood, leading to the sort of disclosures Dad had warned against. Cam, not one to be thwarted, insisted on having some coffee and cake, for old times' sake, and she even played the sympathy card, mentioning that she had no living relative left, now that her father, Cameron Wood, had died of cancer only a few weeks earlier, the same sickness that had taken her mother. Mom was not one to leave anyone grieving without solace, let alone the girl who had loved her unfortunate son.

Mom soon found out how difficult it was to keep the truth of that son's plight to herself, when Cam pointed, once they were seated in the library cafeteria, at the books Margaretta Foster had just checked out. Amazon Indians? Photos from the nineteenth century? Would this have anything to do with what had happened to Fitz? And my mother denying any connection, flailing about for all kinds of nonsense to throw my former girlfriend off the track, until Cam simply said: "I know. He showed me the photo. He showed it to me and fled. He showed it to me and never returned my calls. Didn't even acknowledge the message I sent with my dad. Listen. All I want is for you to tell me how he is. Nobody needs to know we ever met. But it will do you a world of good just to speak to someone about this and oh it will do me a universe, a cosmos, a constellation of good." Typical of Cam, exaggerating, poetical, over the top. And convincing.

A conspiracy was born that day. They shared confidences, like the mother-in-law and daughter-in-law they had been destined to be, could well have been in the future if Mom had not trekked off to Brazil on that cockeyed trip. "I cautioned her not to go," said Cam. "It made sense that there was an indigenous person in the past who had been photographed and was haunting you, Fitz, that fed right into my theory. But there were too many loose ends, things that didn't quite fit. Unfortunately, I was right. Because your visitor doesn't come from Brazil. He comes from Patagonia."

I was trying to digest this when there was a knock on the door. It was Dad. We had already established that this was my sanctuary and that when I locked myself in—almost always, in fact—it meant that he was not to attempt entry. I did not mind, however, if he spoke to me through the closed door. I would choose to answer or not. In this case, he was aware that I had a visitor—not the male demon but a female visitor—and that this was a delicate moment for me. We had agreed not to celebrate my birthday anymore, another anniversary of anathema and damnation, but he did not want me to feel that he'd forgotten and thus his knock was gentle and his voice even gentler as he informed me that he and the boys were going out for dinner. As the rest of the family had done for that occasion for the last few years, even when my mother was alive, given that the special meals she had kept cooking for me remained uneaten, cold, spoiling away uncomfortably at the table. Tonight, Dad added that they would be back late as they were going to the movies after the restaurant to see *Rambo III*. Undoubtedly, the decision to attend that film where Sylvester Stallone rescued some savage Afghan from malignant invaders was Dad's considerate way of emptying the house for some extra hours so that I could freely spend them with the girl who had so unexpectedly resurrected herself, maybe he was crossing his fingers that something miraculous would happen on that day when I was coincidentally and magically coming of age.

"Have fun," I said and he did not respond that I should as well, just murmured, "We love you, Fitz, the whole tribe," and was gone, allowing me to turn to Camilla and Patagonia.

"Patagonia? How do you know?"

She had whizzed through high school and then studied physics and biology at MIT, graduating in a record three years and securing a job as a lab assistant at one of the university labs and also accepting a summer internship at the molecular biology department of the Institut Pasteur in Paris where she had been supervised by the great Dr. Daniel Louvard. He had been so intrigued with her thesis that memory and cell genealogy were somehow associated that he had invited her back to the Rue Vaugirard next year to pursue her research. I listened to all this and more, as she waved her arms around enthusiastically, almost as if she were swimming toward me through the vast water of time lost, not really minding that she was taking her time before divulging the origins of this *carte postale*, taking her time, teaching me to take mine, as we would soon be discovering in my bed—seven years of darkness and perplexity were coming to an end and Lord knows I had waited long enough not to be impatient. And indeed, she finally wound up her rambling about the centenary of the Institut and her advances in the field of intracellular migration and invasion—by triumphantly stating that "if he can invade you, Fitz, soon we'll be able to invade him back if we find the right points in your protein structure," especially now that we knew where he came from.

"Where he came from, yes," I said. "I was wondering when you'd get back to that little detail, when you'd tell me. About Patagonia."

She nodded, eyes misty with reminiscence.

"It was my last full day in Paris and I was on my way from my itsy-bitsy apartment on rue de l'Epéron, taking my usual path to the Institut Pasteur, down rue de l'Odéon where I'd tarry by the antiquarian book shops and browse when the fancy took me."

And that morning—it was just four days ago, in fact—she had drifted to the very back of a store to sort through a tray of *cartes postales* and there it was, the image I was now holding, there he was, the man who had come between her and the boy she loved, returning to her life as he had returned to her dreams and dawning hours, scarred into her consciousness, there he was on paper and sepia, something she could touch and carry and examine and track and hunt down like a wayward cancerous tumor, a palpable sample of evidence from the outside world of history that antedated his incursion into Fitzroy Foster's life and therefore her own, there he was, ready to be bought and transported across the Atlantic, back to the hemisphere where he had been born, the key to my freedom.

"How do you know he is—was—Patagonian?"

The owner of the bookshop was not in that day, but his son André was bristling with data, a clumsy way of flirting with her—"that got him nowhere, Fitz, though I do like it if you're a bit jealous." André informed Cam that this *carte postale*—all the rage in the late nineteenth century, like the *cartes de visite* lying in the next tray—most certainly depicted a Patagonian Indian brought to Paris along with ten other members of his tribe, the Onas. They had been exhibited at the 1889 Exposition Universelle that celebrated one hundred years of liberté, egalité, and fraternité. The owner's son—who claimed to be an expert regarding the iconography of the Belle Époque—had proceeded to sell her a unique and expensive catalogue of that centenary celebration of the French Revolution. In it could be read the story of how Eiffel had constructed his tower, along with many details of myriad pavilions from countries from around the world that were built on the grounds at the Champs de Mars adjacent to it.

Did he know, Cam inquired, the name of the savage in the photo or who might have taken it, as this information was cropped off? The name of the savage was of no consequence, André responded, and would probably not have been on the *carte*, unlike the photographer, who is often identified. In this case, there could be no doubt that it stemmed from the collection of Prince Roland Bonaparte—grandson of Napoleon's younger brother, Louis—whose many séances with exotic races had circulated in diverse visual forms and formats during the late nineteenth century, some of which were available for purchase. Would mademoiselle care to have a drink with him at his favorite café opposite the Luxembourg Gardens so he could explain more about those photos, where they were published and how they could be consulted or acquired? And mademoiselle had thanked him kindly, but she had work to do as she was leaving

Paris the next day, but would be interested in ordering material by post on this subject before she returned next year.

"So you don't know his name?" I said, as if naming my visitor might make him somehow more familiar and release me from his grip.

"It wouldn't be his real name anyway," Cam said. "According to preliminary reading yesterday, the men who snatched such people from their habitat didn't speak the language of their captives and, unable to even pronounce the original names, ended up calling them whatever came into their heads."

"So he was kidnapped?"

"I'd be astonished if he'd traveled to Paris, all the way from the end of the earth, of his own free will. Does he look happy to you?"

He didn't, he never had.

"So what do we do now?"

She answered by lowering the light and then lowering herself onto the bed and then lowering me next to her, she answered by unbuttoning my shirt and moving my fingers to unbutton her blouse, she answered by whispering into my ear that there would be more than enough time ahead to pursue the Ona invader who had separated us, but that now, just now, right now, our time belonged to us and not to him, there were many years to make up for, the birthday present she had intended to give me when I was fourteen was now ready for delivery and consumption, better late than never.

And made all the better by the savage disappearing during the hours that followed, I felt that he no longer existed, extinguished, so far from my attention that I did not give him a second or a third or any thought at all, not even to thank him for leaving me alone with Cam, retire so that we could explore our hungry bodies after so many nights calling out to the other, holding fast against death and despair, he was gone, he was not there as I entered Camilla and she enveloped me, he was not there in her depths or in our pleasure or in the fragile eternity of discovery that never seemed to cease.

Until she finally fell asleep like an orphan in my arms.

Not for me, to sleep. My heart was beating too fast, every cell that Camilla wanted to scrutinize and modulate seemed alive and radiant, my skin glinting with sweat, hers and mine, damp both of us as if we had rained on each other, drenched below and above, inside and outside, been swimming through the infinite ocean of the other. I watched her lips pursed by the breath that gentled in and out—and wished for nothing more than to keep this moment somewhere forever, fix it so I could return to it over the years to make sure it had really existed, was no figment of a fever.

And as that thought overran me with its desire, the mere idea of freezing the instant, possessing her over and over again with my eyes, was replaced by something more imperative.

What if I snapped a shot of myself now, right now?

Wasn't it possible that my true face would be restored to me? The visitor had arrived with my first sexual experience and remained with me during these unwelcome years of solitude. Now that I was twenty-one, now that a woman had shared her body and transparency and sighs, now that I was no longer alone to confront him, and shielded by Cam's loyalty, now that we knew his identity, would he not be thwarted?

I rolled out of bed and walked, naked as the day of my birth, naked as he had been at the instant they had captured his image so long ago, I tiptoed to the penumbra of my desk, where my old Polaroid camera sat, as if awaiting the day when that machine and I would renew our relationship of trust.

I was forestalled from taking a self-portrait by Cam's voice: "What is it, love?"

She was peeping open her eyes, a yawn exhibiting the sweet

cavern of her mouth, flashing the teeth that had nibbled at my shoulder just a while ago.

She did not need me to explain my intentions. The Polaroid camera in my hands was sufficient. Trembling in anticipation, I passed it to her. And set myself at the exact distance he had been when somebody we had yet to determine had snapped the shot, at the exact distance and with my head slightly aslant and my arms replicating how his had hung, one of them by his side and the other crossed downward defensively. As bare as he had been, looking at the camera with what may have been a similar mixture of fear, puzzlement, expectation.

Before clicking the button, Cam hesitated. As my father had not done all those years ago on another birthday, oh if he had known what she now knew, if my mother . . .

"Are you sure?"

I nodded.

"Not too soon, Fitz? Maybe we should . . . ?"

But didn't finish her phrase. We would have to find out eventually. Why not right away?

Again, that click and the shuttering of the lens and the endless few seconds it took for the print to develop and emerge.

And again, he was there.

Just as in every image since I was fourteen. Just as in the *carte postale* that Cam had brought back from the rue de l'Odéon.

Only more uncanny.

Because up till now my clothed body below his face in the photo had always been separately mine, my body and my shirt and my pants kept me in contact with myself, assured me that I still belonged to my century, that there remained a zone of my space and life untouched by his influence. This time, in this recent photo and fresh incarnation that Cam had just snapped, my bare and exposed physique echoed his, copied its pose, reproduced the configuration of the intruder's own uncovered body. His face was, as usual, superimposed on a neck and torso that were mine but in that new image my nakedness minutely recalled and imitated his, allowing him to merge into me with wilder intensity than ever before. It was him in the photo and not him. It was me and not me. The discovery of his ethnicity, the revelation of the rest of his frame hidden until then, rather than distancing this Patagonian from my life, seemed to have drawn him obscenely closer, made monsters of us both.

Even in that dim light, Cam could read my frustration.

What would I have done if she had not been there, had not snuggled me in her arms and grasped the shoulders that were not his but made from my flesh and muscles and bone and skin, with those hands that loved me and that he would never feel, my chest that she held tight against the flowering of her breasts, and that he would never touch or caress, lick or suck or kiss, turn into honey, my body that had been swimming toward her all our lives?

He might have me, but I had her.

I had her saying to me: "It's better this way, Fitz. The slow way. The hard, patient way. It means we have years ahead of us to solve this together, to ease him out of our lives, the five thousand steps that Dr. Land once mentioned to you, remember? Taking our time can only bring us closer to one another."

She had recommended patience but there was one area in which I refused to comply.

"Where are you staying?" I asked.

"At the YWCA on Temple Street until I can find some place nearer to MIT."

"No, you're not. You're moving in here with me. With us, with my family. Tomorrow."

She did not protest. Perhaps she felt comfortable because

Mom had blessed and welcomed her, making her a daughter of the tribe before any of the men knew about that relationship.

And so it was that Camilla Wood entered my life like a whirlwind, reorganizing everything, offering a foundation from which to gaze, unafraid, upon a world that I had turned into a phalanx of hostile stares. Entered my life understates the earthquake of her presence: entered our house, entered my room and bed and mind and heart.

She agreed with my father—whom she instantly put at ease with her cheerfulness and, of course, their mutual veneration of science and progress—that it was perilous for me to be caught by any of the many cameras that roved the world. She cared not a whit for Polaroid's reputation or the photographic industry's future if news of this illness got out. She knew enough about guinea pigs and fruit flies and chimps, enough about laboratories and experiments on animals and amoebas and errant cells to be wary of doctors and engineers and bureaucrats getting their hands on me and even worse if they were betokened to corporations and governments for funding. The fact that my visitor determined a need for furtiveness and clandestinity, did not mean, however, that I should be his slave, genuflect to him, defer and postpone all the delights of the outside world. She would act, she said, as my scout before we ventured out and after that as my buffer, ready to confiscate any indiscreet camera.

She favored, as I did, the most outlandish hours and had always loved the wilderness that I had so missed, insisted on taking long walks through the Massachusetts forests that had not seen the footprint of men or women since the Indians had been driven from this land centuries ago. It was during those weekend outings that I poured my heart into hers, told her everything that had happened to me since fleeing her presence: everything, the masturbation while Peter Gabriel's song played, the terror I had felt at losing her, my years of penitence, the rage and helplessness that had culminated in the near suicide by the Charles River and her miraculous intervention, my memory of our first swim to keep me sane in the time that followed, my mad conversations with the invader, the guilt that had corroded me upon my mother's death. Cam took it all in her stride—you can be a mystery to the world, secrete yourself away from everyone else, but not from me. Even making fun of my need to hide away. A burlap bag? No way. How unfashionable, Fitz. She wrapped me up as a mummy for my first Halloween in seven years—"who cares if it's only this once"—and back home we gave ourselves indigestion feeding each other the candy and caramels and chewy treats overflowing from our plastic pumpkins.

She also arranged for me to reconnect to my estranged brothers, enchanting them with her cooking skills, housekeeping abilities, and penetrating good looks. They wanted a female in the house, had suffered during the recent harrowing bachelorhood all four of us had endured. Made all the smoother when Cam placed on the mantelpiece a memento of her and Mom in obvious camaraderie that she had enticed some kind passerby outside the library to snap. They were both fondling a stray dog, one more thing that joined her to my mother, the love of animals.

Even the weekly photographic sessions were transmogrified beyond recognition. Cam popped herself into every shot, planting a wet smack on my lips or embracing me with an octopus squeeze or simply making funny faces at the camera, *hey, this is Cam, you silly camera, I'm the real Cam camera here*, wiggling her fingers at the lens or the intruder or both—registering an ever more extravagant pose, turning what had been a solemn and excruciating ceremony into a festive occasion, full of jokes that I almost looked forward to.

Almost, because I could not shake the apprehension that such unseemly conduct might be construed by my unwelcome caller as an affront, provoking him to shift his attention from me to my lover, that he or some other Ona ghoul—a female one?—that accompanied him in his netherworld might haunt this woman who was mocking them. What if Cam, like Mom, was unable to protect herself from the curse? When I timidly broached the subject with her, she laughed, waving away any possible threat. "Let him, her, them, just try," she said, sticking out the tongue that had licked me all over. And that was that, if she was enjoying herself so much and lifting my spirits with her clownish antics, why should I be concerned? Later I would kick myself, brood on the debacle that, again, I had failed to forestall.

As if I had much time to worry. Cam had started me on a crash course on the events in our country and the world that I had paid no heed to for all these years—what, you don't know what Iran-Contra is? What? You don't know about the savings and loans mess? What? You don't know what perestroika is, what glasnost? What? You don't know that Grenada was invaded—or that the Falklands War even happened? You don't know that the man likely to be our next president was the head of the CIA? To work, you lazy bum. And back to my schooling as well, that had fallen by the wayside due to a combination of Mom's inattention during hours consumed by the Amazon jungle and my obsessive experiments with pixels and digital images. Why study history or geography if I'd never travel anywhere? Why learn languages?

"Spanish," Cam resolved. It would come in handy, she announced, for our research into the events in Tierra del Fuego.

A quest that we embarked upon the very Monday night that followed my twenty-first birthday, as soon as she had unpacked her few belongings.

There were three major directions for our probe, according to the systematic Ms. Wood: Patagonia and its indigenous population; records of natives from that area forcibly removed to Europe in 1889; and anything relating to this so-called Prince Roland Bonaparte and his photographic collection. Though there was an adventurous, impulsive streak in my Cam, she also had her feet firmly on the ground. I would be constantly amazed in the years ahead at her ability to confront complex situations and swiftly choose the best alternative in a split second, and invariably the one that entailed less danger. No matter how much she wished me to leave my cocoon, she decided it was imprudent for me to accompany her to the Harvard Library. She'd check out books and materials for me to safely peruse at home—increasingly in Spanish to hone my skills—while she, fluent in French and German, reserved for herself the more laborious examination of archives.

"I suspect there will be no straight line to a clear resolution," she said. "Everything worthwhile, in life and science and health, and even in love, Fitz, advances through zigzags, coiling around itself in and out, hiding from us until it's ready to reveal its mysteries, doubling back and forth, groping in the dark before the light comes. Like strands of DNA itself. Like the five thousand steps of Dr. Land. I'd be satisfied if we can turn up enough clues, both about the Onas and your genealogy, anything that will allow me further inquiries once I return to Paris next fall."

A trip I dreaded, though I did not protest, determined not to stand in the way of her vocation. Better to concentrate on what joined us during the year that was left until her departure, tracking down all those clues.

We started with the most notorious and public, and therefore the easiest, of our leads, Prince Roland Bonaparte. Easiest and also a red herring, no matter how fascinating the man's life had been, as we learned from the copious material sent by André from his father's Paris bookshop in late October, not that I was particularly gladdened by any favors from this potential rival.

Thwarted by a decree by the French government forbidding a military career to heirs of the Bonaparte dynasty, the young Roland had dedicated himself to anthropological studies, an increasingly popular field of inquiry in the wake of Darwin's *On the Origin of Species*, published in 1859, the year after the prince's birth. His mentor had been Paul Broca, founder of the French Society of Anthropology and an expert on aphasia and speaking disorders. Besides exploring the brain and measuring craniums, Dr. Broca had decided that photography was the perfect means for regularizing, classifying, and profiling all manner of subjects—from criminals to savages and, eventually, ordinary citizens in need of passports and identity papers, and it was to photography that the prince had devoted his every hour. Not strange, then, that the owner's son had ascribed the prints he'd sold Cam to Roland Bonaparte. A misattribution, according to my love's exhaustive inquiries. The prince had not personally photographed the 1889 photos of the kidnapped Onas. Taken by somebody else, Bonaparte had purchased them for his legendary collection, already filled with other "specimens," as he called them, which he had captured with his lenses: the Kaliña/Galibi of Suriname, the Omaha Indians of the American prairies, Queensland aboriginals, Kalmyks from Siberia, Senegalese, Somalis, Eskimos and natives from what was then Ceylon. Chile was not absent from this mix: from the center of that long country had come Araucanians, also known as Mapuches. No Onas though. Not one inhabitant from Tierra del Fuego.

Anyway, it wasn't possible that the prince's DNA was in any way twisting and turning inside me. His offspring was reduced to one surprising and scandalous woman—Princess Marie Bonaparte, famed psychoanalyst, investigator of female sexual dysfunction and patient first and then benefactor of Freud, having provided the funds that helped extract him from the clutches of the Viennese Nazis. Her two children—Prince George (heir to the throne of Denmark and Greece) and Princess Eugénie (heir to nothing but the title), were certainly not involved with either of my families. As I looked at the photo of Marie Bonaparte, with her dreamy eyes, reclining seductively, all decked out in white and lace, so different from my unclothed visitor, I wondered if she had been taken by her father, at age seven, to see the exhibition of the Onas. Was that image still floating somewhere in that indecipherable mind of hers that had made the venerable Sigmund ask a question that I had avidly first encountered in some porno book that was circulating at school and that I later saw on several T-shirts, all of this before my fourteenth birthday: "What does a woman want?"

A question that only mattered now that Cam had reentered my existence, and which she had no trouble in answering with a sexual frankness that would have awoken jealous suspicions if she had not sworn that she had been as faithful to me over these seven years as I to her. More faithful, as she had no incident with her genitals and Peter Gabriel albums to report nor any last minute dalliance before contemplating suicide by an icy river. Nor did she hold back what she wanted of me, for me: that I should get well, so we could carry out the adolescent plans—marrying, settling down, pursuing careers in biology and math respectively, having children, swimming toward old age together—that my visitor had interrupted.

Just as his own life had been interrupted, though it took us almost a year to establish the circumstances of the abduction—Cam, after all, was working full time at her lab job and could only snag a few hours a week to pursue our research. As for me, I was close to useless: housebound, reading what she happened to hunt and gather on her outings, eager for the evenings when my love would come home and I could discuss my findings with her and slowly piece together the ordeal of the eleven inhabitants of Patagonia. They had indeed, as we discovered, been kidnapped in 1889 to be exhibited in Paris at the Chilean pavilion—Onas, according to most versions, though Cam soon started to call them Selk'nam, the name they seemed to have used for themselves.

This was not the first time, nor would it be the last, that such kidnappings took place in those islands that had been baptized Tierra del Fuego, the Land of Fire, by Magellan in 1520 when he crossed the stormy straits that still bear his name. Besides calling the first natives he encountered Patagones—very tall and gentle and clothed in strange furs—Magellan also ordered two of these natives to be violently taken on board, so they could be exhibited at the Portuguese court—an enterprise that was frustrated by their deaths. Did they die of European sicknesses? Did they resist and then were murdered? Did they commit suicide, jumping into the sea, trying to swim back home? Our readings shed no light on these questions—just that the gentle giants lived on raw flesh, ate rats without skinning them, and liked to gnaw on a sweet root they called Capac. And that before dying they embraced Jesus Christ as their savior—one was baptized John and the other Paul. True or false, these reports? Could we lend any credence to the stories their captors told?

This much, however, was clear. In the centuries that ensued, no nation that traveled to this land of fire—and all Europeans did so, all were bent on the spices of the Indies and the riches of the Orient and control of the route through Cape Horn, they all competed to discover the continent rumored to be at the southern end of the earth, *terra australis incognita*—was immune from the temptation of taking men, women, and children from their original habitat. The Dutch, the French, the Spanish, the Germans, the British, the Portuguese, they all raided those shores and brought home samples of these savages. Except the Americans: they had been content with slaughtering almost to extinction the seals and whales that provided the fundamental food and clothing, shelter and weapons, for the survival of the five tribes that had lived under that inhospitable sky and turbulent sea and freezing climate for over six thousand years.

It depressed me to read these accounts day after day imprisoned in my room.

And more so when the enterprising Miss Wood brought home a book by a Father Borgatello and an album of photos published in Torino in 1907 by the Salesian Congregation that contained, she said breathlessly, a photo I needed to see.

"Him? Is it him? Have you found out who he is?"

"I don't think so, but . . . Here, take a look. It's a Selk'nam."

Sprawled across the bottom of the photo, framed carefully by someone unacknowledged, was the corpse of an Indian, naked among brown and scraggly tufts of grass on the tundra of some wasteland in Patagonia. Genitals exposed to the wind back then and later to eyes, just like mine now, of anyone who came upon the picture. In one hand the dead man clutched a long broken bow, white because it may have been carved from the bone of a whale. In the other, three equally white arrows.

I looked closer at the Selk'nam's face. It was smudged over, hard to identify, except for the snub nose and mop of hair on his head, which appallingly recalled those of my visitor. Above the murdered native stood a handsome bearded man in military gear, casually clasping a rifle, somewhat like hunters tower over the prey they have just shot, though his indifferent foot was not touching the corpse, his body mostly turned away from the lens of the camera, glancing to where three other armed men crouched, their backs to the photographer, intent on shooting at some objective, probably other Indians, on the wide and flat horizon, resisting with arrows perhaps or perhaps just waiting to be killed or simply fleeing.

"That's Julius Popper," Camilla jabbed a finger at the bearded man just above the dead Selk'nam. "Remember him?"

I did. We had come across his name before in other readings, but never contemplated his face yet, a Rumanian who headed an expedition sent to explore the region by the Argentine government in 1886, but also interested in staking a claim to the pastures where sheep could graze, be fattened, and then exported to Europe.

"Eighteen eighty-six," I mused, almost to myself. "So it can't be him, can't be our visitor?"

"Not unless we're mistaken about the 1889 abduction—and there are so many sources insisting that such an event did happen."

I looked at the corpse, just familiar enough to force me to ask questions I'd rather have avoided. How often had I wanted my visitor dead, would have gladly strangled him? And here was someone just like him—who knows, perhaps even my visitor himself if the 1889 date was wrong—supine, helpless, muted by death, no longer defiant, submitted to the iron laws of bullets and the jaws of technology, shot first by a rifle and then by a camera—both artifacts invented and manufactured thousands of miles away, transported to Tierra del Fuego to do their inexorable duty. What happened immediately before that picture was snapped, before that moment was arrested forever? What happened afterward, when the lens ceased to witness and transmit the incident and the boots moved on to other tundra, other murders, an evening meal, the hearty smoke of a pipe next to a fire inside a tent? How to get that dead man in the photo, on the tundra, to respond? Did my visitor know the answer?

"Maybe it's a brother," Camilla said. I think she wanted to fill the void we both felt, the void left behind by that exposed corpse in Patagonia.

"Or the father," I said. "I'll report back once I've read a bit more. Though who knows how much my elementary Spanish and an Italian dictionary will reveal."

As I laboriously went through Father Borgatello's book, trying to catch something pertinent, I found no hint of the dead man's identity. I went back to the photo itself and its lone caption: "This photo of some hunters of Indians in Tierra del Fuego makes us understand better than anything else the unbearable conditions in which the Fueguinos live and how great are the benefits offered by the Salesian Missions."

Cam and I had already learned enough about the predicament of the Selk'nam to understand why the missionaries were publishing the brutal photo of Popper and his victim. By 1887, the year after the execution of that naked native, a thousand indigenous women and children had been herded into the sanctuaries established by these Catholic priests, trying to save what was left of the Selk'nam population decimated by scum from the gold rush of 1880 and then by massacres perpetrated by the owners of extended sheep farms who began paying a British pound for each ear of an Indian brought in. Though the *hacenderos*, noticing Indians trading their furs and baskets without an ear, demanded henceforth that bounty hunters prove with head or testicles, breast and heart, that there was no cheating. The rescue by the Holy Cross of the remaining Selk'nam proved to be a remedy worse than the sickness: by corralling the survivors into squalid and unsanitary reservations, the priests unwittingly opened the lungs of their new congregation to tuberculosis and their bodies to typhoid and smallpox. The Indians could hide from the bullets and the snarling dogs and punitive expeditions and even endure the destruction of the guanacos that were their livelihood and sustenance, but could not hide from the microbes or viruses carried by the foreigners, infestations exacerbated by their close proximity to others carrying the germs. An author wrote that the worse disease for the Selk'nam was sadness, the loss of their culture, their way of life, the open pastures, the extermination of the animals.

My visitor had not uttered one word, had never spoken to me. Maybe he didn't need to. Maybe this was what he was urging me to discover on my own: his story, the story of those he had loved, who had given him birth, who had not outlived him by many years.

There had been 4,500 Selk'nam in 1880. By 1924 there were one hundred left, ten in 1950, and Lola Kiepja, the last of her race of purely indigenous blood, had died in 1962, five years before my birth, Cam's birth.

Gone. Extinct. Disappeared from the face—yes, the face, the face—of the earth.

THREE

I had been wrestling for months with a growing sympathy for this recalcitrant visitor, trying to deny the sort of compassion that had led to my mother's death. But who could shut his eyes to that long heritage of suffering, especially someone like me, who knew what it was like to be abruptly uprooted from normal life? I fought to keep my detestation of him vibrant, I needed to stay angry, a wrath now mitigated by the realization that I might well have acted in a similar way if I had been subjected to the sort of abuse that his people had tolerated for almost five hundred years. More reason not to choose—I wouldn't have, I was sure of that—someone innocent like me to retaliate against. Innocent, unless, unless ... Cam forced me to diligently note down the names of the long line of abductors, merrily declaring that "someday we'll figure out if any of them are your ancestors. And then, then, then, that day," she added flamboyantly—it was impossible to dampen her spirits, she laughed whenever I regressed to my former despondent self—"we'll vanquish your visitor. I'll find the connection, you'll see. Before I come back from Europe."

Europe! Each day and night that relentlessly brought her August departure closer gripped my chest with despair. No matter what pangs of compassion might have been stirred by the plight of my Selk'nam visitor and his tribe, I did not look forward to spending so many lonely months in his ominous presence, no longer protected by my love's smiles and those interludes of sex where he seemed to discreetly withdraw. And oh how I dreaded the return of those tiresome weekly photo sessions, his face overpowering mine without her buffoonery to sweeten the ordeal.

Cam herself found an inimitable way to lighten my mood.

"You know what this is?" she asked, one Friday evening in June.

How could I possibly guess what she held pertly in both hands hidden behind her back. I tried to snatch at it, but only managed—a pleasant enough mistake—to touch her splendidly round and perfect ass. She spun around and slapped me on the cheek with an envelope.

Inside was a letter from the Cambridge County Clerk asking me to appear before him this coming Monday in order to apply for a marriage license. Attached was a certificate from my doctor attesting to the fact that I did not possess a photo ID due to a medical condition, with a waiver from the governor's office specifying that it accepted a birth certificate as sufficient proof. Furthermore, my father was named a Justice of the Peace for one day, July 14, 1989, so he could officiate at the wedding.

I was stupefied as much as I was delighted. That she had been planning this with Dad for weeks, that she had not even bothered to ask me if I was willing to marry her, that she had taken my yes I will yes as a given. How was I supposed to react? Tell her how deliriously happy this made me? Ask her what hoops she had been forced to jump through in order to obtain the waiver?

Instead: "Why July fourteenth?"

"Two hundred years since the French Revolution—when a new era was born. Not a bad date to celebrate the rebirth of our love together, our storming of our own Bastille, so to speak, liberating whatever prisoners we have inside. And one hundred years since those Selk'nam were put on display in Paris, millions of visitors—yes, visitors, Fitz—ogling them. You'll see why that matters when I give you your wedding gift."

For the next weeks, she dedicated many hours to preparing that offering, mostly when I was asleep.

I would wake and see her bent over a huge green volume that easily reached a thousand pages. She forbade me from even glancing at the title, only going so far as to inform me that it had taken her several months and many pleading letters and phone calls to wrest this treatise in German from the library at Duke University, even though it had been consulted only once since being acquired for its special collections in 1931. But there it was in her nimble hands, night after night, testimony to her powers of persuasion and infinite stubbornness. All this gave to the approaching wedding celebration a bizarre quality: nothing substantial would change between us, after all, when the State of Massachusetts, through whatever words my dad might conjure from thin air, pronounced us man and wife. Perhaps that night the encounter of our two bodies, the only honeymoon someone with my condition could contemplate, would reach a more feverish, prolonged, arcane excitement and longing, making up for the many months of absence that loomed ahead. But her gift —what it was I could not predict, that would be a real surprise.

And so, the night of July 14, 1989, after bidding farewell to the guests—Dad and my two brothers—when we closed the door to our room, the only place in the world where I felt safe, and faced each other and whispered the words, to have and to hold, that our hands made real, to have her hold me, to hold me in the having, once I had kissed the bride and she had stroked my hair as if to certify that I was not dreaming, she presented me with the gift.

The book she had been poring over was Martin Gusinde's monumental *Die Feuerland-Indianer, Band I, Die Selk'nam*—the first volume of four dealing with the Indians of Tierra del Fuego. Gusinde, a Catholic priest from the Order of the Divine Verb, had traveled there four times between 1918 and 1924, growing so close to his anthropological subjects that he had been allowed to participate, the first Westerner ever, in the male ceremonies of initiation. According to the transcriptions into English that Camilla had spent many nights working on, this missionary had described countless recent kidnappings of natives by Europeans: a failed attempt to hijack a family of Alakaluf Indians in 1878; a man, woman and child of the Tehuelche ethnic group seized in 1879; another group, a larger one, of Alakaluf forcibly removed to Europe in 1881. Gusinde also mentioned the Araucanians exhibited in 1883 and photographed by Bonaparte. But the crown jewel of Gusinde's revelations—and Camilla's wedding gift—referred to the eleven indigenous inhabitants of Tierra del Fuego who had, in December 1888, been captured in the Bahía de San Felipe by the Belgian whaler Maurice Maître and taken to Europe, "chained as if they were Bengal tigers," Gusinde's exact words lifted, apparently from none other than the infamous Julius Popper. Gusinde not only revealed what we already knew from several pithy sources, that these captives had been shown at the Paris commemoration of the French Revolution, but that the nine who survived the crossing of the Atlantic were billed as cannibals and fed raw horse meat in a cage for the glee of spectators.

In order for Maître to squeeze more money out of his hostages, he next transported them to London to be paraded at the Royal Westminster Aquarium—an exhibition that was suspended after a few days, despite the Indians being "the talk of the town," due to protests by missionaries dedicated to evangelizing South American Indians. Under investigation by Scotland Yard, Maître escaped with eight of his victims to his native Brussels—eight, because one of the Ona women had been left behind, mortally ill and without a stitch of clothing, in St. George's Infirmary, where she died on January 21, 1890. Maître managed to display them a couple of times before the Belgian authorities arrested him and sent the aboriginals back to the Chilean port of Punta Arenas. Only half of them arrived, as four died on the journey home.

I read Gusinde's three pages on this abduction a second time and only then, trembling, asked Cam what this meant for us: Which of these eleven was my visitor? Was there a photo of any of them in this German priest's book?

Camilla passed me a slim annex to this major work, an album of pictures that Gusinde himself had snapped during his four voyages to Tierra del Fuego. Worth examining, she said, in case I was interested in their ceremonies and habitat. But no photo remotely like the one she herself had found in the bookstore, no face that recalled the face that haunted mine. We still did not know anything about which of the captives was our man, nor if he was among those returned to Patagonia.

There was, fortunately, one promising reference that the librarian for Latin American studies at Harvard had discovered: Gusinde had another annex of pictures that she had been unable to retrieve through Interlibrary Loan—who knows where or how it had been lost. The missionary had, however, bequeathed a trove of photos to the Order of the Divine Verb, now stored at the Congregation's Anthropos Institute in Sankt Augustin, a few miles from Bonn. Once installed in Paris, Cam would travel there as soon as a suitable scientific excuse could be found, perhaps a visit to the Institute for Life and Brain, a biomedical center in the German capital. Her intuition was that one of those photos in Sankt Augustin would be crucial to our next steps. We had made real progress, she said, almost crowing with satisfaction. She was leaving for Europe with more clues than could have been expected when our quest had begun, ten months ago.

It was not the only thing she was leaving with.

I also had been hard at work on gifts, though only after she had informed me of our upcoming marriage did I realize that they would be perfect for our wedding.

I had placed, inside some gaudy wrapping paper, a contract. Though secret negotiations had been going on for a while, it was only a week ago that I had signed an agreement with Adobe, a company out in Silicon Valley, to sell them the rights to my patented Imageplus digital image editing program. Adobe had developed, through two brothers by the name of Knoll, a rival method called Photoshop and would be putting this raster graphic editor into production next year, presumably in February 1990. My work would help them to eventually combine in one document pixel images with images that were vector based, a major visual breakthrough. This meant that the newly married couple now had one million dollars in the bank and soon, if the program was as popular as Adobe and I expected, many millions more at our disposal. And, perhaps more significantly: though the program was not yet able to manipulate my photo from age fourteen and make it grow older through Photoshopping to resemble my current face, the technology was just around the corner. Soon I could eliminate my intruder's face from images, receiving a passport. This might well be the last trip she would ever take alone!

The second gift was two personal computers. I booted them up, punched some letters and signs in mine, pressed yet another button, and there, suddenly on the screen of Cam's machine, was a message from me to her: YOU MEAN THE WORLD TO ME.

"We're connected through the Internet," I said. "The World, a company here in Brookline, will soon be selling this sort of access to ordinary citizens, no security clearance needed. Dad got us to be part of their experimental outreach program. Just promise you'll also use the phone, so I can hear your voice. Try it, try it!"

She sat at her computer and, using two fingers like a little bird, typed back a sexy message and I replied with something even more salacious and we squealed like pigs rolling in the mud, life seemed like a sport—so young, both of us, to have the world on a string, the world at our feet. Playing, playing, playing games as if we had all the time in the world, as if we could make up for the seven years my visitor had stolen from us. As if my mother had not been murdered for trying to find out the identity of that young man.

"Perfect," Camilla said. "No pretext for not sending me daily reports, maybe hourly."

"Every minute!"

"Every second!"

"About what? The reports?"

While Camilla uncovered the identity of my visitor and his captors, she wanted me to make a list of every foreigner, from Magellan on, who was in some way complicit, directly or indirectly, whether as a predator or as an observer, in the extermination of those inhabitants, be they Selk'nam, Tehuelche, Hash, Alakaluf, or Yamana.

I protested this onerous task. We knew who had kidnapped those eleven men, women, and children, including my intruder:

it was Maurice Maître, the whaler from Brussels. I didn't know
of any Belgians in the family on either side, but it was worth
sniffing around—as to others . . .

Though Maître's violence against the Selk'nam was paramount,
Cam said, he might not be the precise person we were looking
for. No laziness, no excuses, she emphasized: an extensive list,
so that when she came upon suspects in her European inquiries
we would already have advanced, discarded some, found others
more probable. Every prominent European who had come into
contact with the ancestors of my visitor.

"What, even Darwin?"

"*Stunted, miserable creatures, ignoble, infected, abject, wretched
savages, wild animals.* Who wrote those words? *Devils, troubled
spirits from another world.* Who accused them of howling from
the shores a language that *scarcely deserves to be called articulate*,
eh, who denigrated their *hoarse, guttural and clicking sounds?*
Who spread the lie that they were cannibals eager to eat their
own grandmothers?" Camilla had obviously been preparing for
any vindication of the author of *On the Origin of Species*. In spite
of his prejudice against the Patagonian Indians, I still felt queasy
about placing this scientific hero of ours in the company of
genocidal maniacs. But Cam was adamant: "Fitz: when a detective is trying to solve a crime, unearth the reasons behind an act
of revenge, nobody is innocent. If he had the means, the motivation, the opportunity, Darwin qualifies, no matter how much we
love his work."

"All right, all right. Note, though, that I'm not descended from
him or my parents would have bragged about it nonstop."

"Who knows what Darwin was up to during his travels on the
Beagle, what Chilean wench he bedded, what young American
damsel visiting Valparaíso or Bahia Blanca seduced him, how
his chromosomes may yet pulsate in some faraway American

kid celebrating his fourteenth birthday—the fittest did not survive by abstaining from intercourse, Fitz. And while you're at it,
investigate Robert Fitzroy, the captain of the *Beagle*. After all,
he's far worse than Darwin. On a previous expedition to Tierra
del Fuego, he carted four hostages off to England, even changed
their names. If it had been your relatives, wouldn't that be a
motive to invade some kid whose name was none other than
Fitzroy? And why did your parents give you that name, exactly?
Was it in that man's honor?"

"My Mom liked the name ever since she came across it in
some novel about the life of Henry the Eighth. His illegitimate
son, Henry Fitzroy, duke of Somerset or something or other,
would have inherited the throne if he hadn't died of consumption. Mom always mused about how sickness had deprived this
young man of a chance to show his worth—but that her son
would be different. Maybe that's why she went bananas when I
got sick myself. But my visitor can't be so irrational as to wreck
somebody's life because their name coincides with the name of
the captain of the *Beagle*. He knows me too intimately."

"You don't really have the foggiest idea of what is motivating
your visitor, do you?" Camilla said firmly. "Robert Fitzroy stays
on the list."

I reluctantly agreed. At this rate, most of humanity could
qualify. I imagined the possibility of myriad abstruse linkages,
past and present, between my life and that of an unknown savage
seized from Patagonia. And yet, once Cam had departed for
Paris, I welcomed the work she had plied me with as a subtle way
to ward off the desolate hours alone with my visitor, just him and
me again.

I whispered to him that I was looking for someone who had
done grievous harm to him, his murderer or maybe just someone
who had seen the crime. Yes, I was speaking to him once more,

now that Camilla had crossed the ocean that he also had crossed a hundred years ago. *Guide me*, I said, *let me see through your eyes for even one instant, the eyes that must have seen somebody who tormented you. Or maybe I should concentrate on seeing you from the outside, from the gaze of someone who ripped you from your island or your steppe or your hut, a vision that, alien to your culture, would be closer to my perspective. Where should I start, who sold you for a few pennies, who looked the other way, who would you not forgive?*

I didn't need to tell him, of course, that I had reservations as to whether the gaggle of primary suspects I came up with would yield any real evidence once I sent their names to senior members on both parental sides of the family to see if they rang a remote bell. He was peering over my shoulder, knew about my doubts, as I waded through hundreds of books and articles I had partially digested and returned to now with—yes, a vengeance I guess is the right word.

First off, I filled page after page with every likely culprit and their foulest crimes or sayings. Though who was to say that it was someone mentioned in those books, selected by history? Who were those three military men in the photo, their backs turned to the camera and Julius Popper as they crouched, aiming at unseen victims? Croats, one source suggested—escaping recruitment by the Austro-Hungarian Empire, impoverished, looking for a promising horizon at the tip of South America. Bandits, said another scholar. Rabble, most reports agreed. With so many Westerners flooding Patagonia, slayers of whales, discoverers of islets and passageways, transporters of smallpox, denigrators of those nomads of land and sea, miners for gold and shearers of sheep, how to discern if my ghost did not hold a grudge against one of them?

I wrote my reservations to Camilla, who replied: "Concentrate on the most famous," her message came scrawling down my screen just after she had written it on the other side of the ocean, and this abolition of distance made me feel paradoxically removed from her, how was it possible that her words could travel so instantaneously but not her body? "There's a reason we know their names: due to the great evil—or, like Gusinde, the considerable good—that they perpetrated. The man we're looking for will eventually find his way onto our list."

Two weeks later, I was able to report that the task had been exhaustively accomplished. Without help from my visitor, though I had kept pleading for his participation.

And now that the list was complete, I again spoke to him:

Have I left anyone significant off? I asked, and was greeted, as always, by his silence.

I stared at those hundreds of names. I couldn't very well send them all off to relatives whom I hadn't written to in ages. The accused had to be placed into a hierarchy of guilt, the list pared down to the most egregious criminals.

Violence, I decided. I'd kick off with those who had done bodily harm to my visitor or one of his family or tribe. Six villains, I thought, to start out with, send three names first and then another three and if my extended family responded with bafflement then I'd trickle down the list. Though I found my own decision soon undermined when I examined the naturalists and explorers and found there the disturbing name of Georg Forster.

The twenty-one-year-old son (my age!) of a German naturalist, Georg had accompanied his father on the 1772–1775 voyage of Captain Cook around the world. Besides dubbing the Patagonians filthy, indolent, stupid, uncouth, degenerate, attacking "the whole assemblage of their features that formed the most loathsome picture of misery and wretchedness to which human nature can possibly be reduced," this Forster fellow sneered at them for being insensible to the superiority of European civilization.

I felt like thrashing this pedantic disparager, overcome with a wave of hatred that moved me uncomfortably close, I thought, to my visitor. What if this smug Georg was one of my forebears? What if a great-great-great-grandson of his had migrated to America and lost the *r*, becoming a Foster? What better revenge than to impose the features this Georg Forster had called so abhorrent on one of his remote offspring? Did we not have Teutonic blood in our veins?

When I wrote my concerns to Cam, she dismissed them immediately. "Too easy, too ideological, too remote," she typed back. "Go with violence, your initial instinct, Fitz."

Glad to have instructions to turn my back on the abominable Georg Forster, I obediently complied.

The pyramid of infamy started, of course, with the inevitable Maurice Maître of whom I had already made inquiries, receiving the assurance that no one of that name—or of Belgian origin— had been a member of our family line, but I could always try and dig deeper. Occupying second place was our bête noire, Julius Popper, who had dared to bring along a photographer to commemorate his murders. Not even MacInch, my next choice, the fiercest stalker of the Selk'nam, had done that. Unaccompanied by a camera, he hunted them down for having thieved and eaten sheep, which they considered small and tasty guanacos, prodigiously provided by Nature for the sustenance of her sons and daughters. MacInch also merited a third place on the list due to his justification of the carnage: a favor, he said, to exterminate these miserable creatures rather than prolong a long, cruel, and painful death as captives in the mission. Just as terrible, though less loquacious, was the *estanciero* José Menéndez. One of his strategies was to find beached whales or dead sheep and lace their insides with strychnine, poisoning dozens of famished families that devoured the beasts thinking they were being invited to a feast rather than to a grave. But I shoved him down the list, as there was not even a hint of Spanish or Latin American ancestry in my family. Rumors of some Dutchman, however, had been floated by a second cousin on my mother's side, so I reached back many centuries to Admiral Olivier van Noort who, in 1599, disembarked with his crew on Punta Catalina in order to kill penguins and ended up shooting several dozen Selk'nam, and capturing a woman, who was returned to her island after being raped, while the six youngsters kidnapped with her ended up dead. More than enough reasons to seek retribution.

I added to this dubious company a certain Reverend Stirling, partly because I had a vague recollection that at some point there had been some sort of Anglican clergyman in my granddad's family during the last century but also because I took a particular dislike to him—he had taken four Patagonians to England (two of them died on the return trip).

The sixth man on my list?

None other than Captain Cook. Though he had admired the ability of the Patagonian natives to survive in such adverse circumstances, he entered my hall of perfidy due to casual observations made about Tierra del Fuego, averring the abundance of whales and seals ready for slaughter and commercialization. Those innocent words, when published after his circumnavigation, led throngs of hunters to descend upon the southernmost reach of the hemisphere, depleting the sea of most of its native fauna. While the lamps of Europe and the East Coast of the United States were afire with oil from blubber and the ladies of those lands wrapped themselves in the pelts of sea lions, while the stores filled with soap, paint, medicine, and fertilizers, the Onas began to starve and waste away. Faraway streets and homes were lit, leather polished, grease smeared on steam engines, all squeezed from dead whales. Guess what the cetacean bones, I asked Cam, were used for? Corsets and skirts and buggy whips, tennis rackets and hairbrushes. Modernity was the invisible culprit behind extinction.

"Could you be overreaching, my dear?" Cam inquired from Paris—she who had urged me to put Darwin on the list. "I mean, maybe you're casting the net—excuse the metaphor—a bit too wide. There won't be anyone alive in our countries who didn't benefit from the wholesale killing of every Moby Dick, sea lion, or guanaco to be found. Everyone will end up guilty."

I responded that maybe the ultimate point of so much reading and finger-pointing might be to signal to my visitor that we recognized that it was not only a matter of one man kidnapping eleven, or one stalker killing a hundred, or one clergyman inadvertently opening the door to a raging epidemic, that something more systemic and horrible was afoot. Besides, who was to say that our ghost did not have a sense of humor and would find it appropriate to bring Captain Cook into the equation, even if not directly responsible for the impact of his words on the imagination of the fisheries of Nantucket or the designs of the British admiralty or the owners of French schooners. Was I directly responsible for a Belgian felon abducting a young man from his native tundra? Cook had unleashed this onslaught and his descendants would have to face the consequences, the Flecks and Davisons and Ducks and Carters and Scotts and so many more—oh, his DNA (he had eight children) was rampant everywhere.

"All right, send Cook's name out along with the others, though who knows what your relatives will think."

I had been meaning to write to the family for some time. My two grandmothers, my surviving grandfather, several aunts, the ubiquitous Uncle Carl and other assorted members of my tribe had not even been notified of my tiny wedding, and that event—now almost two months ago—seemed like a good enough excuse. Responses dribbled in: congratulations on my marriage, while informing me tartly that they were unsurprised that I hadn't thought to invite them given my weirdness over the last decade. And not a word regarding my genealogical queries. What they wanted to know was when they would get to kiss the bride, what on earth was she doing in Europe so soon after our hermit-like honeymoon? Was she in Paris to have a good time, all by herself?

Yes, in fact, she was having a swell time. For almost a year now she had been shackled—like a Bengal tiger, I thought ruefully—to me and the visitor I harbored, inhibiting other aspects of her life and postponing the core of her own biochemical research. A prolonged vacation, a hiatus without atrocities and naked corpses and a recalcitrant face in a photo, would be good for her.

And for me.

It reminded me what life could be like if we confounded my apparition and sent him back to the other side of reality. In her emails and phone calls and even occasional faxes, she enthused about the cafés and the free streets of Paris. I did not envy her that stroll through Montmartre or the *sandwich au jambon* she munched in the gardens of the Rodin Museum, "so many places, Fitz, that I'm enjoying because I can now imagine how they'll look when you're at liberty to join me." How to reproach anyone who said: "I feel like a navigator mapping out a territory so her beloved can safely sail here one day. You're with me, my dear, every moment. I'm feeding my eyes and tongue and ears, I'm smelling the fresh aroma of baguettes in the morning for you and wolfing down rich, dense, stewy *boeuf bourguignon* in the evenings, for you, for you, so you can feast on my senses when I get back, drench yourself with my memories."

So I let her live with ferocious delight, enjoy the life she had sacrificed during the last year for me, for me.

And yet, despite these altruistic sentiments, I must admit that I welcomed the news that she would soon be on her way to Bonn, was impatient until she had fixed the date—a few days, she said, before my twenty-second birthday, promising some astonishing revelation.

She called me at noon, that September 11, 1989—six in the afternoon German time.

"Are you ready for your birthday present?" she asked, all bubbly. That stir of excitement in her voice. She's found him, she knows who the hell he is, she was right, she was right! "Are you?"

"Yes," I answered cautiously. "I'm ready if you are."

"Do you want me to tell you what I discovered first and then how I discovered it or would you rather—?"

"Cam, my God, just tell me."

We had been wrong, she had been wrong, that damn André, the damn son of the damn owner of the damn bookshop, had been wrong regarding the hostages of 1889. Oh, they had existed, Maître had stolen them, only four had survived, all that was true.

And here Camilla paused, I could almost hear her swallowing saliva, lubricating the inside of her lovely throat. "But your visitor is not among them."

"How do you know?"

In Gusinde's archive in Bonn she had found a photo of Maître and nine of his Onas. Maître stood to one side, dressed in typical European garb of the late 1880s, bearded like Popper had been, holding a stick or a whip or a pointer in his hand, a white terrier at his feet. To his right were arrayed his captives. "The Anthropos Institute people allowed me to photocopy it, I'll send it by fax once we're done talking, Fitz. But you'll see that none of them looks at all like our visitor. Four women, four children ages one through twelve, and one hunched, older man at the extreme left. Dressed up in furs, staring out at the camera. Snapped in Paris, the caption says, by an unknown photographer. Gusinde notes, separately, that two of the Selk'nam died on the voyage to Europe. So it can't be him, Fitz. Your visitor's a Kaweshkar, called Alakaluf by Gusinde."

"How do you know? How can you be sure?"

Disconcerted by the absence of my intruder's face among the Indians exhibited by Maître, she had kept poking around in Gusinde's papers and, with the assistance of a friendly archivist, had rifled through a number of magazine and newspaper cuttings, finally detecting a copy of *Le Journal Illustré.* "And he was there, Fitzroy. In an engraving by a C. Nielsen—"

"Wait a minute. Not a photo? Why an engraving?"

"They hadn't created the technique yet to print photos in newspapers, so when they wanted to illustrate a story in a broadsheet or magazine they did it with drawings and woodcuts, what they called *gravures.* So this Nielsen fellow depicted the group. Eleven of them, just as for the 1889 exhibit, that must have been what set pompous André off on the wrong trail. These eleven only have three infants among them, and four women, their breasts sagging, and two older men and two younger ones, and one of the younger ones, it's him, Fitz! He's standing just above some of his fellows who are squatting next to a fire, in exactly the same pose as in the photo, holding a sort of spear or stick. Behind him to one side, in the very middle of the picture, an older man crouches in a canoe, while some other Kaweshkar are huddled inside a sort of primitive hut, except for yet another older man, erect next to it, and behind them you can manage to perceive, separated from the nomads by a fence and a moat, several barely distinguishable Parisians, with top hats and cravats. And some children onlookers as well. As if visiting a zoo, and that's what they called the exhibitions, *zoos humains*, human zoos—this was a famous one, the archivist told me, in the Jardin d'Acclimation in the Bois de Boulogne. That's why, in the drawing, there's a bird strutting around the compound, as well as other animals, certainly happier than the natives, all of them miserable, half naked, their backs to the spectators but not to this Nielsen who captured them on paper and then had the image published in this *Le Journal Illustré*. We've found him, Fitz."

"But not in 1889?" I asked dully, unable yet to register such a brutal shift in the direction of our research. A whole year chasing down the wrong crime, the wrong criminal, the wrong date!

"You'll never believe the date that this magazine was published, my dear. Go ahead, try."

I thought for a moment. She wouldn't be asking this if it were not something that made some sort of maddening rational sense, that would resonate especially with me.

"September eleventh," I said. "My birthday."

"What year, Fitzroy Foster? What year?"

It had to be, it could not be any other, it was undoubtedly . . . "Eighteen eighty-one," I said.

"Eighteen eighty-one," Camilla repeated and now her voice was almost singing over the phone, the wire seemed to be burning with her fervor. "One hundred years exactly before he comes to you. I'm sure that the day it was published, that very day someone also must have snapped the photo of him."

I didn't tell her that it couldn't have been the exact day. The photo must have been taken several days before the *Journal* was printed in order to give time for a *gravure* to be made from it. But she was so exultant and I was so excited and there were more urgent questions to ask.

"So what's his name? And who took the picture in the *carte postale*?"

I tried to imagine the scene. Someone speaking to my visitor, ordering him to stand, to grimace, to turn, to frown, to sit.

"Who took the picture? That's what we're going to find out. The past does not die that easily."

Her first discovery, once she had returned to Paris from Bonn, was spectacular.

Again, she could not contain herself, calling me over the phone.

"We found him!" The first phrase, without even saying hello. "It took me a while but I tracked down another magazine, *La Nature*, from November 1881, something written by Paul Juillerat. It's a journal specializing in the sciences and their application to the arts and industry. Juillerat was at the Jardin, he visited them, he has tons of specifics, I'll translate the article for you and send along by email, but here's what matters: we found the bastard!"

"Juillerat?" I managed to stutter.

"No, he's just reporting his observations—well, yes, a bastard, like so many of them, but not the culprit, not who's to blame. He's—but listen, these Alakaluf or Kaweshkar, though Juillerat calls them *Fuégiens*, inhabitants of Tierra del Fuego, people of fire, that's what he—first there's a long historical recounting of their discovery and customs and then this Juillerat guy recounts how his savages were captured. Eleven of them, four women, four men, three children, just as in Nielsen's engraving. They were brought to Europe by a hunter of sea lions, Johann Wilhelm Wahlen, who enticed them on board his ship, gorging them with food and treating them with prudence, that's the word Juillerat uses. When the boat docked in Le Havre, a man named Saint-Hilaire was waiting for them, and took them to the Bois de Boulogne. Juillerat finishes his report by stating that 'Only the future will tell if those who find themselves right now at the Jardin d'Acclimatation will extract any profit from their stay among us. Our opinion is that they will be enchanted to find themselves back home and that the memory of whatever they have seen'—listen to this, Fitz, listen to this—'will remain in their spirit like a dream'—like a dream, Fitzroy—'that was perhaps not completely pleasant.'"

She paused to catch her breath.

I said: "So who is he? Does Juillerat say anything about who my visitor is, which of those we saw in the engraving, his name?"

"Nothing about any of them individually, Fitz."

"So what's the big discovery? Why so excited? You said we got him, we found the bastard. Found who?"

"The photographer, Fitz. The man who took the photograph. That's what's most valuable, besides the names of Wahlen and Saint-Hilaire, you need to add them to the suspects until I—but, listen, there's an engraving that accompanies this article. Against a background of trees—a thicket, full of leaves, to give the impression of something natural—we see five of the eleven. A woman with an elongated breast that falls from her chest, holding a baby, not sure what sex, the child is leaning over, playing with a strand of straw like a typical child of two, maybe three years of age. Squatting next to her is a youngish man, holding a bow and arrow, looking out at us with a dazed expression, and above him, to the left is another woman—seems like one, at any rate, as she has a protruding belly and one of her arms is pressed against a breast, half hiding it. And next to her is your visitor. This time, Fitz, there can be no doubt—I mean, the engraving from *Le Journal Illustré* was a bit blurry and with a distant perspective, but in this new, larger one from *La Nature* we see him just as he is in the *carte postale*, just as he appears in your photos over and over, now we know that rather than protecting his genitals he was carrying a long stick that slants across his lower torso. And the caption below this illustration says—wait for this, listen to this, it's what we've been searching for during this last year, it's the jackpot, Fitzroy Foster—the caption states 'The inhabitants of Tierra del Fuego in the Paris Jardin d'Acclimatation. According to'—*d'après* is the French word—'a photograph by'—note down the name, my love, push it to the very top of your list—'Pierre Petit.'"

"Pierre Petit?" I let the words roll around in my mouth as if they were small pebbles. "Does it say anything more about him? Why he took the original photo that the engraving was made from?"

"Not a word. But it should be smooth sailing from now on. Easy to find that out here in Paris. Also about this Saint-Hilaire who took the eleven natives from the ship. He must be the man running this human zoo at the Jardin or some sort of entrepreneur."

"What about my visitor? And the rest of them? What happened next, after Paris—if they survived Paris, that is, if they—sorry to be so incoherent, Cam, it's just more than I can absorb in one sitting."

"Well, get ready for many more sittings, because now's when things begin to get interesting."

And the disclosures began to roll in like waves, only restrained by Camilla's grueling professional schedule. First of all, by e-mail, clarifications about the two malefactors we had targeted. "There's no sign of this Wahlen fellow so far, but Albert Geoffroy Saint-Hilaire, he has a record longer than Al Capone's. He came from a long line of naturalists, father Isidore and grandfather Etienne, but he was more interested in animals as spectacle than as an object of study, taking charge of the exhibitions at the Jardin. His major innovation came in 1877, when he added fourteen Nubians to a menagerie of exotic beasts, camels, elephants, giraffes, ostriches, dwarf rhinos. Attendance skyrocketed, *le tout Paris* flocking to the Jardin. Next came six Eskimos, then

Laplanders, and Argentine gauchos, Bushmen, Zulus, American Indians—and, in 1881, the eleven Alakaluf."

"So I should write the extended family to see if the name Saint-Hilaire rings a bell?"

"By all means, Fitz," came Camilla's rejoinder, "though I have someone else I've come across, but would rather not divulge his identity quite yet, I don't want to rush to conclusions as I did with Prince Bonaparte—there are two names in fact that I'm keeping in reserve but in case my new leads send me on a wild goose chase, you just stick for now to Saint-Hilaire. Our real objective, however, should be Pierre Petit. He's the one, after all, that we're absolutely certain was on the other side of the lens when your visitor's face was captured. A real jerk. Along with snapping innumerable pictures of exotic humans at the Jardin, he was engaged in a series of more staid and respectable portraits. School groups, for instance, when the students graduated. Members of the Faculty of Medicine. Tons of clergymen, cardinals, abbots, bishops. He was the official photographer of the French episcopal conference and of France's religious orders. So prominent, our friend Petit, that the government commissioned him to register week by week the progress of Bartholdi's Statue of Liberty before the French sent it over to America, he even visited New York several times to take photos of its erection. I wonder what he thought of *give me your huddled masses?* But masses weren't his specialty. He captured a series of notable French artists and intellectuals, Berlioz, Gounod, Gustave Doré, and someone who was even more famous."

"Maybe my grandparents have heard about this Petit guy."

"Hold on," I could almost hear her tapping the words over there in Paris, knowing I would receive them lovingly in my lonely room in Massachusetts, "before you stir the pot, let me check something out. It'll take me a while before I have a free day to go to the Place Vosges, just be patient."

Place Vosges. I looked it up and found nothing that indicated why she wished to visit it—a symmetrical old square in
a corner of Le Marais district, near where the Bastille had been
stormed. More and more I felt that she was on a journey of her
own, speeding so fast that she couldn't find the time to fill me in
on each detail. Or was it that she enjoyed holding back certain
morsels of information, waiting until she could present an irre-
vocable and dramatic picture, in typical Cam style, impress me
with each new pinnacle of accomplishment?

A week later, I got a succinct message: "Fax machine. *Carte
postale* coming in. Kisses and bisses, Cam."

I waited for the fax, heard it whir, saw the page emerge,
half-recognized the features on the postcard she had sent,
couldn't recall where I'd seen that face, a tuft of gray hair above
an ample forehead, two pencils of eyebrows and small dark eyes
peering out from above a middling nose. A mouth encompassed
by an elegant beard, but not exceedingly so, as if its owner wanted
to advertise some gist of disobedience without, however, belying
the overall calm, made all the more serene by the hand that had
been lifted to the right side of the cheeks, bestowing a further
dose of pensiveness. The more I squinted at him, the more I
knew this was not his first appearance in my life, but who, where,
when? And then, finally, the whole photo was in my hands, the
man's gray frock coat sitting loosely on large shoulders, an arm
resting on the contours of a chair. And underneath, at the very
bottom, three words: *Pierre Petit, Phot.*

Was it Petit himself, a self-portrait? No, somebody else, I was
sure of it.

I rushed up the stairs to my computer. As I was mounting
them, before I even read Cam's message, it hit me. I knew who
he was, the man that Pierre Petit had immortalized in that *carte
postale.*

Victor Hugo.

"Victor Hugo," Camilla echoed my thoughts and supplemented them in her next e-mail. "Petit photographed him in Brussels in 1862. One of the most famous pictures of the author of *Les Miserables*. A few months ago I asked your dad at dinner—remember, darling?—about your brothers Hugh and Vic, why those names, and he answered Victor Hugo. So enthused that he had learned French to read him in the original and that his French grandmother, when she had come over for his graduation from high school, had brought along a picture of none other than the great writer, an original, which was up in the attic. So, my dear, up, up you go, with your dad and brothers. Check it out. See if it matches the *carte postale* I faxed. Till soon, your loving, lascivious Cam."

All four male members of the family dutifully trooped upstairs and gathered around the picture of Victor Hugo, the very image Cam had found at the Place Vosges, the very photo snapped by Pierre Petit more than a century ago, the gift my great-grandmother had offered to my father when I had not yet been born, there it was, framed with gilt edges, clearer and sharper than the hazy *carte postale* sent via fax by Camilla.

"Can we take it out?" I asked Dad—as if asking for his permission would make it less of a profanation—and he nodded, carefully dislodged the portrait from its protective glass and frame.

We turned it over.

And read the words awaiting us on the other side.

À ma Thérèse Jacquet, de la part de son arrière-grand-père, Pierre Petit, un portrait de Victor Marie Hugo, son auteur favori.

"*Arrière-grand-père?*" I asked, though I knew the answer, Camilla had known it without even climbing to the attic.

Great-grandfather. Pierre Petit was my great-grandmother's great-grandfather.

The man who had seen through a lens the face that would travel from his French eyes into some hidden recess of his French memory to be transmitted across all those generations until it germinated inside me, one hundred years from when he had snapped that shot, the savage had been captured in light and shadow and those eyes, those eyes, so different from Victor Hugo's, that nakedness waiting for years to make its appearance.

My father was devastated.

I had kept him apprised, from time to time, about our investigation and he knew that we were searching for some ancestor who had been in touch, ominously so, with the young Patagonian he still called a monster.

Now he felt absurdly responsible for what his forebear had done, one click of the shutter of Pierre Petit's machine had repercussions a century later, was still causing irreparable damage to us and our tribe. Why me, why me, why you? The questions we had been asking for over eight years now had an answer, or the hint of an answer. Pierre Petit had spawned both the photo and a family and my father and my brothers and I had the genes of that family tumbling inside us, and yet, and yet . . .

"Why not me?" Dad asked. "Why . . . ?" without needing to complete the thought. Why, indeed? What was so special about Gerald Foster's son Fitzroy that he was selected as a victim rather than his father, who sported the same lineage?

Camilla had a response that tried to assuage my dad's feelings of guilt, spread the blame. "Tell your father that I'm certain that Petit all by himself is not enough to have provoked this apparition, that there has to be something unique to you, a contribution, let's call it that, from your mom's side of the stock."

"And not my brothers?"

"The firstborn always pay for the sins of the past, Fitzroy. But we'll soon take that burden from your shoulders."

She had some potential clues, she said, to the identity and fate of my visitor, and, parallel to that hunt, the possibility of finding what I might have inherited from my mother's German lineage. It had been a German whaler who had hijacked the eleven Kaweshkar and there was one trace in a newspaper clipping about this Wahlen man, linking him to a certain Captain Schwers or Schweers, acting on orders from someone in Hamburg. She'd soon, soonest, report significant progress on all these fronts.

"You know more than you're telling me."

"Of course I do. Since I arrived in Paris, I've been writing notes daily, correcting, adding comments and little meditations, processing each discovery and idea, rewriting the story over and over again so it all makes sense, who did this, why, when, where, how—the typical questions a detective asks, Fitz. But the picture's not complete yet. It'll be ready by the time I'm back— maybe Christmas, definitely before New Year's Eve."

"I miss you, love."

"I miss you too, Fitz. But each time I write something in my report, it's as if you were here in the room with me. Thinking of how I'll read it to you slowly, savor it by your side, see your face as you hear it from my lips, moist and full, the whole story, from the moment they are kidnapped in July 1881 until five of them are sent back to Chile in March or maybe April 1882."

"What? Where did you get that information from? Five of them survived?"

"I didn't say five survived. I said five were sent back."

"Who were they? Is my—?"

"Patience, love. We have to be in the same room together."

"Just tell me this. Did he make it? Did he ever return home?"

"All in good time, Fitz. I can only guess how hard this must be for you, waiting, waiting. But this is what he wants. For me to tell you why he's come, why he chose you. That's what I think he wants and we should respect that."

Did I care, did I really care what he wanted? But I wasn't in the mood to quarrel with her, not over the phone, not ever, in fact—when had she ever lost an argument anyway, my stubborn, glorious Cam?

So all I said was: "Send me anything, something, love—not your report, rewrite that till it's perfect, I understand that, but keep me up to date."

"So you can understand a bit of what's going on, yes."

"So I can be near to you, that's what matters. And I'll be sure to send your way anything I discover, okay?"

Before a packet from her arrived two weeks later, chock-full of photos and some clippings from French journals, translated into English—expedited from Paris by Roberts Express service, only two days for these international deliveries to cross the ocean, how the world was growing smaller by the day!—I had received from my father's mom, Grand-mère Amélie, the confirmation that her own grandmother Thérèse had always claimed the family was related to an eminent photographer. Indeed Amélie had nebulously recounted how she and her mother, Georgine, had visited a dying relative whose atelier was overflowing with photographs and he had signed one for her, the photo of Victor Hugo. As daughters gave birth to daughters, that dead forebear's surname had been diluted and swallowed up by time, but now that I mentioned it to her, yes, the name was Pierre Petit.

"You, child," my grand-mère announced, not understanding full well the implications of her words, "are the sixth generation. Aren't you proud to be descended from such a wonderful man?"

FOUR

"To photograph people is to violate them, by seeing them as they can never see themselves, by having knowledge of them they can never have."

—Susan Sontag

The sixth generation!
What ghosts then would haunt our son or daughter if ever we dared to breed, what would the seventh generation be like? Would the other members of the group that had been kidnapped from Tierra del Fuego and stuffed into my ancestor Pierre's camera find a way into the dreams of my offspring? None of these thoughts shared with Cam as I examined the many reproductions of their photos she had sent me, culled from a smattering of Parisian archives. My visitor was present in a series of collective representations that must have been snapped one after the other, all of them against a background of trees.

Paris in September, an ideal time, Cam commented, for a family outing to the zoo on the train line expressly built to carry innumerable clients back and forth. Animals and beasts mixed together: one of the photos flaunted an ostrich crossing the expanse where the clutch of natives sits. In the next shot, probably a minute later, two of the men have stood upright while my visitor remains crouching, more mistrustful and startled than ever, and he is still in the same position the next time Pierre Petit's camera bags the group that has begun to disperse and separate, a white light from overexposure slicing the scene nearly in half. The light overwhelms them in the ensuing shot, and still he does not move, he continues to stare straight at the man who was my great-great-great-great-grandfather, if looks could kill, if looks could kill. Until in the next take, he is no longer visible, my visitor, engorged by a smudge of infested light. And then, new combinations: there with an older man and woman and a tiny naked babe, and in the following sequences he's standing by a different woman and after that accompanied by an older, fierce man—oh, my visitor was popular, one of Petit's favorites. And of course, of course, the shot that was to be transferred to a *carte postale* and sold for a few sous over a hundred years ago only to end up in a bookshop in the rue de l'Odéon. But it was the others that my faraway wife kept demanding that I look at— who were they, what relation did one have to the other? Was that older couple the mother and father of my visitor? Was that baby his brother? His nephew? The other baby, his niece, his sister? Was that other young man a brother? I interrogated their faces as I had done for all this time with my visitor's and, as with him, their answer was silence.

But on this occasion I had some help, the beginning of a response from the material Camilla had sent over, mainly a long article published by the Anthropology Society of Paris, which tried to understand where these natives fit in the Darwinian scheme of evolution, wondering about their intelligence, how close they might be to the mongoloid race, how far from Asian ancestors. A presentation by Dr. Léonce Manouvrier on

November 17, 1881—"by then," Cam wrote, "they were already in Germany, ten of them, because one of the children had died. The daughter of the woman called Petite Mère, little mother, a name not given to her by Pierre Petit, but by their keepers. They baptized the fiercest looking one Antonio, described by Manouvrier as having *a wild appearance*. The gentle, older man is called the Captain, his wife for some reason keeps her own name, Piskouna. The other women are Lise and Catherine, and then there are the two younger ones, Henri and Pedro. Manouvrier's descriptions don't allow us to fathom which one might be our visitor. But nevertheless, that scientist spent many hours with them on five different occasions, so you should spend time with him, with the pictures, Fitzroy Foster, no better way to get close to those natives and lift the curse, if indeed it is a curse and not, perhaps, a blessing."

These last words alarmed me—was Camilla becoming an apologist for the visitor, like my mother? But I had once doubted my swimmer when she had initially asked those right questions and we had lost seven years of love and companionship due to that mistake and I was not about to tread the same path again. I would let her lead me into this thicket, I would have faith, I did have faith in my darling's guidance. Soon I'd be hearing, in the carnal presence of those moist, full lips, the story she was writing for me.

Meanwhile, Manouvrier's testimony did indeed open my eyes—helping these eyes, so often supplanted by my visitor's, to roam his face and body, probe the habits of his fellow captives. So much that I did not know, in spite of our infinite hours of cohabitation. There was more information about Henri than about Pedro, so I focused on him. His gait, his spindly legs. Advancing, according to Manouvrier, with an odd, uncertain step, bending his legs a little and lifting his feet rather high, in the manner of a hunter who walks with precaution through the bushes. Landing on the outer edge of his feet, just like the native women. A sizable gap between the big toe and the second toe. An overly developed chest, a little convex shaped. Well built, of average stoutness. A nose, somewhat depressed, large at its base, but substantially less flat then a Negro's. Small, quite confined ears. One of the young men (—Henri? Pedro? unspecified) already had had all his wisdom teeth emerge. The teeth are beautiful and well ordered, in spite of the abundance of raw mussels consumed. Skin smooth, of a color corresponding to numbers 29 and 30 of the society's chromatic table, perhaps best described as yellow-brown or a yellowish-red chocolate. No hair on the back, shoulders, chest, except for an extremely fine fuzz, only perceptible when viewed from an oblique angle. The hair on the head, deep black color, straight, glossy, abundant, reaching the eyebrows. Two locks have been deposited in Monsieur Goldstein's collection.

And the eyes—oh the unmistakable eyes—very dark, now I learned that they corresponded to numbers 1 and 2 of the chromatic table. Both Pedro and Henri, according to Manouvrier, under seventeen—so one of them could indeed have been fourteen when the picture was taken.

Could either or both have been the offspring of the women prisoners? The only hint came from an observation about Lise, the youngest female. *This maiden has never had any children. So we were interested in and able to establish the size and shape of her breasts. They are quite voluminous and stand rather upright. The breasts of the other three females droop down, but not noticeably more than those of women of our country who have nourished many infants. We have often observed these natives give breast in the European manner.*

Had my visitor suckled at one of those breasts? Had his

mother put water in his mouth by drinking first from a fountain in Patagonia and then dropping the liquid slowly into his
waiting infant lips, throat, stomach? Had she watched him play
and grow and come of age and now tried to protect him in a foreign land? Or had she been left behind, mourning her son when
he and the others were spirited away?

And then, of course, there were the measurements, a whole
table of them. The individual results had been deposited in Dr.
Broca's lab for further consultation, but there were averages for
each category, quantified according to recommendations in the
Manual of Instructions of the Anthropological Society. I could
visualize the process, Manouvrier's fingers on the measuring
tape and his lips calling out numbers to his colleagues Deniker
and Goldstein, going on to the next angle or limb or protuberance. From the dolichocephalic skull, down the vertex to the ear
cavity, and from the ophryon to the hairline and then to the top
of the nose and the alveolar point. Facial angle from the chin
point to the top of the sternum, and thence to the upper edge
of the pubis, navel and nipple and cervical vertebra and iliac
anterior-superior spine and bitrochanteric line, chest width,
circumference of the thorax under the armpits—did it tickle
my visitor when the examiner prodded under his armpit?—
upper limb, from the shoulder blade to tip of the middle finger,
hand length from the styloid process to the medius, height of
the ankle bone, foot length. Fifty measurements. But not all
the parts of the body were studied.

*Only one thing were we unable to obtain: to examine and measure
the genital organs. It turned out not to be possible to view any lower
than the upper edge of the pubic region. Our insistences on this subject
were unavailing, and whenever we attempted to proceed by surprise
to lower a savage's underwear, which by no means was the Fueguians'
national dress, each would quickly react by hand in order to stop us.*

Manouvrier went on to wonder if this was due to innate modesty or fear of their keepers, *who could well have succeeded in providing them, besides the underwear and the most indispensable notions of propriety, some lessons on decency and proper deportment.*

Probably nothing that I read in this report endeared me more to my visitor and his tribe than this resistance to some stranger scrutinizing their sexual organs. It brought the Kaweshkar to life for me, a process that was already well on its way. They seemed so . . . human, yes, that's the right word. How they laughed when the French experts twirled their moustaches, how they made sure the fire was always lit and barely warmed their food on its embers, the skill shown at forging arrowheads, the fact that they liked baguettes and displayed no interest in coins or silver. Brought to life for me now as life ebbed from them more than a century earlier: each day more dejected and lethargic, apparently because vaccinations had made the whole colony sick, suffering from pustules and glandular congestion. Was this what had killed the child of Petite Mère?

Oh to see through his eyes, once, just once, to see through your eyes, to accompany you on your journey.

Because Cam had discovered their itinerary.

"Listen to this: The day after the baby dies, on September thirtieth, the rest of them are packed in a train and transported to Germany. I'm going to follow their trail, Fitz."

"To Bonn?"

"No, no. Hamburg first, yes, Hamburg is where it all started, that's where they disembarked—not in Le Havre as I thought. And after Hamburg, Leipzig, so that's next if I can get permission to enter East Germany, but there's a lot of turmoil there at the moment, so maybe the Communists won't allow an American to cross the border, we wouldn't want them to accuse me of being a spy or something. Better go straight to Stuttgart, then

Nuremburg, Munich. Not the order in which they made the trip, but it makes sense for another reason and—and I'll leave Berlin for the end, Berlin holds the key, the kidnapping was financed from there."

"You're going to all those cities?"

"And Zurich afterward, that was their final destination."

"Cam! Can't you just tell me what's so important that you—"

She wouldn't budge, said that before feeding me more information piecemeal like this, she wanted to get even closer to them, closer to what . . . Her voice faded away.

"Closer to them! What about getting closer to me, Camilla Foster?"

"Don't tell me you're jealous of that poor young man, Fitzroy Foster! If he's your only rival, a Kaweshkar who died over a hundred years ago, well, count yourself lucky."

"No, seriously—"

"Seriously, just trust me. I'll be in touch every day, only thing is don't ask me for details."

I realized that I had to let her puzzle her scientific way into and out of the labyrinth of my ailment, without the distraction of having to explain each interminable stage, each loose thread, to someone faraway, even if I was the victim. Of course I'd trust her.

And besides, she had a wonderful reward in store, promising to be home by Thanksgiving, with her mission accomplished.

I was delighted at the news that she would soon be in my arms, a delight tempered by what this meant for her career. What about the Institut Pasteur?

"They wouldn't give me the two-week leave of absence I needed, Fitz. So we terminated my contract—quite amicably. They'll be happy to host me in the future, *once you get your affairs in order*. I'd told Dr. Louvard that this trip to Germany, my second since I'd been here, was to help my husband, and he was discreet, raised an eyebrow but smiled and said—oh so French, even for a scientist—*There is only one thing more important than molecular DNA, and that is love.* And I answered that I believed that all DNA is held together by love. And I do, I do. So no worries, Fitz."

She seemed excessively cheerful, even for eternally optimistic Cam. Wasn't this pursuit handicapping her career?

"Not at all," she answered and right away backtracked. "Well, a bit. Dr. Louvard was keen on my teaming up with one of their consultants, this hotshot American epidemiologist from Stanford, Ernest Downey. A legend, already a candidate for a Nobel Prize due to his work on the AIDS retrovirus. But when I met him briefly as I was leaving, he—well, he has, in effect, switched to my field of visual memory and genetic mutations, except that he mentioned that the transmission of images does not only descend through heredity, but may spread from person to person, sexually or via saliva. He said he'd look me up in the States, keep in touch, save humanity from the oncoming plague. Truth is I felt him to be—don't know, creepy, Fitzroy, almost tormented. So your visitor has done one good deed already, keeping me away from Downey!"

Off she went then, deep into Germany.

I heard from her sporadically, mysterious messages of erotic enchantment interspersed with short, almost telegraphic phrases that tantalizingly afforded glimpses into her doings on the road from Hamburg to Berlin via those other cities.

Hamburg: *I know who arranged the kidnapping, Fitz, and much more. Heinrich, they called him Heinrich—Henri's your visitor, Fitz.* Nuremburg: *They were sick when they arrived here from Berlin, Fitz, but still put on display.* Stuttgart: *So sick they couldn't be exhibited, Fitz, not here.*

And then München: *Definitely ill, your Henri, if we trust a Dr. Bollinger who treated him in this city, according to memos among the papers of Professor Theodor von Bischoff.* And later that night: *Now I understand how he died, of what he died, Fitz.*

And, finally, Berlin.

November 7, 1989.

Last link, almost the last missing link, Fitz, here in Berlin where all hell—or should I say heaven—is breaking loose, a new dawn for humanity. But that's not why I came here. It turns out that our Kaweshkar were delivered to Rudolf Virchow, Fitz. Not easy for me to write that name contemptuously, my dear. A friend and colleague of Louis Pasteur, a hero to anybody studying biology and cancer. We owe him the theory of cellular reproduction—that diseased cells originate in healthy ones. Also a terrific social reformer, saving countless lives with changes in public hygiene and the sewage system, one of the most progressive public figures of his time, a believer in full democracy, including for women, and taxing the wealthy and—that's why it's so difficult to believe someone like him could have paid for the abduction. But Saint-Hilaire only came aboard later, once Henri and the others were in Europe. Virchow had been trying for years to get his hands on some Patagons, wanted to examine them thoroughly, up close. More results tomorrow from the Berlin Zoological Society. Love you with every molecule in my blood, Cam.

Heaven and hell were indeed breaking loose in Berlin, where three days before my love arrived half a million people had protested at the Alexanderplatz in East Berlin, demanding free passage to the West. She had traveled "all night in a train from München, through East Germany, darling, was sort of exciting that we couldn't stop because it was enemy territory. I peered out into the darkness and there was nothing, nothing to be seen, I wonder what Henri felt, twenty-seven hours shut inside a wagon with meat and biscuits and a bit of water, from Paris to Berlin." Just a few miles from where she wrote to me, the Politburo of the Communist Party in the East was secluded right then and there trying to avoid a bloody confrontation. Not the best moment to be doing research on other sorts of violence and migrations, other walls erected in zoos a hundred years back, but Cam's exuberance was limitless. "The best time," she cooed the next morning, November 8, "you should see the people in the streets marching to the Brandenburg Gate, thousands gathered waiting for something monumental to happen. Liberation, Fitz, for those people. And for us, we're about to be free as well of the past, you'll see, love, got to go."

And rushed away, not clear if to join the protestors or to delve into the archives Virchow had left to the Berlin Society for Anthropology, Ethnology, and Prehistory.

Next day, she called twice.

First early in the morning. "Henri—I can't get used to calling him Heinrich or Heindrich, one report says he was eighteen years old—which undermines our perfect theory of his being fourteen like you on September 11, 1881. Also that he was, along with Pedro, the son of Antonio, the fierce one—though they both look much more like the one called the Captain. One report adds that Antonio was the husband of Trine, which I very much doubt—nobody in Paris ever suggested anything of the sort. So many lies. You see why I don't want to give you details until I've sorted everything out. But I'll have it all wrapped up by tomorrow. I've just fixed up an appointment at one of the newspapers that reported about the Patagonians while they were still in Berlin. Till later, love."

And with a quick kiss, she was gone.

I waited by the phone for hours, ever more concerned by the situation in Berlin and the nonstop coverage on the radio and TV, and her excessive excitement redoubled my anxiety—did she even look before crossing the street, had she forgotten her promise to be back by Thanksgiving?

The second call came much later that evening.

Sheer gold, she said, the newspaper clippings had all the information we required, she'd leave for Zurich tomorrow evening. So she was in the mood to celebrate and she knew just the place. "It's all coming together, Fitz, our history and the history of this century, two hundred years after the storming of the Bastille, I'll call later, darling. Just remember this. From now on, it's going to be all right. Fitz, we've paid our dues, that's what I realized."

She was rushing out the door, she was zooming away with such speed that I hardly had time to tell her to take care of herself, she was carrying my life as well as hers, take care of yourself, Cam, my Camilla, my Camilla Wood, take care, my love, I don't know if she heard me.

The third call of the day never came.

I waited all night long that ninth of November, 1989, watching the crowds surging through Checkpoint Charlie, the men and women from the East and the West dancing on top of the wall, the first fragments of brick and concrete being thrown down, I watched hoping to catch sight of the only woman in the world I cared about and she was not there, the cameras did not capture her as they had captured Henri and Antonio and Lise and the little child who had died in Paris, there was no call from her that night.

Or the next day, a Saturday.

I had phoned the hotel and nobody in her room was answering. My father said not to worry, there were moments in history when you lose sense of time and space and even responsibility, she'd be all right, he assured me she would be all right.

On Sunday, November 11, the call came early.

I was the only one up. By myself as I had been when the

Consul called from Manaus, again Fitzroy Foster picked up the receiver when an official from another consulate called.

This time the bad news came from Berlin.

FIVE

"The sun did not set only for me."

—Nietzsche, *Thus Spake Zarathustra*

Can I speak to Mr. Foster?"

"There are four Mr. Fosters in this house, sir. Which one do you—" Trying to postpone the reckoning—that voice reminded me, circumspect, neutral, bureaucratic, of that other voice the last time I had—already something was churning in my stomach.

"Fitzroy Foster."

"Who is this?"

"Philip Parker, from the American Consulate in Berlin. Are you Fitzroy Foster?"

"Yes. Has something happened?"

"The husband of Mrs. Camilla Foster?"

"Yes, yes, yes, damn it. What's happened?"

There had been an accident. No, not fatal, my wife was alive, all her vital signs and bodily functions working well, except that . . .

"What, what, what is it?"

Her head. She'd been hit by a piece of debris—that's how
Parker had described it at first, "from the Wall, you know. No full
report yet, sir, but it appears that she was standing underneath a
group that was chipping away for souvenirs, they're called—"

"I don't give a flying fuck what they're—"

"*Mauerspechte*, wall peckers, but some of the chunks can be
hefty and as bad luck would have it—"

"How is she? Where is she? Oh God, he did it! The bastard
did it!"

"Nobody did it, sir. Nothing deliberate. The Mauerspechte
rushed down immediately and called an ambulance. It was just
a celebration. I realize this is something of a shock to you but
if you'd calm down I can pass you the hospital information and
the phone number of the attending doctor. He says she's out of
danger."

Calm down? How could I calm down? My world was collapsing quicker than the Berlin Wall itself—the one person who
had come to save me, who understood everything about my
haunted existence, what if she, what if . . . ?

"I'm calm, Mr. Parker. You're right, it doesn't help my wife for
me to—I'll call the doctor, of course, but if you could tell me
what condition she—is she in a coma, is she conscious, what—?"

"How soon can you get here, Mr. Foster? To Berlin, I mean?"

How to explain that I couldn't, not to Berlin, not anywhere.
No passport, no photo. That I'd hardly set foot outside our home
for almost a decade, that only because of my love, my darling, my
Cam, my Cam, had I started to venture forth. But someone had
to go, someone had to—who? Who?

Parker mistook my silence for something else.

"We understand that it might be difficult to obtain a ticket to
Berlin, of all places, in the next few days. It's become the center
of the universe—everybody wants to travel here, history in the

making, quite exciting, Mr. Foster, begging your pardon, I realize that your wife had joined the festivities and—but what I wanted to underscore was that the consulate might be able to assist you, the airlines have kept seats open for an emergency like this one."

What emergency? How could he dilly and dally like that, offering me no real information, as he meandered on about wall peckers and festivities and the history of the universe. The man was an idiot, undeserving of an explanation regarding my travel impediments, that Dad or one of my brothers, someone else would have to go.

"Mr. Parker. My wife. Can she speak, is she conscious? Please, just a quick update, in case the hospital doesn't answer."

Parker contended that he was uncomfortable offering a medical opinion and there was a strict protocol for dealing with American citizens injured abroad, but seeing my stress—Mrs. Foster was ostensibly suffering from a case of retrograde amnesia, it was called. The physicians would have to elucidate their diagnosis, but basically, when she had awoken this morning—in perfect health, Parker insisted—she had no idea that she was in Berlin or why, not the slightest recollection of the celebration at the Wall or—or—or—here Parker began to stutter.

"So she doesn't remember who she is?"

Oh yes, she remembered perfectly well who she was. Except that she thought yesterday was September 10, September 10, 1981, that is—she believed she was fourteen years old. And that made it hard to even find her husband, because she didn't remember having been married. "She kept asking for her father, a Dr. Cameron Wood, whom we have identified as deceased, but fortunately she had a card with the address of her hotel and in her notebook we found your name and number in the States in enormous letters, inside a big heart, Mr. Foster, so we gave you a call—this call—as next of kin."

I swallowed hard and asked him to repeat the day and year that Cam thought it was. Not because I hadn't heard clearly the first time, but because I needed to digest what it meant. If her last recollection was from the day before I had shown her the photo of my visitor, if her accident had returned her to a time when she had not yet seen his face—well, that was proof he was responsible, he had sought to wipe out any trace in her mind of his existence to stop her drawing any closer to him, he had tried to murder her like he did my mother, he—but now was not the time to waste on Henri, that scum, now I had to tell Parker that my father would be in Berlin tomorrow, the next day if no tickets could be arranged.

"Because you . . . ?"

"I'm ill. I can't leave my bed for now. My dad will ring you as soon I've had a chance to brief him on my Cam's—on my wife's condition."

That night, Dad was on a plane to West Berlin. And the next morning, went straight to the Charité Hospital, where he conferred with the team of doctors treating his daughter-in-law. They recommended that she should not be made aware of the relationship in order to protect her from the shock of realizing that her father had passed away. The nurses had kept her in bed, far from mirrors that might reveal the face of a twenty-two-year-old woman to someone who believed she was a mere fourteen. The idea was to sedate the patient until her return home, where she could be eased into the truth.

Cam seemed puzzled to be in Berlin but too exhausted to be her usual inquisitive self, slightly concerned that her breasts seemed to have grown, that she had discovered more pubic hair than she recalled, that she felt heftier, more "experienced," she said, but attributed that to her "accident," which she did not show much curiosity about either. The doctors assumed that she'd accept any casual explanation for Mr. Gerald Foster coming to get her instead of her father. He should, in an offhand way, state that her dad had the flu and had therefore asked Mr. Foster to fill in for him—a way of starting to insinuate that perhaps all was not well with the father but not enough to trouble the patient. Waking Mrs. Foster up to her new reality was a task best left to her husband.

It was a task I had been readying for. She had arrived almost out of nowhere, out of the swimming dreams of my past, to rescue me. Now it was my turn to return the favor.

The doctors had suggested that there was an outside chance that she would recover her memory as soon as she saw me: instead of being stunned and dazed, everything would simply flood back.

"That could happen?" I asked my father over the phone.

"It's a possibility. There have been cases . . ."

"And if not, how long could—?"

"Weeks, months, even years. It could even—but that's not her case, they think. Something about the hippocampus and the lateral I don't know what . . . The MRI and CAT scan showed no lesions—I can't believe that Polaroid helped develop the techniques that are giving us hope that she'll heal soonest. So let's cross our fingers and pray that one smile from you, son, will do the trick."

When I did regale her with that smile upon her return, it did not jog her memory. It did, however, provoke a smile back, and I felt uplifted, as if the sun had risen after many dark nights. Though barely conscious, she recognized me, of course—the last recollection buzzing inside her, she would confide later in a moment of intimacy, was from the night of September 10, 1981, when we had said goodbye after not making love, pledging to see each other early next morning to go to school together. And here I was, as promised, smiling at her, except I was changed, the features that the camera refused to capture had suffered the modification of time.

"My, how you've grown, Fitzroy Foster," was all she said, coquettishly, as the men lifted her from the ambulance, gesturing for me to come closer to her lips, so she could murmur: "You'll find that I've grown a lot since yesterday, as well, just wait and see what birthday present I have for you," she whispered before she drifted off to sleep and up the stairs and I tucked her into the bed that she could not recognize even if she had bought it. Our wedding bed. The bed had the memories of our life together that she lacked. She thought—but how could she, did her body not recall how it had welcomed me, did the legs and sweat and sex not have a memorial of their own?— that she was still a virgin.

I tried not to despair. What would she have counseled? Look at this disaster as an opportunity, Fitz, that's what. You can experience the joy of my loving you with all my cells for the first time, treat me as a fountain of eternal youth. You missed out, after all, on those seven years, even if each of us was fixated on the other, keeping ourselves pure—and now you've been given the chance to fill in those lost gaps. A great challenge. I'm sure you'll be up to it. Remember, somewhere inside that fourteen-year-old mind is your wife and lover, waiting to be instructed in the ways of the world, ready to start all over again.

Except, of course, it wasn't her speaking to me. It was me speaking to myself, sputtering, abandoned to a void that was dark and endless and empty, the void that she had dragged me from, that she could no longer save me from, perhaps not ever.

Once I ascertained she was asleep, I went down the same stairs of eight years ago. I had expected then to pick her up at her house and head to school together, so much I had expected until one click and a second and then a third one had made that future impossible.

"It could be worse, Fitzroy," Dad said. He let that sink in. He was inhabited by the remembrance of Mom. My visitor had, at least, spared my wife. Maybe he had grown fond of her, maybe she had come so close to him in this last voyage, following in his footprints, that he resolved not to haul her into the blackness where he resided, from which he had been himself awoken— how? She knew, she told me that she knew how it had happened, who, when, where, why, she knew and maybe that was the reason he had silenced her. He didn't want her to read me his story, was afraid that he'd be unable to find his way back into someone who now understood him, excluded forever from my presence.

She had been wrong about his benevolence, his mere need to be recognized, commemorated. He must have panicked as she pursued his shadow ever deeper into the dark heart of Europe, did not approve that she had his measurements, detested that she was getting under his skin, into his eyes, had begun to look out onto the wide captive world through those vampire, puzzled, melancholy eyes of his. Fear, filled with fear, this Henri, with each promise of hers that she would claw him out, convince him with her own dark eyes sparkling like a midnight sun that he should abolish his mission, envious that she loved me so much that he would have to stop the experiment and fold his face back into nothingness or migrate to somebody who deserved to have their life devastated.

Back, back, back to where you came from, you demon, rotting in some European grave, or being eaten by fish at the bottom of an endless sea. You fell in love with her, you contemplated her through my eyes, couldn't bear to murder her as you did my mother, and so you let my Cam live, left me with her and without her, damn you, damn you—but you're already damned, why would my curse or my pain matter to you, why would a ghost give a shit about stealing her soul and mine?

Crazy thoughts—what did I know of what he wanted, what did I know about him? Crazy thoughts, but when you lose someone as I had lost my love, lost our home, you can't go on living if you don't go a bit crazy.

This much, however, was clear to me in the midst of my madness and grief: whatever his plan, it was based on his occupying the center of my existence and attention, proving that he was still my lord and master. Whether he had a lesson of love to teach me as Cam seemed to suggest as her quest drew to its conclusion or whether he hated me, as I had been sure of from the start, in either case, he needed my cooperation to keep thriving.

I would ignore him then, shut him out of both face and body, I would take no more photos, not ever, not one more. I would not breathe any more animation into him. Without me, he was finished.

Only once—the day Dad brought her back from Berlin and waited for me to descend the fateful stairs—only on that one occasion, with Hugh and Vic as quiet witnesses, did I accede to another session.

It was almost as if Dad had been reading my mind, launched a preemptive strike before I could announce any drastic decisions.

"We need to snap a shot."

"No," I said, "never again. Let him stay there, in the dark, see how he likes it. No more passages, no more openings."

"What if—?"

Dad didn't need to finish the phrase. What if that ghoul was now satisfied? What if he had exhausted his capacity to emerge, had wasted his last energy on this horrible intervention? Or if Cam's plight had softened his heart? What if my wife's sacrifice had satiated his lust and cruelty?

Instead, Dad added: "We owe it to her. It's the first thing she'll ask when she starts to remember—and she will, the doctors are hopeful that—Fitzroy, she'll want to know. Is he still around?"

So I succumbed to one more shot, gave Henri one more chance to spirit himself away forever, let Dad click yet another button on yet another Polaroid, one last time, I thought, watching the machine spew out its image.

He was there, of course he was.

Nothing would placate him.

I consigned him to death and oblivion.

If you want to return, you bastard, find someone else.

How to describe the next years?

There was, above all, the slow sweetness of watching Camilla Wood become Camilla Foster again. Unsurprisingly, she was a quick learner. Once she understood her condition, once she had mourned the passing of her father for a second time in her life, once she had wrapped her mind around what the mirror was howling, her irretrievable loss of years and experience, she simply set herself, with calmness and equanimity and self-possession— how could any amnesiac find so much strength inside?—to start all over again, a fourteen-year-old girl in the body of a fully grown woman.

"There are people who would kill," she said, grinning, "to be in my shoes."

At least her sense of humor had not vanished.

On the other hand, all the scientific knowledge she had accumulated from adolescence seemed to have evaporated. Heartbreaking to place in front of her—this was two weeks after her return from Berlin—a batch of her notes on DNA, molecular biology, visual memory. Her baffled expression—"I did this? I have a job at MIT and an internship at the Institut Pasteur, that's in Paris, right?" But she was not one to give in to depression, that had not changed a whit. I eased her into science by focusing on her own case: we studied the brain together and she was an incredibly fast learner.

Her lesion did not appear on the CA1 field of the hippocampus where it should have shown up. But the doctors insisted it had to be a diffuse axonal injury, whatever that meant, and we took it from there, beefing up on where long-term memory is stored and the role of neurotransmitters, how the brain recovers from trauma and the self is formed and incessantly consolidated through what we remember.

"Why was I so invested in memory, especially of a visual sort, how it can be transferred genetically from one generation to the next?" she asked, looking at me with an innocence that made me feel guilty, soiled, so much older—centuries older—than she was.

I told her that she would have to find that out for herself. Best for her to reproduce the intermediate stages of her previous investigation as if she were unraveling each discovery for the first time. Jumping forward to the conclusion would only leave her confused. True as far as it went, my explanation, but a deeper truth was that if I established what had set her off on that path the morning of my fourteenth birthday, I would have to introduce my visitor and his phantasmagoric presence into her eyes and mind, and this I adamantly refused to do.

A strategy that had some snags, as I was to realize when it was too late to amend it. Perhaps a mistake to deprive her of the driving force, the obsession that had moved her away from the study of cancer and deep into the examination of how the image of a stranger could feasibly surface inside the boy she loved. Without this motivation the science seemed distant, abstract, tedious. She obediently read up, went through the motions, continued to be a whiz at chemistry and biology, but the spark had disappeared.

Fortunately, other areas of knowledge attracted her attention. Cam's German and French were as excellent as ever, as were her motor skills, for that matter—but she now took a special interest in Spanish. Before she had come back from Berlin, I had carted up to the attic all the books about Tierra del Fuego and the voyages of Cook and Darwin, Magellan and Weddell, the material relating to anthropology and history. I had also concealed the useless list of suspects, the photos and reports sent from Europe, her messages and photocopies, and then unceremoniously dumped the whole bunch into boxes next to the picture of Victor Hugo that my accursed ancestor had snapped over a century ago. But I had not thought to secrete the Spanish dictionary and grammar book, and very soon she latched onto these and began to work on perfecting her command of that tongue.

"Why Spanish?" I asked.

"It will come in handy," she said, and I felt a chill up and down my spine, a cold that ultimately settled in the pit of my stomach. Those were the very words with which she had justified urging me to study precisely that language. But I could not mention this without exposing why she had preferred me to do so, how she thought we might need that expertise if we someday traveled to Tierra del Fuego.

Not the only thing I hid from her.

Photos, for starters.

Dr. Dalrymple, who was attending her here in the States, had remarked that no surefire therapy for her condition had been found, but using photos was auspicious. There were cases where an image from the past had helped the patient's capacity for recall. And we did indeed ply her with any number of pictures, with her father, then without him, of her graduation, snippets from her Paris trips—and had always drawn a blank, nothing rang a bell.

I sensed that, on each occasion, she wanted to inquire about the absence of my own image from this ongoing collection, not even a shot of our wedding, she wanted to ask that question but had learned, who knows why or how, from what pit of wisdom, to steer away from it, believing me that I was allergic to photography, and that the family had resolved to simply keep me away from cameras—not from my Cam, I joked, the era of my Cam, and she laughed at the pun. Laughing, maybe, as a way of not admitting how mystified all these pretexts left her.

It hurt to fool my love, see how effortlessly she accepted every idiocy I mouthed, as if she were four rather than fourteen—that I rarely went out or frequented the places where we'd danced and partied with friends, that the most outgoing and expansive kid in school was now a hermit, that I had ceased to swim. If she had any doubts, she squashed them, entrusting herself to my guardianship. Very comforting, this love of hers, this confidence that I could protect her. But that was not my Camilla Wood, not the brash woman who had barged back into my life and spent the last year blazing a trail that she thought would liberate me from a demon that I now could not even name in her presence. Secrets, secrets, they were poisoning us like a sewer.

And yet, not all was dark and duplicitous, I am exaggerating, leaving out so much that I still savored.

Sex, I have said nothing about how our bodies rediscovered each other, I have not described how I slept chastely by her side, unwilling to let my experience of what we had done together overwhelm what she had forgotten. It was reasonable to be wary of forcing her into a relationship that another self, a future ego, had chosen for her. Repeating the respect in which I had held her that night before my fourteenth birthday, the abstention all the years after that, keeping my body sacred and clean as if it were a temple. And one night, as we lay there, each absorbed, I supposed, in each other's thoughts, guessing what the other desired, she had almost unobtrusively slipped off her panties and met my mouth with hers and I wondered, as she invited me into her depths again, if this might not be what would return her mind to me as well as her legs and breasts and movements, afraid all of a sudden, at the very moment I thrust myself most privately inside her, crossed the threshold of her flesh and recognized that it was always different and always the same, afraid all of a sudden that I might be making a mistake and that our sexual initiation— the first for her memory if not for her body—could explode her mind, couldn't her orgasm be like an electroconvulsive shock and permanently impair her recollection, make her amnesia worse?

"Are you sure, are you sure, Cam?"

"Silly," she said, as she nibbled at my earlobe and her hands descended down my back to my buttocks and made sure I was firmly inside her, "you are so silly, we'll be fine." Letting our bodies speak after all those months of silence, with each shift of my hips I let my visitor know that there were things he could not take from me, walls he could not erect.

And suddenly, time had been abolished—Cam's welcoming skin remembered what her mind could not recover, I was not the one with extra years of memories brimming with explorations of her pleasure and mine, our gentle rage against death, and she was not the one who was feeling this for the first time, giving herself to me against all the odds of a universe that had wagered that we would never find each other, she and I were equals in our voyage of discovery, I was every man who had ever lived and she every woman, both of us wishing that this interlude would last forever, that it would never cease.

But it had to end, she had to open her eyes and remember that she did not remember, and I had to open my eyes and remember that she did not remember, we both had to admit that there were no shortcuts to the future—as if that mattered, as if our love-making had to have a purpose other than the renewal of our vows and the forgetting that there were boundaries to the human heart.

She fell asleep before I did, I stayed awake watching her, blessed by the wonder of her breath and cascading ebony hair, the sprawl of her legs wet with my semen.

She slept a lot in those days—Dr. Dalrymple said nothing could be better for her dazed brain cells and twisted synapses than to rest. Each time she wakes, he had said, try to find out—not an interrogation, Mr. Foster, no pressure—what she's been dreaming. Her subconscious, after all, may not be affected—that's why hypnosis often works as therapy in cases that are not as serious as hers, why spontaneous recovery can be prompted through past mementos or photos. So what is stored inside or next to her hippocampus might float up in bits and pieces during REM sleep. Just be sure she doesn't feel under any strain.

I was the one who felt the strain. There was so little I could do to cure her, I took the suggestions of Dr. Dalrymple as if they were instructions, trying to always be there when she awoke, spending long vigilant nights by her side, waiting for a miracle.

She never remembered one sliver of a dream.

But watching her there prone and defenseless, I could not help but think of how alone she had been during those hours after the Berlin Wall had crushed her. Specifically, when she was about to reveal the ultimate secret. In a corner of our room, in the bottom drawer of my desk, was the German material that Dad had recuperated from her hotel. As well as the evidence amassed by Cam during her last months in Paris, sent back by the Institut Pasteur along with their best wishes, accompanied by a handwritten note from Dr. Ernest Downey declaring that her accident was a loss for science and indicating he might drop in to wish the patient well if he found himself in the Boston area.

But the real treasure of the trove was a thick blue folder that must have been the exercise in commemoration that she was rewriting each night in order to be shared upon her return—there it was, the contents of her search. But, like her mind, under lock and key. So that not the slightest insinuation of curiosity might trouble my decision to cast my visitor from our world. Like any addict, I needed to go cold turkey, not allow a sip of that Kaweshkar to pass my lips, intoxicate my throat, burn my intestines. Not to be even consulted, her report, I said to myself—she had promised to read it to me with full and moist lips, reiterated this so often that it felt like a betrayal to eavesdrop on her past, open her archives, peruse those words without her jokes and comments and shining eyes. Proof of her love for her Fitzroy, what had brought her to Berlin to meet her violent fate, his power over my love.

His power: he had chosen to hurt her. And her choice: to forget him. The one benefit that crawled out of this ghastly affair was that she could start fresh, be rebuilt in all her purity, take the path she might have picked if I hadn't shown up on that birthday of mine waving the photo. He was providentially gone from her mind, along with the loss of other, more delectable memories, and all in all that was for the better. Never again would I center my life around the existence of those black eyes of Henri's, never again tangle our identity inextricably with his. Maybe he—or destiny or God or history or the fucking fragment of the Berlin Wall—had done us a favor by purging her of any recollection of his floating, sad face, opening the door to my doing the same.

And yet, I could not, as weeks and months stretched into two years of solitary insomnia, waiting for even a glint of those mislaid eight years to glimmer back through the murk of her dreams, I could not stop from obsessing, the same question spinning inside: How had he done it, intervened in the fate of the women

I loved? Or was it just my sick imagination that made him guilty of engineering the death of my mother? And Cam's accident? But Mom had been way off track, whereas Cam had managed to pin down Henri's name, photo, circumstances of kidnapping, itinerary, companions. So one had been attacked because she was far from her objective and the other because she was so close?

The randomness of it was maddening. The more you compared Mom and Cam the less their respective searches had in common. A stone falling on someone's head on a cold November night in the North of the planet, a woman falling into the muddy current of the Amazon in the torrid South, what had one to do with the other? What if they were indeed chance events, as arbitrary as his choice of poor Fitzroy Foster for his experiment, a situation that had no meaning or direction, like evolution itself, simply a chain of accidents that seemed like a pattern to someone like me, born into a species that survived by searching for a higher order, that became mighty and lorded it over nature and reigned over the globe by linking incidents, hammering cause and effect together, connecting spheres that were distant and dissimilar? Why suppose that he had a plan, a goal, a rational motive for any of this? Had Camilla guessed it before the Berlin Wall had—?

Why, why, why the Berlin Wall?

Could my visitor, a practitioner of primitive communism, with no interest in individual possessions, have been displeased that the Wall had come down, that this modern version of communism had failed—and censured Camilla for rushing off to dance on the ruins of the dreams of Karl Marx? But that dictatorial state communism, stifling and bureaucratic, had nothing to do with the free, egalitarian lifestyle of the indigenous people of Tierra del Fuego, there was no real connection between the two. Why should he care what happened in the world? Did he understand the complexities of the twentieth century, he who had lived, for all purposes, in prehistory?

Or was I belittling him by inferring such indifference, pre-judging him in death as his kidnappers, those spectators, those scientists, had done in life? Maybe Henri understood more than I presumed. Maybe the dead received daily bulletins as to how their descendants were despoiling the planet bequeathed to them—and if so, would he not hate capitalism? It had been merchants, after all, who had destroyed him and his people. Entrepreneurs who exhibited exotic savages in human zoos, entrepreneurs who photographed their outlandish features for penny postcards.

Cam would know the answer, of course, she would have been able to separate what was real from what was false, Cam would have, probably already had before her accident, put all this chaos in order, offered a more coherent and grounded explanation.

The one person I couldn't involve in my doleful conjectures.

As the months dripped into one year and then the next one, as she progressed toward whom she had once been at a snail's pace, as the Cam Wood who had greeted me on my fourteenth birthday mingled with the Cam Foster who had last spoken to me to assure me that we had paid our dues, the two Camillas overlapping and contradicting each other and collaborating, as my wife started to assert her independence and ventured out of the house on her own, spent an hour away and then two and then afternoons, I found myself buffeted by hope and despair in equal measure.

As November 9, 1991, that lethal anniversary, approached, I began to absurdly expect some significant change. The doctors had always mentioned two years as a possible limit for curing her—an arbitrary statistic, I knew, an average, a median, and yet that number recurred in the literature consulted. And hadn't dates, their replication, been important, hadn't September 11 recycled itself, hadn't Cam chosen July 14 for our wedding, wasn't I in thrall to patterns, configurations, echoes? Why shouldn't this November 9th bring to a close one cycle and open up another one?

It came and went without the slightest alteration. Well, almost. At around noon, the doorbell rang—and a while later, my Dad came up to say that there was a doctor who had said he knew Cam, had worked with her in Paris, name of Ernest Downey, a professor from Stanford. If we didn't mind, he'd like to pay his respects, and if the patient was not well enough—and in fact, Cam was fast asleep right then—perhaps Mr. Fitzroy Foster might be so good as to offer him some minutes of his precious time? I told my father to dispatch this Downey fellow, recalled that Cam had known him only in passing and that he seemed to give her the chills, "creepy" was the term she had used. What I least wanted was for someone from her past research to come in contact with her.

A few minutes ticked by. I heard the front door open and shut downstairs and from behind a curtain watched the pathway upon which Dr. Downey was walking away, shoulders hunched, eyes glued to the ground, slouching off. And then, suddenly, he turned and stared back at the house, straight toward the second floor from where I was spying on him. Henri had made me an expert in faces and I did not like what I saw, did not like that this man seemed to know what I was up to, my whereabouts, almost as if those eyes like scissors could cut through the curtains and reveal my presence. But he couldn't see me—and his scrutiny of our home and my possible existence lasted no more than a few instants, and then the man was gone.

Except for that hiccup of an incident—quickly consigned to oblivion and certainly not communicated to Cam—I lived that day like every other day since her return and eternal convalescence: inside our premises like captive animals, shut away from the world as if out there a blight stalked the land instead of an infinite array of temptations and potentialities that she seemed to be developing a taste for.

Only in that sense did that date carry any significance.

Though it did allow me, forced me really, to look back over the span of her illness and interrogate its contours. Had it advanced or deteriorated? What had my strategy accomplished? And how long could we continue like this, creating an artificial paradise far from the world's woes, as if she were Siddhartha and I could keep death and disease and terror away forever?

My illness had glued us together, Cam and me, my visitor had ended up making us a couple. Her project in life had been me, curing me, freeing me, imagining a future we could share. And now the roles were reversed and she was my sole project, her healing what I lived for. But she had seen my salvation in setting me off into the unknown world I had feared and been intimidated by, she had sought every means of pushing me out of the cave I had made for myself. Whereas I had done the opposite. I had convinced her, abusing her trust in me, that the outside environment was toxic, a threat to her well-being. I wanted her so much for myself that I had kept her from any possible external influence. And up till recently she had played along. Instead of imitating her altruism, I had reduced the potential richness of her experience to the poverty of my own.

The more I thought about my dilemma and how I had failed her, how my exclusion of the visitor—months and months without his features gobbling up mine—had ended up barring her from any project we could really plan together, the more I admitted how selfish and deficient had been my solution. And the more I felt the answer had to lie inside her, in who she had been, who she truly still was deep inside. She might not be able to illuminate what to do now or next, but she had left me her voice, she had prepared a story for me. Her voice was there, close by, lurking inside the perverse attraction of that thick blue folder from Berlin.

If she woke to her former self, would she not demand why I had not read her long report to me, using her research to help her, to free myself so I could free her?

And then, abruptly, it was the last day of the year and 1992 loomed ahead.

As if she recognized that there was nothing to celebrate, no kiss at midnight, no vows of renewal that made any sense, she fell asleep early.

Maybe it was the fireworks going off in the neighborhood, the early hugs from my father and brothers before they went off to their respective parties, or maybe it was the symbolism of the date, even if I did not realize till later how significant that year was. Am I overinterpreting? Better to suggest that I was simply fatigued, tired of keeping up the pretense that things would fix themselves without some pivot on my part. She was maturing, catching up, becoming ever more autonomous. It was wonderful to see the old Cam emerging again into the light, wonderful and scary to see her challenging me, taking the lead, slogging out of the house without giving details about where she was going or for how long, but that also meant that soon, soonest, soonest, she would begin to press me, cease to tolerate my phony explanations, accelerating my shame, my regret.

Watching her sleep as the new year dawned, ushering in for everybody but us hope for change and renewal, I felt possessed by a sudden urgency to retrieve the voice that had been denied to me since that last phone call over two years earlier. I walked over to my desk, slipped the key in the lock of the bottom drawer—and there was the folder containing the words she intended to read in my presence, that I would now read silently in hers. Was there a better way to spend the night?

The fate of Henri, his fate and yours, Fitzroy Foster, and therefore mine—was determined, as most of our fates are, from afar. From really far, in his case—from the extreme North of the planet and years before he was born.

It was in 1848—a year of revolution across the globe, somewhat like 1789, 1968, and our current 1989—that Claus Hagenbeck, a fishmonger, first exhibited in Hamburg some seals from the Arctic regions. It didn't seem that groundbreaking to show marine animals in large tubs in the backyard of a fish shop, but it turned out to be highly profitable. The seals were next exhibited and then sold in Berlin, launching what was to become a family dealership in beasts that today, 150 years later, is very much alive in the Hagenbeck Zoo in Hamburg.

This success was due, in great measure, to the fishmonger's son, Carl, who had started feeding the seals when he was four years old and whose ambitions went far beyond those of his father. By the age of twenty-two—your age, Fitz—he was running the firm and specializing in African animals: elephants, lions, giraffes, hyenas, raccoons, snakes, and, eventually, apes, showing his catch in a mini-zoo in the two acres at the back of his new house in the Neue Ferdmarket. He was also feeding the demands of circuses, monarchs, and private collectors.

The firm's supply chain was threatened in the early 1870s when the Mahdi, an Islamic prophet-warrior, took over the Sudan, forcing Carl Hagenbeck to look to the cold North for a solution. He recalled that, as a ten-year-old boy, he'd been "notably impressed," as he states in a letter to the American circus impresario P. T. Barnum, by the sight of Zulu Kaffirs paraded in a cage in the Saint Pauli neighborhood of Hamburg. So why not import, along with reindeer from Norway and Sweden, the original trainers of the animals and display animals and humans interacting as if still in one of their villages? If he had been so astonished as a child, might not customers pay for the experience?

Using a Norwegian animal catcher, Arnold Jacobsen, as an agent, Hagenbeck imported a group of Laplanders. These "little men and women" were a sensation—going on tour to Berlin, Leipzig, and other venues. Scavengers who had served the family business in the past were informed that henceforth they should be on the lookout for any exotic folk, not monstrous enough, it was stipulated, to disgust our audiences but not so beautiful that they ceased to be bizarre.

There would follow, Fitz, in the years to come, Eskimos, Sinhalese, Kalmyks, Somalis, Ethiopians, Bedouins—and, in conjunction with American impresarios, Plains Indians. The most noteworthy venture, for our purposes, were three Nubians from the Upper Nile, enticed to Germany in 1876—the first of many collaborations with our old acquaintance Saint-Hilaire, the manager of the Jardin d'Acclimatation—and photographed on their visit to Paris by none other than Pierre Petit.

The need for supplementary savages became insatiable. Not only for clients, but also for academics. The directors of the Berlin Society for Anthropology, Ethnology, and Prehistory were particularly anxious to inspect the inhabitants of Tierra del Fuego, so influential in the formulation of Darwin's theories. Led by . . . my former hero, Rudolf Virchow. Desperate to be the first scholar to find the missing link between ape and man and disprove Darwin's theory, he forms an alliance with Hagenbeck to bring back these "Feuerlanders," providing funds and political backing, the sort of international legitimacy needed in order to kidnap citizens of a sovereign country.

This led to Jacobsen's being dispatched to Cape Horn in 1878. He was on the point of embarking with a group of Kaweshkar, when the governor of Punta Arenas blocked the hijacking. I note with pleasure, Fitz, that I share that governor's surname, Wood—Carlos Wood Arellano. I doubt he is one of my ancestors (so many Woods!), but maybe the coincidence has given Henri a reason to be fond of me, brownie points, in case he ever desired to inflict his dark nefarious arts on yours untruly. Though aren't all we white folks the same to him, just like we think blacks—or Asians or Indians—are indistinguishable from one another?

I sighed. Poor misguided Camilla, making jokes about staying the hand of Henri from the other side of the tomb. But after the first stab of bitterness at the irony, I felt a smile rising to my lips. So typical of her, so full of fun, my woman. And her report, written with such verve.

Good old Carlos Wood! His meddling in 1878 insures that those natives do not end up in Europe. A diplomatic storm erupts. Van Gülich, the German ambassador to Chile, protests, defending Hagenbeck as an honorable businessman, eager to further the cause of science and civilization, helping anthropological societies in his country to study foreign racial types, a study for which young, albeit inquisitive, republics like Chile and Argentina, lacking the adequate resources, should be honored to send indigenous people to Germany. A way of contributing to European research and affording enlightenment to spectators who are the heirs of the legacy of Greece and Rome.

The ambassador is aided by an official letter from Chancellor Bismarck himself. A facetious sidenote, Fitz. Have you heard of the sausage duel? In 1865, Bismarck was so incensed by Rudolf Virchow's criticism of his military budget that he issued a challenge to the eminent Berlin professor. Scholarly Virchow, given the choice of weapons, suggested that each rival consume one of two sausages. The loser would be the one who consumed the sausage secretly infected with a parasite that would cause diarrhea for several days. Bismarck indignantly declined to participate but, thirteen years later, when Virchow's glorious anthropological enterprise is in jeopardy, the Chancellor leaps into the fray to defend science, commerce, and the expansion of German influence.

Though the kidnapping of 1878 is thwarted, this pressure on the Chilean government—whose army was being trained by Prussian officers and whose southern regions, now that the Mapuche Indians had been defeated thanks to the Winchester rifle, were being populated by waves of German émigrés—has its intended effects. In 1879, Jacobsen is able to legally extract a family of three Aónikenk Indians from Tierra del Fuego. Father, mother, and child are examined extensively by Virchow and his colleagues and successfully tour Germany, proving the existence of a major market for Patagonian savages.

The stage is set for our eleven Kaweshkar.

Again, their destiny depends on something that happens under the Northern Lights of our dark planet. Early in 1881, all eight Eskimos from Labrador that had been recruited by Jacobsen for upcoming exhibitions die of smallpox.

Jacobsen, on his way to Australia and Polynesia to collect ethnographic artifacts for Virchow and the Berlin Museum, finds a telegram in Buenos Aires from Hagenbeck with instructions to collect and send some Fueguians to Europe. Jacobsen, unable to do the work himself because he has to continue on to New Zealand, cables back that he knows whose services to engage. In effect, on July 10, 1881, Herr Wahlen, a German whaling captain, captures our group of Kaweshkar, falsely claiming the poor savages were in distress, and had consented to participate in a year-long ethnic tour of Europe to pay off the costs of saving their lives, which, of course, were in no danger whatsoever. Wahlen, the man who, eight years later, will provide Maître with his Selk'nam for the Paris 1889 centennial, knows the operation is illegal. He's careful to transfer the hostages from his small schooner in the middle of the Straits of Magellan to the Thebes, a steamer heading for Europe, an operation paid for by someone called Schweers. Making sure the eleven Kaweshkar never touch land in Punta Arenas, where customs or migration officials might ask prickly questions as to the lawfulness of these proceedings.

On August 16, 1881, the Thebes arrives in Le Havre where the human cargo is inspected and approved by Saint-Hilaire. Three days later Henri—by now "baptized" Heinrich, the name of Hagenbeck's eldest son!—and his band come ashore in Hamburg. Not for long. By the end of that month, the Jardin d'Acclimatation receives these "cannibals" with great fanfare—a last chance to see them in the flesh (and eating flesh) before this missing link of evolution vanishes from the earth.

The first one to vanish from this group, as we know, is the child of Petite Mère. I had presumed it was a girl, but in fact it's a boy of four. Perhaps the brother of Henri. I think of him as he dies, bewildered like any kid who is ill and doesn't even know what sort of sickness is killing him.

Nor do the others understand that something like viruses exists. By the time they reach Berlin, in late October, after having visited, if that is not too ironic a word, Dresden, Stuttgart, Leipzig, and Nuremburg—they are all sick.

I looked up from my reading. Cam had coughed—the first time she had stirred since I had opened the blue folder—a cough that seemed to echo the long-dead lungs of the ten hostages, almost as if my love could, while asleep, probe my thoughts better than when she was awake, when it had been so easy to fool her.

It was hard to accept that the woman who had written all those words, labored over them with such elegance, making such an effort to be both descriptive and lyrical, prepping that text for her lips and throat, it was painful to acknowledge that she couldn't remember one iota of what had been so sedulously collected.

I slid out of bed and tiptoed to the drawer containing the other items from Germany and France. There were tons of mostly illegible notes and dates and chronologies, copies of letters in German addressed to Thea Umlauff (???), articles from journals and newspapers, and several books. My eye roved to two by Carl Hagenbeck, one in German, the other in English, his autobiography. "Beasts and Men" it said on the cover and inside, on the title page, in her careful, carefree script: *For my Fitzroy, so you can read this voice from our past without my having to translate it.*

I flipped through the pages, stopped at the photo of Hagenbeck himself. An impressive, handsome man, probably sixty or so when it was snapped, many years after he had commandeered the abduction of the Kaweshkar. A straight, prominent nose and wide forehead, a distinguished goatee, eyes that managed to be both piercing and benevolent, combining business acumen with the twinkle of humanitarian impulses. He looked more like a civil servant than someone traipsing off to Africa in search of animals.

Could this man really be behind the conspiracies that had uprooted hundreds of unfortunate natives from their homelands? He looked so ... so ... I struggled for the right words. Innocuous, bourgeois, righteous almost, beyond reproach, sure of himself and his cause. But that was probably the case of everyone involved in these operations, and so many more on my endless list, none of whom, save Petit, had any direct link to our family. Or had Cam discovered a connection to Hagenbeck? Or Jacobsen? Or Captain Shweers? Or Van Gulich? Or even Virchow?

As I placed the autobiography back in the drawer with the other materials, a piece of paper floated out from within its pages, with Cam's writing on it. My heart skipped a beat. I had learned to be superstitious. Since Henri's assault on me, every accident and coincidence seemed fraught with meaning.

But it was merely a meditation: *Are we that different from these people, the spectators and the entrepreneurs? What is the difference between the animatronic Indians and dancing bears and costumed Polynesians of Disneyland and what Hagenbeck displayed at his zoo and sold to Barnum and museums? When we rubberneck at exotic folk in nature documentaries on TV or at the movies, are we that far removed from those who flocked to the people shows of the late nine-*

teenth and early twentieth centuries? When I lament the animals extracted from Africa and Ceylon do I include myself as a culprit, my research on guinea pigs and mice and those rabbits in Paris, those rabbits with their red eyes and twitchy noses. Oh, how I wish I could talk this over with my Roy! He'll calm me down, sweet, wise, darling Fitzroy!

I sighed, disturbed by this paradisiacal vision of my virtues. If I had been as sweet as she said, truly wise, I would have refused her call the day she burst back into my life, I would have protected her from the depredations of Henri.

I had failed her.

Something bitter and self-destructive stirred inside and it took a great effort not to close the blue folder that I did not deserve to be reading, that I had kept from her and from myself out of the sort of fear she had not shown while attempting to save me. But its attraction was too magnetic.

On November 14, 1881, Professor Rudolf Virchow delivered a lecture at the Hall of the Zoological Gardens in Berlin to hundreds of excited guests, many of them portly matrons and their numerous offspring. He lamented that two of the female Patagons and their children were too ill to be displayed, but for several hours, Virchow notes in an essay, the remaining women and the four men sat there, half naked, coughing frequently and definitely depressed, staring at the audience, listening to the words in German in which their condition was being depicted. Able to reproduce all those words without their meaning, because they had an astounding capacity for imitation and repetition. I haven't translated the whole speech for you, Fitz, as I did with the Manouvrier because I'll be home soon . . .

Here, I choked back tears. Together, together. She asleep and me reading by myself, a mockery of what she had envisaged. Maybe I had been wrong to trespass on something still incomplete, not up to her exacting standards?

Too late for these doubts. Henri and his mates were there, in Berlin, in that hall, all those people anxious to touch their skin and poke at their flesh, and Virchow was asking the audience to be calm and behave in a civilized way.

. . . and then I'll point out Henri's measurements, each category. Isn't it insane, love? We know more about the length of his arms and thighs and shoulders, the circumference of his skull, than we do about you, about anybody else alive, in fact. Head diameter: 195 centimeters. His second toe was slightly curved and rather pointy, his torso muscles were overly developed from spending most of his life squatting in a canoe, his eyelid slants up, recalling Mongolian models. I'll show you an engraving from a scientific Berlin journal, you'll see how his hair has grown longer since Paris. Lost his vivacious look, less menacing, you know. Virchow also tells us about their diet, how they roast their fish on a fire that they never let die out. He wonders if this is not an attempt, on their part, to reproduce their Patagonian practice of keeping embers perpetually burning in their canoes. He adds that, just as they share possessions and food, men and women also have a communistic attitude toward reproductive behavior, exchanging favors indiscriminately, a charge that I am not sure is true or just made up. How could he possibly know?

What were they sick with? Virchow doesn't provide details, besides blaming the Parisians for allowing the savages to bathe in a freezing pond each dawn. The Norddeutsche Allgemeine Zeitung *reports pneumonia but says they are now well enough for fervent crowds to watch them eat, a process described by the lying* Nationale Zeitung: *the men devour their meat raw and then throw the scant remains to women and children, emitting loud guttural grunts of satisfaction (I think this is sheer sensationalism, meant to sell papers and tickets). Their feeding hours are published in the press, Fitz, as well as a schedule of performances of shooting skills and obsidian arrowhead manufacturing.*

These reports entice so many visitors (the very word, Besuchers, *the newspapers use, Fitzroy), each day more, until on November 8 they are so numerous, 37,000 paying clients, that a riot ensues. The spectators, fueled by rivers of beer, threaten to break down the fenced enclosure, forcing the Patagons to retreat into the ostrich house where they are lodged. The multitude, angered by their disappearance, demands vociferously that the Indians show themselves and start mating. Thousands, kept in check by a strong contingent of police, remain until seven in the evening, shouting, "Bring out the Fueguians, bring out the Fueguians." Imagine Henri and his fellows listening to the bellows of the rabble as they beat against the planks of the enclosure.*

This strong salacious interest in the Kaweshkar's carnal habits was shared by scientists. In München, the captives are impatiently awaited by embryologist Van Bischoff, eager to study the native women's sexual organs, when they arrive there in late November. Other parts of women—such as their brains—were apparently less fascinating to him, as he strenuously opposed admitting the gentler sex into any academic profession. Told that these Patagons had no shame or decency, this specialist in the ovulation of mammals expected to be able to conduct a full cavity probe. But the female Kaweshkar refuse to let him examine their genitals nor, he protests, the hymen of the young daughter.

He feels even more exasperated when informed in early 1882 by a Swiss doctor, Von Meyer, that one of the women who discouraged Von Bischoff's advances has died on the way to Zurich. The correspondence calls that woman Grethe, first time we hear that name. So who is it? I've deduced she must be either Piskouna or Trine (short for Catherine, right?), re-baptized Grethe sometime during the German tour, not sure which of the two or why there is any need to change the name. Von Bischoff is not interested in the identity of the dead, only their anatomy. He reports irately to the München Academy that he's received the information about Grethe's demise too late to demand that her genitals be preserved, but that he won't give up, as he has requested that Von Meyer insure that as soon as any of the female savages expire, their organs be removed, steeped in alcohol, and shipped to him for examination. And, in effect, when two of them die in Zurich, their labia, vulva, and vaginas are cut out and packed away to München. You can see extremely explicit drawings of those body parts, Fitz, when I get back home, but truth is I'd rather you didn't.

This nineteenth-century trafficking in human organs is made possible, according to Von Bischoff's papers, by the death of Lise on March 11, 1882, and Petite Mère on March 13, also in Zurich, followed half an hour later by the leader of the group, her husband, known as the Capitano. In the midst of all this horror, there is a tender moment recorded by the physician attending the couple: as Petite Mère lies dying of pneumonia, she reaches out with her foot to touch and caress the toes of her mate.

And our Henri?

He had preceded them, the first of the four that expired in Switzerland.

But not of pneumonia.

Your visitor, our visitor, died of syphilis.

According to reports by Dr. Bollinger in the München Scientific Society's archives, Henri was taken to the hospital in Zurich on the same day, February 11, 1882, that he and the eight others disembarked in that city. On February 20, they operated on his penis. He expired a week later.

So it's the Treponema pallidum bacterium that kills the young man, if you'll forgive me for going all technical. A highly mobile bacterium that somebody must have transmitted to him. One candidate is Trine, as one source has her dying of syphilis as well when she—but that information is precarious, and I prefer Lise. Maybe because she was single, just as I was when we first made love, Fitz, or maybe because she hadn't had any children yet, maybe because she dies twelve days after Henri did, let's just leave it at that. There's no documentation one way or the other, so I guess it's my choice. How did Lise contract syphilis, a European disease? Almost certainly on board the ship to Le Havre, though we can't discount Paris or one of the German cities. I'd bet on rape rather than consensual sex, Fitzroy, given the mistreatment of captive women throughout history, remote and recent. And while we're on the happy subject of rape, another hypothesis: that Henri was defiled by some male overseer.

Something in my stomach revolts at the thought. I don't think it's because I find the ravaging of a woman less repellent than that of a man. I think it's because I've grown fond of Henri, want to give him less cause for despoiling and soiling you, less reason to be vindictive. Make it easier to appease his rage. Or, or—yes, perhaps I wish to imagine his sexual encounter with Lise as innocent. Did it happen on September 11, 1881, in Paris, the same day his picture was taken? Drawing you closer to one another?

Not that we'll ever find the answer. We can only hope that he received some delight from Lise when he entered her, that she gave him refuge there, in the human zoo of the Bois de Boulogne or wherever else they made love, not knowing that they were also transferring those bacteria, one to the other. That's my hope, Fitzroy Foster: that before he died in Zurich, my hope is that they enjoyed each other as we have, one thing at least that was not taken from them.

Maybe I'll find more evidence in Zurich, Fitz, my next stop, maybe I'll discover what was done with the dead. As to the survivors, I already know that Antonio dies in the bowels of the ship on the way home, but Pedro, the young Kaweshkar we thought might be your visitor, lived on for some years—as did the two orphaned children who managed to make it back to Tierra del Fuego. The sole female to return, well, some versions say it is Piskouna who soon dies of tuberculosis, another one, even less credible, refers to Trine having *died from syphilis. Very sad and confusing: not even in death are these native women afforded their own names. Hagenbeck doesn't mention who they are, just that, disturbed by the four that succumb in Zurich, repeating what had happened to his eight Eskimos the year before, he decides to send the rest of them back.*

He hadn't shown much concern during the tour. He writes to Jacobsen, from Nuremburg, that all is well, health-wise. And that business is good. In another letter from Dresden: Antonio and Pedro have recovered enough to join the others in a public presentation. Even in Zurich the schedule is only reduced from the usual ten hours to four and a half. The show had to go on.

But not for long. When Hagenbeck learns of the death of three more natives in March 1882, he tells Jacobsen that he is canceling the tour. At least some natives, he says, have been saved. Adding that he vows to stick to beasts and not the fabulous animals—his own words, Fitz, I am not making any of this up!—these human animals who have been so profitable.

His words are emphatic, his deeds less so. In the decades that ensued, Carl Hagenbeck organized over fifty more exotic folk displays, built ethnic villages, continued to traffic in primitive peoples. Taking precautions: medical personnel perpetually on call, careful to vaccinate his savages and sign contracts stipulating wages, conditions, benefits. Not sure how much of a consolation it would be to Henri to learn that his death may have saved many others from around the world from suffering a similar fate, as conditions improved, at least somewhat.

Much of this story I pieced together in Hamburg, my first stop, where I spent most of my three days at the Hagenbeck Archive, an amazing collection. It's housed in one of the buildings in the zoo itself—a lovely place, just as it must have been that day in 1907 when it opened to the public, changing zoological gardens forever. No bars, no cages, the animals in a setting that gave the illusion they were in their natural habitat, not free but at least less oppressed than when they had to pace back and forth on concrete day after day, night after night.

I had hoped to meet some of the Hagenbeck family members, who still run the business, direct descendants of Carl and his father Claus, the fishmonger, remember him?—but they were all away for some reason or other. Fortunately, there was Gunther, a diligent and obsequious librarian at the archive—hey, no need to be jealous. Of course, he took a fancy to me, why should that surprise you, of all people? And of course I took advantage of this discreet infatuation to milk him for all he was worth.

And he was worth quite a bit, information-wise, Fitzroy Foster. Not to worry—he didn't milk me. All right, all right, no more vulgar jokes. So listen: on my last day there, I let him take me to lunch—not what it sounds like, just some bratwurst with scads of mustard at the zoo cafeteria.

He had a goodbye present for me. Carl's niece, Thea Umlauff, was not only alive, but thanks to Gunther's good offices, was ready to receive me that very afternoon at teatime.

I can see you shaking your head in disbelief. A niece of Carl Hagenbeck? She must be a hundred years old! Can't possibly be alive! Well, she is exactly one hundred—frail, a bit loony and eccentric, with a wandering mind, but quite alive, thanks.

Thea's father, Johann Umlauff, the owner of a bathhouse where he sold foreign curios, married Carl's sister Christine. The family alliance allowed Umlauff to expand his venture into a full-fledged naturalist shop specializing in authentic artifacts delivered by Hagenbeck's agents from overseas.

Not an endeavor that was impecunious. Many of the most important displays of aboriginal art in museums in Europe and the States were originally handled by Umlauff and people like him, so that by the time he died in 1889, the same year his youngest daughter Thea was born, he had formed a veritable empire.

All three of the Umlauff boys derived their living from the same enterprise. Gustav Jr. carried on the family business, mainly at the World Museum, crowded with aboriginal art. Another son, Heinrich Christian (yet another Heinrich), used those curios and weapons, skulls and instruments and clothes pilfered from the natives, to become a set designer, collaborating with Fritz Lang on many of his early-twentieth-century movies. But the one with the most influence turned out to be Johannes. He became a taxidermist, stuffing many of the animals that died at the nearby premises of his uncle Carl. It made economic sense. The beasts, even after their expiration date, continued to offer a pretty penny, living on as skin and claw and bones. Made into a spectacle from which they could never hope to escape. Like Henri in the Pierre Petit postcards.

Eventually the dead animals—gorillas, bears, antelopes, tigers—were grouped together in tableaux, with painted backgrounds, tufts of false grass, human mannequins—the whole package auctioned off to natural history museums.

We attended those exhibits, Fitz, when we were twelve, remember, at the Boston Museum on a school field trip?

Yes, I did remember. We had been so fascinated that we went back by ourselves, just the two of us. I had kept tapping on the glass wall, as if to awaken the animals, and Cam diverted the attention of the guard who was furious at me for disturbing the peace. What peace? Cam said. They're not at peace, they're not even dead, even that's been taken from them, that's what she argued at the age of twelve, my God, they're just a silly illusion. And the man was flabbergasted, didn't know how to respond, so by the time he turned to reprimand me I'd made my escape. How we laughed at our own impertinence, our youth and foolishness. But now, all these years later, Cam was not in the mood to laugh.

How were we to know, Fitz, that those stuffed animals came from

*the hand and skill of a nephew of the man ultimately responsible for
your visitor's life and death? How were we to know that ten years
later I would be sitting in the Hamburg parlor of Johannes Umlauff's
sister Thea sipping a strong brew of tea and listening to her recollection of her uncle Carl Hagenbeck, that he had a great sense of humor,
that he was so kind to his animals, that he loved performances and
drama and adventure.*

*It was only toward the end of our little séance that something
unexpected came up. As I rose to go, she said: "You're American, aren't
you? Gunther mentioned that, and your accent seemed, well, from the
United States, that great land."*

I admitted that I was from America.

*"They bombed our World Museum, you know. In 1943. Destroyed
our collection, Blown to smithereens. My brother Gustav died soon
after that. Of a broken heart. All those beautiful gorgeous objects,
traveling the world to a safe haven—and then that madman Hitler
turned us all into targets, even the animals. I resurrected the museum
after the war with my niece Christa—she was born the same year our
museum and shop were devastated, 1943, never met her father just
as I never met mine, isn't that strange? You must know her, Christa
Umlauff, she immigrated to America once we sold the shop to Lore
Kegel. You never ran into Christa in New York?"*

*I was trying to get away from the old lady—the next day I had
to rise early to head for Nuremburg—but she wouldn't let me go,
motioned for me to sit down again.*

*"How about Margaretta?" she asked. "If you haven't met Christa,
well, then, maybe Margaretta? The daughter of my cousin Gisela.
Oops, not supposed to mention her, not Gisela. Not after that naugh-
tiness in Chicago. How old are you, miss?"*

I told her twenty-two.

*"Ah well, you couldn't have met Margaretta. She died—in
America, you know, where she was born, just like you. She died in—I*

can't remember, but it was long ago. I was at her wedding, you know, in 1912, oops, not supposed to speak about that either."

By now I was intrigued enough to sit down again. You know how I love gossip, Fitz. After so many atrocities and kidnappings, some good old-fashioned blather was just what I needed.

"Why not?"

"It's a secret."

"After all these years? If you tell me about your Margaretta, I'll tell you about mine. I have a Margaretta in my family as well. My husband's mother."

"How old is she?"

"She died," I said. "Almost two years ago. She was a bit over forty, I think."

"So she can't be my Margaretta."

"No, she can't. What about yours?"

She muttered to herself that her uncle Carl had sworn her to silence. But he'd been gone now for—she couldn't remember, she strained— finally decided it had been seventy-six years ago, added something about the statute of limitations, that he wouldn't mind.

I encouraged her. "If we don't speak for the dead, who will?"

And thus it was, Fitzroy Foster, that she spun out a most implausible tale. This cousin, Gisela, had been the favorite daughter of her father Carl—vivacious, pleasant, pretty, and a whiz with animals, like everybody in that family. "We Umlauffs," Thea explained, "were better at inanimate objects, whereas the Hagenbecks felt all creatures to be their friends, but none more than Gisela. Since she'd been a toddler, her mere presence calmed the beasts, charming the wildness and danger out of them with a look, a smile."

So only natural that her father Carl should take sixteen-year-old Gisela to Chicago, where his grand circus act was opening at the 1893 World Columbian Exposition. Hagenbeck's show was a sensation—tigers on a tricycle, bears tiptoeing across a tightrope, male and female slaves in a triumphal procession, hypnotized monkeys, parrots speaking myriad languages, Roman gladiators subjecting lions.

Enter Stephen Rice, hired by Hagenbeck for his Chicago show because he had trained hippos to dance to Arabian music at Barnum's circus but perhaps more crucially because he was the nephew of a Brit, also an animal dealer, who had married Hagenbeck's sister (what a family!). Delays in the building of a coliseum in time for the grand opening so worried Hagenbeck that he neglected to keep an eye on the dashing, daring Stephen. Or on his wayward daughter. One day, she and the young Mr. Rice simply disappeared. By the time Hagenbeck tracked the couple to New York, through the Pinkerton agency, Gisela was pregnant. And died at the end of 1893 while giving birth to a premature baby, Margaretta.

Carl forbade his daughter's name to ever be mentioned. Erased as if she had never existed. So much so that Thea did not know she had a deceased older cousin called Gisela until a day in 1912, when her uncle Carl, suspecting he had not long to live, told her the whole lurid, scandalous tale. A revelation brought on by a letter from this unknown granddaughter Margaretta, begging somebody from the family to attend her wedding. Accompanied by a resplendent photo—there were the same immaculate eyes and succulent mouth and waterfall of hair that Gisela had transmitted, before dying, to her child.

"And so," Thea said, "Uncle Carl, his weary heart melting at seeing his lost darling replicated so many years later—oh, the magic of photography!—proposed that I go to the wedding. The only member of the family available—and the only one, he said, he could trust to never tell this secret. Because his heart might be melting but his pride was still a cold, frozen, unrelenting piece of ice. He knew I was itching to elude the suffocating supervision of my three brothers and, through his friend Mr. Hornaday, he had obtained work for me at the Museum of Natural History in Manhattan. As a further incentive, he promised to provide a nice stipend in his will. All I had

to do was cross the Atlantic, put in an inconspicuous appearance at the wedding, and send back news of his granddaughter—maybe a photo—offer a hint of reconciliation to an old man on the threshold of saying goodbye to this world. He could never forgive Stephen Rice for kidnapping his daughter, but Margaretta should know that her grandfather loved her."

Kidnapped, I thought to myself. Well, well, well.

"That conversation," Thea continued, her ancient eyes unable to discern the perverse glint in mine, "changed my life. I spent two intensely happy years in New York. Would still be there if war hadn't broken out. It became prudent to return to Germany before America joined the hostilities. But I also brought back with me memories of a friend for life. Margaretta and I became so close that I was asked to be godmother to her son and we kept up a correspondence that only ceased the day she died."

It was getting late. The tea had long since grown cold in the cups and outside the autumn sun of Hamburg was beginning to set. It had been a long day and ahead of me stretched an even longer couple of weeks. I had a question before I left.

"What about Carl Hagenbeck? Did he ever get to see or perhaps write to his granddaughter?"

Thea Umlauff shook her head. She'd informed him of the wedding, of course, without ever receiving an acknowledgment. And wasn't surprised when her brother Heinrich sent a telegram notifying her that Uncle Carl had passed away—that was 1913, so, no, he had never really reconciled with that hidden side of the family, she ended up being the only link.

I thanked her and stood up. It was a sad story but one that I conjectured we would somehow savor together, back home. It didn't occur to me that I'd write it down with such detail as part of my report. Sure, there was some twisted satisfaction derived from Hagenbeck being served some of his own medicine. He spends his life uprooting animals

*and sequestering humans and then someone comes along and uproots
his family and sequesters his own daughter, carries her away so suddenly that he never sets eyes on her again. But I very much doubt that
Carl Hagenbeck ever made the connection, associated his pain with
the pain he had wreaked upon others. Perhaps he went so far as to
realize that he had trained so many beasts to obey him but could not
control the heart and heat and body of his favorite child, the one most
like him. Would Henri have felt any vindication at such a reckoning?*

*It was not something to mention to the old lady. Why taint the
image of her family when she was close to meeting them—and possibly Henri—in the other world. She could ask him personally, resolve
our enigma for us. Oh how I wish I believed in the afterlife.*

*Despite my protests, she insisted on shuffling with me to the door. As
we passed a mantelpiece cluttered with photos, she stopped.*

*"Wait, wait," she said, and handed me the picture of a young woman
in a wedding dress next to an unrecognizably younger Thea—almost
three quarters of a century ago. "Margaretta," Thea said. "Look how
pretty we both were. She was so glad someone had come from Germany representing the family."*

*"You did the right thing," I said, because she obviously expected
me to say something. I really wanted to get back to the hotel, a quick
meal and then soak in a bath for a while and bed, heavenly bed, even
without you, my love—and I also wanted, naturally, to let you know
I was okay.*

*Thea Umlauff was in no hurry. She tarried by the photos, pointing
out this dead person and that one and I had begun to lose patience, felt
an impulse of rudeness starting to rise when she handed me one last
picture.*

*A little girl. Early 1950s hair bobbed cutely. Staring straight at me.
As if saying hello from the past. From the present. From the future
when I will read these words with the emotion they deserve.*

"Also Margaretta," Thea said, noticing my interest. "Called that in

honor of her grandmother. My friend managed to send me this photo of the child—and a few more before she passed away. Would you like to see them?"

There was no need. I could see this one and probably all the others Thea possessed, I could see those and so many more whenever I so desired. In one of your family albums, Fitzroy Foster. Because of course, of course, of course, it was your mother. The granddaughter of Carl Hagenbeck's granddaughter.

So Hamburg revealed its secrets to me. Not just many of the specifics of how your visitor and his family had been taken from their island home, but how your family, your remote family, was responsible for that crime.

The reason Henri chose you to be possessed. You aren't only the descendant of Pierre Petit, but also the sixth generation of Hagenbecks. Both of these lineages came together in you for the first time, an intersection that took more than a century to materialize, the genes of the man who snapped the photo and the genes of the man who gave the order to bring a living body to Europe to be stuffed in a photo.

You were, you are, unique, Herr, Monsieur, Mr. Fitzroy Foster.

I debated with myself back at the hotel, immersed in water so hot it seemed to scald me, whether to let you know right away. But as I dried the anatomy you love so much, touching with a towel the zones that come alive with your eyes and fingers, tongue and lips, I decided that this—and everything else I had yet to discover on the rest of the trip—should be told to you by me directly, both of us in the same room. He will need to make love after this revelation, I will not condemn him to loneliness when he learns of his ancestry, what the sex of others determined through the decades.

We've come quite a way from that fourteenth birthday of yours. Started out with a mere image, nothing more than a mysterious face, and now we've finally answered your question, "Why me?" But not yet mine, really: "Who is he?" We know who Carl Hagenbeck was,

*have reached across time and discovered the identity of Pierre Petit,
your two ancestors, but Henri? We can't even guess his real name, the
story of his parents, let alone seven generations back.*

Nor what he wants.

*Or maybe yes. He wasn't famous like Carl Hagenbeck, he didn't
immortalize with his eyes the celebrities of his day as Petit did. Vanished from history, my love, like most of the billions of the dead of
our world—never registered by memory and writing and imagery
if chance had not set Jacobsen and Wahlen and Schweers and Virchow, and Darwin himself, on his path. If not for the full force of the
German and French publics, hundreds of thousands—surely some of
them were my ancestors, Fitz—of spectators demanding more natives
to be enjoyed on weekend outings. Maybe what Henri wants is for
someone—you and now me—to know what was done to him, tell his
story. But I doubt it, Fitzroy Foster. We have paid our dues, of that
I am convinced. But we still have work to do. I can't wait, my love.*

I took a deep breath.

That she could resurrect the past, bring my visitor's chron-
icle back from the grave he shared with every last man who had
put him there prematurely, oh that my love had been able to use
her detecting skills as a scientist to track down this lost piece
of history, oh that the mind that had accomplished that feat of
memorialization should now be left without memory of a third
of her own life, the years when she had kept me alive from afar,
not even the recollection of our reencounter and marriage, the
contrast between what she had done for Henri and was unable
to do for herself—it was just too much.

I started to cry.

Quiet sobs, I controlled at least their violence—why disturb
her with my pain? But sobs nonetheless, a lament for our ship-
wrecked, caged humanity, for her and me and also, despite my
desolation, for our visitor, dying in that Zurich bed, infected

and alone and forgotten, not even Lise by his side. His image, which I had insisted on banishing for these two years, was the last thing that loomed in front of me as I fell asleep as the New Year dawned, Camilla's story of him and my twisted double link, my double helix link to him had brought those eyes of night back to me. And I greeted him as one would an old friend or a wandering prodigal, still silent, still mysterious, but we could celebrate that what haunted me was the photo snapped by Petit and not the sick one taken in München as he set out for the last legs of his journey, at least he was at the peak of his powers, I recognized the beauty of his dark eyes and the strength of his resistance, how he had persisted through a century to find me, the descendent of two of the men, among so many others, who had determined his destiny, I welcomed his face into my dreams as I never had before, I let him rock me to sleep.

When I awoke, a few hours later, my Cam was next to me in bed, holding the manuscript she had written over two years ago, and that I had misguidedly left open on the blankets. I was about to stutter an explanation, apologize for subjecting her to the violent act of meeting her former self, searched for words that could afford some sort of context for suppressing them for so long, when I realized that no excuses on my part were necessary.

Sufficient to see her face, her old smile, the usual buoyancy in her eyes. And understand that—"Yes," she said. "It's me. All this time it's been me."

SIX

"There's one thing that's truly terrifying in this world and
that's that everyone has his reasons."
—Jean Renoir, *The Rules of the Game*

Of course it was her. Of course she had been there all the
time. And of course the answer had been staring me in the
face all these months, to use her past voice to cure that amnesia,
and only the relief flooding me drowned out the reproach that it
could have been sooner, the day she had been brought back on
a stretcher from Berlin, if only I had not been so consumed by
hatred.

She saw in my face what I was thinking and shook her head.

"No," she said. "You don't understand. It was never about me.
It was a test for you."

What did she mean? What test? And why tell me I didn't
understand, instead of celebrating, whooping in wonderful 1992,
rushing to my dad's room, rousing Vic and Hugh so we could
break open a bottle of champagne? She was back and that was
enough, that—

Cam carefully set aside the blue folder and the manuscript and took my hand in hers. "There's something you need to know." And then started patiently, in excruciating and twisted detail, to tell me about the accident and what had followed.

Nothing new, at first, in her tale. She had indeed suffered from the diagnosed retrograde amnesia due to that chunk dislodged from the Wall, awakening in the Charité Hospital thinking she was fourteen years old. And when my father had walked in, she took his excuses at face value, certain her own dad awaited her at home. Dazed and confused, she had welcomed, she said, some drugs that put her to sleep.

Upon opening her eyes a few hours later—and here Cam paused for the longest while before plunging on—when she awoke, well, she had remembered everything, her whole life, including those last hours in the hospital.

She had healed herself.

I interrupted her, startled, a dreadful bird gnawing at my stomach, bleeding me with questions.

"But—but—why didn't you—if you—if you—these two years, we've—you lost your memory again, right, right away, right? When you came back here you—I mean, you didn't recollect a thing, you still—I mean—"

"No, Fitzroy. I had total recall, even that I'd been afflicted momentarily with amnesia. A bit of a headache, my neck hurt like hell, woozy and disoriented, but entirely myself, twenty-two years old, married to the wonderful Mr. Foster junior, the bride who had just concluded the mission we had planned, all the pieces of the puzzle in place—or almost all of them, I had yet to pass through Zurich—the same person I am now, my identity, memories, love intact."

I stared at her in disbelief. Disbelief was better than anger, than the humiliation starting to poison me in its toxic glow—

impossible that she had been fooling me, us, the doctors. Even to contemplate that she could have perpetrated such a cruel hoax caused me a distress and grief that bordered on insanity. To deliberately allow me to believe she was ill, knowing how my mother's death had disarmed me, no, it couldn't be.

I stood up from the bed. Violently wrenched my hand from her hand. I stood up because I felt like slapping her. Oh God. I had just recovered my wife from near death and I felt like slapping her.

"Sit down, Fitzroy Foster," she said calmly. "I deserve to be heard."

"Deserve? Deserve? You don't—you don't—"

"You think it was easy? You think I did it to hurt you?"

"How the fuck do I know why you did it?"

"Maybe you'd like to hear why. Sit down."

I obeyed her. Damn it. To be so in love with her that I sat down and gave her a chance to explain what admitted no explanation, could never be justified.

If Cam had taken my hand again, I would have rejected her, perhaps even have dashed out of the room. Forever. But she made no such attempt.

Her voice simmered with tranquility, as if she were telling me the result of an experiment in her lab.

When Cam had awoken in that Berlin hospital bed and realized that she was cured, her first instinct was to press the buzzer for the nurse to summon Jerry so he could relate the good news to her husband, who must be out of his mind with worry.

"Yes. I was, of course, I was, I was going crazy—for you to be sick like that and me not able to travel, comfort you. Oh God, why, why, why keep up this sham for so long. How could you?"

"You had already been through the worst, the shock of the accident, the fear I might die—but that was over, I was coming home, one day more or less wouldn't matter. You know how I love surprises. I wanted to see your face when I told you I was well, enchanted that you'd think it was the sight of you that had cured me. The more the idea buzzed around in my head in that quiet hospital ward, the more I savored the strategy. Give you all the delight in saving me. That you should do for me, bring me back to life, what I had done for you. As if we were swimming together again, not in a pool, but in existence itself."

"What? What are you talking about? Swimming apart from each other, that's what—"

She smiled at me with a tenderness that would have mellowed the heart of—of—I searched for someone cold and conniving and genocidal—of Julius Popper. How dared she smile at me like that?

"Listen, Fitz, please listen. If you thought you'd woken me up from my amnesia, it would be great for you, that's how I saw it, a way of activating you, putting you in charge after so many years of being passive. Preparing you for the next stage, now that our research phase was over. Like in science, darling. First comes the discovery, say, of a gene that causes cancer, then comes the more arduous adventure of getting it out of the laboratory and finding ways to apply that breakthrough to something real, make it into a medicine, so it can liberate us from our past."

She was talking as if I were some sort of chimp in one of her experiments—and I told her so in an icy voice.

"That's unfair, Fitzroy Foster. Though I'll admit I was curious, you know, to see how you'd repair me, what parts of my life and yours you'd reveal in order to help me remember. I only intended this to be for a short while, a few hours, maybe not even a few minutes. It was meant to empower you, darling."

"Well, it didn't, your stupid experiment. And my dad and brothers and—you must have realized pretty soon that I had no idea how to heal you, that I was lost without you, your guidance, your—oh what's the use? If you didn't call your little game off once it was clear that I—if you didn't understand then—"

"Because I was baffled, that's why. I never anticipated that you would react by lying to me, treating me as if I couldn't deal with your past or my past, as if I were—as if I were a child or a savage or—"

"That's not true. I was just trying to protect you, from pain, from nightmares, from—"

"From him, Fitz. You wanted to protect me from him. Saw a chance to get rid of Henri, lock him out of our existence, start from zero, don't deny it—as if everything that had happened to him, everything we learned since he made his appearance, didn't matter. You decided to erase him!"

"Damn right! Mom felt sorry for him and he got her killed. You felt even more pity than she did and what did he do? Almost dispatched you! Why not use your accident for something good? Wasn't that our agreement, that we were doing all this to get him to leave us alone?"

"I don't think that's what he wants, Fitz."

"What he wants, what he wants! Again, like the first day I showed him to—who is he? Who is he? Your question. Well, you found out and what did it get us, huh?"

"I wasn't wrong to be inclusive, draw closer to him. And I kept on waiting, since the day your dad flew me back from Berlin, for you to also realize it. Waiting for you to take out the photos, show them to me, open the drawer where you hid all my material and the folder and read my own words back to me, at least respect my work that much. Waiting, waiting for you to bring me into your life, the life we made together. But you were scared."

"And that's when you should have cut this madness short, stopped playing with me."

"No. You had to get there on your own."

Again, I felt the impulse to hurt her, shake her till she fully recognized how harsh she'd been, wake her up—wake her up?!!—to what she'd done.

"So now he's—all this, even this latest bit of insanity—it's all been for my benefit. Is that what you're saying, that it was all for my benefit? You know what's really indefensible? He's turned you against me. You grew too close to him. So close there was no room for me. I should never have let that happen."

"There you go again. As if you can control him, what he means, any more than you can control the image of his that keeps cropping up. He's not going away, Fitz."

"And when were you going to tell me all this? How long did you intend to wait?"

"First, my dear, stop—just stop pretending that this depended exclusively on what I did or didn't do, as if you were innocent of prolonging this misunderstanding. I gave you every chance to come clean. What was one of the immediate things I asked to see? Your family album. And you started with your claptrap and evasions, then proceeded to feed me nonsense not fit for an imbecile. About not liking to go out, not having any of the friends we had shared in 1981, oh, do I have to repeat all those fabrications? You were so glad I was behaving like a good little girl that you never even wondered why I was so gullible?"

"Well, yes, I did wonder, I thought it was, well, endearing, sort of—I loved that you trusted me and, hey, I knew you'd get over it soon, I thought, I prayed it was temporary."

"And I thought, I prayed your reaction was also temporary. He can't keep this up for more than a week. But you did. And I just followed your lead. Remember who was in the driver's seat, Fitz. Up to you how long the journey lasted."

"I trusted you!"

"And I trusted you! Trusted you to reach the right decision, never imagining it would take over two years. But once I'd dug this hole for myself, I was determined to persevere. And you know what? It ended up being all for the better, that's what I began to realize."

"Oh no, now you're going to say it was good for us, for me? All this shit we've been through?"

"Think of this, Fitzroy Foster. Think of what would have happened if I'd come home from Berlin, told you I was all right, and the next night or that very night we'd have—I'd have read my report to you. It would take a few hours—how long did it take you to—?"

"Three hours."

"There you go. Three hours. You'd have listened, we'd have hugged each other as if all our problems were solved, my research all neatly packaged, everything tied with perfect ribbons, but you'd be no closer to him than before, you wouldn't have suffered to get there, paid your dues."

"You said we had paid our dues."

"I was wrong."

"The hell I've been through, losing my—losing you, seven years of desolation, that wasn't enough, you had to add an extra two years?"

"What was worse, Fitz? Having to live with that image imposed on you forever, or having to live without me? What was worse?"

"Losing you," I said. Reluctantly, because I didn't want to agree with anything she declared, anything she was arguing. But it was true. There had been nothing worse.

"Losing me," she said, flatly, without crowing over her victory. "So you hadn't really been through hell. You hadn't touched the depths of Henri's experience. I don't think you have yet, maybe you never will, I certainly will never even approach true knowl-edge. But at least now you are closer."

She was insane. And completely unrecognizable. He had put her up to this. Something far more perverse than what I had orig-inally thought. If he had simply stolen her from me with a piece of crashing stone, then at least she would have remained intact, pure, innocent. But to then resurrect and persuade her not to tell me, keep me in the dark, that was truly evil, to devise ever more dire punish-ments for someone he'd never met. Would he never be satisfied?

She looked at me, saw through me as if I were water. Oh, how I had missed that look, what she had concealed during these months of agony, clouding her vision of any trace of the deep wisdom with which she steered through reality. "You're blaming him again, Fitz."

"Oh, he's not to blame now? Now he's a saint? Like you?"

"A saint would never have done such a terrible thing to you, my love, so no, I'm not, far from it."

"But you think he's a saint?"

"I really don't know anything about him. Maybe he did put the thought in my head. Maybe he does want to screw you over. Or that was his initial plan: seek revenge inside the body that brings together the two rivers that defined his life, the Petit stream and the Hagenbeck stream. But here's what I've been thinking, and boy have you given me time to meditate—maybe he evolved once he got to know you, realized you might be a portal, believes that, given the right environment, you will understand his mes-sage. Maybe he's testing you, your capacity for forgiveness."

I latched onto that last word like a drowning man.

Forgiveness? Forgiveness?

Unforgivable. What she had done to me, to herself, the years of happiness she had filched. Unforgivable. The word I threw at her like a stone, like a wall, like a bulldozer.

As usual, she had an answer.

"Like what they did to Henri? Because if that's truly unforgivable, then he'll never let you go. Why should he forgive what your ancestors did to him, out of greed, pride, ambition, curiosity, indifference? What right do you have to demand it? Are you better than them?"

And so it went for a good while as the first day of the new year stretched past dawn. Everything I sent her way was like a boomerang. She had acted selfishly? So had I. She had excluded me from her life? I had excluded her from mine. So it went, so it went, until I had spent myself, could feel the quagmire of my resentment being drained drop by drop, bog by bog, discovered that the only thing I wanted was to take her in my arms and make love to her and fall asleep when she fell asleep and no more nights as the guardian of her dreams, I had prayed for her return and she had come back, wasn't that enough?

No. I had one more question and I did not want to ask it and I did, I had to. More of an accusation than a question, because I knew the answer, I feared I knew the answer, I feared the answer.

"You enjoyed yourself, Camilla Wood? Watching me sink into misery, desperate for your advice, shut off from the source of all comfort, you enjoyed that?"

She took her time responding, as if she had been waiting for many months for someone to ask this, brooding about it in the loneliness of her own hours.

Then: "Yes."

Just that word. And then: "I enjoyed it. I didn't want to. I wanted to hate myself for turning into this spectator of your anguish. I discovered that inside me there was this dark, demonic self. It was a relief, not being as perfect and flawless as you made me out to be. Being more like them."

"Them?"

"Petit and Hagenbeck and Virchow and Jacobsen and Saint-Hilaire and even like Julius Popper. Maybe I wanted to cast off my feeling of smug superiority—oh me, I would never do something like they did, I hope at least I wouldn't. I told myself that I persisted in this experiment out of love for you, but the truth—I think something in me relished wielding all that power, unburdening myself of that image you have of me, that I'm oh so impeccable."

I was shaken to the core and yet, and yet, had I really expected that our relationship would always be like that morning when we had coordinated our swimming, together, together, before even one word had been exchanged? She had always been too good to be true. To accept that there might be, that there was, a twist in the fabric of her personality might be an obligatory, unavoidable step in the difficult process of becoming an adult.

Or was I simply rationalizing, suppressing my rage because I couldn't stop loving her, because I had been itching to shout hallelujah since I'd awoken to find her by my side just as I had seen her when she had left for Europe two and a half years ago, because the other alternative was to live forever in shadows, to lose any future, all hope.

I was at a crossroads. For the first time in my life.

Up till then, everything had just happened to me, as if I were a mere receptacle. Even before Henri. Coasting along since my first breath, drifting from one birthday to the next, what the family album exposed, from event to event as if every problem could be resolved like an algebraic formula, cruising into adolescence with the confidence that someday I'd understand what life was all about, rebelling just enough against my parents to give myself the illusion that I was determining my fate, whereas I was really just fulfilling whatever plans they had laid out for me, kindergarten—oh what a cute little monkey—elementary school—our monkey is growing up!—middle school—I guess we can't call you a monkey anymore, Roy—and high school. And me next to the Arc de Triomphe and in the Jardin d'Acclimatation, not knowing what I was seeing, what had darkened any of the places I passed through, museum visits and swim teams and baseball games and parties, even Cam—even her, like everything else, an accident that befell me, nothing actually of my own doing, bothered slightly by that excessive normality—but not bothered sufficiently to break out and do something original, become someone else and other and unrecognizable, surprise myself. Perhaps that act of solitary sex, my first real choice, something I could take full responsibility for.

And then, almost immediately, Henri.

He'd come visiting and never left, and my life became even more acquiescent. Aware, oh so aware, that I was chained to circumstances I had not selected—but now not even harboring the misapprehension that I could change course, now married to my sickness, now submissive to a fault, caught, like Henri himself, in a world not of my making, made into a stranger, a pariah, a victim.

Cam had not transformed that fundamental dynamic, that I had always complied with what fate had dished out to me. She had been the active partner: her phone call years ago and her *carte postale* the next day, and then directing the quest and the research and even the date of our marriage. And when she had suffered her accident and I was handed the chance to be in command, show initiative and help her heal, I had simply retreated, let things take their course, a spectator of my own pain as if there was nothing I could do to alleviate it.

Well, now I was confronting a real choice.

I could dwell and sulk in this outrage done to me or I could climb out of that anger and chart a new map for my life. I could take control of the only thing that truly belonged to me—not Cam, nobody owns anybody else, I had just been taught that ruthless, necessary lesson—the one thing for which we should be judged: how to react when you have been damaged, when you feel betrayed by the one person who was the foundation and scaffolding and architecture of your very being, how to live with that and not succumb to despair and mistrust.

Did this mean that I'd forget that my Cam had let me twist and turn and had even, by her own reluctant admission, somehow enjoyed my plight? No, that festered inside me and would perhaps never be entirely assuaged. But that was what growing up meant. That we are imperfect beings, that we do stupid, incomprehensible things to one another, that we justify doing such things because we are too afraid to see our true image in the mirror. The contradictory truth I had to face: that we cannot live trusting anyone and that we also cannot live unless we renew that trust every day, because life without love is not worth living.

Cam was right. It was up to me.

She must have seen something shifting inside me, the seed, the hint, the dimmest lightning of an idea. If I could forgive her, might Henri not forgive me?

Now she took my hand and was not mistaken, because I accepted the temple of her offering, the refuge of her lips that followed and everything else, everything else that I had dreamt of for seven lean years and then for the months of her absence in Europe and finally during these last two years of loss and distance, how I had always wanted to greet the dawn that was renewing itself as we were, as we were.

And the first thing she asked in the morning, before we went down for breakfast—we had agreed not to let my dad or my brothers know that she had been playing a game all this time, preferred to greet them with the news that the miracle we had been awaiting had finally blessed us—her first question under that cold snowy January sky was:

"What year is this, Fitz?"

"Nineteen ninety-two," I said, fighting the concern that perhaps she had elapsed back—this time for real—into amnesia land.

"Nineteen ninety-two," she repeated the number with delight, rolled it on her tongue as if it were my mouth in her mouth. "You don't think it's significant that we're ready to restart our adventure precisely five hundred years since Columbus set sail for the world which Henri's ancestors had walked and inhabited and also sailed in canoes for thousands of years? Can there be a better date to figure out—together, Fitzroy Foster—what your voyager expects from us?"

I pondered this question as we descended the stairs hand in hand and as Cam received my dad's jubilation and the rapture of my brothers, and continued to ponder it through a sumptuous brunch as my wife filled the rest of the family in regarding the Hagenbeck ancestry, congratulating Dad for his lineage no longer being solely responsible for the haunting. And Dad had answered by proposing a photo session, the first in over two years, perhaps this cannibal would leave us alone now that the family had acknowledged our ancestral participation in his fate, perhaps he was feeling benevolent, it was the New Year, after all, 1992.

So there it was, again, that date, and its possible relevance looming large when I sat down for my portrait, as if I were Victor Hugo in person and Dad were his distant forefather Pierre Petit. I did not protest this futile exercise or bother to tell him that I knew what was going to happen. No consternation when those features of Henri emerged, crowning my body with his unforgettable eyes, confirming that our knowledge of his exact itinerary, mistreatment, and death did not mean that the journey was over for us. Or for him. You know that, Fitz, his face seemed to be whispering, don't tell me you really believed it would be that easy. I've missed you the last two years, man. Isn't it great to be together again?

I smiled at his cascade of words inside me, insanely winked at my visitor in complicity.

My father caught me in the act—as he had so often when I was a child, and just like back then, now he was not pleased either.

"What? Getting chummy with the ghost? Recovering your wife hasn't made you all sentimental and gooey and forgiving, has it? All of a sudden this demon's benign?"

The rancor in Dad's voice, contrasting with the serene, impassioned conversation I had held with my darling that dawn, bared something he had not wished to express when Cam had materialized in all her glory: I had my wife back and he had lost his, the monster had spared one and taken the other. But more crucially: we could not count on my father to second us in any effort at reconciliation with the savage who had ruined our family and left him bereft.

I could see Cam on the verge of trying to reason with him. She didn't realize the endless abyss of his hatred, something dark and dank flaring in his breath, the overflowing rage of his fingers as he ripped the Polaroid print into pieces and cast them onto the burning logs of the fireplace. Even when he laughed—it was more of a cackle than a laugh, more of a sob than a cackle— Cam seemed oblivious, intent on saying something, wanting to include him in the next stage of our search. He had lost so much, he didn't deserve to be left behind.

And yet, Cam finally said nothing. Just looked at me.

She needed me to enter the fray, respond to my own doubts by responding to my father's. She needed me to publicly commit to the path we were about to go down.

"You could be right, Dad," I said. "It's certainly a possibility that he's a demon. But there are other ways, more benevolent ways, of looking at him."

Dad was not in a mood to ask me what I meant.

"The bastard murdered your mother! He tried to kill your wife! And you're on his side now? How can you—oh God, you, of all people—what do you need? For him to start exterminating the whole human race, everything we love?"

Since infancy, I had learned to recognize danger signals, when his anger was on the edge of turning to rage and from rage into fury. Mom had helped me to navigate the endless sea of his mood swings, recede before the wave exploded, make sure that he never got physical. Mom had been an expert at this, the only one in the family who knew how to defy Dad without trying his patience.

But Mom, of course, wasn't here. The whole point of his outburst was that she could not help us anymore. All I could do was guess what she would have said, how she'd have calmed him. That he was a man who believed in science and that the law of statistics and probability indicated that two events—such as a boat capsizing in the Amazon and a piece of mortar falling from a wall in Berlin—were not necessarily part of the same pattern, even if both victims were related to the same human being, and had been on similar missions of discovery. That the interpretation of those events, the decision to interlock them, depended on the perspective and outlook from which we started out. If someone, like my father now or me as I had been for all these years, understood Henri to be out for revenge, then that is what we would predictably discern in whatever befell us, regardless of whether he even had the power to enact those assaults and misfortunes. If, on the other hand, we thought that his intervention in my life was not malignant—a stance that Cam had increasingly adopted, a position that I was on the brink of adhering to—then everything changed. Rather than Mom being killed by my visitor's desire to liquidate the great-granddaughter of Carl Hagenbeck's estranged granddaughter, Henri had been striving to protect her. And we could construe Berlin in the same way: it had been his intercession there that had averted a similar tragedy killing my wife. Or maybe all of us were mistaken and these accidents were no more than that, accidents—and Henri had nothing to do with either of them, and we were being distracted from what really mattered by presuming that a youngster who had been so helpless in life was a master of the universe in death.

That's what I should have explained, composedly, to my father.

And yet, given that we could not agree on the fundamentals, was it not useless to enter into any substantive discussion, why even go through the motions of a deliberation, why not avoid altercations altogether? That is what Mom would have concluded, that is what she whispered in my ear. Don't make matters worse. Keep the family together. Be as happy as you can because you never know when some tragedy will strike you, at a birthday breakfast or on the Amazon river or at a celebration in a city no longer divided by a wall. Indulge him, Roy. And find your own road to peace with the woman you love.

The consolation of hearing her voice inside me, my mother's ability to persist somewhere, anywhere, could not prevail over the grief that it was not her mouth saying it, her lips blowing the words to me, one hand in mine and the other holding onto my father.

That's when, in order not to start crying, not to open the new year, Mom's favorite day of the year, with tears, that's when I took a step forward and hugged my father. He tried to break loose but I wouldn't let him, Cam joined our embrace and then my two brothers became entangled in that messy jumble of arms and torsos, all of us simply exulting in our communal breath, rejoicing in the possibility of loving each other enough to leave it at that and go our separate ways.

But which way was ours?

That was something that Cam and I now set out to discover.

Discovery was the key word, of course. Five hundred years since the discovery of America, though there were already many who were derisively calling it something else and declaring there was nothing to celebrate—especially the descendants of those who had existed for millennia on the continent incorporated into the Western world so abruptly, so violently, so unexpectedly on October 12, 1492.

Something had opened up in the history of humanity that day, when the world changed forever, when Henri's fate in the South and our fate in the North had been determined. Columbus had started it all, returning with six Arawak Indians to be flaunted in the court and streets of Spain, he was the first to call them cannibals, the first to decide that their earth and trees did not belong to them, the first to describe with alien eyes what he saw.

If Cam hadn't been hit by the debris from the Berlin Wall, if she hadn't feigned the amnesia, if we hadn't lost over two years, that date wouldn't have entered into our discussion of what to do with the knowledge brought back from Europe, but as it was . . .

"It's got to be a signal," Cam said cheerfully—her optimism really was astonishing, how I had missed it, how I beseeched it to lift me up, now more than ever, now that the pangs of betrayal kept simmering somewhere in my soul. "Look at it this way: we've been given a chance. That whatever we have to do to atone will coincide with the commemoration, for good and for bad, of the half millennium since the first Indians met the first Europeans . . ."

Her words triggered in me an idea: What if we journeyed to Zurich and—

And I enjoyed her eyes opening wide with wonder, was I seriously proposing to travel?

I walked over to yet another drawer of my desk, also locked, and extracted something, concealing it behind my back, daring her to guess. An elephant? Wrong! A flying carpet? Wrong! An invisibility cloak? Wrong!

She came to kiss me and then snatched what I had in my hands and squealed like a monkey.

"A passport! How . . . ?"

"Well, I couldn't tell you about this, could I, given that you supposedly didn't even know a visitor was invading my—"

"Fitz, let's not go there."

Right! So I explained that, after abandoning my experiments in Photoshopping for most of the last two years, I had recently returned to them, concerned that if my love were to have another crisis or needed urgent care some place faraway, I needed an ID. The techniques of image manipulation had, using the very patent that made us rich, taken great strides forward. Many nights, while Cam slept—or was she just feigning that as well?—I had, starting from that old picture of myself at fourteen, constructed a model of how I looked now, like a plastic surgeon operating on his own face in front of a mirror. I did not confess to Cam that there was a certain perverse pleasure in this exercise of slowly aging the digital image—fuck you, Henri, look at me recover my identity in spite of you, look at me force the picture to conform to what Cam and my family see. But more important than the gratification at excluding my enemy was the certainty that this was my ticket to freedom.

"My doctored photo," I said to Cam. "It fooled the bureaucrats, they promptly approved the passport."

Great, but public places, Cam cautioned, were still perilous. If anything, she said, her exploration of human zoos had made her even more fearful, oversensitive to what might happen if powerful people ever learned about the image that was haunting me. Just as Virchow had measured the skulls and Von Bischoff had prodded the genitals, so there had to be many scientists who would love to get their hands on someone like me to experiment on, unravel a phenomenon that had no rational explanation. "I know them, Fitzroy," she said fervently. "They'll be out to extract some commercial value from your tragedy, Henri's tragedy. We'll only travel if absolutely necessary, if the rewards outweigh the risks."

Zurich, I argued, returning to my initial idea, seemed to fit the bill. If we could find the body of Henri and the others who died there, if we could retrieve them and carry them home, reverse the journey they had taken over 110 years ago, if we could then give them burial on the island from which they had been abducted, if we could find some relative who—"A lot of ifs," Cam objected. "I doubt that anyone knows where those bodies were buried—though I'll admit that this was why I was going to Zurich after Berlin, to complete the investigation. But let's say the bodies can be located, what right do we have to ask for an exhumation, let alone cart them away? It would be kidnapping them all over again, even if we had the best intentions—just like Hagenbeck who, after all, claimed he was educating the public, providing a service to science. And you'd end up in the spotlight. No, Fitzroy Foster—good try, but there's got to be something more feasible."

Over the next weeks we searched for another project. Go to Europe, confront the Hagenbeck relatives in Hamburg and whatever Pierre Petit descendants we might be able to find in Paris, enlisting them in some sort of private or even public act of penance. But if it had taken me eleven years to begin to decipher that my visitor might not be an enemy but perhaps a collaborator with benign intentions, how difficult, then, would it be to

convince those distant members of my family to assume responsibility for something they had not personally done?

Then Cam timidly came up with the idea of working with Survival International, following my mother's example. But it made
me uncomfortable. Undoubtedly, the best way of redressing a
wrong done in the past was, as Mom had put it, to make sure it
was not repeated in the future—and yet, that solution was too
abstruse and self-satisfying, too removed from Henri's individual
suffering and story. Save an Indian now to compensate for one
massacred a century ago. No, whatever we came up with had
to address his life, his motives, his extinction. We would have
many decades ahead of us to make the world a better place. There
was only one October 12, 1992, and we had to do something that
explicitly focused on that special date and dealt with my special
visitor.

Cam responded to this demurral on my part by designing
a gigantic cage, which she proposed to build in front of some
major institution that had profited from the exploitation of
Henri—like the Hagenbeck zoo or the Jardin d'Acclimatation
or the Berlin Museum or even some bank where the profits from
these human zoos had been deposited—and she, Camilla Foster
Wood, intended to dress up like a native Patagon and there, half
naked, gnaw on bones and utter guttural sounds and—It was
so easy to shoot down her initiative that I felt a surge of pity as
I said: "How about me? I'm the one who's haunted and you're
exposing yourself? If this—this happening—were to work, well,
I'd have to be in the cage with you, be photographed by any passerby and be carted off to jail as a public nuisance. And besides,
Cam, we can never be Henri, we can't really replicate his ordeal.
Because, my dear, we can escape from that cage whenever we
want. Now, if you really wish to turn into him, go with me to
Patagonia and live with what remains of his tribe, spend the rest

of our life trying to become a Kaweshkar Indian. I think that's nuts, but at least it isn't a performance, at least it would be the real thing. Only problem is that I don't believe it's what he wants."

All our incoherent plans led us back, always back, to the same question. What does he want?

Forcing us to realize that we needed to draw even closer to him, at least try to understand where he had come from, what sort of life he would have led if Hagenbeck had not created human zoos, if Columbus had not stepped on an island he did not yet know was part of a new world.

Let Henri guide us. Give him whatever agency we could in this quest. Make him part of it.

And that was the reason why, toward mid-February 1992, Cam returned to the Harvard Library to find an answer to our problem in books and materials and maps.

And came back with a different sort of problem.

Mrs. Hudson, the librarian, after congratulating Cam on her recovery, had suggested they go to the cafeteria, where she confided, in a conspiratorial whisper, that an official from a government agency had come by a few months ago, in early November of last year, to inquire about the books and documents Miss Wood, later Mrs. Foster, had requested in 1988–89. When Mrs. Hudson had refused, citing client confidentiality, the administration had intervened and ordered her to cooperate, for reasons, they said, of national security. She had complied with the bibliography, not allowing the man, however, to take the books from the library's premises. This agent, Danny Makaruska, he said his name was, returned the next day accompanied by an older man who had spent hours perusing those volumes and taking notes and often photos. A strange fellow, a bit creepy, Mrs. Hudson commented, and sad, as if perpetually on the verge of tears.

Cam had asked if the man was tall, gaunt, bald, with red-rimmed eyes? Yes, that was right! A melancholy man, very silent, hunched over his labors, very concentrated. The agent had referred to him, quite deferentially, as Doctor.

"Dr. Downey," I said.

"It's got to be him. Ernest Downey. How did you guess?"

I told her about his visit to our home on November 9 of last year, a date coinciding with this stranger's incursion into the vaults of the Harvard Library.

"Why do you think he's stalking me, him and this—this Makaruska agent?"

Later that evening, we held an emergency family meeting. Even if Dad disapproved of any initiative of ours that might presume Henri was a friendly force, he was even more infuriated by the idea that someone was shadowing us.

"How dare the bastard go snooping around!" Dad exploded. "I've a good mind to seek him out and—no wonder he gave me the jitters. National security? I very much doubt it!"

We agreed, however, that it would be better not to alert Dr. Downey that we were onto his spying.

"Maybe he thought there was some sort of clue in those books as to where my scientific research was going," Cam ventured. "That's what he seemed obsessed with when we met briefly in Paris."

It was something that also obsessed me. Ever since she had awoken from her false amnesia attack I had started to press her to resume her work, retrieve all that lost time. More so now that it seemed that this Downey fellow was out to steal her ideas.

"So what? If he finds the gene that allows visual memory to be transmitted from one generation to the next, good for him, great for science, terrific for us. But listen, even if he—or I— were to find the link inside someone's DNA, that still won't solve the enigma of your visitor. It will just depict how he did it, how nature did it, how memories transfer. These years you keep calling lost have, in fact, helped me to realize a fallacy in science: we keep thinking that if we uncover the how of something we'll have solved its mystery, get it to speak. But Henri will still be silent, we'll still not understand what he wants and why. I've brought back more books and material from the library, on the Kaweshkar, their language, their history, their customs, their spiritual ceremonies. We'll never get inside Henri, see the world as he did, that would be so arrogant, to presume that we can abolish time and history, undo our own identity and desire, turn into natives, in fact impossible to embody him entirely, possess him all over again, but we can essay a respectful approximation, that's where we have to put our energies. Chromosomes will always be there, ready for exploration."

All through the next month and a half, as we plunged into everything published about the Kaweshkar—so much written about a tribe that did not itself have writing, that believed in words that were hurled into the wind and kept alive by the waves and the rocks and the birds—I kept bringing up how strongly I felt that she should at least set up an appointment at MIT and see if some sort of job might be open, and she kept on postponing such an interview. Until one day, I cornered her: "I think you're afraid that your research is no longer valid, no matter how much you say that you don't care, and I'd be the first to grant that such a fear is legitimate, Cam, but look at it from my perspective: every day that passes makes me feel guiltier for having blocked your career. So, please, even if it's just to allay my own remorse, please, please, speak to your friends at the lab."

My anguish convinced her—and she came back in mid-April from MIT, with an expression that hesitated between joy and concern. The good news was that she was welcome to start right away, collaborating with the genome project. The bad news was—who did I think was in charge of this unit, parachuting in from Stanford?

"Downey," I said.

"Downey," she confirmed. As soon as he'd been informed that she was requesting a job interview, he'd mentioned how eager his team would be to fit her in, in view of her pioneering work at the Institut Pasteur. He would, in fact, be visiting soon, and had expressed an interest in getting reacquainted, hoping to take Mrs. Foster and her husband out to dinner when he was next in the Boston area.

Cam had not lost her cool for one instant, playing along, accepting the relayed invitation, but not just yet, as she would only be returning to work later in the year—she lied to them as she had lied to me, feigning that she was not completely well, under doctor's orders to go easy on strenuous mental and social activities.

"I wanted to consult you first, Fitz," Cam said. "Should I set up a meeting to sound him out?"

"No way," I responded. "I don't like the idea of you even getting near that weirdo."

"So how can we find out what he's really up to?"

Neither of us would budge—adventurous Cam against cautious Fitzroy. Fortunately, Vic was home from Chicago Law School for Easter holidays and he solved the impasse. A classmate, Laura—and he blushed at her name, so we realized he was studying more than jurisdiction with the girl—was the daughter of Barry Cunningham, a former police captain who had set up a private eye agency. Why not turn the tables on this mysterious Downey and scrutinize his past and intentions?

By early May Cunningham, a beefy, affable man with brows so bushy they almost overshadowed the mischievous sparkle in his eyes, sat in our living room with a preliminary report.

There had been nothing furtive about Downey's research until a few years ago, when he had suddenly moved from epidemiology and public health studies—he had been instrumental, along with the Institut Pasteur, in discovering the cause of AIDS—into the diverse area of visual memory and its genealogical transmission. That recent research was classified as top secret by the Pentagon and Pharma2001, the gigantic German-American company, the entities subsidizing Downey's work. So Cunningham had told the detective assigned to the case to back off, though feelers had gone out to a contact in the FBI for further information.

Laura's father was able to provide, nevertheless, compelling details about Downey's personal life.

At about the time Downey had switched his field of interest, a corresponding sea change had occurred in his character. From a cheerful, amiable, back-slapping colleague, considerate with others to a fault, he had transmogrified into a misanthrope, fanatical about his work, haughty and difficult to deal with. And then, suddenly, a few months after this remarkable transformation, tragedy had struck the scientist's family in Palo Alto. He had come home one evening and found both his wife Anna and his eighteen-year-old daughter Evelyn dead, hanging from two belts. That double suicide pact had deepened the shift in Downey's personality, made him even more introspective and lugubrious. And he had thrown himself into his work with fury, the only consolation left to a man whom everybody agreed was beyond brilliant, a perennial candidate for a Nobel Prize in Medicine.

"Yes, yes, yes," Cam said. "That's it, that's got to be it!"

Before we could even guess what she meant, she asked Barry Cunningham to please dig up details about Downey's lineage, as well as his wife's, back at least five generations. And would say nothing more on the matter till, two weeks later, Dad received a packet from the detective agency—at his office, as Barry had intimated that our house might be under surveillance.

"I knew it," Cam exclaimed when we had finished reading. "No wonder she killed herself."

"Who?"

"Downey's daughter. No wonder her mother . . ."

I read through the report again, passed it to Dad.

Ernest Downey descended directly from a famous photographer, William Ernest Downey. Born in 1829, a favorite of Queen Victoria's, he'd immortalized Prince Albert, the whole royal family, and innumerable viscounts and earls and notables of that age. Awarded a Royal Warrant in 1879, most of his fortune, like Pierre Petit's, had come from postcards. Our Dr. Downey's grandfather had been the grandson of this original Downey.

"Fitz, Jerry! See? The sixth generation! Evelyn! And look at her mother Anna's side!"

Anna Farini prided herself on tracing her ancestry back to William Leopold Hunt, known far and wide as the Great Farini, a Canadian who had been one of the world's great showmen and acrobats in the late nineteenth century. He had walked a tightrope across Niagara Falls on stilts with a fat woman on his back while juggling swords and soon became famous for daring circus performances with Lulu, a boy who, for years, had been disguised as a girl. Farini had eventually reinvented himself as a major entrepreneur in London, displaying freaks and bringing friendly Zulus from Africa to the Royal Aquarium. Besides adopting Lulu as his son, Farini had two boys of his own, one of whom was the great-great-grandfather of Anna, Downey's wife. The Great Farini fathered no daughters but had given his name to a girl from Laos.

"Don't you see, don't you?" Cam was beside herself with excitement. "A notorious showman and circus entrepreneur on one side of the family and an eminent photographer on the other, their blood coming together after all those generations, just like you. So it's got to be—yes, yes, yes, that's what it's got to be. Lulu or the girl from Laos or . . . Wait, wait, wait."

And before Dad or I could question her further, she was out the door. Dad grinned at me. "Married life," he said. "I think she's terrific."

I spent the rest of the day perusing the report again. Evelyn Downey's genealogy resembled mine to a depressing degree. Had Petit crossed paths with this first Downey, did Hagenbeck have dealings with the flamboyant Farini?

Dad and I were preparing dinner, had laid the table, when Cam breezed back in, pushed aside plates and cutlery and plopped a large book down, opening it to a page marked with a feather.

An image stared out at us.

"Krao," she said. "Gentlemen, please meet Krao Farini as photographed by William Ernest Downey in 1882."

The sight struck dread into my heart. The child—perhaps seven or eight—was almost entirely covered with a dense coating of soft black hair about a quarter of an inch long, through which a brown-olive skin gleamed faintly here and there. Her cheeks were full and pouched, made more gruesome by a low and short nose with excessive nostrils. Though hunched forward in an ape-like pose, her eyes were large and beautiful, sad and immensely human.

Cam turned to another page.

Krao had two arms and one leg wrapped around a distinguished bearded gentleman—the Great Farini, my wife announced triumphantly. This time the girl was clothed in pajamas, forlorn as she clung to her adoptive father. He responded by holding her tenderly, carefully, like a doll.

Next page.

Krao by herself again, fully clothed, showing off teeth which seemed more like those of an animal than of a female child, sharp and separated, a grimace meant to ingratiate but mostly repulsive. With those eyes, those eyes.

Cam explained that Norwegian explorer Carl Bock had heard on one of his Asian trips that there were tribes of these savages deep in the Laotian jungle, akin to apes, the possible missing link of Darwinian fame. In 1881, Farini paid for a new expedition by Bock to bring back a specimen: none other than Krao, called thus due to the plaintive cry emitted by her tribesmen when she was forcibly separated from them. This little orphan (her father, abducted along with her, had died on the trip to Europe and the mother had been forbidden to travel by the king of Siam— the same one made notorious by the musical *The King and I*) had caused an unparalleled sensation in London and later in the States and—"get this," Cam enthused, "was examined by good old Virchow and Von Bischoff." Despite the latter testifying that the girl was not a missing link, simply born with a sickness known as hypertrichosis, she continued to be billed as "Living Proof of Darwin's Theory of the Descent of Man," drawing hundreds of thousands of spectators till the end of her days at the age of fifty-four.

"A very intelligent girl," Cam went on, "who spoke, in adulthood, many languages, and was described by fellow performers as one of the sweetest people alive. What is strange is that all accounts describe her as content with her lot—whether this is true or not, we have no way of knowing. But that she might be happy is strange."

"Strange? Why?"

"Because she haunted Evelyn Downey. That's why Evelyn killed herself. Didn't you almost commit suicide?"

"Yes."

Dad gasped. He must have suspected that I'd contemplated taking my life, but, like so many of my secrets, we had skirted talking about this one.

"And wouldn't you have done so if, instead of Henri, the photo were that of a disgusting child that seemed an animal, would your sanity have withstood an invasion by someone like Krao, if you felt that ape-child crawling inside you, demanding sympathy?"

"I'd rather die."

"And the mother, Anna," Dad asked, "what about her?"

"The difference with your family and Downey's is that they knew right away about the ancestry, the past was not a blur for them as it was for you Fosters. Imagine Anna when she realizes that the freak the Great Farini kidnapped was colonizing her daughter, seething inside her own child."

"And another difference," I said. "Downey. As a doctor, he—"

"Must have decided to experiment, run tests on her, find out how these incursions transpired. And when he lost his loved ones he persisted, tried to turn his tragedy into a major scientific achievement."

"He went mad," my father said. "That I understand."

"He went mad," Cam said. "And he's dangerous. Don't you see, guys? If we've been able to track him down, well, what doesn't he know about us, given his means? We hunt down Henri and his victimizers, he hunts us down. He knows, Fitz, he's discovered who you are. Once someone like me has established the genealogy, anyone following my itinerary will deduce why I'm doing this, find out I have a husband who drops out of sight, out of camera range, at puberty. Downey knows what that means, his daughter must have had some sort of sexual experience as an adolescent that triggered this, made her feel she was to blame. But that's not all, my dears."

We waited expectantly.

"If you are not a solitary phenomenon, if Evelyn repeats your visitation, there must be others. You're not alone, Fitzroy Foster. Who knows how many men and women are also haunted by ghosts from the past, just waiting for us to find them."

SEVEN

"... why all the living so strive to hush all the dead ..."

—Herman Melville, *Moby Dick*

Over the course of the next months, Camilla became unrecognizable. She threw herself into an endless quest for those she called Henri's brothers and sisters, searched voraciously for the men who, like my ancestors, might have victimized those natives.

Realizing she was serious, I remonstrated with her. Wouldn't we have heard if there were that many cases like mine, surely somebody would have gotten a whiff of their existence?

Not necessarily, she answered. Some might have foolishly revealed themselves to the authorities and were now quarantined in some hole or laboratory, rotting away, being dissected by Downey's avid hands. Others might have followed the path of Evelyn and killed themselves. But it made sense that some, like me, must have squirreled themselves away.

I decided not to contest her newfound mission. Maybe this was just a pretext to get out of the house where she had been confined—albeit by her own foolish choice!—for two years. Maybe it would be good for her to compensate now with a mad dash of activity. Who could blame a vibrant woman like my wife for wanting to spread her wings again?

She'd leave early in the morning and come back late at night, full of dates and exhibition notices, names of entrepreneurs and explorers and photographers, copies of postcards and drawings, charts and newspaper clippings. Most of the victims were anonymous, forgotten by history except for a solitary snapshot, while those responsible for their captivity had led well-known lives. Kidnappers like Willy Moller and his Egyptian caravans and the French entrepreneur Jean Tauver and his Kula tribe from Equatorial Guinea shown in Madrid, and Xavier Pene, the owner of a plantation in Dahomey, who transported sixty-seven Africans against their will to Chicago in 1893. And of course, the omnipresent Jacobsen and another partner of Hagenbeck, Joseph Menges. The victims were harder to identify, as always in history, Cam said, even though they far outnumbered the criminals. Javanese dancers and headhunters from Borneo and wild women from Somalia and wild men from Togo and Samoa, wild anything and anybody from the Philippines and Indonesia and Abyssinia and the Sudan, the Bella Coola tribe and Zulu performers from the Transvaal, Bedouins at Brighton Towers, a New Zealand Maori chieftain frowning from his portrait, captives from Formosa and Okinawa, Lilliputians from the Caucasus—a perpetual planetary tour of horrors. Blind Ashanti boys and girls. Miserable Andaman Islanders from the South Pacific. A Negro cretin from Fouta-Djallon. Only a few sported names. Saartje Baartman, the Hottentot Venus, whose immense posterior was more famous than her face, paraded in cabaret acts and circuses, promoted in caricatures and postcards and lewd jokes, her skeleton preserved after death, her likeness copied in wax at the London Wax Museum. Also embalmed in London, Julia Pastrana, a goateed indigenous woman from Sinaloa, whose beard Darwin had admired. The Congolese Gemba, Kitoukwa, and Sambo who, after dying at the Brussels International Exposition in the summer of 1897, were buried among suicides and adulterers when the townspeople of Tervuren stoned the funeral procession that would have lowered them into consecrated ground. Maphoon, a thick-haired African woman who was photographed in Manchester in 1855 breastfeeding an angelic child. No names for the Danaki tribesmen that Carl Milano caught with his camera in Turin in 1884. Just one more of what seemed an endless list of photographers. Jules Grand and Julien Damoy and Julien Lecerf and countless other Jules and Juliens. And Jesse Tarbox Beals, Ferdinand Deslisle, Matthew Brady, Nicholas Henneman, Carl Gunther, Charles Dudley Arnold, and Harlow Higginbotham, even some women like the Gerhard sisters, official photographers of the St. Louis Exhibition of 1904.

So many names, so much suffering, began to take a toll on Cam, annexing her nights and dreams. I was patient, hoping that, like a fever, it would soon subside. But when she ran out of kidnappers, and started adding scientists and abettors, middlemen and clergymen—can you believe what this missionary Sam Philips Verner did to his Congolese pygmy?—I decided to confront her.

If Downey had been unsuccessful in finding others like his daughter with all the resources at his disposal, what chance did she have of accomplishing anything different?

"Oh, he's probably found them," she said dismissively. "But he can't appeal to victims like you can, not with a daughter who killed herself, not if he did not protect her. They'd react as we have—wanting nothing to do with him."

She was feeding the fax machine with a request to Barry

Cunningham's agents to pursue potential genealogical links to a series of suspects. On the list was a certain R. A. Cunningham who had snatched groups of aborigines from Australia to sell them to Barnum and Bailey—"Ha, maybe our detective will discover that he descends from this guy who's responsible for those poor people ending up destitute in Drew's Dime Museum, wouldn't that be insane!" Always on the trail, my Cam, that hadn't changed—forgetting each morning that a few hours earlier I'd been forced to wake her from a storm of nightmares.

"So let's say," I persisted, "that the faraway progeny, the sixth generation, results from the coupling of some eminent kidnapper of a victim and some equally eminent photographer, what then? Hi, I'm Cam Foster-Wood. My husband has your syndrome. This happened after he masturbated, so I'm wondering, sir, miss, about your first sexual experience? No problems with photos? Oh, my mistake, sorry to have intruded on your life. But say you did stumble upon someone like me, what's next? Would you care to join forces with us? Join you, ma'am, to do exactly what? I doubt you've even started to figure out a plausible response, right?"

She didn't seem to listen to a word I'd said. "Oh, Fitz, don't you see that they have to be the key to what's ailing you, how it happened. Don't you see? If there's only one of you, it can be a fluke. If there are two, like you and the Downey girl, it can be an accident. But with more cases, a pattern can be established, bio-historical causes can be tested, a deterrent discovered."

"Didn't you say that the deterrent was to draw closer to Henri, particularly in a year as significant as 1992?"

"Keep at it," Cam said. "We'll be working on parallel tracks. Until our paths meet up. I'm sure of it. Here, look at this photo."

I looked. Several jet-black African women looked back at me. Sticking out from their mouths were colossal labrets, plate-like lips larger than cocktail trays, offensively, shockingly, derisively jutting forth. While white women, tourists, posed for the camera, their polished, manicured nails probing those dark, alien faces.

"How many creatures just like these were exhibited, Fitz, give it your best guess. Twenty-five thousand," she rushed to answer her own question. "And each captive was burnt on some retina, each and every one is seeking a host. Henri and Krao may just be the tip of the iceberg, the scouts who spy out the lay of the land before the major invasion. I can't let Downey get to them before I do, I won't."

I shivered. Rather than the woman who had spoken lovingly of Henri and his plight, she suddenly sounded more like Downey, as if, in a twisted way, she had started competing with him. She hadn't seemed to mind in Paris when he had been chasing some vague idea of transmission of visual memory through the generations or via saliva, but once Cunningham's detectives had revealed Downey's private stake in this investigation, Cam must have taken it as an affront and a challenge. As if he was violating her exclusive territory, which by virtue of my existence and our relationship belonged to her and no one else.

It was true that she wished to find the brothers and sisters, far-flung and near, Bedouins and Dakota and dwarfs from Okinawa, who accompanied Henri from the darkness of the past. It was true that she grieved for their uprooted lives. And true that she hoped to alleviate the malady of their young victims. But her deepest and fiercest desire sprang from the need to beat Downey at his own game.

The fact that Downey had at his beck and call so many assets, corporate and governmental, seemed to spur her on. She felt that advantage to be somehow unfair, unsporting, an outrage directed at her personally—and was determined to even that lopsided playing field by exercising her outlandish talents, inhabited by the supreme self-confidence that the imagination of one human being can overcome an army of adversaries.

But watching her feed the fax machine with frenzied page after page of queries and photos and biographical data, I told myself that this explanation of a cutthroat competition was insufficient. Maybe there was something more fundamentally wrong with her, maybe all this time she had been as flawed as I was, only without a visitor to make the condition manifest. Or maybe that debris from the Berlin Wall had affected her more than either of us allowed and she had been, in effect, amnesiac all through those two years. I could picture her awakening in that first light of 1992 with that folder sprawled on the bedspread, I could see her reading those pages and sluggishly returning to her own old true self. I wouldn't put it past her to have decided, before I myself woke up that New Year's morning, to invent, for my benefit, that she been well and in control for the duration, always wanting to be in control, my Camilla Wood.

This much, however, was certain. If I did not rescue her now, if I let her just meander through a labyrinth of endless genealogical crisscrossings and horrific photos and atrocities, if I let Downey invade her as Henri had invaded me, I would be failing yet again, failing her and myself, and this time there might be no absolution.

From the moment we had met up again she had criticized what she called my lack of initiative, an opinion reenforced by my recent passivity during her own ailment. Whenever I ventured that she might be going overboard in the search for fellow ghosts lost in the wilderness of world history, she irrefutably answered: So what do you propose, my love?

She would soon find out.

While she ran races with Downey, I had stayed steady on the course of exploring the Kaweshkar, faithful to the idea that once we had deciphered what Henri wanted, able to look at the world with his eyes, from his eyes, a plan of action would follow.

I tried to imagine him the day he was abducted as he watched the coast recede mercilessly and then that night, the first night in the dark hold of the ship.

I decided that the women would be the first to console him. I decided that they would act as the guardians of the group's memory, describing each rock they had lost, each island, inlet, seal fur, obsidian flint, withered shrub, scraggly tree; I decided that they would sing the landscape back into being, each word part of a net, each object like a fish in that net, each memory to be cleaned and gutted and stored and nibbled till it had become part of their collective landscape inside, the coves and the beaches and the bleached bones of a whale, and how the bite of the breeze and the drizzle of the rain below the clouds reveal when a tempest is coming, and how they used to throw stones into the sea warning the weather that they'd had enough of wretched never-ending storms. As if, with the effort of those who spoke and sang in the ship's cavern, and the attention of those who listened and responded and repeated, through the magic dwelling of their tongue, they could shelter the stolen environment and ensure it would still be there as the distance and the miles and the waves accumulated, waiting, fluid and intact, for their footsteps and their fingers. Night after night, day after day telling and retelling each other stories of the land and the sea, the canoes and the hunt, the fire extinguished and the fire relit, like incantations against the fiends of forgetfulness, urging the adolescents not to despair, teaching the smaller children winds and words that they had hardly been able to breathe, giving them a home in the language and a home in the remembrances they shared until the day when that home could materialize out of the mists and be touched and walked and navigated, until they could bathe themselves in the freezing currents and emerge as if reborn, as if this trip were only a bad dream that would never return. Trying not to forget their homeland so it would not forget them, the berries and the surf, the tinamou and the seasnipe and the penguins.

It was that fierce and tender resurrection of their past that opened the door for the adult males to take the young men, Henri and Pedro, under their wing. If Antonio was their father and the Capitano their leader, perhaps their shaman, they had much to impart. Perhaps that instruction had started aboard the ship, but I suspected it had really become important once they were all imprisoned behind the fences and staves of the Jardin, once they were forced to perform all manner of fraudulent ceremonies for the entertainment of those gawking Parisians. So as soon as the last show was over and the last spectators had paid their last admission fees and returned to their apartments in the shadow of the wide boulevards, the elders had whispered to the two young males what their duties should be, what genuine rituals they had missed and should be preparing for.

It made sense that they had been captured while at sea, because Hagenbeck's agents wouldn't have been able to find them on land, discover the caves where the Kaweshkar would have hidden. The whole group, wandering as water nomads do, in search of better fishing grounds. More likely, I resolved—and it was up to me, I had to visualize what Henri could not tell me—that a whale had foundered in one of the coves, the signal for the dispersed families to convene so that foundational rites could commence, now that meat was guaranteed for many days. Were Henri and Pedro, therefore, on their way to participate in the ceremony that would have marked their transition into manhood, had their lives, like mine, been truncated? That's what I wanted to think, that Henri had been blocked, as I had, from the definitive rite of passage that would have made him a full member of the community, wanted to think that was the reason he had chosen me. Because it helped me to conjure up how Antonio and the Capitano had approached him with the secrets that only they knew.

Most of what the boys learned had been kept from the prying eyes of even sympathetic anthropologists and missionaries, but enough had seeped through for outsiders to divine the outlines of what ensued inside the ceremonial hut. Given their age, it was conceivable that Henri and Pedro had been through the *kálakai*, a first initiation for the young of both sexes that Lise would have participated in, though females would have been forbidden from the next stages, sanctioned only to bring food to the entrance of the sacred hut. Henri and Pedro, on the other hand, would already have been assigned a task, to ensure that mothers and sisters, grandmothers and daughters, did not even peep inside, scaring the women away by dancing furiously in front of them in the guise of spirits, their male bodies painted with stripes, their faces covered with leering masks. If they performed well, they soon might be invited to undergo the *yinčiháua*, as long as they had given proof of readiness.

Proof that he could use bow, arrow, harpoon, and fashion them from wood and clamshells. Proof that he could manufacture a canoe and build a hut and provide for a family, make fire under the rain and in a vessel that immense waves covered and spun. That he could find each crevice in the worst sleet storm and how to tell when the weather was about to turn really nasty and where one can find fresh water where the deer and guanacos and foxes would come to drink, how to forage for birds' eggs and mollusks and *erizo* sea urchins without depleting them all, without stopping the cycle of regeneration. And afterward, in the hut itself, during the *yinčiháua*, go without eating for days, survive many hours crouched in the fetal position until his muscles cried out, as if he were in his vessel pursuing the seals that would offer meat and oil and fur, terrible trials but nothing compared to what they were subjected to on this other trip to the land of white strangers. Yes, the boy must have been trained in Paris by the two male adults in the group so that upon his return he might immediately restart his initiation at the point where it had been interrupted, pretend a miracle would deliver him.

A miracle nobody visited him with back then, that I could not give him now.

But the more I thought of Henri on the ship to Hamburg and Henri in the Jardin d'Acclimatation and Henri being photographed and paraded and Henri on a suffocating train to Berlin and Henri being examined by doctors and scientists and Henri on his way to Zurich and Henri dying alone in that hospital as Dr. Seitz tried to save him, the more I thought of what his experience might have been and his need to share with others his unfulfilled longing, the more and more I thought of Henri dreaming an alternative existence, another possible life, as the end drew near, the closer I drew to his desire and loss and expectation, the more I realized what was being asked of me.

I would go where he had been unable to journey.

South, to his birthplace.

EIGHT

"Home is where one starts from."
—T. S. Eliot, *Four Quartets*

That bay in Tierra del Fuego from which Henri and the others were taken, his home, that's where we needed to be on October 12.

Find his descendants and ask them what they remembered from that violent past, what the great-great-grandparents had told their children so they could tell theirs, so some trace of that suffering remained alive in memory. What did they feel, those left behind, when, from one day to the other, their loved ones suddenly disappeared, were never heard of again? Vanished, as if they had never been born. What had the four Kaweshkar who came back in 1882 related of their trip, did any of them recall Henri writhing on the floor of a Zurich hospital, drying up with dysentery, his innards burning? Did they pronounce his real name? Did anyone recall it? Had the only woman to return, Piskouna or Trine or whatever her name was, had she at least whispered something about his fate? Had Pedro, who might have been Henri's brother? Isn't that what brothers do?

And once the distant relatives of Henri had spoken to us, then this distant relative of Petit and Hagenbeck would speak, I'd tell them our story, we would show that the forgiveness we were asking for was not fraudulent, came from our own sorrow, my penitence for what my ancestors had done to theirs. Perhaps they would lift the curse, perhaps they had the power, perhaps there was still some healer among them who recollected how to quiet the fire of revenge, how to sing the dead into the next world, how to lay to rest the spirit of Henri. And then maybe we could help them in a more concrete way, create a foundation in my visitor's name for the last survivors of the Kaweshkar ethnic group, finance a museum for their objects, pay lawyers to demand reparations, something, anything, anything to atone.

Among the books I had laboriously read in Spanish about the Alakaluf, as they were insistently called, was one delving into their spiritual world that I particularly treasured. The author was a historian by the name of Frano Vudarovic, who taught at the local university in Punta Arenas.

Would he appreciate my writing to him in his native Spanish, however stilted mine might be, awkward, excessively formal, scattered with grammatical errors? My hope was that he'd appreciate that effort as proof of my sincerity—important, as so much of what I'd be telling him was deceitful. On a recent trip to Paris, I wrote, my wife and I had come upon a postcard of a striking young Indian (I included a photocopy of the *carte*). Because we couldn't forget his features, and above all his haunting eyes, we had spent many months tracing the subject's ultimate fate, *su destino*. After briefly summarizing this young Patagonian's voyage and death, I asked Professor Vudarovic if he might provide us with information regarding any possible living relatives of this man who had been called Henri by his captors, as we were interested in contacting them to see if a ceremony might be performed to help his soul find some respite, given that his body probably couldn't be found and buried. I enclosed a self-addressed, prepaid express mail envelope for any possible response.

It came back five days later.

Written in impeccable English.

Dear Mr. Foster:

As you may know, the Kaweshkar believe—or at least did, when there were enough of them alive to believe in something collectively— that the soul is made of air. Xolás, their Supreme Being, breathes that soul into the body at the moment of birth. When the body, a mere perishable creation of the parents, dies, the soul lifts up, light as the wind, rides up and ever up into the stars and beyond, where the vast hut of Xolás serves as the abode of the dead. When the soul arrives at the enormous door above which Xolás presides, it is overcome with trembling and shame and swears, even if this is not so—"I have not done anything really bad."

Xolás does not deign to listen to these words. Instead, their god asks them to look back: "Reflect now on your life and actions." And once the soul has done so and is ready to tell its host the truth, then Xolás opens the great door to the immense hut and says, "Now you may come in."

If the world followed the advice of Xolás to tell the truth, it would be a far better place and I would not have been forced to write this response. It is advice, dear Mr. Foster, that you have chosen to ignore, though I conjecture that your motives are not sinister or malevolent, just guided by trembling and shame.

I called a colleague at the linguistics lab at MIT, with whom I had studied while completing my doctorate at the University of Sussex, and he informed me of your wife's recent accident and recovery and also that it was rumored that her husband was a recluse, had not been seen in public for years due to some strange illness which made him agoraphobic. In short, you could not have traveled to the center of Boston, let alone to Paris.

I am told your wife has no parents and you yourself sound bereft, and though I am not myself a Kaweshkar I have learned much from them; in this case, to revere their tradition, by giving refuge to you both as orphans. And am thus most willing to help you, sir, but can only do so if you are equally willing to share the truth with me. Then I will welcome you and your wife into my abode and my life with all the respect you deserve.

I await your further instructions.

Cordially,

Dr. Frano Vudarovic

P.S. There are no direct descendants of the man you call Henri, whose fate—as that of those kidnapped along with him—is a legend among the older members of this ethnic group. It is likely, however, that his blood—or that of brothers and sisters left behind—courses through some of the few pure Kaweshkar who still survive and are on their way to dying out.

His letter did not really surprise me. It was as if I had wanted to be found out, maybe had blatantly lied in order to receive an admonition demanding that, like the lost soul in the Kaweshkar myth, I pour out the truth to a stranger.

I began to feverishly write back. In English, naturally. After so many years of hiding from others, skulking in my room, entombed with Henri's face, it was a relief to express my story with no ornaments attached, freely and forthrightly.

When I was done—seven pages later—I felt fresh, renewed, invigorated—and more so when my letter was dispatched the next day. Remembering what Cunningham had said about the agent Makaruska who had interrogated Mrs. Hudson at the library and the possibility that we might be under some sort of surveillance, I asked my father—he did not demand an explanation and I did not furnish one—to mail it from a post office with no return address. It would be unlucky if our confidential information fell into the wrong hands. Given such a confession of my vulnerability, I did not doubt that Professor Vudarovic would defer to my directives and send any response care of my father at his work address.

It took a while for the reply to arrive, but when it did, the news gave me yet another lift.

If my wife and I were able to arrive in Punta Arenas, despite the problems that I had with travel, two Kaweshkar elders were ready to welcome us and perhaps perform a ceremony that might offer some relief to the dead and also, perhaps, to the living. There was only one thing puzzling them. They were not *owurken*, shamans—most of the ancient rituals were no longer practiced in a semi-urban environment where the young were frequently disbelievers. If I was indeed possessed, they feared they did not have the knowledge to dominate demons and drag them out of my body, even though certain remnants of the ceremonies, like the language itself, had been transmitted from the past. If they were to engage in a burial ritual, what exactly was being given its final resting place, given that the body itself had been lost, perhaps forever, as well as anything that might have belonged to the dead person?

I spent several days mulling over how to respond to this query, when my dad offered an answer.

The joy he had received from his daughter-in-law's New Year's Day recovery had gradually eroded as Cam's conduct became more obsessive and erratic. At first, perhaps channeling Mom, who would have counseled prudence, he reined himself in, but changed his mind when Vic called toward the end of July, confiding that Barry Cunningham was concerned about my wife's increasingly shrill demands, putting excessive pressure on the agency. Perhaps the blow to the head had not completely healed? But when my father at last voiced his doubts, he did not blame her but me for indulging her manias.

"And what would you have me do?"

"Burn them."

"Them?"

"The photos. And the documents, notes, photocopies, sources, the whole shebang, everything. But first of all, the photos. Down to the last one."

I didn't understand how that would help us—or get Cam to cease and desist from her research.

"The photos," Dad insisted. "That day, on your fourteenth birthday, remember how I pleaded with your mom to get rid of them? And she convinced me, damn it, to preserve them. Oh, if I'd—oh, I blame myself for not having had the balls to turn the fuckers to ashes right then and there, prove to this savage that he had no power over us. Instead, we let him grow each time we—"

"But you were the one demanding sessions, one after the other, so we could find out if he was still—"

"I know, I know. My mistake, stupid, idiotic, imbecile, to ignore my gut instinct. Keeping that poison in our home! And when your mom was murdered by him, I should have gone straight upstairs and burnt that savage like a witch, see how he liked being licked and consumed by fire like we were by his fucking face, blacken his fucking face, turn it to cinders, scattered to the wind, ground into pieces, drowned down a toilet. And I would lie awake at nights—by myself, by myself, reaching out a hand to where your mother used to sleep. Eyes wide open in the dark, thinking that those images were close by, in a box, seeping through the floorboards like a serpent, spitting at you, at me, at us. Gathering my courage to incinerate the motherfuckers, but always held back by the memory of Margaretta, her project, her hopes, not wanting to betray what she had dreamt of as a way out. And when Cam entered our lives, well, I quenched that desire, because she was like your mother. I could see that she was being seduced by this monster, but I fooled myself into believing she could tame him. And then he caused that amnesia—and even so, I held back, it wasn't fair to trash the photos when Cam couldn't protest, participate. And when she awakened, well, I thought maybe he's satiated. But now, now it's clear he's cast another spell on her, engaged legions of other fiends, and we have to intervene, drastically, you have to show him who's the boss, you're the one—not me—who has to do it."

He was wrong. That road of revenge and anger would not assuage Henri. It had led me nowhere for many forsaken years.

And yet, Dad's outburst supplied me with the response to the question the Kaweshkar elders had transmitted via Frano Vudarovic.

The photos!

Take them down to Henri's birthplace, the island where his life had been interrupted, where we would get the last Kaweshkar to honor Henri and his story. Even if it didn't free me, it was the right thing to do. His body might be irretrievable, but his images—they were the greatest outrage. Pierre Petit had made immortal and perennial his humiliating captivity. But we could reverse what was done to him, at least symbolically, at least indicate that we understood. Take him home.

But how to get me out of the country without my photo being snapped or my face filmed? All airports were under surveillance, with hidden and not-so-hidden cameras everywhere. Though Cam had hinted that she had some ideas about how to circumvent that security, probably had contrived some harebrained scheme to—No, I wanted to present her with solutions and not problems. She was right that I was depressingly dependent on her initiative. And besides, who knows if she would abandon her quest for Hindu acrobats in London and Tuaregs in St. Louis long enough to look for a way of smuggling me out of the United

States, she'd probably shelve my idea indefinitely—whereas if I had it all disentangled ... Which I did more promptly than I could have expected—thanks to some inspiration from Henri, who must have whispered the solution that had been staring me in the face, his and mine.

He had left his home by sea and we would get there by the same means, of course. Arrive in Tierra del Fuego on a boat, avoid troubled, congested public areas and Downey's presumably ubiquitous spies. For that we needed a ship seaworthy enough to get us there, run by somebody we could trust—if not with all our secrets, at least with the fact that we were not only in danger from treacherous currents or hurricanes but from human enemies as well. Someone ready to take risks and bend the law a little, with decades of experience sailing every ocean, preferably an older man whom no one would take on as a skipper anymore, perhaps slightly insane, ready to cater to the whims of a young couple who were more than a little insane themselves. Someone who wanted the job so urgently that he'd be loyal to a fault.

And how in the hell can you, Fitzroy Foster, unable to move out of your house, find someone like that?

The next day—it was a Sunday—Barry Cunningham providentially solved my problem.

He called to let me know that he happened to be in town. Would we mind if he stopped by to pay us a visit?

The first thing he did when he stepped up to the door was to flash Cam and me—Dad had gone fishing for the day—a piece of paper on which words had been written: at the top, in capital letters, ACT NORMAL, and below, *pretend I've come to talk about possible wedding plans for Laura and Vic. While a technician sweeps the house for listening devices. Nod if you agree.*

We nodded obediently and he flashed a signal to someone waiting in the Ford he'd rented. A tall, stooped, gloomy man emerged, blinked his eyes at us as a way of saying hello, and proceeded to make sure the house was clean. It was, I could have told Barry that. I did tell him that once we could speak freely, sure that nobody was eavesdropping.

"I'm always at home," I said. "I haven't left this place in years. So they—whoever they are—can't plant their devices."

Better safe than sorry, was Barry's clichéd but unassailable reply. More so, when we heard why he'd come to warn us personally of the discovery made by the detective assigned to Cam's genealogical inquiries, who had confirmed that everywhere he went a man had preceded him. The description of this person corresponded to Danny Makaruska, the agent who'd been to the library to interrogate Mrs. Hudson. Barry's source at the FBI had indicated that this was all part of a hush-hush Pentagon project—Operation Memory Redux—and that Camilla Foster Wood and her husband were among its targets.

This meant that someone could be listening in on our phone conversations, opening our mail, examining packages sent out. If we had revealed confidential information in recent calls or encounters, he suggested disseminating contradictory versions in the weeks ahead in order to confuse our pursuers.

As to the investigations initiated on Cam's behalf, progress was negligible. Collating all those names in search of a common lineage had turned up only a few possible leads and even those had fizzled out. He thought, frankly, that we were wasting money and resources. His firm had more normal cases to pursue, adultery and fraud and missing children, and hoped we didn't mind if he desisted from tracking down the far-flung progeny of circus impresarios and photographic hacks. If any other need happened to arise, he'd still be in town for a few days.

Neither Barry's warning nor his withdrawal from the investigation had any effect on Cam. On the contrary, she seemed even more resolved to stick it out, engaging another agency if necessary. "We're so close, Fitz, I can feel it." Nor did she care if Downey and his henchmen were spying on us—"So what else is new? Just proves that we're nearing success, that he's worried we'll get to all those people before he does."

I was, however, shaken. Did our adversaries know of my contact with Frano Vudarovic, had they intercepted my confession to him, his invitation to Punta Arenas? I would have to throw them off the scent, as Barry had counseled—one more task awaiting me, along with hiring a skipper and vessel to take us down there.

The next morning, as soon as Cam was on her way to the library to check out who had photographed a nine-year-old Hottentot girl exhibited in Paris and a phony Swahili tribesman in Basel and some early film by the Lumière brothers in Lyons, I called Barry Cunningham at his hotel and asked him to come over right away, see if he could help us get to Europe by sea.

As he had told us that the less he knew, the better, I didn't mind lying to him about our destination. Le Havre, I declared, we wanted to arrive in that port by early September—a voyage by sea, as the air might help my wife recover from her sickness. Our intention was to visit Zurich and then board the same boat and cruise the North Sea before heading to the Caribbean in time for the five-hundredth-anniversary celebrations. Perhaps he could locate a sea captain, preferably someone slightly shady?

A few hours later I called Barry, notifying him that it was Hamburg and not Le Havre we were sailing to, hoping that whoever was recording the call would take due notice.

"Hamburg, eh?" Barry said, emphasizing the word, he had probably guessed that this was some sort of trick on my part.

"Hamburg," I confirmed, relishing how Downey would receive the news, prepare his cohorts for a European excursion. He'd assume we were going there to interview the Hagenbecks and visit the Jardin d'Acclimatation and then on to Zurich to disinter some Kaweshkar body.

"I'll find the right person," Barry said.

That Captain London Wolfe was indeed the man for the job was obvious to me one week later during the first five minutes of an interview that was to last for several hours. Before we even sat down, in fact. He had not called ahead of time, just showed up at our door, banging on it as if funneling a gale. A tall and burly man, face burnished by wind and brine and sun, with a white beard out of some novel and knuckles the size of hammers.

"You must be Fitzroy Foster," he said, pumping my hand genially. "Was told you never leave the house so why bother letting you know I was on my way, huh? Though if you never leave your house, not sure why the hell you and your wife want to cross the Atlantic and cruise other seas and then sail around the Caribbean in hurricane season—and hey, a vessel before the end of August, not much time to get ready."

"Before I invite you in, Captain . . ."

"Name's Wolfe—Captain London Wolfe. Born in Nantucket, smelled the salt and the sand before I even knew the taste of milk, like six generations before me. Been sailing since I was a lad, lied to the skipper of my first boat about my age, he thought—or maybe not—that I was several years older—done every ship, every shoal, every sea. Served in the Coast Guard, sailed the Norway fjords and the depths of Sumatra, cruised the Great Lakes as master boson, speared sharks and hunted marlin, towed vessels in Korea and Singapore and Rio, can fix any electrical and mechanical problem, deal with boat maintenance and engineering, first aid and CPR certified, one-hundred-ton endorsement, you won't find anyone better equipped."

"Then why do you need this job so desperately, Captain Wolfe?"

He measured me as if I were lightning on the horizon. He must have liked what he saw or maybe he was, in fact, so desperate that he would have liked me if I had been Godzilla or mad Ahab.

"You asked for someone who knows the ropes but nobody will hire. Now, if you're not interested, let's not waste each other's time. I'll go my way and you—well, you'll never find anyone like me."

I was soon to find out how true this was.

We sat down together—after he had refused a cup of coffee, the tilt in his eyes telling me that there would be plenty of time to share beverages and warmth once we reached an agreement.

"So, you asked me a question, Fitzroy Foster, sir, and here's what I propose. You're hiding something and I'm hiding something. If you tell me the truth, then I'll retaliate. You tell me your plans—your real plans, not the bullshit you fed Barrington Cunningham—and I'll tell you why nobody else will hire me."

I liked that. Though no way was I going to reveal all my secrets to this stranger, certainly not the existence of Henri. Just as I did not expect him to come completely clean. But other things he would get to know in due course if we engaged his services, so I explained that Hamburg was a fraudulent endpoint, meant to fool anyone who meant us harm—here, the captain's features lit up with bliss at the possibility of a good brawl, I noticed approvingly how he clenched his robust fingers into a fist—and that as soon as we were in extraterritorial waters, we'd deviate from our course to Europe and head south until we reached Punta Arenas, so we could visit one of the most inaccessible islands on October 12.

"Patagonia," Wolfe exclaimed. His eyes—squinty from having faced windward for so long—opened a tad, brightening even more below a forest of bushy eyebrow outcrops. "Went there on my first ship, I was just fourteen—" And at the sound of that age my eyes began to sparkle as well, this was the sort of adventure I had dreamed of during my humdrum early adolescence—"when I escaped to sea, following in the wake of my pa and grandpa, whalers both of them from Nantucket. Climbed the masts on that whaleship, swabbed the decks, peeled potatoes, slept in the filthiest quarters reeking of bilge and seaweed, did anything the first mate commanded and several things that he didn't. I've been back many times since, in every capacity, I know those reefs and inlets, coming from the Atlantic and from the Pacific and under the worst gales, but also enjoyed some days that were gloriously sunny, fewer than anywhere on this earth, but oh so translucent and bright. So I'm your man. It was meant to be. I have contacts with the Coast Guard who will facilitate that change in course, I know somebody in the International Maritime Organization who will help us avoid collisions but not pass the information along, frustrating reconnaissance by the pursuers out to cause you mischief. I'm your man, I say. The Straits of Magellan! And I'd thought I'd die without braving them again."

I reminded him that we had a bargain: no deal until he opened his life to scrutiny.

"Fair's fair. I can't get a job because I was caught smuggling refugees into our resplendent land of the free. From El Salvador, to escape the civil war—a few years ago, you know, when … It was for money, I'll admit that any day, though the truth is I'm proud of saving those families caught in the middle of a massacre they wanted no part of and didn't understand. They caught me, my former buddies in the Coast Guard—caught me, but the charges couldn't stick. Some idiot had deported all the Salvadorans so the evidence was gone, they couldn't be cross-examined by my attorney who's as sharp as a cutlass. So I got off the hook on a technicality—far from heroic, but I'm not complaining. My license was reinstated, they couldn't deny me that, but the bureaucrats made sure nobody'd ever touch me again, not with a ten-foot anchor. So, enough said?"

What would Cam have done? She'd have pressed him for more. I needed to play the tough guy.

"What are you holding back?" I asked.

"Okay, okay. I smoke and I drink and I whore around—yeah, even at my age, but you don't want one of those goody-goody squeaky clean seafarers who swears that they're as pure as the Virgin Mary, blessed be her soul. So that's me: slightly over seventy, and no job. There you have it. I've told you as much as I'm willing to tell, just like you told me only a wee bit of the truth, but enough so that each of us knows who we're dealing with. You need a boat that can survive the roughest squalls and the most treacherous rocks on this planet? I can have the perfect craft in a few weeks' time, along with two mates I'd trust my mother's life with, if she were alive—one's a hand deck, the other's a cook, ready to help in case of an emergency. Just give me the word. And a deposit."

He had me and he knew it. But there was still one more condition he and his crew needed to agree to before we could sign a contract: no cameras on board, not one picture taken, not one.

London Wolfe shrugged. He'd seen stranger requests. He'd never been partial to photos anyway—they always lied.

I had never met anyone like him. An understatement. My tiny world of Cam and Dad and my two brothers was about to expand explosively with this stranger who seemed to have emerged from one of the adventure tales I had read as a child. Who knew such people really existed? And would Cam find him as attractive as I did? We shook hands and its roughness felt like yet one more auspicious sign that change was coming. It had been sailors like him who had handled the ropes and rigging and currents that had taken Henri from his home and now would carry his photos with us to the southernmost tip of our hemisphere. Would Wolfe be able to deliver on his promises?

Two weeks later he returned and I had the response in my own rather more delicate hands. A series of pictures of a magnificent cruising sloop. One sail, two diesel engines, three cabins—one for me and my wife, a smaller one for him, the last one with berths for the two crew members, toilet a bit compressed, but what the hell ... A Delanta Dehler model, forty feet. Slick, sturdy, nobly built—another auspicious sign—in 1981, slipping into the sea at about the time Henri was slipping into the waters of my mind. And with a name—*The Southern Cross*—that made my heart leap. Snug inside if it was raining, ample decks if the day was bright with blue and the cloudless nights full of stars.

I tried to contain my excitement, sound business-like.

"And how long would it take to reach Punta Arenas?"

"Thirty-three days, eighteen hours, and two minutes—at ten knots a day, but taking into account weather delays, stopping for repairs and fuel, water and supplies, calculate a month and a half to get there by early October, as per plan."

I computed all this rapidly in my head. "But that means we'd have to leave by this Saturday at the latest. Four days from now."

He nodded his head, yes, that's what it meant, adding: "We'll tell the authorities that before we head for Europe we'll sail the Caribbean first and then my contact at the IMO will cover for us when we keep going south. Just the right window of time to escape Hurricane Andrew as it diminishes and before Bonnie, that vixen of a storm, blows us to kingdom come."

"Good plan," I said, as if I understood what he was talking about. "Saturday's fine."

The captain passed me a sheaf of papers to be read and signed, along with a budget detailing overall costs. This little adventure was going to cost us close to $300,000—if we did not run into any unforeseen trouble.

The enormity of that sum, so nakedly exposed, startled me out of my grandiose reveries. Was it worth it, to spend so lavishly, based on a capricious intuition on my part, a plan not so much as whispered to the woman I loved and who would be asked to join me on the high seas four days from now? All this money, time, and energy expended, and there was no guarantee—quite the contrary, really, given the record of the last eleven years—that taking the photos to Tierra del Fuego and burying them in some island which might not even be Henri's birthplace would appease my visitor. Wasting such a fortune might be deemed by Henri as proof that I had learned nothing, was just a spoiled brat who deserved to be persecuted by those eyes till the day of his death and beyond. He had been abducted for money and photographed for money and raped for money and touted through Europe for money and probed for money and now my money was supposed to save me, buy my freedom. How would the men and women and children of the world, enslaved, starving, dying for lack of water, dying from curable diseases, judge me? How would Cam? And Henri? Wouldn't he have preferred that I use the funds to help the few indigenous people left in Patagonia?

I must have gone pale, shown signs of dizziness, because Captain Wolfe had to steady me with his strong arms.

"Having second thoughts, eh, lad? Can't say I blame you. It's one thing to get all excited about going to sea, another to face the storm when there's nothing to save you but your own two hands and whatever mates are by your side and just damn luck. Lord knows, the South is calling to me, but if you don't feel up to it, just pay me for my two weeks of prep and I'll go and spend it at a nasty dive I haunt in Boston and then it'll be goodbye—as long as you also compensate my buddies Jim and Wellington. No harm done, except to my dreams and yours—and mine have been frustrated enough times for me to be vaccinated by now. Yours, well, I won't pry, but I can recognize suffering when I glimpse it on a man's face. Whether this voyage will placate whatever demons are plaguing you, that I can't say and you'll surely never know. Unless you sign on the dotted line."

I signed, of course I signed. Feverishly, until every consent had been agreed to, the lease of the ship, the bond in case anything happened to it, the insurance, the three contracts with Wolfe and his mates, the escrow fund to cover future costs, an array of fees we'd encounter on our way, I signed each document with a flourish and then a hefty check, and handed the whole lot to him.

"Now," I said, and my hand was trembling but not as much as my heart, "there's only one thing left for me to do."

"Oh. What's that?"

"I need to tell my wife we're departing in four days' time."

"She doesn't know?"

"Not a clue."

"You're a brave man, Fitzroy Foster, I'll say that much for you. Though I wouldn't want to be in your shoes when the missus hears what you've got her into without her say-so."

And now I really panicked.

That independence of mine that gave me such pride, it broke the unspoken pact and consonance we had automatically established since those first strokes in the water of a pool more than half a lifetime ago. Now to be tested in waters that we would navigate under the guidance of an old man whose main merit was his expunged criminal record. I was putting Cam's lovely, lithe body, not to mention my more cumbersome and awkward one, at the mercy of rough waves and someone I really knew nothing about. I could already hear her: *You what? Three hundred thousand dollars? Pretend you're going to Hamburg and end up in*

Patagonia? Back out, Fitz. There's got to be a clause that allows it. Or do you really believe I'll just hop on an unknown boat with a drunken, whoring smuggler? With all those photos of yours and Henri? Giving Downey the chance to grab you?

"Can you wait here a sec?" I said to the skipper—and rushed upstairs to the attic. The photos were there, nestled in a box. The imagery and itinerary of my life. Those eyes of his that had bewitched me and that now wanted to convince me to take them thousands of miles away. A final act of perdition, that was Henri's deepest desire, to destroy me as he had done with my mother and tried to do with Camilla. Burn them, my father had urged, burn the damn things and be rid of the specter forever.

I closed my eyes, beset by turmoil and confusion.

My hand reached into the box and extracted a photo.

Filled with apprehension, I forced my eyelids to open and he was there like a corpse or a newborn child, as unspeaking and demanding as the first time we had met, almost eleven years ago. And I knew that I could not burn him anymore than set fire to myself and my loved one and our home.

I would follow my plan through to the end.

Only one way to cast aside all doubts, make it impossible for Cam to persuade me to withdraw from this mad scheme: to do something even more foolish and bold than the voyage on *The Southern Cross* itself. I scribbled a short letter and then placed it in the box, alongside the thousand and one images of Henri monstrously twinned with my body. Next I wrapped it with brown paper, taped the edges and seams and addressed it to Frano Vudarovic at the University in Punta Arenas, Chile. And asked Captain London for a favor. "Can you send off this box by express mail? Taking care that nobody's following you and that you pay with cash, as credit cards can be traced. Can you do that for me?"

He accepted with alacrity.

Cam would be, I thought, a harder nut to crack.

Downey, of all people, unwittingly smoothed the way. He had, that very afternoon, tracked Cam down at the library.

I had never seen her so agitated.

"He knows Barry's detectives have not come up with any other victims like his daughter, he knows Barry came to visit, he calculated that now we might be more receptive to his offer to join forces. He wants to use you, Fitz, I knew it, I knew it, didn't I tell you what his plans were? He's got some horrible experiments in store, tap your blood, sample your skin, scrape your retina, graft your hair, extract marrow from your spine, he'll—"

"Wait, wait, wait. He said he intended to do all that to me?"

"He didn't need to. I know what he's up to. He spoke about his daughter, how she could have helped him stop the invasion if she hadn't lost hope, but there were others out there, close by, very close by, he said, who could thwart the enemy before they get their hands on the process—sometimes he seemed to be speaking about the Russians or the Chinese, other times he hurled insults at savage creatures who were infiltrating cameras and photos and synapses."

"Did he tell you anything else about his research?"

"He said that he had just recently detected the first tentative signs of a pandemic, a game changer that made his work more urgent, something he calls the next stage."

"The next stage?"

"He spoke about finding some combination in the blood, the bones, the optical membrane, an aberrant gene. That if we could prove it was recurrent, if we had enough cases for a scientific comparison—just as I had told you, right, how important it was that you not be a unique specimen, right?—if we discovered this mutation, we could stop the plague from becoming widespread, advance to the next stage, our faces, our faces, he said over and over, and not just the photos. He grew more excited as he talked, as if he'd forgotten who he was speaking to—we can do it, we can do it, he kept repeating."

"Do what?"

"Isolate the strain of that virus so as to find an antidote before somebody introduces it into our food or water supply. Worse than the Black Death, he said, our whole way of life could collapse into chaos, the social fabric that holds together our civilization. And then you know what he said? He said he couldn't wait to meet you, because he'd heard you were so brilliant at computing and that you'd find the solution. And then he took a step back and looked at me, leered at me, as if stripping me naked, Fitz, I'm not embroidering this, and said, *No, not find. Your husband won't find the solution. Fitzroy Foster* is *the solution.*"

"And that makes you sure he wants to get his hands on me."

"But he won't. I won't let him. As long as you stay put, don't venture forth from this house, we'll be fine, we'll be protected."

I took a deep breath. We had exchanged roles. Here was my love demanding that I never leave the nest and here was I, about to tell her that four days from now we would be on a small vessel on our way to Patagonia. A deep breath as a prelude to revealing everything I had been up to while she was busy chasing down duplicate victims. She listened quietly, anxiety and alarm draining from her face as if my words were a transfusion of energy and courage and serenity—could this really be me formulating these plans?—there was none of the fury or dismay I had expected.

She took it all in her stride.

"Good for you," she said. "It's wacky, of course, and risky as hell, and will probably end in shambles, but it sure makes sense. More than what I've been doing, can't dispute that. Good for you," she repeated, "and also for me. I love it that you've fixed this up, that you did it without my help." And then: "But not through the Panama Canal, right? Down the Atlantic Coast."

"Like Henri," I said. "The same seas he was forced to cross . . ."

"But in reverse, undoing his route, yes."

She was back, she had returned to me, the two of us were again thinking the same thoughts!

"Only one more question before I start packing—winter clothes, as it rains all the time—what did you write to this Professor Vudarovic in your letter?"

"That we'd arrive there by boat a few days before October twelfth. That we felt that the photos were safer with him and the elders of the Kaweshkar in case anything happened to us—so that if we did not show up, they could go ahead with the ceremony. To please be careful because we were under surveillance and he might be as well. And I apologized for burdening him with all of this, but he had said he would welcome me if I told him the truth, so I was only appealing to Xolás and the tradition he had invoked."

Four days later, on a gray imperfect misty dawn, we set sail from New Bedford for the islands Magellan had first sighted and claimed for a European king, the islands that Henri's ancestors had inhabited for thousands of years.

Without knowing who was awaiting us there.

NINE

"All we can do is return. We have no more tasks. Our days are over. Think of us, do not erase us from your memory, do not forget us."

—The Maya Book of Counsel

We arrived in Punta Arenas with barely three days to spare, on October 9, 1992, a Friday morning.

The voyage had been both more and less eventful than anybody could have forecast.

It had been no trouble to sneak on board *The Southern Cross* in the middle of the night, nor did the port authorities or the immigration and customs people give us a hard time, hardly casting a cursory glance at our passports and certainly not questioning our navigational plans, probably judging us to be a couple of spoiled American yuppies out to spend Daddy's money.

And just as Captain Wolfe had promised, our change in course, he announced triumphantly, was duly noted without questions from the maritime organizations. It was our business that we headed south once we passed Martinique, instead of veering north-northeast. Not a sign, either, of any watercraft fol-

lowing in our wake and we doubted we were important enough
to warrant satellite spying.

The weather, for the most part, cooperated to make the
journey glorious and without major perils, though with enough
rain and choppy seas to give us a thrill. And even a scare, when
we hit a squall that seemed to threaten to sink our ship, and
damaged the foresail. So there was some time lost when we had
to undergo repairs in Montevideo, and also one tense moment
when we were accosted by an Argentine patrol refusing us entry
to Bahía Blanca, but our captain and crew did not seem fazed
by this obstacle—they simply headed to the nearby Falklands to
restock before the long haul down toward Antarctica.

"Just as we planned," London Wolfe used to exclaim at dinner
when he would show us the nautical miles advanced as we
sat down to spicy dinners, prepared with flair by Wellington's
Jamaican hands, whose specialty was the fresh fish caught by Jim,
a tall and cheerful Australian who ended up teaching me the joys
of struggling against a forty pounder so that I might become the
main provider of that fare. Like Hemingway in these very seas,
Jim said. And I answered in my mind, like Henri, like Henri!

If the itinerary was what the captain had minutely planned,
the exhilaration of the voyage itself was a surprise.

Until I stood at the bow of the boat that first morning, holding
hands with Cam, the canvas in the sails flapping from the mast
at our back and filling my expanding lungs and heart; until
the spray dashed onto that skin of mine that had been drying
and withering in the seclusion of my room; until the eyes that
had blinked away at computer screens and mathematical algorithms and binary codes greeted the tinges and hues and shades
of waves rippling on the stern and the cathedral of the sky so
clear and lofty; until the ears that for eleven years had only registered nature through recalcitrant birds chirping above dreary

urban streets began to decipher the sound of wind and seagull and the cries of our first dolphins urging us on toward our destiny; until we tasted the salt and the unfathomable depths, until then and so much more, I had not really measured the inhuman deprivation suffered by my senses. That Cam herself had never boarded a boat in her life, that this was also an adventure for her, everything startling and unexpected and enchanting, what a gift to again be sharing, like when we had first met, the rhythm of reality.

That communion with each other and delight in the ocean billows was enhanced by the growing health of our young and robust muscles, too long confined to stuffy, overheated or air-conditioned rooms. Despite the tossing and rolling and heaving of the ship—and it would get worse, Wolfe gleefully admonished, worse than the storm we had survived, worse, he insisted, the closer we got to Cape Horn—despite so much turbulence neither of us was attacked by the sort of seasickness that had floored poor Charles Darwin when he had embarked on the *Beagle* in 1831. So bad that the young naturalist could only combat it stretched out horizontally on a table for days, his nausea worsened by the screams of sailors being whipped with the cat o' nine tails, a punishment that my namesake, Captain Robert Fitzroy, imposed upon his crew to ensure discipline.

I knew about this barbaric practice—and Darwin's disgust at it—because my father had given us several books as a present before we left. Cam insisted that we confide the real itinerary to him, though we had been careful not to divulge fully what we intended to do in Tierra del Fuego. Instead, I explained that among the Kaweshkar a dead person's possessions couldn't be inherited by the living, even his canoe left to rot by the seashore, clothes, ornaments, amulets, his very hut, consumed by flames. "Brilliant," he said, assuming we had taken his advice to heart and were determined to finally burn the photos. "The only thing he left behind were his images—so you get rid of them in the place where he was born and poof, he's gone as well!" He'd been so pleased with the idea that he'd bought us some reading material. "The sea," he exclaimed, ever the advertising man, "doesn't exist only as nature. It's also something created by the mind, the pens and imaginations of men who explored it and then sold it to readers who craved going to sea, investing in oceanic trade. You won't only be navigating water. History, you'll be navigating history."

The diaries of Columbus, the journal kept by Pigafetta as he rounded the earth with Magellan, Darwin's logbook of his own years on the *Beagle*, an anthology of sea tales, and, to top it all off, *Moby-Dick*.

"Thousands of pages of ballast," Captain Wolfe snorted, when he saw our little library. "Didn't I warn you to pack light?" But despite protesting that it was a shame to be reading about an ocean when it was there to be experienced, he ended up enjoying the historical references we came up with.

"Do you know why this is called Puerto Plata?" I asked him as we docked at that port of the Dominican Republic in order to refuel and stock up—and celebrate my twenty-fifth birthday!

"Because they charge you lots of *plata*," he answered, rubbing his fingers together significantly, "moola, doubloons, pesos, for everything."

And opened the narrow straits of his eyes wide when I enlightened him. The natives in another part of that island had told Columbus—eager to get him to sail elsewhere—that there was a bay nearby where the land was made entirely of silver. And, in effect, it had seemed to the approaching Spanish fleet as if the shore was ablaze with precious metals—one more illusion foiling Columbus, produced by the sun reflected on untold leaves as they fluttered and swayed in the breeze, but the name, silver, *plata*, had survived the ages.

"A mockery now, that name," Wellington remarked, as he peeled some potatoes for a luncheon chowder with which we would continue celebrating, after the walnut-crusted waffles he'd cooked that morning, this special September 11—and pointed his knife bitterly toward the hordes of beggar boys diving next to a nearby wharf for coins flicked by passengers on a gigantic ocean liner. "Go ashore, follow those kids to their hovels or the streets where they're exploited by pimps, and you'll see the face of human misery. Some of them are probably even called Cristóbal, in honor of Columbus. Columbus, my black ass!"

My priority was not the face of human misery but keeping the face that Henri had bequeathed me from thousands of tourist cameras roving the town in search of a souvenir. Cam did descend, mainly to call my dad and enthuse about the Caribbean, where we'd tarry a bit soaking in the sun while we waited for Hurricane Bonnie to race by. And not to worry if he didn't hear from us till we reached Cadiz at the end of September. Taking care to speak extra loud to throw Downey's aides off the trail in case they were eavesdropping. We didn't want our pursuer guessing we were on our way to Brazil and would soon cross the equator.

The equator! That moment when we passed into the southern part of our planet on our *Southern Cross* boat. So ecstatic that we did not resent the dunking the crew gave us, chucking both neophytes overboard. We astonished them by swimming together, stroke by stroke, like two superb swordfish, round and round the unwavering ship. Just one more form and shape and manifestation of togetherness—to be renewed on dark moonless nights in our berth, keeping as quiet as clams as we let our lower bodies express what the day had drifted into us and left behind, muffling our own whimpers and endearments and especially the heartbeats that could have wakened a regiment. Trying to still the sound of our lovemaking not only out of a desire for privacy, but also because it seemed prudent not to flaunt my privileges to the other males on board. Until Wolfe took me aside one twilight evening. "Not to worry," he said. "Enjoy! You're young and we will be relieved in the next port just as we were in the last one. If you were not married, I'd show you the most affectionate whores this side of paradise. To each his own."

And thus did the days pass so placid and pleasantly, the nights with such warmth and passion, that I almost forgot the purpose of our mission.

As soon, however, as we hit Brazil and entered the bay of Sao Salvador and saw the docks overflowing with dark-skinned bodies, stevedores and fruit merchants and prostitutes, Henri reminded us of his existence. As did Darwin in the journals Cam and I were reading. He had recorded the words of despair uttered by an African slave in that very port of Bahía, *If I could but see my father and two sisters once again, I should be happy. I can never forget them*, anticipating like an obscene echo what Henri must have felt fifty years later.

That was how South America greeted us, with black faces in Bahía and black memories of lost souls, millions of them, who had never returned home, in whose name, perhaps, Henri was rebelling, motivating me yet again to navigate toward a funeral that he and they had never been afforded in their place of birth.

And Henri came to me again a few days later in Rio, though for different reasons. In this city, I said to Cam somberly, my mother had landed on her way to the Amazon. I felt like jumping ship and walking the streets she had walked a week before her death. She had written, in a last letter sent from this very place, how the vitality and beauty of Rio animated her, its botanical garden, the Cristo Redentor, the Pão de Açucar, the wide beaches of Ipanema bursting with surfers and youngsters playing soccer, *oh my darling Roy, I took photos of them, soon you'll be as free as they are. The city of the River of January, Rio de Janeiro, tells me that I will not, cannot, fail.*

And here we were, fulfilling her promise, bringing Henri inside me to the South, ever to the South, Montevideo and the Falklands, until finally cooler winds and larger and more permanent waves and far-off cliffs announced that we were at last nearing Patagonia, nearing Henri. The same seas he had crossed and gales that had said goodbye to him. With this difference: no fires from hill to hill that had alerted Darwin to the existence of the savages he could hardly conceive of as human, no fires now from one clan to the other communicating the arrival of *percherai*, strangers, no fires because there were no longer any hands to light them, any lips to pronounce astonishment at the intrusion of foreign ships, no eyes to examine the invaders with curiosity. And this other difference: Henri's ocean had not been choking with plastic, he had not passed carcasses of fish and birds poisoned by the slick from oil rigs, and the sun in his days had not been dangerous to the human skin, his ozone was not depleted, there was no rust crusting the waves. How would he have grieved to see the ocean which had given his people sustenance for millennia turned into a garbage dump, the sewer of the world. Perhaps he would have considered that crime more unforgivable than his kidnapping—that violence, after all, had affected eleven Kaweshkar but at least back then the sea had remained intact, the great mother had not yet been assaulted. "Maybe that is what he has come to warn us about," Cam whispered, divining, as always, my thoughts. "Maybe that is what he wants us to understand. That we shall all become *percherai*, strangers on this planet, unless we stop this madness."

I could only hope he had such benevolent intentions in mind.

At any rate, it was not to sadden him that we had come so far. Better to let him drink in, through us, the scenery that would have still been recognizable to him, made, as we were, of the same clay. The cone of snow on jagged distant mountains, the blue glaciers rearing out of the water like white leviathans, dark ragged clouds rolling down between gulfs in the fjords, strong outlines marked on a lurid sky. And the cries of gulls and far away, when a lull in the wind allowed, the howling of some animal. He would have welcomed the way sea and coast merged under a rain so icy that each drop seemed to pierce the skin—we were not protected, as he and his people had been, by the thick oil from the seals, we used deodorant and soap and indoor plumbing, we had forgotten what it meant to be at the mercy of the elements, we had forgotten that we were once mineral.

For us, in love with the color green above all, biking from a young age by the lush rivers of New England, the bareness of Patagonia was both repellent and attractive, those naked islands rising from the sea with trees and bushes scant, scant and blasted and stunted and gnarled. How had Henri ever survived? We were in October and the Southern Hemisphere days were growing longer and the seas rougher, testing our endurance with waves that washed over the vessel as if it were a toy boat, and then, a sudden calm and the springtime sun would peep through the overlaying of cloud upon cloud, once in a while the wind would die down and the rain would cease for a few minutes, how could anyone survive in a lone canoe during winter nights seventeen hours long, when the temperatures dropped and smothered the tundra and froze the fingers that had learned to carve utensils from the great marine mammals, how could these tribes have survived the extraordinary hostility of nature only to be destroyed by their fellow humans, hunted down, exterminated, and, in the case of some, carried off, never to return? The wrong question, the wrong way of looking at this land of fire with no fire, this land of the Patagons without any Patagons left, this land, this land—the wrong question because he had loved it here, this was his home, this was what he had yearned for on those warm Parisian nights and then in Berlin during the autumn and finally in that aseptic bed in a Zurich hospital as the snow fell outside, as his life ebbed he had dreamt of these channels, these archipelagos, these breakers he knew as we knew the television channels and the avenues and neon of our cities. And perhaps, if we were lucky or deserving enough, some representative of his people would greet us not as strangers but as friends come to learn, come to listen under the rain that had been his constant companion.

That is what Cam and I thought, promised ourselves, hoped for, as *The Southern Cross* approached Punta Arenas. It had started to snow—more mellow than the icicles that had fallen upon our ship just the night before and driven us shivering to our cabin. The soft white flakes brought with them a descending hush that seemed a benediction after the relentless sleet hounding us since our ship first ventured into the Straits of Magellan.

Chilean policemen and customs officials were waiting at the wharf. They were less perfunctory and far more inquisitive than their American counterparts; London Wolfe had no buddies in this country. What were we here for? How long did we intend to stay? Our place of residence? Anything to declare?

Cam and I, with the assistance of captain and crew, had rehearsed our answers. We'd come to see the baby penguins hatch, streaks of yellow already adorning their necks, and when we'd had our fill of that marvel, maybe explore some islands. Staying no more than a few days, at the hotel Cabo de Hornos on the Plaza Muñoz Gamero. As to declarations, I had to bite my tongue not to tell them, declare to the winds of Patagonia the joy my wife and I felt at alighting with someone hidden inside me who'd been stolen from these very shores over a century ago thanks to the lack of oversight of the Chilean state, but I kept quiet, smuggled Henri across the border, as I chortled to Cam later, once we had collapsed on the ample bed at the Cabo de Hornos.

That bed, the hot shower, the champagne promptly delivered by room service, the radiators steaming warmth, the phone, the radio, the television, the gym on the top floor and the bar at the bottom—and outside, streets with cars and lamplights, asphalt and discotheques. A city! The southernmost of the world, with all the charm of a frontier town—it reminded me of settlements I had seen in Westerns—but stocked with everything modernity, not to mention tourists, demanded.

After more than forty days at sea—like Noah!—to step into a late-twentieth-century town, steady and dependable and civilized, was a shock. I had grown accustomed to sharing Henri's view of the world—if not from a canoe, at least from the perspective of a skiff that, in spite of our provisions and gadgets, was still at the mercy of massive waves and sudden spasms and perils of the weather. So that, as I let the devices and luxuries sink in, I was still able to access, though with increasing remoteness, Henri's wide-eyed amazement when he had seen Hamburg and then a train and then Paris, the dizziness he must have felt at finding himself in a universe so removed from his previous experience. It lasted only a short while, this sharing in Henri's bewilderment—yes, that was the word, because for him the industrially produced world was a wilderness and his tumultuous ocean was normality—whereas we belonged on this hotel bed, we were being returned to our privileges and comfort zone and could not truly understand how divorced he must have felt from his new world.

And even so, something of his disorientation and perplexity

remained with us. Just scant hours ago, we had been exposed to a hostile environment, real danger no more than a compass point away, a turn of bad luck. Aware of how easy it would be for our fleeting civilization to melt away, for my body to become like Henri's and Cam's like Lise's, Adam and Eve at the start of time, naked under the last savage ribs of the Andes. The only thing really separating me from my visitor, I realized, was that he did not require cameras and computers and combustion engines and satellite readings to get through the day. If ever a catastrophe swept away all the inventions mankind had placed between itself and the encroaching jaws of nature, we would all have to become Henri or perish. Virchow, Hagenbeck, Pierre Petit, Darwin himself, would not last a week if stranded on these bleak beaches, all their belief in progress and commerce and improvement and industry, mere smoke and mirrors, ephemeral as a dream. In that respect, Henri was far superior to them—and certainly to me. One had only to consider him, not as a piece of anatomy to be prodded in a lab or a spectacle to be gaped at, but as a wondrous human perfectly adapted to his circumstances, admirably adapted, highly intelligent and gloriously free.

If we had merged transiently with him during our voyage and our common, underlying humanity had been revealed and prized, yet now that these pillows fluffed our hair while we viewed the Straits through double-paned windows manufactured in some factory far to the North, another lesson, a lesson about the distance that separated us, was being learned. In effect, I had no desire to live forever chained to a boat and buffeted by chance. I was a man of my time and clime and this room was paid for by my skills at coding and Photoshopping, and Cam was wedded to her microscope as much as to me, loved splicing and enzymes as much as she loved the body of her Fitzroy. It was a delusion that we could ever truly go back to what he was and how he had endured. I should be grateful that my prosperity had given me occasion to draw near to Henri under that rain, but I had to acknowledge how inseparably far we were from his precipices. He was unreachable and not ever returning.

All of this we explained that very evening to Frano Vudarovic as we dined with him on the delicacies of the zone prepared by Elba, his lovely, freckle-faced wife: the king crab *centolla*, then *cordero magallánico* with local potatoes and greens, topped off by a choice between British bread pudding with homegrown berries or an apple strudel. They must have known that, in spite of whatever wonders the cook on board our ship had been able to rustle up, we'd be famished for this kind of hearty home fare—and for the conversation with someone willing to discuss my dilemma without subterfuges.

Vudarovic understood what had guided me to him more intensely than I could have hoped for. Now that we were face-to-face he could admit that his cordial reaction to my desire to atone obeyed deep, personal reasons.

A kidnapping, he said, had brought me and Cam to Tierra del Fuego. Well, a kidnapping—of a different kind—had done the same for him. In 1881, the same year that Henri and his fellows were abducted and taken to Europe, Frano's great-grandfather, Anton Vudarovic, had fled that very Europe in the opposite direction. Perhaps their boats had even crossed somewhere in the Atlantic. Like many Croatian males, he was escaping the forcible impressment into the Austro-Hungarian Army. Most of those migrants wound up in the nitrate fields of Chile's Atacama desert. But Anton was also anxious to evade the fate of his family, dedicated since Roman times, so legend had it, to mining salt from the extensive shallows of their native island Pag—*Vudarovic* meant "son of a miner" in Croatian. So Frano's great-grandfather jumped ship in Punta Arenas and let his brother and other compatriots continue north up the Pacific to seek fortune in drier climes. Anton worked for a while at one of the recently launched sheep haciendas, but once gold was discovered, he drifted into his forefathers' profession: with his mining experience, he soon amassed enough capital to marry and establish a shop catering to his former gold digging comrades, as well as to whalers and the general public.

"I am the beneficiary of that prosperity," Frano Vudarovic said, puffing on a pipe that jutted out from a prominent brown beard. "My university education, both here and abroad, derives from that business and the generations that kept it going. Moreover, I was emboldened to become a historian by my great-grand-father's activities during the three years before he set up shop, which family legend vaguely rumored to have been infernal. When I tried to find out what had been so hellish about that time, all I received back were evasive answers—and soon resolved to arm myself with instruments to force the past to reveal its secrets. Later, I learned from my mentor at Sussex, the great John Lyell, that history seldom responds to our queries. History, he would say, is like a cemetery with unmarked graves, quiet and unyielding but if we look hard enough we will always find atrocities and victims, and they are far more interesting than the perpetrators. Was Anton one of the latter? I'd like to think he had no direct involvement in the killing fields of Patagonia, no blood on his hands. It would be sad if he had escaped from using the emperor's Mausers against his fellow Europeans only to turn them on defenseless Patagonian Indians who were massacred by the thousands. Once back in Punta Arenas, knowing where to look, I noted that there was no reference to Anton's participation in that violence in newspaper articles or letters. Though he most certainly sold the guns that did the killing. I saw the ledgers: between November 1893 and December 1895 he provided the

Sociedad Explotadora de Tierra del Fuego with twenty-seven rifles and eight revolvers, all of them .44 caliber, and twelve thousand five hundred bullets for the rifles, nine hundred fifty for the revolvers. And the knives, biscuits, fishing nets, clothes and boots, everything that was used in the mass slaughter on the sheep farms and on the nomad islands. An accomplice. And so, my dear friends, like you, I have something to atone for, a past that drives me."

The sorrow we saw in his eyes had been there for a good part of his sixty-odd years.

"And yet, I ask myself, who is not the product of some crime committed in the past? I ask if there was ever a dynasty built without a murder, the pain of someone else, the erasing of that guilt? If so, then what matters is not what your ancestors did—which cannot be undone—but how you react to that, what you freely do, as Sartre once noted, with the life that was given to you. And here I am, the great-grandson of Anton Vudarovic, dedicated to keeping alive the heritage of the people he, at the very least, collaborated in exterminating." And now that sorrow of his turned into a sort of bizarre elation. "So there's the question for you, the real question that Henri might ask if he were alive, because he belongs to a gentle and not a vindictive race: what will you do with this knowledge you have acquired, this experience, this journey?"

Before I could open my mouth, Cam intervened: "First he has to be free enough to walk down a street, make a life for himself."

Frano Vudarovic nodded, begged our pardon. "Yes, that's what matters now, you're right, that's why you've come."

"And they're ready, the Kaweshkar elders are ready to help?"

"They'll do what they can," Frano said. "The Kaweshkar Council—an entity that's only a few years old—has given its approval for a ceremony near Puerto Edén, where the few surviving members of the ethnic group now live. We'll leave for that island on Sunday the eleventh—give you tomorrow to rest after your long voyage. We should arrive well in time for your October twelfth deadline. The photos are already there."

"And they understand the significance of the photos, the date, our request?"

Frano sighed. "You know, Fitzroy, your life has revolved for many years around the past, your head turned backward. But the remaining Kaweshkar are concerned with the present. Like most people on this earth they want health, education, access to goods and transportation, and, particularly, security. Given the choice of lobbying, some decades ago, for a teacher who could teach the children elements of the Kaweshkar tongue or a police station in Puerto Edén, they went for the station. Memory is a strange creature, my friends. The massacres, the abductions, the epidemics in the missions, the bounty hunters, the onslaught of the whalers, the extermination of the sea lions, what happened a hundred years ago, that is the stuff of legend and deep trauma, but the fears of the Kaweshkar today are of more recent vintage. What the older people remember is how they were, for decades, the prey of bandits, the worst sort of scum, hiding out in the impenetrable labyrinth of coves and inlets. These strangers— many from the island of Chiloe, farther north—would force the natives to fish and hunt for them, ply the women with alcohol and trinkets, rape them. Theft became common and even murder—the kind of violence unheard of among them at the time of Henri's kidnapping. So defending themselves from law- lessness was a priority—like you, they have understood that first you survive the most imminent danger, get rid of the shackles, so as to be free to pursue other goals and needs."

"Needs? What sort of needs do they have now?" Cam asked. "Perhaps we might assist."

"Jobs. They're lobbying for a communal fishing area, an exclusionary zone that would forbid the big companies from depleting the marine reserves, a strategy designed to eliminate middlemen so artisanal craft can be sold directly in Punta Arenas and Puerto Natales. Not much you can do to bolster that project. But there's the prospect of an ethnical kindergarten which might revive the indigenous tradition among the younger generation, as well as a new grammar and oral history they are working on with me—I was so bold as to pledge, on your behalf, a donation."

"It was the right thing to do," I said, though I also expressed a certain discomfort at the thought that we were, well, buying our way into the hearts of the surviving Kaweshkar.

"Oh, they're authentically interested in helping you," Frano said. "Anyone who cares about them and the mistreatment they've suffered, anyone who values their identity, at times more than they themselves do, is welcome. But they have come to comprehend, through tales told by their grandparents and their own experience, that tomorrow you, the visitors, will be gone and that they'll be left with the legacy of centuries of exploitation. They have no illusions as to a permanent relationship with you. They don't expect someone like you—or me—to save them. They may even see you as part of the problem, rather than a solution."

"What do you mean?"

"If, once the ceremony is over, a youngster from Puerto Edén were to ask for a lift to Punta Arenas, how would you respond?"

"That we'd be delighted, how else should we respond?"

"All over the earth," Frano Vudarovic said, "villages like Puerto Edén are becoming depopulated, the young are migrating to nearby towns and from there to cities and from those cities to other countries, the largest migration in history, culminating a process that started massively with the Industrial Revolution. The Kaweshkar Council keeps demanding more connections to the world, more traffic than one ferry a week. But the road that brings modernity is the same road the young use to leave. And you are, inevitably, with your curiosity and your need for a ceremony from them, with your devices and latest gadgets and clothes, a beacon and a magnet and even, once you agree to transport one of their people to Punta Arenas, a facilitator of the process that is erasing the universe that your Henri inhabited, erasing him from memory. The young are leaving now, not because they are being kidnapped, as in the past, but because they're seduced by what people like you and I can offer. Wouldn't you be seduced? Don't you want to be free of your visitor so you can enjoy your own century rather than be imprisoned in his? Wouldn't Henri want something similar if he were alive today? But we should talk more about this in Puerto Edén. You'll see for yourselves on October twelfth where that inaugural visit by Cristóbal Colón has landed us."

I did not have to wait that long. That very night I got a taste—a bitter one—of the dilemma he was describing.

His glum diagnosis of the illness besieging the indigenous people of Tierra del Fuego did nothing to dampen our enthusiasm for the mission we had launched. Back at the hotel, Cam took me in her arms and snuggled me under the covers and we were able to voice our cries and sweet talk so unavoidably subdued during those many days in the tossing sea. The expression through throat and mouth and lips and teeth had opposite effects on Cam and me. It exhausted her and she fell asleep almost immediately, whereas I felt awake and alert and marvelously alive.

A while passed, with her soft black hair breathing on my shoulders—and when I realized I would not be able to nod off, I rose from the bed.

There was a chill in the air, despite the radiator going full blast, and rather than blunder back into pajamas, I got dressed—perhaps I could go down to the bar and enjoy a nightcap, perhaps the captain was there and he could inform me more about Sunday's itinerary.

I looked out the window at the wide expanse of the city and the waters that Magellan had crossed and Henri had explored and Captain Cook and all those whalers had watched, as I did now, shimmering under a ghostlike moon.

And then a figure caught my eye, moving slowly, shuffling along uncertainly, through the plaza below.

A young man.

Somehow familiar, something that I—and then his face, as he stumbled and paused under a streetlight, for no more than two seconds, before he submerged himself in the shadows.

It was Henri.

Or somebody extraordinarily like him.

I thought of waking my love, having her validate my sighting, but she was deep in another dimension and the young man had staggered off into the dark and I had only this one chance to follow and find him.

If all those days at sea had not emboldened me, if the freedom of the waves had not still been carrying me forward, if I had not been inspired by glaciers from the times of Genesis and enchanted by birds flying with forever as a horizon, if the reckless wind had not taught and taunted me, I would never have dared to risk such an adventure. But that momentum from the immediate past, the independence with which I had proven myself, been able to organize this trip without anyone's help, flung away any misgivings—I was like a hunter who would not ask his mate's consent to go out in search of a quarry.

I crept out into the night.

It felt good to be on my own, unshadowed, grown-up.

What could possibly go wrong? Who could possibly photograph or identify me?

I had seen, from my window, where the man had been heading and that is where my steps carried me, peering into doorways and around corners, somehow inhabited by the conviction that I would track him down, wherever he was, whoever he was, I had spent more years with him than with anyone else on this planet, I knew him inside and out, I knew where he would go.

And stepped inside Sotito's Bar.

There he was.

Not really Henri, of course—some distant relative, some of my visitor's blood had to be coursing through his veins. A slightly less flat nose, the hair trimmed differently, but the eyes, the eyes and the cheeks and the mouth. The mouth! I had never seen it moving, opening and closing, any sounds coming from that throat, that tongue. How often had I imagined this scene, the moment when his photo would materialize into reality, when at last he'd speak? But not like this, a man sitting by himself in a bar in Punta Arenas, so much like Henri and yet not him, not him.

For a moment, I hesitated. Behind me, I heard the door to the bar reopen and a vicious wind blow in and then a voice, probably a tourist, because he said, "Sorry, buddy, you're blocking the way."

I took a step to the side, felt the man, burly and gruff, accompanied by a blond-bleached woman reeking of perfume, brush by me, install themselves at the bar, not far from where I—

Where I should be.

I walked to the young man's table, stood by it. Seeing him up close, the resemblance was less evident—he was older than Henri had ever been, for starters, and the skin was lighter, perhaps tinged with some white blood, but that only made his presence more disquieting.

"*Con permiso,*" I said, in my rudimentary Spanish.

"Want to join me?" he said, in English, though heavily accented and somewhat slurred with an excess of liquor. "Sit."

And when I did so, he signaled the waitress, lifting two wavering fingers. "You sit, you pay," he said.

I nodded.

He reached into his pocket, fished out a flyer, and passed it to me. It was a bit rumpled but handsomely printed.

NOMADVENTURES it stated, in red letters at the top—red, the color that indicated one is welcome in the Kaweshkar community, or maybe that was a mere coincidence. I liked the way it played with words, "nomad" and "adventure" and also indicating this would not be mad, this adventure. Reassurance. Underneath that introductory banner, a photo of Henri's double, smiling broadly, settled between two foreigners—a tall Scandinavian male, hair as yellow as cheese, and, on the other side, a pretty brunette, her eyes alight with pleasure. Then came several words: EXCURSIONS. TOURS. PENGUIN ISLAND. KAYAKING TO GLACIAR PARK. HORSEBACK RIDING. HUNTING. FISHING. And in smaller print: NATIVE CEREMONIES UPON REQUEST. AUTHENTIC. EXOTIC. And at the very bottom, a name: JEMMY EDÉN WALAKIAL, GUIDE, ENGLISH-SPANISH. With a phone and fax number.

"Jemmy Edén Walakial," I said. "Your name?"

"*Así me llamo,*" he said, in Spanish, yes, that was his name.

"*Como Puerto Edén?*" I asked, showing him that he did not need to continue in English.

He ignored the invitation. "Born Puerto Edén."

"We're going there soon," I said.

"No penguins?"

"No," I said.

"Nothing in Puerto Edén. I show you the penguins. Mating, Hatching. Isla Magdalena. I show you lots of things."

The waitress, a tired-looking, drowsy woman, brought the drinks. Two whiskeys. He downed his in one gulp, indicated that

I should drink mine. I shook my head. He reached across the sharp angle of the table, grabbed the tumbler, finished it off. He waved to the waitress: two more.

"Your name?" he asked.

"Fitzroy," I said.

He snorted. "Like big sailor boy. You also big sailor boy?"

"No," I said.

"No penguins? What you want Puerto Edén? Nothing there. Snow gliding? You like snow gliding? We got snow gliding."

"No," I said.

"You want shipwrecks, flamencos, guanacos? We got guanacos. We got foxes, black swan, many ducks. You want to hunt?"

I shook my head.

"What you want?"

"Kaweshkar," I said.

"Kaweshkar," he repeated unsteadily, but his eyes narrowed. "We got dance. Ceremony. Real shaman. Initiation dance. I teach you. But it cost you. Or maybe you like pretty girl, pretty Indian girl. Real thing. Young. But gonna cost you. Not cheap, Indian girl."

"I don't want an Indian girl," I said.

"Indian boy, then."

"No," I said.

"What the fuck you want then?"

I wanted to reach out to him and touch his arm, feel its weight, make sure it was real. But that gesture would have been too easily misinterpreted.

Instead, on an impulse: "How do you say 'forgiveness' in Kaweshkar?" I asked.

"'Forgiveness'?"

"*Perdonar*," I said.

He looked at me, for the first time he truly looked at me, through me, into me, as if realizing that I was no ordinary tourist.

"Don't know," he muttered.

"Skin," I said. "How do you say 'skin' in Kaweshkar?"

"*Káwes*. Also mean 'body.'"

"And 'face'? How do you say 'face'?"

"Why you care?"

The waitress was back with the two drinks. He drank one, waited, drank the other one.

"Face," I said. I took out a twenty-dollar bill. "How do you say 'face'?"

"How you know I not lie?"

"Face," I said.

Jemmy frowned and pursed his lips. I never found out if he didn't like the question or was simply holding out for more cash, because we were interrupted by an unexpected voice.

"I heard what you said," and it was a loud American twang, Midwestern and male and intrusive, "about the penguins and such. We've got our tour arranged already, buddy, but we were wondering how much you charge for a day, your other services, I mean, if we wanted one of those, you know, ceremonies, dances, stuff like that."

It was the burly tourist who had walked over from the bar where he had installed himself with that bleached-blonde woman.

"We're busy," I said, eager to turn my eyes back on Jemmy Edén, almost worried that if I lost sight of him he would disappear.

"Wiggins," he said. "Jasper Wiggins, that's my moniker. And over there, that's my lady friend Matilda. Matilda Nordstrom."

She flapped a glass of wine at me. Her face was pasty and had too much rouge, giving her a slightly clownish aspect. I didn't like her, didn't like her pert snub nose and her false eyelashes and her toothy grin, I didn't like anything about her, but especially I didn't like the fact that she was there, at that bar at the end of the world, staining and polluting my encounter with this Henri lookalike, this chance to have a conversation with one of the victims of my forefathers.

Wiggins must have seen the derision and disgust in my eyes and a dangerous glint embittered his.

"Not very friendly, are you, buddy?" He retreated a step or two, scraped against a chair. "I'll be back later then, when you've calmed down, we'll be around—me and Nordstrom there, we'll be around for a while."

I turned back to Jemmy, who had not reacted to this exchange between foreigners.

He took the twenty-dollar bill and pocketed it.

"*Jeksórtqal*," he said. "'Face.' Add *ak'iéfkar*, 'white face.' Yours. Mine like fire. You want to know how we say 'fire' in Kaweshkar?"

I put down another twenty-dollar bill.

"*Afčar*. And 'night.' Night I give you for free. *Ak'éme*. 'Night.' My face. Fire and night. My face painted. Red, you are welcome. Black, not welcome. You want to see my face painted, my body painted. Like old times. You pay. How much?"

"Nothing," I said.

"That your word? 'Nothing'? No, no, no? You see this eye? You see this"—he searched for the word—"cloud?"

I looked into the eye he was pointing at, the eye that was the exact replica of what I had been peering at desperately since my fourteenth birthday—and the only surprise was its irrefutable existence, no cloud that I could discern.

"Moon was born of an eye. An eye—*cortado, sacado del sol*."

"Gouged out of the sun," I said.

"Yes. Night tells us this. The sun is a woman and Kaweshkar are her children. Me. I go blind. Soon. Like my mother, my grandmother. Soon. First one eye, then this eye. Sickness."

He looked down morosely at the empty glasses, played with them for a few seconds, clink, clink, clink, signaled for more. And then he began talking in Spanish, more to himself than to me. With some words in English and some in what must have been Kaweshkar. He had left Puerto Edén, hoped he would leave the blur, *la nube*, in his eye behind. But it was inside, *adentro*, like a moon in his eye. Did I understand what it was to have something inside that wouldn't go away? Like a broken stone that was at the bottom of the sea, that you can hear hissing forever like a serpent. And then murmured something about the sky being sick and collapsing, the sea going blind. *Pena*, he said. *Pena*. He had been born near the Golfo de Penas.

He stopped, fixed on me those eyes that were going blind as if to ensure that I was still there.

"You know what that mean? Pena, *penas*?"

"Pain," I said.

"Sadness," he said. "Sad, like when somebody die."

"Grief," I said.

"Grief, yes."

"Gulf of grief, that's where you were born."

"*Soledad. Solo, solito y solo.* Alone."

"I'm sorry," I said.

"Why you care?"

How to even begin to answer that?

He was the first Kaweshkar I had met. The first indigenous native, in fact, of any ethnic group, tribe, race whatsoever. I had spent eleven years with one of his ancestors inside me, my incessant companion. A good part of my life brooding and researching and learning about the indigenous existence, but it had all been book knowledge, secondhand experience built out of intermediaries, all those pages and documents and travelogues and photos, all those reports and measurements from observers. To be face-to-face—yes, face-to-face—with a real human being, with real biceps and intestines and flesh, real blood and bone, real eyes that could see me, was unbearable, seared me through and through. And moreover this man, of all possible people, this Jemmy Edén Walakial who bore such an uncanny resemblance to my visitor. And for me not to know what to do, what to say, what to demand. Here was the pain I had been seeking, here was the anger, here was what I had been looking for—and I was paralyzed.

Disappointed.

Because I realized that up till then I had harbored the hope that I would find some sort of salvation on this trip, that it would end as fairy tales do, with a magic wand that would solve all the problems, bring peace and harmony.

Impossible. Impossible in this bar with this man, selling everything and anything he could get his hands on, selling his heritage as if it were a trinket. Impossible because there was no way to make amends for what he had been brought to, this last of the Kaweshkars, no way of reversing the course of extinction. The only thing one could do, as with all those who were destined to die on this earth never to return or wake again, was to keep them company, sense their sorrow. Perhaps for their sake as they faded, certainly for one's own. Struggle together against the *soledad*, the grief, *solo, solito y solo.*

Again I felt the urge to touch him, cross the slender space that separated us and take his hand, for the first time in my life touch the skin, the *káwes* of this lost and desolate man who was of Henri's lineage, touch the skin I knew so well and did not know at all. And I was about to do so, throw all prudence to the winds, show some faint flame of compassion that would not help him at all and that he did not need, but try I must, anyway, try and the hell with anyone who misunderstood. I was about to do so, break down the infinite distance between us, when I was interrupted by a different hand clamping down on my shoulder.

It belonged to—who else—Jasper Wiggins.

He stood, as before, at the angular corner of the table, peering down, not even glancing this time at his idiot lady friend at the bar. Swayed for a couple of seconds, as if unsteady on his feet, and then laid his other beefy hand on Jemmy's neck.

There was a flash of light.

One I knew all too well, that I had suffered far too many times, but not like this, not far from home, not—

It came from the bar. From the Nordstrom lady.

In her hands, a camera.

"Say cheese," she said, focusing again.

Another flash. Another picture. Of us. Of me. Of me.

What should I do? Cam, Cam, what should I do?

But my Cam was sleeping in a hotel bed, full of my semen and love, Cam wasn't here to ward off the camera, the photograph of my face that I had been avoiding like the plague.

Calm down, Fitz, that's what my wife would have whispered in my ear. Don't call attention to yourself, just ignore it. Who cares what two drunken American tourists capture with their stupid camera at midnight, what does it matter?

It mattered to Jemmy Edén.

"Fifty dollars," he said to Wiggins. "First photo, fifty dollars. Real Patagonian Indian. Second photo, discount. Thirty. Eighty, you owe then. You want five photos, more discount. One hundred for five. You take three more, only extra twenty."

"Sure, buddy," said Wiggins, taking out a hundred-dollar bill. "Let's snap a few more. Nice souvenir."

I sprang up. "No," I shouted. "No more photos. I'll buy them back from you. A hundred each photo. And two hundred for him." I fished into my pocket and put all the money I had on the table. I didn't know how much was there but certainly not four hundred dollars, not even close.

Jemmy examined Wiggins with interest, suddenly sober, all business.

"You pay more?" he asked.

"Yeah," Wiggins said, and flashed a thick wad of bills. "Now it's you turn, Mr. Friendly Face."

"Back at the hotel," I said. "I have enough money."

"Put up or shut up, Friendly Face."

I fled into the night.

Trying to convince myself that when that Nordstrom bitch developed her photos, they would be flummoxed by the result, thinking the bar Stoppito's was bewitched. Next to the real, authentic, exotic Indian there would be another one in the place of the American who had obnoxiously dissed them, two Kaweshkar side by side. They'd show the photos in question to their friends back in Little Rock or Nebraska or Topeka and make jokes about voodoo magic and the strange guy who wanted to buy back his photos, as if we were trying to steal his soul, can you believe it?

Sneaking into our hotel room as if I had committed adultery, betrayed Cam's trust, I tiptoed to the bed. She had not moved from where she had lain an hour ago, the same position, tummy down and innocent and breathing gently into the pillow. I should have woken her and blurted out everything, but I didn't want to spoil our expedition, listen to her berating me as a fool for going out, I couldn't stand her exasperated look, her sighs, once again poor old helpless Fitz, untrustworthy. The day after tomorrow, in less than thirty-six hours, we would be at sea again, heading for Puerto Edén and she would be none the wiser.

The next day—Saturday, October 10—I stayed in the hotel room all day, overcompensating for last night's misadventure, while Cam sallied forth, keen to tour the city, the cemetery, a museum with a replica of the *Nao Victoria*, Magellan's ship, another museum run by the Salesian brothers—"that way I can show you the sights when we come back here from Puerto Edén." That's how sure she was that the ceremony awaiting us would liberate me from my phantom, "but we don't want to risk someone photographing you, Fitz, confusing you with a penguin! Not when we're about to cross the finish line."

She returned full of enthusiasm and little anecdotes several hours later—"Good you didn't come, there were quite a few tourists snapping shots of everything they set their eyes on. And you would have been indignant, Fitz. There's a mansion open, where the Brauns used to live, the richest family in these parts— all about how they brought progress to Patagonia with all those sheep, but not a word about the natives who had to be cleared off the land first, not a word, Fitz."

Cam nattered away and then stopped, wondering if I wasn't feeling claustrophobic, stuck, "obediently, so patiently," she said, in this room after all those weeks of basilica skies and the open witchery of the ocean, her words, she was getting ever more poetical, ever less scientific as the journey advanced. "How about if we creep down to the hotel bar? No one there just now when I passed it—and anyway, who snaps photos inside a silly bar when outside they have the most spectacular vistas in the universe?"

I declined. I knew all too well who might snap a photo in a silly bar. What if the infernal Wiggins and his mate were staying at the Cabo de Hornos, what if they spilled the beans about last night, what if Cam discovered, through *them*, oh Lord, my dishonesty? No, better to stay here, lapping up her praise of my discretion.

It was a relief, then, when Sunday arrived and we were able to check out of the hotel without trouble. Not a nosy tourist in sight at four in the morning. Only a canopy of stars above. Not even haze in the sky to mist over the brightness with which they shone. Another favorable sign. I reminded Cam that, according to the Kaweshkar legends, the souls of the dead were up there, behind those celestial bodies, soon to be joined, if we were successful, by Henri. Or perhaps Henri was already there, up in that intense firmament, guiding us to his home.

Our real guides were, of course, waiting for us on *The Southern Cross*, Frano and his wife Elba—delighted to come along for the ride.

It was smooth sailing out along the Straits—into the Paso Ancho and past Bahía Agua Fresca and then Dawson Island.

"Dawson," Vudarovic said, meditatively. "The missions were there, administering the last fatal blows. Dawson."

Elba whispered something in his ear and he shook his head and she insisted and he turned to us. "My wife wants you to know that I almost ended up there myself. The military turned the island into a concentration camp for political prisoners back in 1973, after the coup. I had been agitating for the rights of natives, so they thought I was, well, dangerous, but Elba's father was a colonel and he intervened and here I am. It would have been strange—to be shut up where all those Patagonians I had been studying and writing about had been enclosed and—Oh, look."

He pointed at the mountains, where the sun was tingeing the virgin snow on the highest peaks with faint but ever-deepening color—contrasting with the foliage, rocks, and glaciers still wrapped in the steepest shade. Then the pink summits of the mountains changed to gold and yellow, and then to dazzling white, as the light crept down into the valleys, illuminating all the dark places, and bringing out the tints of olive-greens, grays, and purples, in the most wonderful combinations. How many mornings like these had Henri contemplated from his canoe, the pinnacles he called his rising from huge domed tops, and his those vast fields of unbroken snow and had he seen, as we did as we advanced into the *Paso Inglés* the glaciers running down to the edge of the sea? And all of a sudden we were blessed, as he must have been, by an iceberg crashing into the water a mere hundred feet away and then floating past us. And each bank and promontory richly clothed with vegetation of every shade of green; and the narrow channel itself, blue as the sky above, dotted with small islands, each a mass of verdant splendor, and reflecting on its glassy surface every object with such distinctness that it was difficult to say where reality ended and the image began.

And it was at that moment, when we thought there could be nothing on this planet more magical, then it was that a whale rose in all its majesty and stayed above the vast, turbulent horizon for what seemed an eternal minute and then gave a cry out of heaven itself and disappeared into the deep. By now we were beyond enchantment. Here was yet another magnificent sign that all would be well, that nature was sanctifying our enterprise, that not everything had been corrupted since the days more than a century ago when Henri had witnessed a similar kind of miracle.

And then, like a mocking echo, we heard the whir and thunder of a machine—Jim pointed a finger to the north. A giant helicopter was speeding toward us, then hovered over our craft.

"He wants us to stop," Captain Wolfe yelled above the din. "Stop and be searched."

"Stop then," Frano said. "These Chilean navy people can be ferocious."

"Not Chileans," Captain Wolfe said grimly. "Americans."

And idled his engines.

A ladder descended from the helicopter and a Navy SEAL climbed down it. As soon as he hit the surface of the ship, London Wolfe sprang at him, with startling agility for a man of his age. The Navy SEAL, however, had no trouble in subduing our champion, though the old man, now face down on the deck, his arm pinned behind his back and an enemy knee immobilizing him, kept cursing with every insult in his extensive vocabulary. Only quieting when his left arm was twisted to a breaking point, supplemented by the words, "Please don't force me to hurt you, Captain Wolfe."

And then the Navy SEAL waved his free hand and two more men came slithering down the ladder, fully armed. And behind them I saw, to my consternation—it couldn't be, but yes, there they were, in the full horrible light of day, Wiggins and Nordstrom, clambering their way down the ropes, landing next to me and Cam.

Its human cargo delivered, the amphibious helicopter moved away and then perched nearby on its pontoons, as those whirring dreadful asps rocked the waves that had been so calm. When the engine was hushed, the ensuing silence felt even more foreboding than the previous racket.

So Wiggins's voice carried loud and clear. There was not a hint of the Midwest in it. On the contrary, it sounded very much like someone born and bred and educated in New England. And it was soft and polite with just an intimation of irony and amusement.

"Mr. Foster, Mrs. Foster, if you'd be so good as to accompany us."

"Why? What have we done?" Cam asked, indignantly.

"Agent Nordstrom and I have not been authorized to disclose the purpose of our mission. Only to deliver you safely to the destination chosen by our superiors."

Frano Vudarovic exploded.

"You are in violation of Chilean sovereignty, sir. We are a free and democratic country and I will see to it that this outrage is reported and punished, be assured of that."

Wiggins wearily extracted a piece of paper from inside his jacket. "There's really no need to show you this, Professor, but seeing as there's nothing you can do to stop us, what's the harm? Authorization from the head of your Armed Forces, General Augusto Pinochet Ugarte, your very own former president— and cosigned by Minister Correa and Minister Rojas. Given the National Security Pact subscribed to between Chile and the United States, blah, blah, blah, the American Navy is allowed to apprehend two fugitives from justice, blah, blah."

Vudarovic did not deign to look at the document.

"But you can't detain me, a Chilean citizen. I'll denounce this travesty at the nearest port."

"Hey, Nordstrom," Wiggins said, with a toss of his head, "didn't the Chileans warn us that this guy was a troublemaker?"

"Indeed they did," she answered. She seemed to be enjoying herself. Around her neck hung the satanic camera that had forced me to flee Sotito's bar. I eyed it nervously, absurdly more afraid that she would reveal my escapade to Cam than of being arrested.

"And didn't they say that the professor here had learned a lesson back in '73 and that he'd been given a second chance then and wouldn't want to misbehave again? So, no publicity, Professor. Or there will be consequences. And now, if you'd stop playing the hero, we'd like Mr. and Mrs. Foster to gather their belongings and come with us."

"Where are you taking them?" Wolfe asked, still pressed to the deck, speaking from the side of his furious mouth.

"All you need to know," Wiggins said, "is that the Fosters won't be returning to the States in your ship, Captain. How you deal with that situation is not our concern."

He signaled to the Navy SEAL to release his prisoner.

Captain Wolfe refused the hand of assistance offered and stood up on his own. He brushed himself off, his eyes slanting down- ward, not wanting to meet mine—it was as if he had been stripped of his identity, his masks and pretensions. For all his bluster, he had not kept his promise to protect us, defend his ship.

"Captain," Cam said. He didn't react. "Captain."

He turned to her, his face congested with shame.

"Captain," Cam said, and there was a bizarre alacrity in her tone, almost as if she was taking pleasure in this episode. Did nothing ever dampen her spirits? Couldn't she see how truly fucked we were? "I want you, dear Captain Wolfe, to proceed with Professor Vudarovic and his wife to Puerto Edén. The elders are awaiting him and the donation he will be delivering on our behalf. Once you've completed your mission there, please return our Chilean guests to Punta Arenas and continue on to New Bedford. If we can join you at some point during your voyage home, we will do so, but I don't believe that is likely."

Was she just trying to put a good spin on this utter disaster? Or was her joy authentic, surging from some mysterious reason only she could divine, some implausible silver lining?

"I let you down," Wolfe said. "It's my fault. The Falklands, the damn Falklands! Idiot, idiot, idiot! I should've known. Never trust the fucking Brits."

Wiggins nodded sagely. "You shouldn't and we don't. But they did alert us, you can say that for them. So Nordstrom and me, we had to leave Hamburg and fly down here—missing Oktoberfest, how about that! But if you'll excuse us, we have some photos to retrieve."

"What photos?" I stuttered.

"We have information that you are traveling with a set of important photos. Our instructions are to confiscate said photos before leaving the ship."

"We burned them," Cam cried out. "We burned them back in Boston."

"They're here," Nordstrom piped up. "On this ship. And we'll find them."

Our captors, of course, despite a prolonged and thorough search, came up empty.

"Somebody I know is going to be pissed," Wiggins said.

Nordstrom shrugged her shoulders. "Not really. He's so pleased with what we already sent. No big deal."

"Let's hope you're right," Wiggins replied. "I mean, we've done our job. Without those photos in the bar, they wouldn't have given a greenlight for this operation, so . . ."

Cam frowned, perplexed. "What photos? What bar?"

"Secrets, secrets," Nordstrom smirked. "I love it when couples lie to each other, just love it. Gives a *je ne sais quoi* to our work, spices it up, you know. Here, take a look. Two nights ago, Sotito's bar. Recognize your husband?"

Quick as a viper, before I could stop her, Nordstrom placed copies of the guilty snapshots in Cam's unwilling hands. There was Wiggins in the middle, one brawny hand on Jemmy Edén Walakial's neck and the other on my shoulder, except it was not my face there, atop my body, but Henri's. Wiggins between the two of us, the three of us, Henri and me and Jemmy, twins, triplets, an eerie and repellant picture.

"Until I saw it, you know," said Wiggins, "I didn't believe any of this. Thought the boss was insane and that we were on a fool's errand. But these two snapshots, they convinced us. And more than us. They convinced the top brass to give the go-ahead, the final phase of the operation. The last nail in the coffin. So thanks to you, Mr. Foster, for making it all so easy."

"How about posing again, huh, with your lovely wife," suggested Nordstrom, lifting her camera. "Say cheese."

Cam, my Cam, was also quick. She jumped at Nordstrom, grabbed the offending device, and threw it into the sea.

I gasped, pulled her back, protecting her body with mine, seconded by Jim and Wellington who stepped forward, ready to make a last stand. And a swift and brutal retribution would have been exacted if Wiggins hadn't intervened.

"As long as you don't throw him overboard, I don't care about the camera. Where you're going, there are lots of cameras, more than you've ever seen. You two! Pack your bags."

We went down to our cabin.

I ventured: "Cam, I'm so sorry, I—"

"No, Fitz, what you did—it's fine, it's . . . better than fine. It's perfect. Don't you see? It happened to Henri—maybe right here, maybe on this very bay. The kidnapping, Fitzroy Foster—these imbeciles don't know it yet, may never realize it, but they're helping us, they're collaborating by—"

"But Downey," I protested. "Downey needed a photo to pull this operation off, that's what my stupid excursion in Punta Arenas gave him. And I didn't tell you. About Henri's lookalike, there was a man who—God, I'm so sorry I didn't tell you, I didn't trust you."

"Well, trust me now," she said, planting a wet kiss on my lips. "And trust Henri."

I suspected she was dreadfully wrong, but I certainly didn't have the right—or the time, for that matter—to refute her. Still, I failed to see any lasting parallels between Henri's kidnapping and our own detention. He had no recourse, no language to defend himself with, no knowledge of his captors and their wiles. And no habeas corpus, which my father would interpose on our behalf as soon as Vudarovic called from Puerto Edén. Nor were we bound for extinction. And yet, I was glum, less from the assault we had suffered than from the depressing encounter with Jemmy Edén, which had haunted me with more ferocity than Henri, perhaps because it showed me what any of his alter egos might have become a century later. If I had been him (and who was closer?), I'd have no longer wanted to go home to the island of my debased ancestors. Maybe he was relieved that the odyssey had been interrupted. Or maybe he was frustrated that such violence kept on repeating itself endlessly and despaired of there ever being a solution. Whatever I might speculate about him, only one certainty remained to guide me. I had to believe that Cam was right, that, quite simply, we needed to trust him.

I held tight to that idea as we were lifted forlornly into the air, and held tight to that dimmest hope as we watched our friends waving goodbye while *The Southern Cross*, our home for so many weeks, became a speck below, lost in a sea tenanted by islands and dolphins and cragged twisted spires and an iceberg that crashed from its glacier mother like a child being slaughtered by the wind; even held onto Henri as an anchor as we crossed Patagonia eastward, the peaks and plains that he had never seen with his own mortal eyes from the heights we were flying; and kept that belief alive until we landed in an airfield in the Falklands.

And then felt it all melt away as soon as we observed the lank, solitary figure of Dr. Ernest Downey loping to greet us even before the asps of the helicopter ceased their murderous rotation. He was beaming, veritably hopping with joy, did not hesitate to embrace me, so hard that he seemed to be squeezing my body dry. I felt Henri's loathing couple with mine, and it was all I could do not to vomit on the man who had chased us to the southernmost tip of the earth.

"My boy, my boy," he murmured in my ear. "Finally, oh finally, we meet. And before the plague advances to the next stage, what a relief." He reluctantly let me go, but kept speaking as he turned to greet Camilla, who took a step backward to avoid his hug. "And you, my dear Mrs. Foster, how kind of you to join your husband, share his glory and mine and what will soon be yours, this great occasion in the annals of medicine and science. If only my poor girl, if only my poor darling Evelyn were alive to be part of this celebration, if only she had been wise enough, given the right advice by her mother, but guilt is never the right counselor, we should never act out of guilt, never, never, but from the purest love of humanity and progress. Huxley said it, if you know the truth then you can do no wrong, didn't he say that? T. H., I mean, because Aldous had it all upside down, didn't he, antiscientific bastard, deriding the brave new worlds we have been forging. But we mustn't detain ourselves further with allusions and quotations you may not be familiar with. Come, come, our transport awaits, men of significance and imperium are gathered to marvel at Operation Memory Redux, this giant step forward that Pasteur and Watson, Crick, and Miescher would die to witness, come, come."

He gestured, still speaking, half pulling, half pushing us toward a large military plane on the tarmac, its motor humming as it was refueled by an energetic group of men in uniform.

"And agents Wiggins and Nordstrom, well done, well done. The photos, the photos in the bar, no one could have managed a better couple of shots, not alerting Mr. Foster to the game that was afoot, oh it would have been more complicated if you had been forced to barge into his room dressed as hotel personnel, well done indeed! I cannot describe my elation when I received them via fax. That was it, that was enough, the final visual proof I needed to convince our sponsors, rid them of that last pinch of skepticism, oh when they saw, when they saw with their own eyes what I had been promising, the truth that could no longer be hidden, oh, they were ready, they were ecstatic, oh, you will be commended, be assured of a raise and a commendation and a footnote in the book I am writing, such service is not forgotten. But come, come, come, destiny awaits."

Ushering us all into the bowels of the aircraft, sitting us in some rather uncomfortable seats and placing himself directly across from ours, and still talking and talking and talking.

He kept at it all night long as we overflew the continent that Columbus had bumped into almost five hundred years earlier, the plane covering in one night what it had taken us a month and a half to navigate by sea, Ernest Downey did not cease his tirade even while he ravenously ate—we refused to partake of even one morsel—the tepid meal served a few hours after we departed the Falklands, he kept at it when Cam asked him to please be quiet and even carried on by himself when I stood up to relieve myself.

All the reports Cunningham had assembled indicated that Downey was a taciturn man, a melancholy man, who seldom opened his mouth except in reproach or when hurling out orders. True, he had engaged in a long rant with Cam at the library regarding his research plans, but nothing that predicted the ebullience that now possessed his vocal chords, a veritable Niagara, Amazon, Mississippi, Pacific Ocean of words cascading from thick, sensual, starved lips.

Cam soon enough learned to ignore that buzz and curled up by my side, snoring gently away, but not me. I was fascinated, in spite of my disgust. Meeting for the first time someone touched by the same tragedy that had afflicted my loved ones. As if I were perversely gaining a new family member, an older relative, insane though he might be, who could grasp what I had been through, the trials of my parents, someone who had been as shocked and puzzled and as determined—even more determined—to find a solution, a way out. And he seemed to recognize in me a similar affinity, treating me with the kindness, solicitude, and confidence of a father. Able to pour his heart out, confess to someone like me the emotions he had suppressed for years.

He talked of the grand voyage of discovery we were about to embark upon, the days and months and decades ahead—and how this would change the future of humanity, only akin, he said, to the discovery of America half a millennium ago, was this not a sign from God. And God, he talked about God and America as God's chosen nation to lead the world out of poverty and backwardness and ignorance. Though his faith had been tested by Evelyn's sickness. Because at the end, it wasn't only the photos. Her face, her face had started to show signs of black bristles, tiny spikes of hair seemed to be protruding from her cheeks, and her nose beginning to flatten like a monkey's, in those final days Krao threatened to take over Evelyn's features, that's why the girl had killed herself. But when his daughter had died, he had not buckled under, he had assembled a team and deepened his knowledge of the affliction that had taken her—and then, realizing the medical and scientific implications of his research, worried about the possibility of a next phase in the plague, attacks on faces rather than mere photos, which was bad enough, terrible enough, he said; worried about the future of mankind, he had contacted the people at the Pentagon he'd worked with previously on contingency plans for epidemics, how to handle evacuations and quarantines in the case of germ warfare. They had already stumbled upon a case, Jedediah Grant, a youngster who, like Evelyn, had also ended up killing himself. Here, Downey's rant became murky and more confused, alluding to an army of names, some that vaguely resonated with me, like Jesse Tarbox Beals, and others, like Madison Grant and Topsy (Topsy?) that I had never heard of before. Convoluted genealogies, the Bronx Zoo, Coney Island, Australian aborigines—victims and lineages tracked down by national security agents. "Too late, too late," Downey lamented, "I always arrived too late. But not you, Fitzroy Foster, not you, thank heaven and Pasteur's spirit, not you." And then, again more names and then praising me for not having succumbed to despair, exalting my choice of Camilla Wood as wife and companion, someone who, unlike Downey's own spouse, had sustained and nurtured my efforts, had journeyed into the wilderness of the double helix in search of answers. And on and on he talked and always he kept returning to what really obsessed and wounded him: his own heartbreak. And the more he circled back to his daughter's dead body and his wife's betrayal, the clearer it became that this was the major motor of his hunt: only a victory over the sickness, only a triumphant outcome and scientific breakthrough, could justify so much pain, erase it, assuage the guilt he would not admit.

His grief was like a black hole, swallowing everything in its wake. The neck of his little girl, he kept coming back to that broken neck, her corpse dangling from a belt that he had bought for her on a shopping spree. He lingered on their good times together, he evoked the first occasion she had boarded a merry-go-round, her squeals of delight as the wooden giraffe glided up and down, held fast by her father as if there were no mournful tomorrow, and then an elephant and a camel and every other animal on that carousel, and the photos, he had snapped picture after picture with his Polaroid, he had acquired it because of her, so she could enjoy herself twice, in reality and then in celluloid memory. That merry-go-round was encrusted in his brain, he couldn't purge it from his life, the music, the image of Evelyn rising and falling, he was the merry-go-round, he circled back to it over and over, all night long, to the one thing that really mattered, that his daughter was dead and there was nothing he could do, despite all his knowledge, to resurrect her. Unless, unless, unless, she endured in his visual DNA like Krao in hers, unless, unless, the debris of atoms she had breathed in and out in her oxygen was scattered somewhere, inhaled somewhere, reconstituting itself, water molecules that came and went, particles that could be recuperated like the dust of stars. So alone, he said, so alone—echoing Jemmy in the bar and who knows if Henri at night in the Paris zoo and me before Cam appeared to save me from the dark, so alone, so alone.

And yet, for all his suffering and loneliness and guilt, for all his theories and experiments and hypotheses, his mad, groundless suspicions about a next stage, he had learned nothing from his journey, nothing about himself and nothing about the ultimate victims of violence and photography and greed and blind science. And now he was making me his victim, he was joining the chain of oblivious oppressors, taking my life from me, interrupting the one chance I had been given, I had given myself, to atone and lay to rest the crimes of the men whose genes were spliced inside me. How dare he act like a god who decided my fate from his certainties and civilization, how dare he use me to allay his own trauma. "You're making a big mistake," I said impulsively, not thinking he would listen but because I needed to tell myself that I had tried, had afforded him the opportunity to step outside the bubble of his megalomania and self-confidence. Suddenly finding inside myself, whispered from who knew what twilight of wisdom, terms that he might, as a scientist, consider worth at least bearing in mind. What if the appearance of his daughter's visitor, and mine, was not a virus that signaled a degeneration in our bodies, a regression to savagery, but a slight evolutionary step forward, one timid way in which the species was searching to free itself from the limbic system governed by fear and loneliness, heralding the need to develop the zones of the brain where compassion and empathy and trust reside? What if we treated my visitor as a prophet and not a plague, a challenge instead of a tragedy? What if the genes lodged in me and Evelyn had come to warn us of humanity's fate if we kept destroying one another? What if Downey had greeted his daughter's ghost as an angel rather than a demon? I would have done my best to elaborate, would have tried to articulate a theory about this possible mutation towards kindness, but just then Wiggins came by to let us know we were about to land.

Outside it was dawning, the sun was rising on October 12, 1992. I caught a glimpse below us of a bright blue sea as the plane banked and began to descend.

Wiggins woke Cam—quite gently, to my surprise—and asked her, as she yawned and stretched the slim branches of her arms, if she'd like some coffee, a roll, some orange juice, which Nord- strom, all rouged up for the day, mascara applied thickly, had begun serving to Downey and me.

Cam nodded, thanked Wiggins, and turned to me. "What have I missed?" she asked.

"Nothing," I said. "He's making a big mistake." I addressed Downey. "You know, it's not too late. There are other ways."

"Other ways?" Downey asked. "No. It's perfect. Isn't it per- fect?" He gestured toward the plane, the scenery outside, the mug of steaming coffee in his other hand, perhaps the plans and projects he had for this day and every day till the end of time. "Isn't it fucking perfect?"

I wish I had been given the time to explain to him what I meant. A message I would have liked to deliver to Pierre Petit if I could go back in time, mutter to Carl Hagenbeck and all the rest of them—all the men who had made me and the world we inhabited, I would have liked to speak to them through Downey. Because they were dead and he was alive, they had made their mistakes and convinced themselves that it was fucking perfect, and he still had the chance to acknowledge how deeply flawed his life was, how fucking imperfect despite all the terrific reasons he kept feeding himself, I would have liked to persuade him that it is never too late for any of us to understand.

For an instant I thought it might be possible. Incredibly, he turned to look at me, and seemed genuinely perplexed by my intensity and, more crucially, was silent, stopped talking, as if he were seeing me, not as a piece of flesh to be probed in his lab and paraded anonymously in scientific journals, but as a fellow human deserving care and attention, respect and kindness, simply because I had been born, as he had, from a mother and a father and a long line of men and women who had hoped for something better. As if he sensed his daughter speaking through me. Was that a glimmer of serenity bathing his eyes? Or was I deluding myself, projecting onto him what I would have wanted him to feel? Or maybe he was just exhausted, gathering strength for the day ahead?

I never found out.

We were on the verge of landing. Below our plane, a frothing ocean landscape and then swaying tropical palm trees and then, with a thud, a tarmac with barracks on both sides. And no sooner did Cam feel American soil, what she supposed was Florida, beneath the plane's wheels than she intervened, hijacking the conversation and turning it in an altogether different direction.

"My husband's right, Dr. Downey. A big mistake. Have you heard of habeas corpus? Filed by Jerry Foster on our behalf, I have no doubt. So get ready to release us. Court order. And start thinking about finding somebody else's life to screw up."

Downey smiled at this outburst. "And here I am, thinking you wanted to celebrate the sesquicentenary in one of the places that Columbus encountered, that he mentioned as Puerto Grande in his Third Voyage—where he partook of baked fish and *huitas*, a sort of rabbit with the tail of a rat."

"You didn't answer me," Cam insisted. "You can't just kidnap people here. Now we're in America, damn it!"

"Yes and no," said Downey.

"What do you mean?"

"You're under American jurisdiction, that's true, but with none of the guarantees accruing to a US citizen."

"Where are we?"

The plane had cruised to a stop and the hatch now opened. Outside we glimpsed a military jeep speeding toward us. I saw it veer suddenly to avoid running over an iguana, and then screech to a halt next to some stairs that were being rolled toward us.

"Where are we?" Downey stood up and once again smiled. "At a Naval base, outside the territorial United States. Welcome, my dear Fitzroy, welcome, Mrs. Foster, to Guantánamo."

TEN

"Two souls, alas, are dwelling in my breast."
—Goethe, *Faust*

Guantánamo!

They could do, Downey explained, anything to us here. Not that they intended to—on the contrary, we were his guests and would soon meet some other prominent hosts, come especially to celebrate our arrival and the wonderful discoveries that lay in the near and far future. He recounted their names and titles as we mounted the jeep and headed off to the other side of the bay, where a large building loomed: Phillip Clarke, the CEO of Pharma2001, along with a couple of his German acolytes, the secretary of defense himself, the subdirector of the Center for Disease Control—to which soon would be added the words "and Prevention," Downey assured us, as soon as Congress voted on the new designation—a fundamental step forward for the funding of his own project. And as we were on the subject of funding, two bankers would be in the auditorium, whose names he preferred not to reveal, as well as a high operations officer from the Central Intelligence Agency. And an eminence, Professor Saltmacher, in charge of Biosafety and Toxins at the National Security Agency. Several scientists and Nobel Prize–winning economists, whose names, though I didn't catch them, seemed to suitably impress Cam. And, of course, the academic world was also in attendance, through a member of the Board of Visitors of the National Defense University who was, at the same time, here to represent the Project for the New American Century. And, of course, Admiral Peabody, who would be our primary host.

I interrupted Downey, pointing at a large barbed-wire compound behind which dozens of black people, half naked, were grouped, watching us go by, cheering our jeep as if it were a presidential cavalcade.

"What's that?"

"Oh, that's Camp Bulkeley. Haitian refugees, rescued on the high seas by our Navy—fleeing their country after the recent coup d'état. The United States can't let them reach our shores and can't let them die in the ocean, so here they are till things settle down in their own land or we find some place that will accept them, though who knows who'd want the poor devils. I've been sending them extra food rations—maybe that's why they're waving to us."

And then he kept on salivating about the renowned men who would be there for my presentation, as he called it, but I had lost all interest in his preening, couldn't escape the image of those men and women pressed against the railings, eyes boring into mine like black candles under the same sun that had seen Columbus go ashore on an island like this one five hundred years ago.

At about this very time of day. He had waited for dawn because the night of October 11 lights had been sighted—lights like eyes in the darkness, like a wax candle rising and falling—he had waited and ordered the crew to sing the Salve and called the island San Salvador and the trees were very green and there was water and fruits of diverse kinds. And he leaped on the shore and was soon received by the inhabitants of that island, who brought parrots and other goods. The natives were well made and handsome. And they were naked.

Five hundred years had gone by and everything had changed and nothing had changed.

I looked at Cam to gauge if she was feeling my sadness but she seemed to be animated by the same sparkle of cheerful buoyancy that had gripped her since we had been assaulted just outside the Straits of Magellan, since we had first met, if you came to think of it, in that swimming pool so long ago it seemed to have happened in another lifetime.

My despondency only grew when we met Admiral Thomas Peabody, from the Joint Chiefs of Staff. Another admiral, I thought, another man of the sea, greeting us effusively and with who knows what venomous second thoughts in his head, like that other admiral, Almirante Cristóbal Colón, back then greeting the natives, the Arawaks soon to be kidnapped and exterminated and enslaved—not one left anymore on any of these Caribbean islands.

Cam, on the other hand, was delighted with Peabody.

Not because he was jolly and rotund and received us as heroes, thanked us for so willingly serving our country, apologized for the abruptness of what he termed the "invitation." But because she obviously perceived in him a possible ally—why? what flicker in his eyes justified such an assessment?—although she waited till Downey had hurried away to attend to preparations, waited for the door to close behind his receding footsteps, before pouncing, letting loose a wild purring animal inside her.

"You know that all this is a hoax, Admiral."

"What's a hoax?"

"That my husband has this sickness that Dr. Downey has been selling. That his body contains the cure to it and the cure to God knows how many other ailments and problems. It's a lie, smoke and mirrors."

Peabody held his ground. He had survived worse storms than one woman, no matter how bewitching. "Begging your pardon, ma'am, but I've seen the photos, the damning evidence—and the results of Dr. Downey's experiments. Not to mention his reputation. You have your credentials, but you're not in line for a Nobel Prize, eh?"

"What if the photos you have are a fraud, Photoshopped with a technique created, by the way, by my husband? What then?"

"They're not. They were snapped by two of our most reliable agents—and they fit into everything else about Mr. Foster's life—and other proof amassed regarding other cases."

"If they are a fraud, what then?"

For a second, a cloud passed over the admiral's face. Then he recomposed his features, hardening them back into certainty.

"Listen, Ernest Downey, he's the first true genius I've ever met. A bit eccentric—and difficult to please when he's in anger mode or overdrive, I'll give you that. But fraud! I've gotten to know him quite well these last years, and more so while we were working to get this facility ready for your visit. You're surprised? He anticipates everything, told me as soon as you recovered from your accident, Mrs. Foster, that you'd both be heading down to Tierra del Fuego. That's when we started prepping Gitmo for your imminent arrival, the auditorium you're about to see and the three labs with state of the art technology where Mr. Foster will be residing until the tests are completed—"

"For how long?" I interceded.

"For as long as it takes," he answered. "But the point is, he doesn't make mistakes—"

"But he thought my husband and I were going to Europe, he sent the agents there . . ."

"Let's not quibble about tactics. Strategically—and that's what matters in a war, not minor skirmishes and maneuvers—he always hits the nail on the head. He told us to investigate the genealogy of the victims we had found with the same syndrome exhibited by your husband, and he was right. His paradigm works! And the research is flawless! He wouldn't convene some of the most powerful men in this country—and abroad—if he weren't certain of his data. Those two photos are irrefutable. Now, I understand you want to protect your spouse, but the needs of the nation and humanity supersede individual rights, so—"

"If it's a hoax, will you let us go?"

Peabody was getting impatient, his civility about to turn sour. Why was Cam provoking him? We were at his mercy. I reached out to her arm, hoping to dissuade her. She shook me off.

"I want your word of honor, Admiral, that you'll let us go if Fitzroy proves useless to you. That you'll immediately return us home so we can peacefully continue our lives."

The admiral sighed, won over by her passion, her stubbornness—not surprising, it had happened so often to me.

"All right then. If Mr. Foster is useless to us, and you can prove that, then, yes, we'll let you go. I trust you'll accept my word of honor."

"What I'll accept doesn't matter. It's whether you'll stand by it that matters here."

"I will stand by my promise. But you're in for a big disappointment."

And as if this were a signal, the intercom buzzed.

"Here we go," the admiral said. "Showtime."

He escorted us down several winding corridors until he reached a door, guarded by none other than Agent Wiggins. "Remember to

keep Mr. Foster out of sight until Dr. Downey gives the go-ahead,"
Peabody said—and before I could object, he had grabbed Cam by
the elbow and moved away with her. Wiggins opened the door
and, bowing to me, indicated that I was to enter.

It was a projectionist's booth, looking out onto an auditorium.
Reading an issue of *Hustler* magazine sat a huge-bellied black
man—oversized for such a small space, even more so now that
Wiggins and I were squeezed in. "At last! The guest of honor," he
said, leaving the magazine open at a particularly pornographic
photo of two naked women making out. "I'm Ensign S. Henson,
go by the name of Sleazy Steve, but seeing as I'm in charge of
making sure you look good under the spotlight and the cameras,
all that stuff, you can call me plain and simple Sleazy."

I told him I would rather address him as Ensign Henson
and he shrugged complacently and invited me to make myself
comfortable—would I care for some reading material, he had
a stray copy of *Bound and Gagged* and *Screw Magazine* and, if
I cared for more sophisticated fare, some *Playboys*. I declined,
more interested in the auditorium: a hundred seats, twenty-some
filled with men in suits, looking up at a podium, behind which
a giant screen glowed in the penumbra. The walls were cloaked
in darkness, a mass of curtains covering what was behind them.

I saw Admiral Peabody steering my wife into the auditorium.
They stopped in front of the assembled men and he introduced
them one by one. She seemed at ease, the only woman in the
room, relaxed, flirtatious, joking. I felt a surge of jealousy until
she looked up in my direction—guessing where I was—and then
gifted me with a little wave of her hand, mouthed the words,
Trust me, it's going to be all right, before returning to some sleek
oaf with silvered hair and rim glasses who must have been the
rep of the Board of the National Defense University or some
such nonsense.

Cam and Peabody stood for a while, chatting with the other attendees, until the lights dimmed and everybody took their places, side by side, expectantly gazing at the podium where a bright beam of light announced the arrival of Ernest Downey—a spectacle engineered by Sleazy Steve who, as he fingered buttons, barely looked up from the photo of a petite Asian woman, full frontal and breasts budding.

"My friends," Downey said, "we are gathered to celebrate a breakthrough with tremendous implications for the world. Thanks to your support and the organizations you represent we are about to set forth on an odyssey that will revolutionize the way in which we comprehend and replicate our bodies and our history, influencing how we practice biomedicine and warfare, helping to avoid a potential apocalypse. Decoding visual memories embedded in our genetic makeup will allow us to recuperate a past apparently lost forever, with enormous commercial benefits as well as major consequences for our national security. You've been frank enough to admit, at one time or another, a residual skepticism regarding this enterprise. Those lingering doubts will now be laid to rest."

I was struck by how unruffled and rational Downey sounded. The frantic lunacy of our transcontinental night flight seemed to have drained away, depleted on my hapless ears. Aghast as I was by his procedures, and fearful, despite Cam's reassurances, of what the impending experiments might mean for me, I couldn't help being drawn into the serene vortex of his arguments, the conviction with which his speech was delivered. I looked at Cam's face to see if she was equally mesmerized, but her left foot was nervously tapping the floor, a sure sign her mind was elsewhere. What could she be thinking of, scheming, strategizing?

"You all know," Downey continued, "that Operation Memory Redux derived from a personal tragedy. I do not wish to subject you, and definitely not myself, to the recollection of those sad circumstances. I do not intend to exhibit images of my little girl before and after being assaulted by the monster Krao. But you do need to see photos of other victims of this pestilence from the past, this alien invasion of innocent lives."

At Downey's gesture, Sleazy Steve set aside his reading material and pressed a button. On the giant screen, a photo of a young mulatto boy in basketball garb appeared, eyes ecstatic as he hoisted a high school trophy.

"Jedediah Grant," Downey intoned. "At age thirteen."

He signaled again and Sleazy responded by making another photo materialize, with its all-too-familiar contours: the body still belonged to the boy we had previously seen but the round face was that of an African midget, eyes dancing merrily in skin as black as tar, teeth out-jutting and sharply filed as he grinned for the camera.

"Jedediah Grant, now age fifteen," Downey said. "Invaded by Ota Benga, an African pygmy enticed to the St. Louis Fair in 1904 by a missionary and entrepreneur. Photographed by Jesse Tarbox Beals and displayed two years later in the monkey cage of the Bronx Zoo along with an orangutan. Puts a bullet through his heart in 1916, when, abandoned by those who had profited from his shows, he is unable to secure passage back to the Congo. Why Jedediah? His lineage, of course. On his mother's side, a direct descendant of the photographer Tarbox Beals. On his father's side, a bit more complicated. The second in command at the Bronx Zoo, responsible for the pygmy's ordeal, was Madison Grant, a man later famous for having written a racist tract that inspired Adolf Hitler, warning of the threat to the Nordic race posed by inferior forms of humanity. Grant was supposed to have died childless. Not true. Ironically, he spawned an illegitimate child with a Negro striptease artist, and that son was

Jedediah's grandfather. By the time I received this information from the Pentagon, Jedediah had shot himself. A pity. The dead are useless to us."

Downey lifted a finger and again Sleazy lifted his own finger and pushed it down, again the screen was lit up, first with a white girl in a white dress—and then the same girl, this time with the enormous head of an elephant mounted on her shoulders.

"Mary Fielding," Downey said, "the great-great-granddaughter of Adam Forepaugh, a circus entrepreneur who brought the elephant Topsy from Africa in the 1870s. Topsy ended up at a Coney Island amusement park where, in 1902, she crushed a spectator who had burned her trunk with a hot cigar. The elephant was subsequently electrocuted by Thomas Edison's company, a process filmed by Jacob Blair Smith who is—naturally!—an ancestor of poor Mary Fielding's mother. Again, I was too late to save this child for science. She suspiciously died a few months after Topsy's head invaded her photos. We lack proof that it was poison as her parents promptly had her cremated. A third death that left us with no live DNA, no blood or skin for sampling, no organs to X-ray or transplant. Just when we feel the danger of infiltration of our photographic system and even of our faces themselves may be growing, just when recent research indicates the possibility that this plague of natives and, worse still, the innumerable animals abused by our species could strike millions of victims. Regardless of their specific lineage. Your sons and daughters."

Downey paused for this to sink in.

I saw Admiral Peabody lean over toward Cam and whisper something in her ear. She didn't answer, turned to look up toward where she assumed I was watching, must have guessed I was desperate for reassurance. She nodded her head at me, smiling, and then let her smile vanish as soon as her eyes returned to Downey. If looks could kill.

"The eventuality of an epidemic of biblical proportions, my friends, made it all the more imperative to find a living, breathing, vibrant specimen, someone who might illuminate our search, a missing link, so to speak. A while back we learned that there was indeed such a subject, an American citizen, no less."

And here another signal and Sleazy obeyed and this time it was me up there, the very photo that I had pinned up to remind me of what I innocently looked like before my visitor had come, the image snapped just before my fourteenth birthday. There was something obscene about being exposed like that for this audience of strangers, having them delve into my private life and strip me of the anonymity I had wasted so many hours protecting. I wanted to reach across the keyboard and press another button, but Sleazy's large bulk dissuaded me—he'd only press the button again—and there was Wiggins breathing down my neck. Cam had half risen as if to place herself between those gaping men and the image of the boy she had loved enough to come back to save, but she must have thought better of it and collapsed into her seat—was she also giving up, did she now realize we had lost, that we were as orphaned and helpless as Henri and his fellows in that hall in Berlin while Virchow rattled off measurements and theories?

"An American citizen," Downey went on, with evident satisfaction, "giving us an advantage over our global rivals—though the Russians and the Chinese have less of a chance of winning this race anyway, lacking the sort of zoos and universal exhibitions of more developed and civilized lands. Recruiting such a valuable asset was made more taxing by the complete isolation in which he lived, hidden from the eyes and cameras of the world. In spite of courteous efforts to coax him out of retirement through approaches to his wife, herself a promising young researcher of the intersection of DNA and visual memory, no signs of willingness to cooperate were forthcoming. To justify using more aggressive means of persuasion we required indisputable, physical proof that he was indeed afflicted. Luckily, he made the mistake of traveling abroad where our agents managed, a few days ago, after pursuing our quarry halfway across the globe, to secure a couple of damning and definitive photos. Maestro!"

"Oh, yes," Sleazy Steven Henson whistled, pressing a button emphatically as Downey motioned his hand with a flourish in the air like a magician, and there they suddenly were, side by side, the photos procured in that bar in Punta Arenas.

I missed Downey's explanation about who I was and my genealogy of Petits and Hagenbecks, because Wiggins hissed: "Now it's your turn to shine."

He nodded a goodbye to Ensign Henson, and led me out of the projectionist's booth and along a corridor to the backstage area of the auditorium. I could hear Downey's voice droning on—and then Wiggins gently shoved me forward, pointed to a curtain that my old buddy Nordstrom was prying open.

I stepped through it.

"My friends, my friends," Downey said excitedly. "I give you . . . Fitzroy Foster."

The audience rose and applauded, as I saw the curtains that shrouded the walls lift and reveal multiple screens, blank for the moment, blank but not for long. Not for long: dozens of cameras had surfaced as if out of nowhere, all of them pointing at me.

I had spent the most significant years of my life dreading this very situation, scared to even be caught momentarily by some passing stranger. Dad and Mom and Cam had been right to warn me to be careful. All it had taken to deprive me of liberty was for two fraudulent tourists to snap my picture in a bar in Punta Arenas, that's all it had taken to shipwreck me here, in this Cuban bay plundered by Columbus and appropriated by the US Navy.

There I was now, there was Henri, there was Jemmy Edén, all three of us displayed like pieces of meat on a screen for our enemies to feast on. There I was, for them to do with me as they pleased.

I panicked—and yet could not run, my limbs and lips paralyzed by that phalanx of Guantánamo cameras pinning me down, strangling my face, ready to invite Henri into me yet one more time. A thousand insect eyes on the walls, flattening my torso and arms and legs into celluloid, preparing me for the tests ahead. The ultimate showdown, these cameras that had been waiting out here in the perilous air since my fourteenth birthday, if looks could kill, oh if looks could kill, waiting for this moment of truth when I could no longer evade them, the looks or the cameras.

My time had come.

"Ready for your close-up, Fitzroy Foster?"

I did not answer, tried to will myself away, sealed my eyes and hoped against hope that when I opened them I would be in Puerto Edén where perhaps at this very moment the photos Henri and I had created between the two of us were being given the ancient burial they deserved. But it made no sense to keep those eyes locked—it was a tactic that had never warded off Henri, he would overwhelm me no matter what obstacles I placed in his path. And what hope was there that he would act differently now, why would he not want to show his persistent defiance of these military and pharmaceutical and scientific denizens, prove his power?

I was fucked.

I forced my eyelids open and I was, of course, at Guantánamo and Dr. Ernest Downey, descendant of a Downey who had photographed Krao and Prince Albert, lifted his arm and brought it down as if he were flagging the end of a race and I beseeched the gods to let me die, that a flash of lightning would obliterate me from the earth, destroy me utterly, end it once and for all, but no, no such salvation, up there a man improbably called Sleazy clicked a button, one more click in the endless snapshots of my captive existence.

Not just one click. All the cameras clicked, one after the other after the other, like sharp drops of dirty rain falling, as they had over eleven years ago when my dad had tried to capture me on my birthday. It felt like all the cameras of the universe since Daguerre and Eastman and Land had perfected this art, it seemed like every eye in history, my ancestor Petit and my nonrelative Prince Roland Bonaparte and Tarbox Beals and Jacob Smith and the Downeys, all of them and thousands more clicking away in the past so I could be the center of attention, so that Henri could make his stellar appearance and again perform his assigned role, again perform tricks in front of a select audience.

Except he didn't.

The image that almost instantaneously took shape on the screens, spread out through that bending hall of mirrors, that image was the immaculate image of Fitzroy Foster.

For the first time since my fourteenth birthday, my startled face stared back at me, back at the audience of military brass, boring into the eyes of the CEO of Pharma2001 and his devotees, parading in front of everyone else, but above all befuddling, astonishing, enraging Dr. Ernest Downey.

Henri had disappeared!

As a murmur rose from the spectators, Downey cried out, "A glitch! A glitch!" and ordered Ensign Henson to try again—"and this time make sure you get it right!"

This time there were no coy remarks, no asking me if I was ready for my close-up. He just grabbed hold of my arm as if I were about to escape him, as if that could guarantee a different outcome. I did not attempt to free myself, did not even have the presence of mind to seek Cam's reaction—I was too fascinated with that face of mine that I hadn't seen in a picture for so long, too stunned that it should seem so wonderfully unrecognizable.

My initial shock changed into something else, delight, vindication, understanding, the hint of merriment in my throat, when the next clicks sounded in the cavern of that auditorium and yes, once more proof that Henri had retreated from my existence, only Fitzroy Foster grinning from each screen, grinning in the photo and grinning in reality, and then I heard a laugh and I knew it was my Cam, I knew that I wasn't dreaming, I knew that we had won this battle, that Cam had been right to trust Henri.

Next to her, Admiral Peabody stood up and lifted his arms to placate the assembly, their murmurs of displeasure turning into irritation as they also rose, more indignant at themselves for having fallen for this scam than at Downey for daring to perpetrate it, and yet ready to indulge the famous scientist one last time, still willing to believe him when he begged them to return to their seats.

The third time—oh that third click, just like the definitive one all those years ago that had separated my existence from its past, now separating me from Henri as if cutting two Siamese twins down the middle. He had said goodbye to me, left me alone with my own identity and image, here in 1992, while he, my visitor, my Henri, returned to his existence in *cartes postales* gathering dust in Parisian bookstores and Old World libraries, concealed in grubby attics and arcane collections, Henri was no longer present, trapped back in 1881 forever, in silence and death forever.

"A hoax!" Cam yelled out now. "Those other pictures—Photoshopped, gentlemen, using my own husband's computing skills to defame him, abuse him, ensnare him. As you can see, the only evidence Dr. Downey has for his farfetched hypotheses and accusations are two doctored photos of two Patagonian Indians, probably brothers, maybe cousins, a hoax, a hoax!"

Pandemonium ensued.

Admiral Peabody barked out something that must have been some sort of order, because I found myself hustled away by Wiggins, was still too dazed to object until I saw Cam dragged along by two Navy officers and that was it, I'd had enough, I began flailing and screaming, calling out to her even when she was no longer present. Nordstrom rushed over and helped to subdue me.

"Hey," Wiggins said. "Hey, you won! You wouldn't want your children to see you with a black eye in the family album, would you? Enjoy your victory!"

"Where are they taking her, you bastard?" I said.

"To the admiral's office, just like you. Come along nicely and you'll both be all right."

I realized that it made no sense to get beaten up, give him that satisfaction.

"What happens to us now?"

"If I had to guess, I'd say you're on your way home. But under what terms, well, you'll just have to be patient, Mr. Foster."

I decided to heed his advice and was rewarded by Cam, more ebullient than I had ever seen her—and that was saying something!—embracing me in the admiral's office and then, without the slightest sense of ridicule, dancing with me. Not stopping when Peabody and Downey abruptly entered, she seemed to be savoring their amazed faces as we swung around and around the room.

Until she realized that our victory waltz was provoking the officer who still held our destiny in his hands, and she ceased the twirling and said to him:

"So, Admiral, when do we leave?"

"Right now. I'm a man of my word."

Downey was not happy. "Against my express recommendation. I told him, I asked the Admiral"—again, Downey seemed to be speaking more to himself than to anybody in the room—"how can we be sure this isn't a temporary lull, that tomorrow—or right this minute—our patient won't have a relapse? And even if that were not the case, you, Fitzroy Foster, you're still valuable, irreplaceable, unique. Not useless. No, no, no. If I could have just a year, just a few months, with his body, Admiral, we could examine what residues remain dormant, what vital signs have been altered. A month, Admiral."

Peabody just shook his head. "You promised proof and didn't deliver. And I promised they could leave if there was no proof and I will deliver, I will keep my word."

"Listen, listen," Downey said breathlessly. "This is what happened, I figured it out. I overreached. I'm to blame for frightening him out of his wits"—pointing at me—"cornering him into a near-death experience. You know what war is like, Admiral, when you're bombarded, when someone comes at you with a knife, you know what the body does in order to survive, how the brain's amygdala reacts automatically. If he had been alone like my poor daughter, he could have killed himself, like she did, in order to kill the marauder inside. You saw his face, you saw him pray for death. Didn't you, Fitzroy, didn't you?"

"Yes," I answered, even as Cam tried to shush me.

I felt sorry for him, that's how much I had mellowed, that's how much I had learned that revenge only destroys us, that's what Henri had taught me before leaving—yes, I actually felt sorry for that Downey son of a bitch. He simply didn't get it, never would. He was unable to fathom that Henri's disappearance could not be reduced to the iron laws of biology and chemistry and physics. He would never believe that a far-off ceremony on an island lost at the southern end of the world, a burial of photos, might have any effect on this other island thousands of miles away. He did not believe that Henri—or Krao or Ota Benga or even Topsy—had agency, had a say in when they appeared and where and why. I said yes to Downey because I felt he needed some sort of consolation, he had to unearth a scientific explanation or he would go crazy and I would be responsible, I would have to carry the guilt of his darkened eyes for the rest of my life.

"You see, Admiral, you see," Downey exclaimed. "Under surveillance twenty-four hours, unable to commit suicide, like my daughter did. So, instead, his cells accelerated and then exterminated all visual traces of that intruder from his memory and skin, an all-out attack on the enemy virus. Don't you see, Admiral, if we keep him we can fight this plague, find a vaccine before it strikes again. Because that monster's waiting out there, they all are, to bring down our civilization, don't you see, don't you see that there's no other recourse?"

"No," Cam said. "Bad science, Admiral. My husband never had any visitation of any sort. Those last photos prove how boringly normal he is. And even if we were to admit—we don't, there's no evidence, not one substantial piece that would stand the test in an American court or a laboratory for that matter—that he once had a hint of this sickness—by now it's clearly been burned away and expelled. He's just like any other human being."

Downey turned to me. "Stay," he pleaded. "I can't lose you, my boy. Not again."

"What do you say, Mr. Foster?" Peabody said. "Because if Dr. Downey happens to be right, it's your children and grandchildren you'll be saving from a possible pandemic. Would you be willing to sacrifice a week, contribute to the cause?"

"I think the cause will survive fine without me," I said. "I'm really, really tired."

"How about your wife then? Now that she has no fears regarding your future, maybe she'd care to join us?"

"You're continuing with the research?" Cam asked, with genuine interest.

"Of course we are. The Pentagon was investigating this outbreak before Dr. Downey was installed as head of the team. This initiative remains one of our top priorities."

"I think," Cam said, "that I'd rather go back to working on cancer. I've been toying with a different approach, a less warlike one, to a cure. I mentioned it, in fact, to Mr. Clarke, the CEO of Pharma2001, and he said to get in touch with him if I needed preliminary funding."

"Not if I can help it," said Downey. "And you're not leaving this base until certain conditions have been met." He set out the terms in rapid-fire sequence. We were to sign a binding document stating that any revelation of the research in which Dr. Downey and associates were engaged, or our experience since our boat was boarded, would be in violation of the Espionage Act of 1917, and subject to immediate imprisonment. Second, Mr. Fitzroy Foster agreed to be photographed once a week by emissaries of the Pentagon's choosing. And third, if the visual disorder recurred in the patient, he would promptly be retained at a site determined by the Center for Disease Control.

As soon as Cam and I quite willingly signed the document, Downey grabbed it, held it aloft triumphantly. "Because he will be back, you know that, right?" he crowed. "And when you relapse, there'll be no getting away."

He tried to follow us as we left the room, but Peabody seemed to have had enough for one day and closed the door firmly in Downey's face. "So where do you go from here?" Peabody asked as he escorted us to a jeep waiting outside. "What's next?"

The questions—so apparently innocent—terrified me.

This liberty, this freedom from Henri, was all that I had dreamed of since that lethal birthday in 1981 and now that the dream had come true, the truth was that I did not know what to do with my life, where I was going from here, what was next.

Henri had protected me from having to answer or even ask those questions.

And now I was alone.

Solo, solito y solo.

I missed him. I missed Henri.

He had left me, as the dead always end up leaving us. Leaving me without guidance and company. How could I possibly know what came next?

Cam, however, had ideas, was chock-full of plans and projects. She had never been inhabited by Henri and could not possibly realize how suddenly bereft I felt now that he had vanished, gone without even so much as an explanation or a goodbye or a last word of advice. Cam would soon enough tell me about all the wonders that lay ahead of us. For now, though, it was up to her to answer the admiral's question, up to her to point north. "Home," Cam said, laughing. "That's next. We're going home."

Her enthusiasm, spilling out of her all through that trip to Boston, should have been infectious.

She spoke of returning to her research on the cancer that had deprived her of both parents—if Henri had been persuaded through kindness and empathy to cease his malignant growth inside me, perhaps this was a model for a different pathway, perhaps aberrant cells, instead of being bombed like an enemy, could be coaxed into becoming healthy again, could become partners rather than tumors. And then she spoke of my genius for code writing and computers and why not, now that I didn't dread cameras, invent a way of creating three-dimensional representations of the inside of the body, why not create a phone that sent pictures instantly, why not break down the one-sided way in which pictures are produced, why not offer people control over their visual images so they would no longer be trapped by others as I had been trapped, why not? She spoke of the charities we could create and the millions we could help if our work and fortunes prospered. She spoke of starting to live together like any other couple today, of concerts we could attend and friends we could recover or make, of barhopping and how to enjoy the bloom of youth that had been forbidden us for so long. She spoke of dinner at exquisite restaurants tasting dishes I had never savored and excursions to museums and public squares and seaside resorts in a car that she would teach me how to drive. She spoke of Paris and Berlin and the beaches of Bali and the mosques of Morocco and the heights of Tibet, a wide-open Earth whose sights we could drink in, the resplendent artistic heritage of our species, without fearing the everlasting snapshots of a thousand tourists gone berserk. She spoke of building a house of our own and sallying forth arm in arm to furnish it and choose from every color in the rainbow, and scout for appliances and the right neighborhood, and that there needed to be a room so we could care for my dad when he was too old to live by himself, care for him as one should every elder member of the tribe. She spoke of taking care of the future as well, opening a family album inaugurated by a picture of the two of us holding hands and smiling at the camera or maybe a snapshot of our bodies racing in unison through the waters of a pool or a lake, she spoke of pictures of children we would bring into the world and their children and, if we were lucky, our great-grandchildren, and photos of Hugh's wedding and Vic's first baby and anniversaries and bike rides and PTA meetings and political marches brimming with other bodies, and dancing, dancing, dancing. She spoke of that night of love in Punta Arenas and what was singing inside her, how just and ethical and appropriate it would be if the seventh generation of Pierre Petit and Carl Hagenbeck were to have been conceived precisely there, were to start swimming toward the light in a place so close to where their crimes against humanity had originated. She spoke, bless her, as if all our troubles were behind us.

Full of the life inside and outside her, my Cam was already starting to forget Henri.

He had disappeared, that was true, and equally true that the living should not dwell among the dead, and also true that his refusal to cooperate with Downey and Downey's sponsors was already a message sanctifying our future, telling us to relish the days and years left to us before we joined him in the great stillness.

What could possibly be wrong with the pursuit of happiness when there was so much cruelty and misery in the world? Had we been saved in order to feed on sorrow till the end of our days?

And yet, if the face of Henri had vanished from my photos and was no longer, for good reason, a priority for Cam, that face had not abandoned my memory or my life. It was still somewhere inside me. And other faces. The face of Jemmy Edén drunk in a bar, going blind, pimping his past to make a living. The faces of the Haitians behind their barbed wire, so close to the sea they could taste it in the wind but unable to set sail, as we could, for whatever horizon desired. The face of Captain Wolfe pressed down onto the deck, treated like a criminal because he had dared to defend his passengers and his ship and his dignity. The faces of Krao and Ota Benga and Topsy, all those who had not been given the chance to withdraw peacefully, compassionately, as Henri had, those faces that had been captured and uprooted and confined and given no redress, not even the distant satisfaction of thwarting the plans of their jailors. The face of the earth itself, the earth and the sea, speckled with oil spills and plastic bottles and rotting fish and broken birds, the face of the waters from where, according to Darwin, we had emerged. And the face of my mother who had died in a foreign land so that the land would not be foreign to those born on it since the beginning of time.

The beginning of time: when everything was sacred, the whole world a temple.

Maybe it was enough that one person had understood, really understood.

Was that, is that, enough?

If I ever tell this story, how soon will it take for Henri to fade from the memory of those who deign to listen? How long before he and I are forgotten, his love for me, what else to call what he did, his act of mercy, his quiet farewell, the reservoir of his trust in me? How long before we are forgotten?

So easily are the hearts of men, the hearts of women, smashed.

"It's going to be all right," Cam said—as if she had read my thoughts, the silence with which I greeted her words of prophecy and celebration, my darling always full of hope for our many tomorrows. "Twenty-five years from now, our children will live in a different world, a better world, shining and brave. You'll see, Fitzroy Foster. Just wait and see."

I pray she is right.

I pray we have learned something.

I pray we have fully, deeply, definitely learned something.

And that Henri will not have to come back again, one last final time.

When it may be too late.

Will you need to come back, my brother, my brother?

He does not answer.

ACKNOWLEDGMENTS FOR THE LIVING

Though ghosts inspired this story, taking possession of me during its long inception and writing, the words would not have existed if not for people made of flesh and blood, sinew and heart.

First, of course, is Angélica, my wife, love, and partner, to whom this novel, like most of what I create, is dedicated. Her company and encouragement have been as essential as her endless readings of one and another draft in English and Spanish over many months, correcting, suggesting, fine-tuning my prose and helping me to draw near to the elusive protagonists.

This is a book about violence that demanded a modicum of peace in order to be completed, as well as mountains of research, and for both of these, I am grateful to Suzan Senerchia, our friend and my assistant. She was seconded in her labors by the efficient, cheerful, and forbearing librarians at Duke University who supplied me with many materials essential to a novel so grounded in real history and pain.

My agents at Wylie, Jacqueline Ko and Anna Wood, and before them, Jin Auh, have been fiercely loyal to this idiosyncratic and stubborn author of theirs, and have managed to find the right haven for this novel.

That home was Seven Stories Press and its host was my friend and editor there, Dan Simon, with whom I have enjoyed a fruitful relationship for almost twenty years. He has pushed me to make this book better, with care, deliberation, and affection, never letting me off the hook, but always showing the utmost respect for what I was trying to achieve. I am also grateful for Lauren Hooker's meticulous copyediting and oversight and to Jon Gilbert for his devotion to the text and its design.

Two of our many dear friends read this novel in its original draft, and this is an excellent occasion to recognize their cordial comments and queries. Deena Metzger, a great writer who is also the closest person I have to a sister, has been a compassionate comrade for many decades. And Max Arian, our Dutch brother-in-arms, has shown a faith in my work that has invigorated me since we first met in exile in 1974. A third friend, Queno Ahumada, provided me, from Santiago, with valuable information that I required about Patagonia and its history, as well as a companionship that has lasted since childhood.

Of course, there were many others close to us for whom this story will be a surprise, even if they fortified me during its composition with their love. I cannot mention them all by name, but I do need to at least list the members of our immediate family, who give us the sort of joy that Fitzroy seeks and Henri deserves: Rodrigo, Joaquín, Nathalie, Ana María, Pedro, Patricio, Marisa, Isabella, Catalina, Primm, Ryan, Sharon, Kirby, Kayleigh, and Emmy.

Thanks to all for helping me give birth to this tale of sorrow and redemption.

ARIEL DORFMAN is considered to be one of "the greatest Latin American novelists" (*Newsweek*) and one of the United States' most important cultural and political voices. A Chilean-American author born in Argentina, his numerous award-winning works of fiction, nonfiction, and poetry have been published in more than fifty languages. His play *Death and the Maiden*, which has been performed in over one hundred countries, was made into a film by Roman Polanski. Among his works are the novels *Widows*, *The Nanny and the Iceberg*, *Mascara*, and *Konfidenz*, and the memoirs *Heading South, Looking North* and *Feeding on Dreams*. He recently published a collection of essays, *Homeland Security Ate My Speech: Messages from the End of the World*. He contributes to major papers worldwide, including frequent commentary in the *New York Times*, *El País*, the *Guardian*, *Le Monde*, and *La Repubblica*. His stories have appeared in the *New Yorker*, the *Atlantic*, *Harper's*, *Playboy*, *Index on Censorship*, and many other magazines and journals. A prominent human rights activist, he lives with his wife Angélica in Chile and Durham, North Carolina, where he is the Walter Hines Page Research Professor Emeritus of Literature at Duke University.

ABOUT SEVEN STORIES PRESS

Seven Stories Press is an independent book publisher based in New York City. We publish works of the imagination by such writers as Nelson Algren, Russell Banks, Octavia E. Butler, Ani DiFranco, Assia Djebar, Ariel Dorfman, Coco Fusco, Barry Gifford, Martha Long, Luis Negrón, Peter Plate, Hwang Sok-yong, Lee Stringer, and Kurt Vonnegut, to name a few, together with political titles by voices of conscience, including Subhankar Banerjee, the Boston Women's Health Collective, Noam Chomsky, Angela Y. Davis, Human Rights Watch, Derrick Jensen, Ralph Nader, Loretta Napoleoni, Gary Null, Greg Palast, Project Censored, Barbara Seaman, Alice Walker, Gary Webb, and Howard Zinn, among many others. Seven Stories Press believes publishers have a special responsibility to defend free speech and human rights, and to celebrate the gifts of the human imagination, wherever we can. In 2012 we launched Triangle Square books for young readers with strong social justice and narrative components, telling personal stories of courage and commitment. For additional information, visit www.sevenstories.com.